Praise for Shelter

'Beautiful'
Adele Parks

'A tender and illuminating novel, written with warmth
and eloquence'
Carys Bray, author of *A Song for Issy Bradley*

'Powerful and moving. Connie and Seppe are amazing
characters. So well nuanced. I loved her feisty courage.
And such heartbreak! This compelling debut shows
how outsiders in a time of war seek to rebuild
their lives again.'
Essie Fox, author of *The Last Days of Leda Grey*

'I LOVED it. Seppe is one of the most refreshing
portrayals of masculinity I have ever read'
Shelley Harris, author of *Jubilee*

'A lovely hymn to the woods and the men and women
who worked there during the Second World War'
Lissa Evans, author of *Their Finest Hour and a Half*

'One of the year's hottest debuts'
NetGalley, Book of the Month

Shelter

Sarah
FRANKLIN

Zaffre

First published in Great Britain in 2017 by

ZAFFRE PUBLISHING
80–81 Wimpole St, London W1G 9RE
www.zaffrebooks.co.uk

A CIP catalogue record for this book is
available from the British Library.

ISBN: 978-1-7857-6299-4

also available as an ebook

1 3 5 7 9 10 8 6 4 2

Typeset by Palimpsest Book Production Limited, Falkirk, Stirlingshire
Printed and bound by Clays Ltd, St Ives Plc

For my parents

'Where is the Forest of Dean? It's still back there. It's a sort of mythic Forest of Dean . . . a strange and beautiful place . . . a heart-shaped place between two rivers, somehow slightly cut off from the rest of England . . .'

Dennis Potter

' . . . women replaced men in every branch of (timber) production. They drove tractors and lorries, they worked on sawbenches, they felled, they measured, they even sharpened saws. They became forewomen and acquisition officers. They became in fact an integral part of the great production machine. Without them the targets could not have been achieved.'

Russell Meiggs, *Home Timber Production, 1939–1945* (published 1949)

Forest of Dean, Gloucestershire

May, 1944

CONNIE STUCK OUT HER tongue at the face gurning at her from the faded looking glass on the tallboy. Mud was everywhere, in her eyelashes and streaked down her face like bad rouge. It was going to take some serious spit and polish to get spruced up. For a moment she couldn't remember why she'd agreed to go to the dance in the first place. But Hetty would kill her if Connie missed tonight's final fling before the other trainees scattered, and it had been too long since she'd been out dancing. Time to make sure she still knew how.

Connie found the edge of the washcloth, spat on it and rubbed her cheek, twisting sideways to see if she'd improved the situation. Not a hope. She was scuppered – time to brave the water. She moved over to the chest of drawers and poured water from the jug that sat there in the porcelain basin. It was as clear as spring water and as cold, too. Nothing like the brown trickle you'd get back in Coventry.

Connie tangled the brush through her hair until it was stick-straight again and tugged off her drenched socks.

When she'd been in the hostel, before she'd been billeted here, some of her fellow lumberjills had made a big song and dance about getting changed as soon as they were home from the woods. They'd swan around putting on dainty tea dresses, or the clean skirts and blouses their mothers had sent them.

Some hope of that for her. Connie yanked open the wardrobe door and stared at its contents. The cupboard still smelled of the forest; maybe she'd stop noticing once all her clothes whiffed like that too.

Nothing would fit. She'd have to wear that yellow dress, though she should have got rid of it months ago. Connie pulled it out, hangers jangling. The trousers and overalls that belonged to Amos's son bumped into her uniforms, releasing another pong of the countryside into the air.

Connie draped the frock against her overalls and dragged the rickety chair over to the window, craning to catch a glimpse of her reflection. Behind the panes, finger-like twigs tapped at her and she jumped. This place gave her the willies, always something creaking or scratching. Whoever thought the countryside was still and calm hadn't spent any damn time in it.

She twisted on the chair to get a better look at the dress and nearly toppled over. Hmm. The dress was made for someone else and it showed. It was going to be a hell of a squeeze to get into it after the time on the farm.

She gritted her teeth, willed the stampeding thoughts away. The yellow dress would have to do – and perhaps the music would snap her out of these doldrums.

Connie dropped the dress onto the bed. In no time at all she'd be out there on the dance floor, whirling around, and for those few hours nothing else would matter. Not this war, not what the future held, none of it.

She lay back on the bed for a moment, the counterpane

scratching her cheek, and screwed up her eyes. She'd loved the dances back home in Coventry, had lived for that tingly moment when the factory's closing siren would rise in duet with the shrill clamour of the girls. They'd all dash to the lavs shrieking with the fun of it, the foremen yelling at them to pipe down a bit but them paying no real notice. They'd cluster round the sliver of mirror above the sink and chatter like magpies as they did themselves up, then head out into the city.

Invincible, that's what they'd been. But then, before they'd even known what they had, it was shattered.

Connie shivered. 'Right, let's get this thing on.'

She discarded her overalls and squashed herself into the dress, its faded cotton soft against her skin after the lumber-jill dungarees, a reminder of when life was all dances. She twirled and the full skirt span out around her like a chink of light escaping from a blackout. There was no full-length looking glass anywhere in the cottage, so Connie had to trust that she wasn't flashing her scanties where the buttons that ran down the bodice gaped and strained. She'd get Hetty to check at the hostel, cover up any dodgy bits with a brooch. Wouldn't be the first time they'd been on display, admittedly, but things were different now.

Jagged thoughts crawled along the edges of her mind. Connie took a deep breath to shoo them out. Better hang up those sopping wet socks in the window to try and dry them out before tomorrow's shift. She just couldn't be doing with drawing stocking seams on her legs tonight; she was licked. Anyway, it itched when she did that, and she'd forget the pencil was there and rub one leg against the other, like she always did. She tiptoed down the stairs, trying and failing to avoid the one that creaked. She jolted past it, the wood cold where the carpet had worn down, and paused at the bottom, one hand on the newel post.

She'd better go and say goodnight to Amos, or try at least – keep kidding herself that they actually spoke to each other rather than circling like Heinkels waiting for the signal to start the bombing. She pushed open the door into the little back room and the homesickness roared out at her so strongly that she stepped back again. The air in here was heavy, tangy; Connie could almost taste Hillview Road again in the stewed tea and ash from the grate.

'I'm off out, then.'

The old man nodded, so she persisted, bellowing over the wireless.

'You doing anything nice this evening?'

What a daft question! She wanted to bite her tongue the second it came out. Amos never went anywhere once he was home from the sheep, as far as she could tell.

Silence.

Connie shifted feet. 'I'm off dancing with some of the girls from the hostel, down at Parkend Memorial Hall. I haven't half missed a good dance.'

She was babbling now. Amos had made it clear as day more than once that he didn't want her there, so the right course of action was to do them both a favour and button it. For as long as he kept a roof over her head, however grudgingly, she'd have to learn to make the most of a bad job.

By the time she'd fetched Hetty from the hostel in Parkend and they'd walked up to the Memorial Hall, there was a queue winding right round it, coats flapping open in the promise of this late spring balm and making them look for all the world like the bats that swooped out at them from twilight perches. Music warbled from the hall as they inched their way past the pebbled edges of the building and before Connie knew she was doing it, she tapped her hand against her bag, the beat invading like a swarm of Messerschmitts. Connie's feet were numb, the chilblain on her big toe itching like mad, but there was a dance in there, a bevy of blokes and girls finding their rhythm and losing their minds, just for a while, and she was going to be part of it.

Connie had never had any truck with the idea of packing your troubles in your old kitbag, as the song went – your troubles were your troubles – but she'd been away from dance halls for too long, had forgotten how music could lift you up. She could almost smell it, for crying out loud, couldn't wait to be a part of the glamour and the glee. Amos only put the wireless on for the news and the one time she'd suggested the Light Programme he'd glared at her as if she'd suggested dancing naked on the pavement. Not that there were any pavements in this bloody forest.

Connie grabbed Hetty's coat sleeve and stood on one leg to scratch one foot against another, but it was useless through her gumboots and she splashed dirty puddle water everywhere. Just as well she hadn't bothered with those seams. 'Watch what you're doing!' hissed one of the other hostel girls.

Connie stamped from foot to foot, banging the feeling back into them. 'What are they doing up there? Can't take this long to let us in, can it?'

The girl in front turned around, the mud-splattering apparently forgiven. 'There's a crowd of new GIs up ahead of us; don't have small enough notes yet so it's taking forever to give them the change they need.'

Hetty perked up, shoe woes forgotten. 'GIs? It'll be worth the wait, then!' She prodded Connie, who fought the urge to jab her friend hard in the ribs under pretence of jollity. Had none of them ever met a Yank before? Obviously not.

Connie's thoughts slid to Don and her heart slipped into her guts. No sense in pinning your hopes on a GI.

It was proper crowded inside the hall, every space jam-packed with music, with sweat, with jostled mugs of beer and with the oversweet, over-perfumed girls bunched in corners waiting to be plucked to dance. God, but she'd missed this! The weight came off her, dissolved into the music.

Connie looked around for a seat, her feet already pushing forward and back, finding the pattern in the music. There was a spare chair behind a pillar; she waved vaguely at Hetty and wandered over to it. After the day she'd had out at the site, she needed to sit down for a minute before she hit the dance floor, whatever plans her feet had.

She wriggled out of her coat and the lightness enveloped her. One of her dancing shoes fell out of the pocket onto the floor. She smiled at it, but just the thought of squeezing into such a dainty object right now made her chilblains sting. Best to wait until she'd had a gin or two, then go for it. For now, her gumboots would have to do.

The band was on the makeshift stage at the crowded end of the hall and she squinted at the round sign in front of them. 'George Thomas and his Gloucester Accordion Band', apparently. Must be using all the accordions in Gloucester, wherever that was; there seemed to be hundreds of the things.

Connie relaxed back into her chair and took in the scene around her. A bit hick, but a dance was a dance. She felt the fog in her head clearing, giving her a chance to be herself again. She beamed, fond of everyone in this moment.

'Mind if I join you? You've found the best seat in the joint.'

She looked up through the smog at the man in uniform in front of her.

'Be my guest.'

He found a chair at another table and pulled it across, the metal legs screeching against the melody of the band. She grinned at him, swung her boots in time to the music. It still got to her, fizzing until she had to get up, had to get moving. That hadn't changed a bit.

'Shall we?'

The true woman finds her greatest joy in
life in building up a 'happy home for
her husband and children'.
Advertisement, *Dean Forest Mercury*,
7th April, 1944

FOR SALE: 2 Goats in milk. Apply D. Hodges,
Hangerberry, Lydbrook. 10378
FOR SALE: quantity good sound Shallots,
cheap. Hatton, Allastone Cross, Lydney x623
Advertisements, *Dean Forest Mercury*,
7th April, 1944

Spring, 1944

One

April

WHERE WERE THE HOUSES? This would never work if people didn't actually live here. Outside the window, in the gathering twilight, rows and rows of trees lined up like the Coventry terraces before they'd been blitzed. It was a wonder the train was finding its way through at all.

Connie blinked, her lashes hot and wet, and dashed her sleeve against her eyes. It reeked of sick and she nearly gagged again. She needed to get that under control before they arrived.

The train's whistle shrilled and she pulled herself up on tiptoe to peer out properly, the chatter of the other girls in the carriage fading as she poked her head out of the window, sucking in the damp, fresh air. They were pulling into a tiny station, smaller even than the one in Worcestershire. The trees mingled now with little white-washed houses and Connie sighed into the strange, furniture-smelling breeze, blowing out all her nerves. Her plan might just come off if she played it right. Then she'd be free to get on with her life.

The train juddered to a halt and Connie lost her balance, stumbled backwards into the crowd jostling behind her. One of the other Women's Timber Corps recruits – were they really supposed to call themselves lumberjills? – stamped on Connie's chilblain and with some effort she bit her tongue. No need to give her a piece of her mind; it wasn't the girl's fault that Connie's back was killing her and her mouth was sour. Not long now until she'd be shown to her digs. With a bit of luck she'd wangle a bath then get under the bedcovers. Maybe her billet would be as cushy as that last place, a couple of hours south of Coventry, when she'd still been doing farm work. There, the farmer's wife had doted on her, made all her meals.

Until . . . well, what's done is done, and it was probably all for the good that she'd had to move on. This endless war wasn't all bad; it gave the likes of her the chance to shift around a bit. And as long as there were a few houses here and there, these woods would suit her better, sprawling on for miles as they did.

Connie stepped off the train and quietly joined the throng of nattering girls as they trailed off the platform towards the station entrance. This wasn't like any station she'd seen before, more like a rundown bus shelter, really. There was none of the bustle you'd see at Coventry station of an evening, even with the war on. It gave her the creeps, but she'd keep her opinions to herself for once. She needed to behave, make a good impression; this next billet mattered like none before.

Her hand was cold against her own cheek and smelled of grit and fumes.

'Girls, girls! Gather round, please.' The crowd piped down and Connie shivered into the weird silence. No sirens, no machines whirring, no shouting over them. It was so bloody quiet. There was a muddy little road in front of them, stretching into the murky light. All around, closing in on them like enemy troops and swallowing up the day, were trees. So many trees! She thought there would at least be a proper town or two here, but it seemed to be the arse end of nowhere. Her stomach tipped again despite herself.

A woman with a horsey face and hair the colour of gutter-water stood in front of them beside a small, wiry man with a flat cap. He was leaning heavily on a stick even though he didn't look that old. And he was missing a finger. Connie stared, pulling her coat around her. It was cold for April in the shadow of the trees.

'I'm Mrs Marsh, your Area Rep for the Women's Timber Corps. Congratulations on your recruitment – the WTC has proven far more successful than we'd imagined. This . . .' she tipped her head towards the man '. . . is Mr Watkins, the timber foreman here in the Forest of Dean and your boss for the next few weeks. Training starts tomorrow. Right now, we need to get you gals to the hostel.' Horsey-woman clapped her hands and the bloke called Watkins moved forward.

What was that behind him? One of the other lumberjills, shiny and keen in her stiff new overalls and beret, beat her to it and called out.

'But that's a horse and cart!'

The wiry man spoke up. 'Course it's a horse and cart. What d'you expect, a chauffeur-driven car?'

If Connie ended up on that contraption she'd be sick again for sure. She made her way towards the bossy woman who was checking them off on a clipboard as the dozen or so girls clambered into the cart. When Connie didn't say anything, or move, the woman looked up, brow furrowed in irritation.

'Name?'

'Constance Granger. But you don't need that for this.

15

I'm not getting on behind that thing, and I'm not going to no hostel.'

Horse Face's pen dug into the clipboard so viciously it was a miracle she didn't break the nib. 'All Timber Corps trainees live in the hostel until their permanent locations come through at the end of training. Didn't you read your recruitment materials?'

Connie almost laughed at that, but this was no laughing matter. She'd heard the 'permanent billet' thing before. She'd met Land Girls who'd been stuck in a hostel for months, all crammed in together and freezing their bits off. If they thought she'd put up with that, they had another think coming.

The wiry man stepped forward. He had a limp to go with that missing finger and a faded blue neckerchief that clashed with the brown check of his flat cap. He might not take kindly to her pointing that out, though.

'Everyone goes to the hostel to begin with. It's not so bad, you'll see.'

She scowled at him and stifled a yawn. She was worn out after all the time in this country air. Everywhere she looked there were trees closing in on her. God knows what they were supposed to do with them, in this timber corps of theirs.

'When do we get out in the woods?'

The wiry man laughed and jutted his chin at the trees all around them. 'How much more forest do you want? You'll be out there soon enough. But only if you're in that hostel tonight.'

She squared up to him with the last of her energy. Nobody told her what she did and didn't do. 'What if I won't?'

Horse Face laughed and Connie fought the urge to pinch her. 'It's a proper question. There must be billets some-where.'

'Not for you trainees. If you don't want to stay, that's up to you, but you're on the next train out of here, and that's not till tomorrow, so you'll have a long night alone on this platform. And there's rain coming.' As she turned away, she pointed up at the thickening cloud, low against the endless trees.

Connie didn't mind a fight, but she knew when she was beaten. And a bed was a bed. She peered at the horse and turned to this Watkins fellow. 'He's not going to bite me, is he?'

'What's he want to do that for? Better things to eat out here than stroppy wenches.' But the man's smile was kind, and for the first time since they'd got off the train her shoulders dropped a tiny bit. This might work out after all.

Two

He'd thought the thickening silence in the truck was every man finally accepting that he'd been captured, that he wasn't being sent back to battle. But now he understood it was because they were being slowly gassed. Whoever had connected the pipe hadn't thought about the truck's canopy. The fumes caught under the tarpaulin and muffled the men as they rocked on the benches, last in their convoy. They'd been breathing in the gases for hours, ever since the interrogation ended. They'd left the holding camp by the ferry port just as the sun stretched upwards. It must be afternoon now; they had been handed something to eat a couple of hours ago but nobody had the stomach for this stodgy English food and the guards had muttered, 'Suit yourself,' as they took it back.

Seppe had been the last one on to the truck, shoved aside by the rest of them as usual. From here at the back of the truck he had a good view of the exhaust pipe. He'd been staring at it for hours, fogged into stupidity, assuming the nausea he felt was merely the same nausea that had

18

accompanied him through the months in Africa, intensifying cruelly every time he'd shouldered his weapon. But overlaying the nausea now, overlaying, too, the anxiety of what might lie ahead, was dishonourable relief that they were truly done with fighting. Nobody was sending him back out there into those sheets of dust, that suffocating cacophony of shouts and weapon fire. It made him a bad patriot, but he'd been a bad patriot for a long time. He was in the war for shameful reasons, pretending devotion to Il Duce, to Italy, like the men he matched step for step.

The truck veered abruptly right and jolted along a rough path. Was this the end? Seppe pulled his greatcoat tighter, but the chill of dread wreathed him still. The fear his father had beaten into him had only become more piercing during those months of battle, marching endless miles whilst the flies buzzed around his head in bitter haloes. And now he was a prisoner of the Allies and about to be made to pay for the sins he'd been compelled to commit.

The juddering slowed and Seppe looked out through the gap at the back of the tarpaulin. It was all greens and browns, swaying – or was it the truck swaying? He blinked through the fog in his brain. They were at the heart of an avenue of interlocking oaks; tentative green buds reached for each other. He inched aside the tarpaulin, heavy and cold, and peered out. Trees mazed together, trunks twisted and bent towards invisible hope. English trees. Oaks, but beeches too, and spiky-fingered yew – *tasso* – filling his nostrils. Yew was supposed to heal.

'Oi, mister! What are you doing in there, then?'

The English. The enemy. He hadn't understood what they had said but it couldn't be good. They wouldn't know he didn't believe in the cause he'd been made to fight for; they'd only want to harm him. Seppe jerked and felt his pocket for the whittling knife. Beside him his compatriots shifted dopily on the bench as the unfamiliar language met their ears too.

'Deaf as a post, this one is!' A stick flew up and Seppe flinched. It missed him by inches and he picked it up, turned it in his hands, wondering. The bark was pliable, rough against his palm.

He looked at the two boys loping alongside the truck. They were only youngsters, maybe eleven or twelve. The one nearest to the truck pulled a face at him, not quite hatred but certainly antipathy.

'POWs, aren't you? The baddies! Seen that Mister Hitler out there?' The boy goose-stepped across to his friend, who grabbed the side of the truck and hopped onto the running board. He was much too close; the only thing Seppe could do was squirm out of his way. The Italian opposite him, a devout follower of *Il Duce*, muttered in disgust and leaned forward. Seppe tensed. The British surely had no love lost for the Italians, not even now they'd been downgraded to 'co-belligerents' since Italy's capitulation.

'Look at him, all scaredy! No wonder them did get themselves caught.' The boy swung in, his leering face too close. Seppe turned away, couldn't show a kid that he was intimidated. His seatmates muttered, ignored it.

'Won't be able to escape from us, though. Not in *our* forest. Goes on for miles and miles. No way out for you, prisoner.' The boy spat, his breath warm and earthy.

The running-board boy inspected Seppe more closely. 'Them aren't no Jerries. Wrong colour uniform. I reckon you're Eyeties, right, mister? Muss-o-lee-nee? That ent so bad, you know. They ent fighting any more.' The boy jumped off the back of the truck and saluted, stiff-armed.

'Hey, you two – scarper!' A guard had appeared. He must be a guard; he was in uniform, though not one Seppe had seen before. The boys laughed up at the man and Seppe's stomach looped. They'd surely be thrashed for such behaviour.

'Keep your hair on, Ern. Only wanted to see real live POWs, we did. We're off now for our tea.'

The guard tutted at their retreating backs and stuck his head into the truck.

'Crikey-oh, man! Don't half stink in here – what the heck's been going on?'

The guard's nose was wrinkled; was he talking about the fumes? His words were slippery, nothing like the English they'd learned at school. They rumbled through a giant set of iron gates that clanged shut behind them.

'Here we are then, out you get.' The guard didn't sound vicious, but that could be a ruse. He wrenched open the tarpaulin and cold air doused them all as they staggered down from the truck. Seppe's legs wobbled and he grabbed the running board. *E adesso?* What would happen next? The stories had flown round their first camp in Alexandria: tales of beatings, of prisoners paraded through the street, crowds jeering and spitting. On at least two separate occasions captives had been stoned by angry townsfolk. This war just got worse and worse and Seppe had long known that to trust was to suffer.

'Cripes, look at the state of you.'

He mustn't look up, mustn't anger the guard with insubordination. Better not to react to the hand that gripped his elbow. 'That's it, lad. Bringing you over here.' He went where the guard led him, shocked by the softness of the tone, the steadiness of the grasp.

The noises were so different here. His truck mates were still muted by gas and defeat; there was no firefight, no outburst of rage. Instead birds cheeped and whistled and leaves hushed each other like prayers. The sun hung high

21

in the sky and a breeze played across his cheeks and soothed the graze there.

Seppe risked a quick glance around. Whatever else his childhood had delivered, he knew how to take the temperature of a situation, to read people and surroundings for danger. He was right; there was no apparent threat. He frowned. This couldn't be so.

The gates they'd entered through bordered a perimeter fence that curved in either direction. The camp stood at the top of the hill, and stretching off into the dusk in either direction were trees, so many trees, silent and dark. He looked more closely, careful to keep his place in the formation they'd been loosely assigned to, shivering as the sun moved behind a cloud. They seemed to be standing on some sort of parade ground. The earth beneath the thinned leather of his boots was scuffed and dry, though moisture was in every breath he took, the skies heavy with protective cloud.

To one side of the parade ground a clock tilted lopsidedly above a noticeboard and, despite his exhaustion, the nerves and the uncertainty, Seppe had to ball his hands not to break away, to go over there and right it. The parade ground was flanked by long, corrugated iron huts and from time to time one of the doors would clang open and a man would slouch out. They must be other prisoners, arrived before them, but even from this distance they didn't have the haggard, wary look he'd become used to seeing in the holding camp. Seppe must still be fogged from the gas; he couldn't parse what he saw, couldn't correlate these relaxed-seeming figures with the certain knowledge that he was a prisoner of war in Camp 61 according to the paint daubed on the main building. The confusion clattered in his head and he looked towards the trees again to quieten his mind.

He was behind gates, and beyond the gates were the

trees, leaves swaying in welcome. They were a skein, a living barrier between him and the world out there. Let them contain him if, by so doing, they held at bay the chaos of war, of home.

Seppe sighed, a long exhalation of relief. His war was over. He no longer had to pretend to believe in things he abhorred. Who knew what lay ahead, but for today, at least, he could breathe.

Three

CONNIE SLUMPED INTO THE last chair going in the hostel classroom and squinted crossly at the blackboard. Nobody had let on that forestry training would be like school. But they'd been in this mouldery classroom for a full two weeks now, twenty-four of them from around the country learning how to tell one tree from another, how to sweep brush, what went on in the sawmill. The other girls nodded and bent over their books to write things down, but for Connie it was all a sludge of words that didn't mean anything. Book learning had never been her thing.

'Tardy again, Granger?' The tutor, a buttoned-up old codger whose hands were the only thing to tell you he'd ever seen an honest day's work, squinted at Connie. What had happened to that Watkins they'd met on their first day? He'd seemed all right, not like this classroom bloke. A full two weeks of this she'd had now, the same sarky dig each day. She couldn't get down to class any faster because she had to wait for the other five girls to leave the dorm before she risked getting dressed. Even with those wooden partitions between each bed she couldn't be sure the others weren't gawping at her. She missed it, getting ready in a gaggle of girls, but this was nothing like those clocking-off times at the factory.

To begin with she'd heard a few smart whispers from a couple of the other lumberjills about how she thought herself a cut above, was too standoffish to lower herself to mingling in the bathroom with the likes of them. She'd bitten her lip, even though she was desperate to join in; she'd learned her lesson at the farm. After a couple of days they'd left her to it and now she could get on those overalls in peace. They were carefully friendly the rest of the time; life was too short to hold a grudge.

But she was hardly going to tell all that to Mr Hoity-Toity. She was struggling enough in the classroom as it was, and she needed this posting more than she'd ever needed anything.

What gobbledegook was he putting them through today?

The words scrolled past like a bookie's ticker tape.

Softwoods – larch, pine, spruce, fir – fetch 1½d per cubic foot.

Hardwood – ash, beech, chestnut, elm, oak, sycamore – are 2½d per cubic foot.

Pit prop lengths: four sizes; 3 foot, 4½ foot, 6 foot, 9 foot.

Why did they need to make it so complicated? As far as she was concerned there were trees with leaves and trees with needles that were a pain to get out of the rugs after Christmas and made Mam even more shouty than usual. Connie's insides twisted as she copied it down; she'd figure out what on earth it meant later. She knew it was all part of the war effort. She'd copped on that some of the trees were needed for pit props, since coal production was increasing. Some became telegraph poles, some were for rebuilding, and some would be used as ships' masts, but she was no closer to remembering which was which, or what the holy Moses she'd actually be doing, than she had been two weeks ago. She needed to get this stuff straight – and sharpish. There was a test at the end of it, and if she didn't pass, she'd be out on her ear. And she couldn't be moved on again, she simply couldn't.

If only she hadn't cocked things up on the farm. If only she'd been able to stick it out back at the factory in the first place.

Connie swallowed hard. *Get it together.* That was just the tip of the 'if onlys', but the others were best left well alone or she'd start bawling right here in this crappy little classroom.

The scraping of chairs snapped her back to the present. Connie grabbed the arm of a dark-haired girl pushing past.

'Where now?'

The girl – Hetty, that was her name – shook her head and smiled. They pushed out of the classroom into blissful fresh air, the door clanking shut behind them. 'You didn't listen to a word in there again, did you? We're off out into the woods. Time to see whether any of this classroom learning has sunk in, apparently.'

Connie's stomach lurched. 'What if it hasn't?'

Hetty shrugged. 'Other war work, I suppose. Can't say I'm too fussed one way or another, tell you the truth.' She tugged at a piece of ivy that coated the grey stone of the hostel walls, crawling up them as if trying to escape.

The hostel towered over the other buildings, such as there were, as if to show the importance of the forest even in this poky excuse for a village. Back in the day it had been the engine house for some ironworks or other, so they'd been told, but since the last war it had been a training centre for foresters from around the country.

Connie looked around her at the stone-built post office and the faded curtains in the window of the postmaster's adjacent house. She knew that what she must be looking at was a village, but she couldn't make it fit her idea of where people really lived. There were no uniform terraces, no craters, not even really any grime, just a bunch of trees with little yellow flowers hiding underneath them like people queuing for a public shelter.

Beyond a line of stone cottages, so low they appeared to be crouching, there seemed to be a park. Or perhaps it was a bit of what they called a village green here. It was tricky to tell what was forest and what was green because none of it looked like Coventry or any street Connie had known. Even all the noises and smells were wrong; it had her right at sixes and sevens.

The pub sign swinging in front of yet another grey stone building on the corner was the only thing she'd copped on to that looked like anything from home. Where were the buses, the people, the families giving each other hell in the street? Not that she'd be seeing her own family any time soon. She stared at the pub sign, blinking hard until she could move on up the street.

Today they seemed to be trudging in a new direction, away from the cluster of cottages. The girls rounded the corner from the hostel and the narrow street gave way to a wider road – or wider by the standards here, at any rate. Sheep were wandering across the road like they had a death wish, but nobody was paying them any attention. Connie skirted round them – it wasn't right, seeing animals all over the place like this – and concentrated on following the others up the hill.

Now they really seemed to be into the forest. It was darker – no, that wasn't it. The light was somehow *rounder*, like every part of it had absorbed the curve of the trees' bark. Connie looked up. She turned around and already she couldn't see the road. The trees had completely swallowed her up. She trembled. She needed to stick close to the others or she might never find her way out, left abandoned in the forest with nobody expecting her back and nobody to notice she was gone.

Connie put her head down to get away from this weird, rounded light. The softening ground between the trees was a wild purple, and it smelled clean, like soap. They surely shouldn't be walking on these delicate little things. Connie stopped still. The girl behind looked at her askance and pushed past. 'Haven't you ever seen bluebells in a wood before?'

Connie bent down, let the other lumberjills stream past, her fear superseded by curiosity. Little purple flowers, hundreds of the things, all packed together around the trees. They stretched as far as she could see. She'd only usually see flowers outside in pots if somebody posh was coming to open a new bit of the factory, didn't know they could please themselves like this, roam free. It was gobsmackingly gorgeous. Mam would love this.

'Come on, lass, or you'll be copping it again.' Agnes, the cheery one from Derby, pulled her back into the line and she scrambled along, trying not to tread on any of the flowers.

It was a relief when they stopped, not least because, there in front of them, was that Watkins bloke. She'd know him anywhere with that missing finger and a way of favouring his good leg that she'd clocked that first night. He'd have a story or two to tell. He stood beside what looked like a battalion's worth of weird weapons.

'Rightio, ladies. I'm Frank Watkins. There's no standing on ceremony out here, mind, so you're to call me Frank. Time to see what you can do, never mind that book learning.' Connie perked up.

'Line up – that's it, get where you can see me.' They shuffled into place, a bit too close to the sharp edges of the weapons for Connie's liking.

'These are your tools of the trade. Dangerous if you don't use 'em right, and lethal in the wrong hands, so listen up.' Frank walked along the row of tools. 'Axes for butting. Cross-cutters to get 'im down. Spokeshaves for bark stripping. Loppers . . . well, them's obvious. Fretsaw for snedding. Billhook, canthook, bushman, sledge, wedge.'

Connie's head hurt and her whole body was rigid. Birds were flittering about like butterflies, squawking away and making it hard to think about what Frank was telling them. She'd been wrong; this was so much worse than indoors. Screw it up with one of these baffling deathtraps and you'd be done for.

Get a grip, Connie . . . An axe; she recognised that. That little triangular metal thing must be the wedge, and there were two saws, one with one handle and another one that had a handle on either end, so they must be the fretsaw and the cross-cutter – was that what Frank had called them? God only knows which was which, though. Could the loppers be those massive shears? This bloody Frank calling it obvious – it was all clear as mud to her. She sucked in air again, tried to look at one instrument of torture at a time. They hadn't even made sense as words, never mind matching them to the various metal and wooden contraptions in front of her. She'd never ever keep any of it straight. Connie swallowed and swallowed again. She *had* to make this work.

'Like every forest you'll be assigned to, there's a crew of men here, full-time timber workers, that you'll be working alongside. Some of them have been here for years, but lots of our best men have been sent to the front now, same as them forests in Scotland and Yorkshire. We've got enough men for the real heavy work, more or less, and they'll fell the trees for the most part. Up in Scotland they've brought over Canadians to help out. Only a very few of you will get the hang of tree felling, mind, but don't you go fretting about that. There do be plenty other jobs to do in a forest. Once them trees are cut down you need to get rid of the branches with a billhook and then we burn 'em. Careful, mind; the dry weather's round the corner and we don't want nobody setting off a blaze with a forgotten fag end or getting any ideas about campfires in the woods.'

Frank stooped forward, his expression more sombre than before. His voice was nothing like them at home and Connie leaned in to follow the curls of his sentences, looping up and down, in and out like these bloody tools in front of her were no doubt supposed to.

'Now you listen to me, my girls. Don't go thinking that forestry's easy work, or that every tree's the same. There's a lot as goes into cultivating a woodland like this one; it's been around for centuries and it'll still be standing once this war's over and we're all dead and gone, whichever way things turn out. This is more than just war work. This forest do matter more than any of us.'

There was fire in his words.

'Those of you fit to be measurers, you'll mark up the tree according to what it's being used for and then the rest of you will cross-cut to the right lengths. When that's all sorted you take the bark off with the stripper and load it ready for freight.'

Connie shifted from foot to foot, trying to concentrate. Once she was actually doing the job it would surely all start to make sense. She'd never met anyone who knew their job so inside out as Frank, who cared about it as much as Frank seemed to, not even the farmer and his wife at the last place. At the factory, nobody had given a monkey's, not really. It was a laugh, a way to get a wage packet at the end of the week.

Frank paused, shifting his weight off his gammy leg. 'We'll be keeping an eye on you all these next couple of weeks and deciding which forest you're best suited to. They do need lots of help up in Scotland at the moment on them pines, so most of you will be off there when you're done here. But that's nothing for you to be thinking about now.'

Moving again? Connie pinched her eyes shut. She couldn't. She didn't have the time for more flitting around; the next few months mattered like nothing else if she wanted to get herself sorted. But before she had a chance to speak up, Frank came amongst them, dividing them into pairs. He looked Connie up and down, assessing her without speaking to her, then pointed at Annie, a lunky girl from Brum who always seemed to know her stuff.

They were all right, the other lumberjills had seemed friendly enough except maybe those in her dorm who thought she was stuck up. But she couldn't risk anything going wrong again after that fiasco on the farm, so she kept a bit of distance. Soon enough they'd followed her lead, somewhat to her dismay, and kept theirs too.

'Right then, ladies. We'll start with cross-cutting the spruce for these pit props; nothing too tricky.' Frank led them across to row upon row of tree trunks lying on the grass like an obstacle course. 'One of you either side of the timber . . . that's it. Find the measurers' mark and that's where you put the teeth.' He stepped between the rows and pointed at a white cross. 'One of the long ones you've got here, girls.'

Connie squatted beside the log, one leg stretched in front for balance, and picked up her end of the saw. 'Like the original see-saw, this is,' she called across to Annie.

You could feel the saw biting when it was in the right groove, and then it was a matter of pulling as strongly and steadily as you could, and pushing – well, you didn't really push, you guided your part of the blade as your partner pulled it through. Easy, really, supposing neither of you cocked it up and you could find a decent rhythm.

At the other end of the saw, Annie couldn't get it though, not at all.

'Here, let me show you, girl.' Frank took her place, squatted into position and signalled to Connie. The blade flew away from her, swift and certain through the wood, then paused, like a swing flying through the air and stopping at the top for that secret, stomach-jolting second.

This was her cue. She pulled down on the saw, not too deep, but deep enough that the weight of the wood came up her arm, flew into her. Up, up, up it came . . . there it was. Top of the swing again. The air filled with a sharp, clean smell, like furniture polish again.

'See it now? Nice and steady, like; don't want to rush it, you don't.' Annie nodded, but she looked like she might cry. Poor cow. No good being all book-smart if you couldn't do this bit.

Frank nodded across at Connie. 'Nice work there.' She looked around but he really did mean her. Nobody had ever praised her for work before! She puffed out, just a little.

Frank came over to her side and watched a minute longer. Up close like this she could see how heavily he was leaning on his good leg.

'You done any timberwork before?' She shook her head, watching the blade, checking the line matched to the pressure coming through her knuckles.

'Factory, then dairy farm.' If she closed her eyes she could still smell the farm, the hay and manure mingling with the surprising sweetness of warm milk. No way she was going to close her eyes with a saw in her hand, though.

'Is that right? Might have to try you on a softwood in a bit. No time to waste with the amount we've got to get down.' He scrutinised her face, then moved away. 'Another hour then dinner break, ladies. Make it count.'

The girls huddled round the campfire, taking it in turns to fill up mugs from the billycan. Connie had got in quickly and now she leaned back against the stump of the old oak and stretched her legs out until they nearly touched the fire in front. She yawned and the bark dug into her back as it arched, cold and scratchy.

Beside her, Hetty pulled a face at her tin mug. 'It's warm and wet but I still don't know how they get away with calling it tea.'

Connie laughed and reached behind her for the twist of sugar they'd all pooled their rations for. It was precious, this sugar; seemed like years since they'd been able to just spoon it in willy-nilly. But she was having a good day at last and chatting to Hetty kept the collywobbles at bay. Connie needed that more than she needed her sugar ration right now.

'Here, put some of this in it. It'll take the edge off.' Who ever had proper tea any more? But in the couple of weeks she'd been in the Forest there'd been no mention of rations, not really, though the girls had all handed in their books at Horse Face's command. All the same, the hostel barely seemed to run out of things, which was more than could have been said for back home. Was it just that these local types were better at making their own stuff? Those baskets from the hostel were full of hunks and hunks of fresh white doorstops with slabs of dead sharp cheese in them, and it didn't half go down a treat after a morning's hard graft. That didn't explain the tea though; maybe the hostel's cook bartered it with some of them foreign prisoners who didn't believe in a cup of hot brew. Poor bastard Eyeties. It'd be bad enough to be actually out there, dodging bullets, not knowing if you'd live to see the next day, never mind getting stuck afterwards in a wire pen in the middle of a forest, with less freedom than even the sodding sheep seemed to get here. It's not like they were the Jerries, after all. She was a bit hazy on the facts but the Eyeties hadn't started anything, as far as she knew.

Connie squirmed against the stump, picked up her mug and gulped. It was bitter without the sugar, but she tried not to mind.

'What with the fire, the snap and now the sun, it's a miracle I'm still awake. Better cop on quickly before Frank gets me out there with those leftover forestry blokes of his. There's no way they're better than me at getting trees down, that ragtag bunch of leftover soldiers. Half of them look older than the trees, and Frank reckons some of the trees are hundreds of years old.'

Now it was Hetty's turn to laugh. 'As if being a bit dozy would cause *you* any hassle. You're running rings round most of us already. I shrieked when you got that first tree down; couldn't believe they'd let any of us do something like that on our first morning out.'

Connie's eyes lit up. 'Nor did I! I think Frank was trying to prove a point to his men, tell you the truth, show them a girl can learn it too. I don't care though; I love it. That feeling when the saw hooks in and you skip through the wood; and the point where it starts to tilt and you know you did the first cut just right, positioned the wedge at the perfect angle for the tree to fall right where you need it. You have to think it through and at the same time it's just gut. It gave me a proper kick to get it right. Didn't know I could like a job like I do this one.' She took another swig of tea. It was less bitter this time.

'I joined the factory in 1941, when I was fifteen, but it almost felt like more school, just with a bit more of a laugh at the end of the day. I've been itching to do something that feels like I'm properly helping, d'you know what I mean? What if this is it? Making munitions was all right, reckon a few of the parts I made might have ended up in a plane or two that knocked Jerry out of the sky, you know? But really I was just part of the line.' She snorted. 'And squeezing a cow's teats to make sure the last of the milk came out? That was just peculiar. But when that tree came down earlier, I thought, that's me. I did that. If I hadn't been here, done that, that tree wouldn't have come down. I could be helping out the navy, Hetty, with all this wood. Frank might say forestry's not just about the war effort, but I've seen the war up close, not like he has down here, and I *want* it to be war effort. It can be whatever Frank needs it to be too, long as he keeps me out here.'

Connie threw her arms wide. What a load of nonsense she was spouting. But finally she was doing something to help rather than just a series of cock-ups that took her further and further from any kind of decent life, war or no war.

'I dare say I'd feel like that about it too if I was half as good as you.' Hetty reached for the sugar again, tilted it so that the last grains ran from the twist of paper. She threw the paper onto the fire and it flamed blue from the residue.

'Finished it. Sorry.'

'Nothing to be sorry for.' You took it where you got it; Connie couldn't begrudge Hetty that sugar.

Connie glanced across the clearing. Logs were arranged around the fire, and at the edges were great piles of leftover twigs and branches – brush, she was supposed to call it now – ready for burning or for taking to the sawmill to be turned to woodchip. Frank's hut stood off to the left, flanked by two giant gnarled tree trunks, which must be what he called old-growth to judge by their size. She didn't have the foggiest what kind of trees they were, though, just old ones.

The hut looked to be made out of oddments that would otherwise have gone on the fire, and she was amazed that it didn't fall down, all those planks seemingly just laid one against another. The door was propped open with still another bit of wood, one of the boughs from lopping that should be on the clearance pile, by the looks of things. Frank was at his table in the middle of the tiny room. He had his head down over a pile of papers and didn't seem to be bothering with his food, even though Connie's mouth watered just to look at it. She was starving all the time these days.

Just then he stood up, stretched as if kip was a long way off yet, then stepped outside the hut and heaved the door-prop bough out of the way.

'Ready to get started again, Granger? Give it another couple of days and we'll try you on the felling sites proper. It's not every girl that gets the hang of it but looks like you might.'

Connie stood and twisted round to rub the small of her back. Pride bubbled, mixed in with relief. Frank didn't seem the sort to mess around and it had been a long time since anyone had thought she was up to much. She'd been right to sign up with the WTC, not that she'd had much choice in the end. Her arms were heavy and the insides of her fingers were rubbed raw, but the weight of the worry had eased off, ever so slightly. If all this shoving around of logs solved the other thing . . . that wasn't so bad, either. These aches were good ones. They'd replace the ones that crowded in if she let herself think.

Four

Gloucestershire Regiment
Shropshire
12th April, 1944

Dear Father,

I trust this finds you well. Isn't that how you're supposed to start a letter? Been years since old Miss Turner taught us that at school. Mind, she'd have me putting 'Dear Sir', but it seems a bit daft to go all formal.

Feels funny enough to be putting pen to paper to you at all, but here I am outside the forest and there's you tucked in it, and this is the only way I can find my way back to it until I get some leave. Don't reckon that'll happen for a good while, neither. Best we can hope for is that this war is done soon and I'll be back in time for next year's lambing, even if I've missed it this year. Don't go overdoing it. Frank will send one of the lads to give you a hand if you give him the nod. I know you don't like to ask for help but the sheep traipse miles up and down the forest, and even with Bess it's a lot of ground to cover.

I'm sorry for any words that came out harsher than they should have. You weren't wrongheaded to tell me to stay safe in the mines instead of enlisting, and I shouldn't have accused you of wanting me to take the coward's way out. You've never raised me like that and I'm sorry, Dad. The trees is the safest thing I know, and working underneath them kept me pretty protected, I do see that all right.

But I couldn't stay put any more, reserved occupation or not. To my mind, the best way to save our oaks is to get out there and fight for them. When Mr Churchill talked on the wireless about fighting for the land, I barely had to look out the window to see what he meant. Frank told me before I left that those London people are ordering him to cut down more and more of the old-growth every week for the 'war effort'. They're butchering the forest, our Dad, plain butchering it. The sooner I help stop this war, the better. If my war effort saves our trees – saves the way we live our lives – that's got to be worth summat, don't it?

They told us out here at basic training that anything we write home about our situation – where we are, where we think we do be going – is likely to come to you all blanked out by the censor, and I'm doing my darndest to avoid that. I'm up north a bit, think I can tell you that, and the likelihood is that we'll be shipped out somewhere soon. I'm fit and well, and the other lads stationed with me seem a good bunch. The river here joins up with the Severn, so when we get to stand down, as they call it, I go out and sit beside it and fancy it's telling me of home.

I've put the address at the top of the letter again in case you'd mislaid it. I know we had words, but I do hope I do hear summat from you soon, all the same.

I'm going to stop here and wish you good night. I'm looking forward to the day when I can be out trampling down bracken again, whistling for our lost ewes or helping out Frank. Say hello to him for me, and to the rest of the miners, whoever's left down there.

Your ever-affectionate son,

Billy

SARAH FRANKLIN

Hawthorn Cottage
Lower Yorkley
Glos
23ʳᵈ April, 1944

Dear Billy,

Seems odd to be writing to you when I'm used to just shouting over the garden wall. I was so glad to get your letter that I told Frank the tea would have to wait. As you can imagine, Frank's none too pleased about playing second fiddle to a bit of pen on paper, especially after a day out in the spruce stands trying to teach those new lumberjills one end of a saw from another. All the same, he said to send his best and that you should give Jerry hell so that that crowd in London stops demanding more timber. You'd think they must be building an ark to put the population of Britain in, at this rate.

You'll be wanting to hear about home. First things first: don't be fretting too much about your old dad, will you? I've known Amos for most of my life and all of yours, and he can be as stubborn as an old ewe at dipping time. Nothing changes in the forest, and that's the way Amos likes it. You're all he's got, and he'll have worked himself up about something happening to you. There're plenty of us here keeping an eye on him though, even if he don't like the idea. I take his coupons up to Cinderford when I do my shop so he doesn't have to be bothering about that. You're not supposed to, but Foresters don't abide much by other people's rules, you know that. We look out for our own and that's the way it is.

Seems to me that half the forest's waiting on news of someone at any one time, and it isn't always the news they wanted, neither. I've got to be honest, it do break my heart, it really does, and it's about the only time I've ever been glad the family situation didn't work out for Frank and me the way we wanted it to. And now, of course, with you out there as good as family, it worries me silly, it really does.

Hark at me carrying on! I'm supposed to be cheering you up, not unfolding all my nonsense on you. Frank'd have my guts for garters if he knew he was waiting on his tea whilst I moaned on to you.

Fancy you, a private in the army! I hope they're treating you half-decently. We've been listening extra-careful to the wireless in case they mention your regiment but they're pretty tight-lipped on that official stuff. Suppose you never know who's listening when they shouldn't be. Careless talk cost lives; that's what they tell us, don't they?

I laughed when I heard that, I did, and said to Frank, well, whoever wrote that hasn't never been to the forest. Who'd be yapping on out here? And who'd hear it except them trees? Mind, even the forest's jam-packed at the moment so you don't know any more, you really don't. Those evacuees are still out here, causing chaos in the school. And since you've been gone we've got Yanks in the Forest, whole regiments of them, apparently. Frank's tearing out his hair because they keep building these enormous tracks right through the newgrowth. You can imagine Frank's response to that, can't you? He doesn't hold with trucks thundering through the forest, not natural, he says.

The other big change out here is that we've got

POWs up at Broadwell. Not Jerries, don't worry. I do reckon there'd be a mob if it was Jerries, given how many of our boys we've lost to that Mr Hitler. No, it's Italians, and do you know what, Billy? I was walking up to Coleford last week and I heard what sounded like the wireless, right there in the middle of the road. I looked around, it was two of these Italians, cutting the hedges and belting out opera they were, there in the lane, not a care in the world. I had half a mind to join in with them, tell you the truth.

Other than that, there's not much to report here. Frank's bad leg's giving him gyp from all these extra hours out with the trainees, but he doesn't mind as much as he lets on. The stories he tells about the youngsters, Billy, it'd make you laugh to hear! I keep reminding him: these girls are no older than our Billy, and here they are miles away from home, learning to do physical labour that's been passed down for gener-ations. It's only right that they get in a muddle sometimes

I'd better go and put the tea on before Frank's really got something to complain about. You write to me any time you like, Billy. It's not a patch on having you next door but needs must, eh? And we'll keep an eye on Amos for you, fear not.

You look after yourself, mind, and try and tell us when you get posted on. We look at the paper every day, trying to guess where you might be sent, but it's a fool's game. Just remember there's a whole forest here waiting for you when you get back.

Yours truly,

Joyce

Five

BILLY'S LETTER CRACKLED IN his father's pocket as Amos picked his way back home through the gathering dusk, the sheep all accounted for until the morning. The oaks were starting to fill out, this time of year, and lime light spread through them and up over the spruce-flanked ridge Amos would have to climb to get home. Behind him, the sheep grazed peacefully down the hill. The ground beneath him was still just about purpling from the last of the bluebells, but it wouldn't be long now before it withered back to the brown of last year's leaf fall.

Amos brought up a fist, joints swollen with the damp, his eyes smarting with the last of the sun's rays. Bess trotted faithfully ahead, the collie showing no signs of tiring even after a day of herding and rounding the straggling ewes.

Amos jutted the tip of his crook into a birch root and heaved on up the slope. No need to bring the letter out – he knew these words better than the nightly prayer he'd got his Billy saying. But he'd keep this one close until the next one arrived, keep the lad safe and out here in the forest with him.

When Amos had walked Billy to the train up in Cinderford on that day two months ago, the boughs were still bare. The earth and bark of the forest had been scrubbed away from the boy too, replaced with starched white-and-blue, the smell of serge and carbolic soap. Amos shuddered, turned his gaze outward again.

Wouldn't be long until shearing time now. You could see it in the branches, feel it in the softening underfoot. The leaves were unfurling again and winter had mulched away those great big drifts that the sheep liked to wander into. All very well until they did turn around inside the leaf piles and start panicking. The daft blighters didn't seem to learn from one year to the next, and it was hard to find them when mist thickened the spaces between the trees. Fourth year of the flashlight ban and he still hadn't got used to it. As if Jerry was ever going to find them down here, let alone bomb them. Taken seriously though, the ban was; every week in the *Dean Forest Mercury* he saw more and more notices of people brought up before the county court accused of shining lights where none should be, slapped with fines people down here could ill afford. So instead Amos had to examine every last shadow, standing still beside the briar to judge if that shape or this was sheep or bush.

Amos didn't set much store by wishing for things; that was only a way of borrowing trouble from tomorrow, far as he could see. But it ran through him like a seam of ore, this deep longing that by the time the oaks were stripped of leaves again, this war would be done and Billy would be back where he belonged. Everything had its season. But it was all off-kilter nowadays. People didn't leave the Forest; why would they? All the life you'd need was right here.

What had he done to make Billy want to leave? It stuck

to Amos like a burr. What had he missed? The boy had seemed contented all right, grafting in the mine, sitting outside on a summer evening with him and Frank and a pint of cider. But sometimes if you looked at a thing every day, you stopped seeing the changes.

Amos skirted the remains of a fire pit. Started earlier by those new Eyetie prisoners and their funny ways, no doubt. No Forester would build a fire in the middle of a copse to keep warm. But now the forest, *his* forest, was being overrun with evacuees, with POWs, with GIs. Worse than the last war this was an' all, far worse; seemed like there'd be no rest until half of England was crammed in amongst the trees, and it just weren't intended that way, the forest. Women were coming on their own, too. It weren't right; anyone who knew the forest could see that.

According to Joyce, who did make it her business to know everything, these incomers were flocking to the two forest towns demanding things never needed in forest homes before: inside lavatories, water from a tap. They might as well ask for the forest drift mines to yield gold instead of coal, or for them to have them fancy elevators the deep mines did have 'stead of being built for walking into. Forest homes were two up, two down, built with stone from the quarry to fit the family as originally lived in it, more often than not. Even in Cinderford and Coleford and the towns you wouldn't find anything fancy. Forest folk didn't have need of them things.

In the centre of the fire pit, amber and ochre splashed against grey embers, molten tongues of ash and yew singing their scent into the crackling air. Amos tutted again, poking smouldering sticks with the tip of his boot. He arced patterns in the ash with his crook, strewing the embers over the base of the fire, making sure each last flame was extinguished.

Amos whistled to Bess and trudged the final steps home. There they were, his cottage and Frank's, where they'd been for generations, ever since their grandfathers had worked together to build the two of them, laying stone and digging gardens where before had just been a rough gap in the trees. You could do it like that then, mind.

The door didn't want to open again tonight so he put his shoulder to it. The weather was in the wood, swelling the door, making it uncooperative. Not likely to get proper rain, they weren't, not this late in spring, but you could tell where it had been, despite the onward march of the forest down through the seasons.

The fire had long since died in the grate and his breath puffed white into the gloom of the hall. Amos hung his coat up on the peg beside Billy's, hooked the stick beneath it. It bodged Billy's and the hall filled up with the smell of the boy, of dust and apples and horses and bits of straw. Nothing else to fill it up, mind. The house was as empty as it had been nineteen years ago, a sweltering summer when May lay dying at the infirmary up the road in Cinderford and Billy was in isolation whilst the doctors waited to see if scarlet fever would claim him too. Heartsick and scared to his bones, Amos had tended the sheep day and night, same as he ever had. Weren't nothing else he could do. It hadn't helped, but that weren't the point of it. Every teatime he'd cut a bit of bread and walked up to the Dilke to look in on May and Billy. Then he'd gone back into the woods to get the sheep sorted out before coming home to a house ghosted with absence.

He glanced up at the pictures above the coats. The paint was lighter around the edge of May's photograph, marking time where the silver frame had once held it. 'I tried to stop him, May, honest I did. Tried talking to him but it was no use. What did he have to go off to war for?' He nodded at Billy's picture, pinned up beside May, just barely touched his fingers to it, then moved away.

Amos sat down in his chair and stared again at the letter from Billy, in case the words had changed. '*I couldn't stay put.*' Amos shook his head at the page. Billy should be here now, talking about how them new lambs were doing up near Drybrook, not so many miles up the Severn he might as well be in Timbuktu.

The sudden banging nearly made him rip the letter clean in two. Right ruddy state that would have been. Bess pricked her ears but it wasn't an animal; she slumped back down. Shouldn't have the dog inside, really, working collie like that, but Billy had always snuck Bess in and Amos didn't mind the company, truth be told.

The front door knocker banged again. Couldn't remember the last time anyone'd used that. The noise blasted down the hall, carried on empty air.

'Keep your hair on; I'm coming.' He was slower up than he used to be since his Billy had gone. His feet didn't want to move anywhere once he'd made it home of an evening.

'Joyce. Don't expect you at the front door, all formal like.' Funny to see her in her coat this time of evening, though her hair was still tucked into its headscarf as usual. She filled the doorway like she always did. Bonnie woman, Joyce: you knew when she was in a room.

She was wearing that look that Amos had come to know all too well over the years. She wanted something, did Joyce, and she'd stay put until she'd got it. He steeled himself. Two could play at that game.

Some raggedy young woman was splayed beside her like a half-terrified yearling trying to put a brave face on it.

'Amos.' Joyce had one hand up already. 'I know Frank

spoke to you last week but I've been up at that site today and things are out of hand. Frank needs the help.'

Joyce shoved the girl forward and she smiled at him, hope in her eyes. Amos twisted away from her.

'I told your Frank, and I'm telling you, Joyce. That's our Billy's room and it's no being taken over by no wench. Someone else can have her.' He folded his arms, elbows firm against the doorjamb.

Joyce wasn't having any of it. 'Now listen, Amos. The whole forest's full up. Frank needs this, you know he does or I wouldn't be here. If we had the space we'd take her ourselves, but we don't. The spare room's full to bursting with all the sewing I'm taking in, and the longer we have to Make Do and Mend, the more stuffed that room becomes.'

Amos's bunions were giving him gyp, all this standing around. 'I'm not doing it, Joyce. It's our Billy's room, and that's that. The war'll be over soon enough.'

That brought a splutter from the girl. Full of kerfuffle she was, for someone who evidently had no home to go to.

Joyce came in closer and he drew back, away from the doorway. 'You can't go keeping that room as a shrine; it doesn't help anyone. If I know you, you haven't touched a thing up there since Billy's left, have you? Bet the door's shut tight to keep all of him in.' She was in the hallway now, the girl as well, bunched up like ewes trying to get through a gate. That young woman was more like a goat in the sheep pen, come to think of it. She was jittering about as if figuring out who to butt next, too brash, too colourful, in that bright lipstick of hers. His eyes hurt.

Joyce nodded up at the pictures of May and Billy, tugging at the belt of her coat as if missing the cardigan she would normally wrap around her. 'What would May here think of this? All these years you've kept your Billy alive, brought up that lovely strong man we all love, and now you're acting like he's dead already, keeping his room all shut up like a mausoleum.'

Joyce had a point, but Amos was darned if he was going to admit it. If May were here she'd be on at him to fill the blessed room, especially if it was to help out Frank and Joyce. He ran a forefinger over the rough edge of the photograph, looked up and saw Joyce had caught it. Eagle-eyed, that woman was; didn't miss a trick.

'When May passed away and it looked like your Billy was going the same way, we did help out, didn't we? Gave what we could to keep that baby in the hospital until he was cured. Just like you helped out me and Frank when his leg got trapped under that oak and he couldn't work for months.'

Joyce put her hand on his arm. His body strained with the effort of not moving it away. 'Nobody's asking you to sell any more silver, Amos. All we need is a roof over this Connie's head, stop her getting any more daft ideas about sleeping in Frank's forestry hut. She's a good little worker, Frank says, and he doesn't make those claims lightly, as you know. You know how riled up he is about all these extra timber quotas sent down by them blokes who don't know how to manage a forest. Frank needs all the help he can get at the moment, and that includes keeping this one here, so it seems.' Joyce smiled briskly at Connie and the young woman returned her smile.

Wasn't often he saw Joyce plead, however used he was to her notions. His firm intentions mulched. That girl must have something going for her, if Joyce could see past the sickly scent and the bright lips.

'You have to have her, Amos. Can't leave her to her own devices out there. We wouldn't if she was one of ours, would we?'

There was no point arguing the toss with Joyce, not when she'd got her teeth into something.

'Can she cook?'

'Doubt it, but I'll teach her a few bits. Least I can do.'

'Aye, you do that. Want someone who can pull her weight a bit.'

Amos tipped his head at the stairs, led the way up. His hand shook on the banister. Joyce was right; this was what Foresters did, gave each other a hand. But it felt all wrong. What if something dreadful happened to Billy out there in that war of Mr Churchill's because Amos had moved life on without him? He wasn't sure he'd be able to bear it.

Amos pushed open the door to Billy's room, nodded the women in, his head aching slightly. He couldn't pretend Billy was coming back any time soon. And that didn't sit right, didn't sit right at all.

Six

WHOEVER HAD OWNED THESE boots before they were issued to Seppe had loved to play football. The leather was scuffed almost into oblivion at the right toe, the heel worn down where this mystery man had angled time and again for the ball. But they fitted Seppe as if they'd been waiting for him.

He resisted the urge to scuff the other toe so that the shoes matched up, and continued his walk around the perimeter fence, urgency setting in now he'd nearly arrived at the right spot. The sheer height and length of the fence spoke of hordes of POWs yet to come. Italy's wartime losses must be more severe even than they'd seen in the desert. More imprisoned Italian troops meant more Italian factions, more arguments about the dominance of the northern *fasci* over the soft, partisan south and whose fault it was that they were now incarcerated. Already the staunch *fasci* were making themselves known, even though they were in the minority here, forming a choir and lustily belting out the 'Giovinezza' as 'resistance'. The guards took

51

no action, even stopping sometimes to listen, feet tapping along. Seppe, for whom the song raised instant hackles of apprehension, couldn't believe the guards let it continue, reasoned that it was because they had no idea of its potency as a fascist anthem.

The night terrors had returned. He dreaded the days, the lies he had to tell to avoid being pulled in to the growing band of fascist troublemakers here. But the nights were worse. Violent colours clashed and screams rent the fabric of his soul so that he woke grasping for his knife, his garments soaked with sweat. He had been lucky, that's what they'd told him, his capture relatively bloodless, the Allies ambushing them before first light and surrounding them so that the only recourse was surrender. But still the wounds and horror of battle played nightly, a prelude to the memories of Alessa, rendering sleep futile and every day jagged and uncertain.

Seppe had managed to turn down an invitation – more of a command, really – to join the inmate choir by hinting that he'd smuggled a weapon into the camp and was thus doing his 'resistance duty'. But it was a patch of a lie, destined to wilt away the moment his compatriots saw this 'weapon' in action.

How he needed to find it now. The knife was the sole thing that could sustain him and he felt its absence in every muscle of his arms, in every vivid nightmare. Seppe glanced over his shoulder, apprehension never far away. Would the guards think he was trying to escape?

But none of them were watching; they'd joined in the game of five-a-side starting up on the scuffed parade ground. Perhaps his boots had belonged to one of the sentries before they'd made their way to the uniform stores.

He held his breath as he turned around, to stay less visible. What about the watchtowers? In the holding camp by the ferry, and before that, in that first camp in Egypt, the barrels of the rifles had poked out, a constant, oppressive reminder that they were captives and alive only at the mercy of their captors.

But there were no watchtowers here. It had taken all of his first week for this to really sink in, so discomfited was he by the discrepancy. But he couldn't wait any longer. He had to do it today. This had been the longest period he'd been without the knife; the desert had yielded long patches of waiting around for the foot soldiers such as himself and he'd managed to use it daily despite the salt gumming his fingers from the sweat and the heat, the anxiety coursing through his fingers out into the smooth handle.

Only with the knife in his hands again would he gain some sense of self, some calm.

Seppe lined himself up so that he was opposite the ablutions barracks and dropped to his knees. In the confusion of their arrival he'd buried it somewhere here, in one of these mounds of earth that looked like a misguided escape attempt. 'Molehills,' the guard had told him. 'Can't stop the blighters.'

The molehills had multiplied in the few days since he'd used one as a hiding place. Seppe scrabbled at the first heap of earth he came to. It was damp and surprisingly silky, but yielded nothing.

Nothing in the second one, either. In the third, his increasingly desperate fingers met something hard and he pulled it out in relief, but it was a piece of stone, worn smooth from years of mud.

Seppe's pulse met his fingertips and his breath quickened. It *must* be here. Nobody else had noticed him bury it, he was sure of that. He straightened and looked again at the camp. No guards were in sight. He bent to his task again. Off beyond the fence a hawk called, the eerie bleat of a lost child.

His nails found it first, clinking against the blade. His fingers curled around the handle and relief surged through him. *Ecco*. Even covered in a pile of dirt, he knew this was it. Seppe lifted his hands and pulled out the knife. Perhaps these disturbingly relaxed guards wouldn't have confiscated it; maybe he hadn't needed to bury it after all. But he couldn't have taken that risk, his English not good enough to explain how he needed this knife, what the weight of it in his hand did to his soul. Seppe's breath eased as he shook the clinging remains of the dirt from the blade and slipped it into his pocket.

Now, if he could only find a piece of wood he could make a start. Anything would do. He paced the perimeter, his breath coming fast now, eyes sweeping like the searchlights. But the weather had been calm and still since they had arrived at the camp a few days ago, and the imposing ranks of trees beyond the perimeter fence hadn't given anything up.

He found what he was looking for at the furthest end of the camp, away from the locked gates and the parade ground, beside the ungainly structure of brick and concrete that was apparently on its way to becoming yet another sign of Italian dominance. An elbow of wood unable to support its spring foliage. *Perfetto*.

Seppe bumped down the knots in the wire until he was sitting on the ground. He turned the wood over in his hands. It was scaly against his palm, the lichen betraying its age. What did it smell of? Of the earth, of damp, and of something else that must be the scent particular to this timber. He studied the cluster of leaves, sticking out of the far end of the wood like a bunch of flowers at Holy Communion. Tiny hands, reaching out to greet him. This was oak.

Allora, finalmente. He fished the knife back out of his

pocket and tested it against his finger, then against the wood. Renzo's voice echoed in his ears, still clear and calm after a decade. 'Not quite sharp enough, not yet. Never start with a blunt blade.' With a rush he was in Livorno again, outside the stables at the port with the men rushing trolleys to the ships, the shriek of the seagulls and the brine of the sea against blue skies, his hands clamped around the blade's handle, the only place they didn't tremble.

The knife was his guardian, the bright thread that showed him how to be himself. Caught between these English guards and his volcanic, trapped fellow-prisoners, it was more vital to survival than ever.

Seppe ran the knife against the wire, wincing at the screech of metal against metal. He glanced around again: surely this would bring the guards running? He needed to be careful until he knew he could explain properly about the knife in English. But the football match was still in full flow, any noise he made drowned out by the shouts of outrage and success.

This time when he greeted wood with metal, the knife pulled through cleanly, despite its time in the soil. Seppe rotated the wood, sizing it up, slicing through soft layers of moss and bark, finding the rhythm of the grain, his breath slowing, his hands steadying, his mind calming.

The wood was softer here than he was used to. *L'acqua satura il legno.* He heard Renzo's voice again: there's water in the wood. But despite the unfamiliar quality of this English oak, the knife grounded him, carried in it all the memories of the happy times with Renzo, their backs warming against the sun on the stable door, knees up, forearms resting as they sat side by side with their knives and their carvings, taking a break before getting back to the 'proper' carpentry Renzo was paid for by the Livorno port authority.

Seppe's heartbeat settled. Gently, gently he carved,

twisting and turning the wood, humming, content, his fingers, thumbs and palm forming his own personal lathe. A soft gust of wind blew up over the hill and a timpani of fallen twigs rattled against the wire. He smiled to feel the reassuring ache in his fingers as they found the grooves of the knife, the grooves of the grain, and his breathing slowed, a tune came slowly to his lips.

During the interminable, confusing months in the camp in Egypt, he had carved by the light of the same unforgiving moon that had led to their capture, not daring to show the knife in daylight for fear of dying by it. The guards there had been brutal, unprepared, didn't take kindly to the hundreds of Italians thrust upon them, the near-constant escape attempts. *Certo* they would not have played football with the inmates. This English camp was an inexplicable place. There was talk here of some prisoners being sent out into the forest on work duties.

He peered at the dark outline of the trees just beyond the camp. To work outside, to carry the illusion that you were a free man, to be soothed by nature during the course of a prison day . . . To return each evening to this camp, which, despite the poisonous choirs and aggression that bubbled below the surface, threatening any moment to erupt, was proving to be a place of uneasy but nonetheless reassuring containment. Seppe shivered at the thought of it, dared to dream.

'Where did you get that knife?' A shadow fell over him. Now the trouble would come.

A guard, panting slightly, whether from the football or with self-importance was hard to assess yet.

'Thought I saw a funny glint and then we realised we had one missing from the roll call. Come on, Sonny Jim.'

Seppe put his hand over the blade the way Renzo had a decade earlier, but he didn't offer it up.

'No, no!' He gritted his teeth. The knife must stay with him. The guard would never understand. Even in Italian he couldn't have expressed this.

'What do you mean, no? Up here with a knife and half a blessed tree, by the looks of it? You want to tell me what you're up to?'

Seppe couldn't follow all the words but he had been an expert gauge of his father's tone since before he could read, and this man wasn't angry. He sounded curious. Seppe forced his shoulders back, met the guard's eyes.

'Is from friend, the knife. For make this.' He opened his palm. There in the centre like a communion wafer, was a thumb-sized acorn. It wasn't anywhere near finished yet. The bowl needed nicking with the inverse edge to dapple it, and the nut itself was too symmetrical. But it was a start.

'Crikey Moses, lad, you made that in the time it took the rest of us to have a bit of a kick about? Well, I'll be blowed.' Seppe's shoulders sagged.

'You'd better come with me. Hundreds more like you arriving these next few weeks and we haven't got anything like the furniture we need. The boss is in two minds if we're going to need to segregate you all, too. From the sounds of things it'll be them from the north of your country coming next, and from what we've heard on the wireless here, them's the ones that love that Mussolini. Reckon they'll be a whole other kettle of fish from these soft southerners we've had in, we do.'

The guard beamed.

'Anyway, reckon you could build a table or two?'

Seppe had built his first table, with only minor interventions from Renzo, when he was fourteen.

'*Certo.*'

The guard smiled again. 'Reckon you've got yourself a

job then, boy. And if you prove to be half decent, not one of them troublemakers, I'll see my way to getting your knife back to you.'

He had no choice. Working in the woods was only a dream, not something for someone like him. 'I start now.'

Seven

May

SHE WASN'T IN COVENTRY any more. Amos's house was her home for now, if you wanted to look at it that way. Perhaps it would feel more like home once she'd been to this dance tonight, started living a bit more like she used to. Not that living totally like she used to was an option any more. Connie smoothed down her yellow dress and shook her head to stop the bad memories landing. She pushed open the door into the little back room and concentrated on the biggest difference between here and home: the wiry black-and-white dog splayed out in front of the fire. Connie had never lived with an animal before and was surprised every day by that jolt of happiness when Bess nudged her rough nose under Connie's hand. She found herself wanting to say things to the dog that she couldn't say aloud to anyone in case she crumpled, and it made her pleased and terrified all at once.

Amos was shrunken into that wingback chair of his, head cocked to one side to catch the wireless despite it being up so loud that Frank and Joyce must be able to hear it from their side of the wall too. Connie sighed, sympathy for Amos inflating her. He might not say much, but he didn't miss a bulletin. He spent a lot of time poring over a very crumpled envelope, apparently always in his pocket.

'Billy. His only son,' Joyce had said one Saturday afternoon when she'd come over to show Connie how to pluck a chicken (Joyce had killed it herself! She'd shot right up in Connie's estimation for such daredevilry).

In a flash Connie had got why Amos wasn't one for gabbing on. Even after all these years of war, it only hit hard when it came for your family.

It wasn't cold out, but Connie pulled her cardigan closer over her dress as she skirted the shadow-filled garden to get to the road down to Parkend and Hetty. It went on for miles, that garden; you'd fit another row of houses at least into that garden if this were Coventry. At the end, where there should be brick walls backing on to terraces behind, fuzzy green stone walls were locked in ownership battles with trees. All these trees! And Frank was worrying about getting down enough to fill some daft Ministry of Supply numbers. Frank felt about these trees the way Amos felt about his son; he was sending them off to a war when all he wanted to do was keep them safe.

There was the path. Wouldn't be long now. A gin and the music would perk her up.

This dance might yet be worth the trouble of sprucing herself up. The Yank looked a bit surprised at being asked to dance, but he recovered quickly enough. He was a pretty slick mover, too. Connie wanted to put her head back and howl at the sheer joyous rightness of it, but he'd probably do a runner. She ducked and twisted, smiling, staying at arm's length, the tiredness shucking off with every swoop, every twirl.

A slow number came on – who knew you could play slowly on seven accordions? – and the Yankee moved in closer, pulling her towards him.

No.

The panic of the bombs was upon Connie again without warning, sending sparks into her speech.

She pushed away and the GI took a step back, hands outstretched. 'Hey, no offence meant.'

She smelled a trace of his Lucky Strikes and swallowed, her mouth slick and watery.

She needed to get out.

'Sorry . . . sorry . . .' She hustled her way to the door.

'Watch it, you!' Connie didn't stop to see who was yelling like that, or why.

That tree with the big splayed leaves, opposite the hall, would have to do. Connie braced herself against its trunk and heaved up all the jolted memories along with her dinner. Nobody was queuing outside now, thank heavens, and even George Thomas's accordions were muted from this distance. She stood gingerly upright and leaned against the tree, backhanding away tears.

She'd been so excited about coming to the dance that she hadn't bargained for the way the music would slice right through the shell she'd been forming. Connie leaned over the branch and retched again, speckling the shadowy grey-green of the lichen with vomit. And the Yank's accent, as he had got up close, it had been too much. The tears were back, streaming this time. Nothing to do but to let them out.

If only she could go back and change it all, she'd be dead – and that'd be easier than this. Easier than toughing it out and carrying on alone. If she could only will the bombers back. Connie looked up into the sky, but all she saw were the tops of the tree laced with soundless stars.

There hadn't been any cloud cover *that* night either.

January, 1944

The Coventry doormen are old hands at ramming them all through at double speed before their light and laughter betrays them. There's barely room to hop on the dance floor. It's heaving, joyous. Connie, spruced up in the bright yellow dress and on her second glass of gin and water, has already lost the girls from the factory in the crush of it all. What does it matter, though? The band, some local outfit with bad teeth and good tunes, is playing the 'Chattanooga Choo Choo' with as much spirit as Captain Glenn Miller himself, and all around couples are whooping and swooping. The music ripples through Connie and she laughs. Mam was expecting her home by teatime. She's supposed to be minding the littluns whilst Mam goes to the bingo to win the family fortune and Dad slopes off to the workingmen's club to drink it. But then Cass, working beside her on the munitions belt, started on about the dance.

'It's your Friday night too, you know; and God knows we've worked for it this week. I feel like we must have built twenty new tanks between us.' Cass has a point; they've worked like the devil was at their backs this week. To stay on top of their production targets the munitions factory has had them doing overtime whether they want it or not, the whole line of them.

'Aw; I dunno; I'm all done in and I've got nowt to wear.'

'What d'you think those dresses hanging up in the ladies' are for? For times like these, that's what.' Cass grabs her arm and pulls her across towards the lavs, grinning that grin that means mischief is afoot. 'You don't really want to go home, be honest. You want to come and have a laugh with us.'

Cass is right; she does want some fun. So Connie borrows a dress from the spares in the lav, pinches her cheeks for the appearance of rouge and paints on her favourite red smile. Anything's possible.

And here she is, in the heat and the dark of the dance hall, ready.

'Looks like you've got it all figured out, lady.' Warm hands wrap themselves around Connie's waist and a lick of flame heats her thighs and her belly. She smiles at the familiar voice, arches and hooks one arm easily around Don's neck, brushing his cheek. Her forearm tingles at its smoothness. He must spend hours in front of the mirror making sure he hasn't missed a patch.

'Wondered if I'd see you here tonight,' she says, and twirls to face him as if they're already dancing.

'Is that right?' Don bends down, kisses her full on the mouth with beery lips. 'Well, it's your lucky day, lady.' He's a cocky sod; she fell straight for it the first time they danced. And he doesn't care that she matches it. Most blokes expect her to mind her P's and Q's, but this Yank seems entertained by her outspokenness. She'd ribbed him when he'd told her his name that first time they met in this very dance hall: 'Don Wayne? Where's your horse, cowboy?' but secretly she's glad of a way to remember it. And she's glad to see him, too. He reminds her that there's more to life than Coventry and the factory, that she can make it out of here and she's right to dream big.

Connie turns into Don, her body still swaying to the music. She can picture Mam sucking air through her teeth, muttering 'fast'. As if she herself hadn't been three months gone with Connie when she and Dad had got hitched! And there's a war on. Life *is* fast in wartime, especially after those early years when the bombs were pelting down reminders every night. 'Fancy showing me how it's done?'

'Are you talking about the jive?' Don presses against her in a way that's got nothing to do with the dance move. Won't catch her complaining, though. His scrubbed soapiness twists through the smoke and clears her mind of anything but him.

'Let's start on the dance floor.' She flashes him a smile. And then they'll see. Whenever Connie meets up with Don it's as if he switches on ninety hidden flashlights all at once. She glows so strongly the ARP wardens'll be over soon to throw a bucket of water over her. It isn't only what she can feel under his uniform, though that doesn't harm. It's that way of talking he has, like someone out of the pictures. It gives her goosebumps. Like the real John Wayne himself coming out of the screen and showing her she could get out, have a different life. And get out she will. Connie isn't about to beg Don to take her back to America, but he's made her see that another life is possible. Ever since she's been knee-high to a grasshopper, no bigger than their Barbara really, Connie's had an itch that there must be more to life than their street and the factory. She hasn't got any idea what form that takes or how to get there, but she knows she needs to do it. And now, with the war moving people around all the time, she's started to formulate a plan. She'll get to London and take it from there. The big city will sort her out. Just as soon as she's saved enough, she's off.

Connie pushes against Don on the dance floor, his sweat salty on her lips. The waves of the jives throw them apart and her hips and belly scream their disapproval. The music swoons her back towards him and she laughs, Don laughing back. This war won't last forever; perhaps after London she can get out to America, find a job with a bit of glamour, jive like this all the time. Who knows, they might take her for a film star with her accent: the Yanks never tire of telling her she speaks 'cute'. Why not? She scrubs up all right and it's the Land of Possibilities, that's what they're always telling her.

The band stops singing about trains and segues into 'White Cliffs of Dover'. Don grabs Connie's hand, pulls her away from the dance floor and out through a side door. She curls into him, breathless and laughing, as he steers her further down the alley into a doorway. Frost crisps the empty fag packets littering the alley; she shrugs closer into Don.

'Here.' A couple of steps lead down away from the street.

'Down there? It'll be full of cats and pee, and cold enough to freeze the brass balls off a monkey.' She knows this city better than to get all soppy about backstreets, but she's desperate for him really, needs that body back up close against hers, and here is as good as anywhere. Won't be the first time she's stooped down some alley for a quick knee-trembler.

Don laughs again, that bellow of his that's bigger than any she'd known before. 'You're such a romantic. C'mere.' He pulls again, insistent, not buying the innocent act for a second.

What the hell? You only live once. This week has been all about other people – her messed-up shifts, the buses home all over the shop, even Mam wanting her home for more endless looking after the littluns. But this moment, right here, this is about her, about living a bit, about a yellow dress on a dank grey night and doing something that feels good because she knows it's wrong. Those Jerries can't take away all her fun even now they've started bombing London again. She'll show 'em. She follows Don down the steps, giggling. 'Shh!' But he's laughing too. The music is in them still and they sway together, her arms up around his neck. Her fingers push into his hair, finding him as he finds her; her breath becomes harder and more insistent as Don's hands move down her body, palm away her yellow skirt and trace their way up the top of her stockings. Her own hands trace their way up his thighs, explore. There's nothing now, only this.

From above, the sky splits with the laments of the siren. The door they've escaped through fills with shouts, laughs; the warmth of bodies hitting the night and racing to carry on Friday night. She should pull away; they should head for somewhere warmer, carry on the party. But the voice in her head is coming from far, far away; has nothing to do with this Connie right here, right now, her hips forward, legs curving around Don's, beyond caring about cold or propriety. Every part of him pulses in her. The air is thickening, with the siren that won't stop, with the frantic crossing of the searchlights. The urgency of the city mingles with his taste on her tongue. Don's fingers are separating her; her hands, her cheeks, her legs are slippery with need. Her thoughts are panting, her body racing, her mind far away and here, here, here.

She stayed there with Don, collapsed onto him, concertinaed, until dawn on the back steps of the dance hall that sloped down into the alley, swigging something smoky and bitter from a hip flask he produced and chain-smoking those Yankee ciggies until her throat was sore and her eyes were as gravelly as when the iron filings spangled the factory. She didn't want that evening to end, which goes to show what she knew. *Got your wish in a way, didn't you, eh?*

When a fox shows its snout down the steps, a scraggy vixen nosing for scraps to take back to its mangy cubs,

Connie yawns, stretching along the length of Don, and stands up. Her breath billows out, warm against the early morning, and she laughs, a dragon ready to take on any comers. Just as well.

'Time to get home and see what damage faces me.' He grabs her fingers, languid, greedy, but the oozing need has turned gritty in the grainy morning light and she shakes her head. 'It'll be ugly but I can face it. Better to get it over with now.' She blows him a kiss full of sunshine despite the proper nip in the air and clambers up the steps, no looking back, beaming as she marches forwards. No ties means no ties. And no shame means no shame.

She struts to the bus stop, despite the pinching of her dancing shoes and the chill in her bones now she's not all snuggled up beside Don. Should she circle back to the factory and collect her lace-ups? No, best get home and get it over with. Mam will read her the riot act, no doubt, but she'll stand there and take it. Connie has promised she'll always try and get word home if she's staying out, especially with all the raids and sirens. But last night she'd known Mam would be mardy that she wasn't coming home like she'd promised, so she'd 'forgotten'. There'll be hell to pay when she gets in, and she probably won't get any kip for ages, neither. Worth it, though. Her smile widens.

The conductor looks at her oddly when she steps on, hands over the fare and asks for Hillview Road. Is it that obvious? Is there some pitch to her voice that sings *see what I've done, see what I've done*? Can he smell it on her, that mingling of sex and dare? Her joy at his disapproval bubbles up into a beam. But the conductor simply shakes his head. What is that look, anyway? He isn't having a go, isn't criticising. She looks at him again as she jams her purse back into her bag. It's pity.

Pity!

Connie bridles. Judging is one thing, but to feel sorry for her after the night she's just tasted and smelled and danced in? He's off his rocker. She strides to the nearest seat and plonks her handbag beside her on the bench, smooths her coat over her borrowed yellow dress as the bus pulls away from the kerb, the vibrations low beneath her thighs. It's her lucky dress now so she'll hang on to it, 'forget' to take it back to the factory. The girls understand about lucky dresses; nobody'll mind. Her coat's dusty where she'd balled it up for a pillow on the steps last night, a bit damp too maybe, but nothing worse than you see after a night in the shelters.

Already she's scheming which dance Don might next show up to, whether it would be too bold to persuade Cass to come up with her to one of the hops held near the US base at Grafton Underwood. Her body aches with the absence of him. More than that – as if that's not enough! – she feels better when she's with Don. The very fact he made it all the way over to England shows her that her path to America isn't just a pipe dream. All she needs to do is get to London. And from there the world's her oyster.

Everything in life is improved by time fooling around with Don. Today she's unbeatable.

She rummages in her bag for her lipstick. Warpaint's what she needs now. She'd better get ready; there's going to be a doozy of a battle once she gets home.

The conductor taps her on the shoulder. She peers up at him. He's still got that strange look on his face.

'This is your stop, miss.'

She's been so wrapped up in thoughts of Don that she hasn't paid the blindest bit of attention. And she still hasn't found that lipstick. Have to deal with Mam barefaced, then. Connie claps the bag shut and marches down to the end of the bus.

SHELTER

What the hell's happened here?

Dust is everywhere, dust and freezing damp and the clanking of shovels. But Hillview Road is no more.

Eight

THE STENCH OF SIXTY men's sweat and excretions was a small price to pay for solitude.

The accommodation barrack was empty. Blocking out the disputes and shouts of '*gol!*' from the parade ground, Seppe eased the door closed into a frame that it didn't want to fit. He should bring the plane to it.

Seppe made his way down the rows of bunks until he reached the one he shared with a friendly southerner, Gianni D'Amato. Gianni seemed to understand without pressing the point that Seppe's sympathies lay less with Il Duce than one might expect from a northerner. It was only around Gianni that Seppe's shoulders relaxed, his hand less often seeking the security of the whittling knife.

Seppe dug under his pillow and pulled out the knife and the rough piece of oak he'd salvaged from the last set of chairs he'd made on the camp commandant's orders. In the three weeks since Seppe had arrived, trucks had rumbled in every day, as many as ten at a time. It was just as the guard had said: more hollow-eyed northerners brought

70

over from Africa where they'd been detained in the camps all over the continent for months, even years, now. Northerners were trickier, more belligerent, even if it was the southern Italians who'd been known as 'co-belligerents' since last year. Seppe thought of his father, of Fredo, of every Livorno Italian he knew bar Renzo. They were all fiercely proud of Ciano, Livorno's son and father of Tuscan fascism, and since his death a few years ago seemed hell-bent on keeping his memory alive through their fervour. If Seppe were a good citizen, more northerners should make him hopeful, uplifted, he knew this. But more north-erners meant being reminded again of home, and that was a subject he couldn't touch on. These northerners, he knew, would root out his lack of patriotism, and this quiet but precarious life of peace amidst war would be over.

Already the rows of Nissen huts were filling, the calm of the camp lost to shouts and jostling. Even the theatre, over on the other side of the parade ground away from the latrines and the sleeping quarters, seemed less of a folly and more of a sensible diversion now there were men enough to use it.

He pressed the blade against the oak and the handle bit into the soft skin between his finger and thumb. With every stroke the hundreds of his countrymen crowding into this place disappeared, along with their avowals of the greatness of the system that had overshadowed his whole life and brought only fear and dread. With every stroke he heard more faintly the strangled cries of his dying countrymen in battle, spread out in futilely thin lines along the desert so that Allied air troops couldn't kill them in one manoeuvre. With every stroke, Renzo came back to him and Seppe's breath slowed.

Seppe's hands were beds of splinters like when he was a boy, his thumb crimson where one had become infected.

71

He put down the pipe he was crafting and sucked, though it would make no difference. He was ten again.

March, 1934

An undercurrent to his father's voice signals impending danger as he returns from a meeting of the Livorno *fascio*. Seppe gets as close as he can, to listen, without being seen.

'You'd think even the workers, especially the workers, would support Ciano's ideals. What more do they want from our local hero?'

Seppe's mother lays a tentative hand on the Major's arm, appeasing. 'But your rank amongst the leadership continues to rise. This is something to be proud of.'

He bats her away without so much as a glance in her direction. 'Don't contradict me. These are matters about which you are ignorant. These riots are infuriating and something must be done.'

Seppe shrinks against the wall. That 'something' doesn't bode well for anyone.

His father marches into the formal drawing room and closes the door pointedly behind him. A moment later, a bark: 'Vittoria! The newspaper.' Seppe's mother scurries to find the paper and Seppe sees his chance. He lifts up an edge of the tablecloth and crouches.

'Careful! You've moved the baby. She will start to cry.' Alessa is already under the table, playing a complicated game with the 'family' of tassels that hang down. It's so musty under here – he doesn't know how she stands it.

'Sorry. There, she's quiet again now.' He drops the table-cloth and crawls under. Not so easy to do at ten as Alessa finds it at eight; he is getting taller, even if Fredo still taunts him for being the weediest in the class.

'Do you want to play?' Alessa bears no grudges. He wishes he could be more like her, enjoy life without complication.

He gestures up through the tablecloth into the poisoned air and shakes his head.

'Papa's in a mood. I'm going down to the port.' He hesitates. She's big enough to come, and if he were a good brother he'd take her. But the port is his place.

If it were the other way around, would Alessa take him? He sighs. Yes, without question. He stretches out a hand, whispers to her.

'Come with me?'

Alessa twists a corner tassel, studies it. 'I'll stay under here. I need to look after the babies, or nobody will care for them.' She beams up at him. 'See you later.'

Seppe is filled with tarnished relief as he eases open the front door, slips out and makes his way to the industrial port to wait it out. The grand white houses, their columns and begonias bright in the warm sunshine, make way to smaller rows of small-windowed houses tipping towards the canal, which discharges him at the port. His father never deigns to come down here unless it's on official business to berate and intimidate the workers into signing up to Ciano's party of fascists. More often than not he'll send henchmen to make his point more starkly.

The drays are all out on delivery when he arrives at the stables and he slips in to the side, the hay smelling, as it always did now, of sanctuary. That's how he found this place, following a dray home after its delivery one day. He settles in. Folded into the corner of one of the stables, he's invisible, free to dream of a day when his life will not be dictated by his father's moods, by politics, by the *fascio* movement. He listens to the day going past; the horns on the ships coming in and out of the harbour, the pace of the men's grunts as they heave crates onto carts, underpinned by the lapping of the water in the neighbouring canals. By the time the noise abates, his father will have spent his fury and Seppe can go home. And Alessa knows to be sensible and stay where she is.

That burning Livorno afternoon, thirst gets the better of him and he dips out of the stable as far as the horse trough, cupping the water and taking quick, parched slurps before resuming invisibility. This time, just as he makes it back to the safety of the hay a hand grabs him by the cuff.

'I've been watching you, lad.'

But the owner of the voice is smiling. He's an old man, older than Seppe's father, in rough working clothes that the Major would consider an indicator of inferiority, and a heavy apron of some sort.

'I don't know what you're hiding from, but I do know you can't keep it up forever.'

Seppe's mouth runs dry. The man hums 'Bella Ciao' as he waits for an answer. 'Bella Ciao', the song of the resistance, of the folk who don't believe in Ciano's dominance and aren't afraid for it to be known. The Major's fury will be unassailable when he finds out that not only has Seppe run away but he has also kept company with a traitor to the cause of fascism.

'What's that look for?' The old man squints and loosens his grip on Seppe's collar. He smells curiously of cooking oil and his fingers are broad, the nails blackened.

Seppe considers his options. He could make a break for it. But if his father were to find out he wouldn't even stand up to these 'peasants' things would only be worse. Seppe's hands are shaking. He stuffs them in his pockets and clenches his fists. It doesn't stop them.

'I caught a glimpse of something shifting a couple of

weeks ago when I came in here to fix that rubbing door. Thought it was a rat, but now I know better.' The old man considers him. 'Don't want to be home, is that it? Well, I can understand that, had the same trouble often enough when I was your age.

'We'd better give you something to do, make you useful.' He dug into a pocket and drew out a knife. Seppe jumps back and the man flips the knife, offering it, handle out, to Seppe. '*Calma*. I'm not going to hurt you. Take this.'

It's warm from the man's pocket, and tiny, no bigger than a butter knife, but the blade winks in the salty harbour light and speaks of its power. Seppe balances it in his palm, not daring to look up. What does this stranger want him to do? The ports are chock full of crooks, another reason his father despises the place. The Major has been accused by some of double-dealing to gain his place in the Livorno *fascio*, and the battle to clear his name has left him implacable if faced with anyone he considers immoral; the ports are the epitome of this, in his view. And he has many methods of enacting this rage.

Seppe rolls the knife in his hand, the weight firm and steady. No bloodstains. This is a good sign.

The man rests back on his heels, watching. Seppe risks a glance and the man smiles. Grown-ups don't normally smile. They use their special 'obey me' voice (his father), cower (his mother), or do as his father demands (his teachers, the padre, the neighbours).

'I'm Renzo. I'm the carpenter round here, keeping the carts steady, the stables safe. I don't know who you are, and it's probably better that way, but I need to call you something.'

It's beyond Seppe to lie, not about something so fundamental. But he can leave off the family name and that might protect them both. The shame he feels towards being his father's son is complicated; if he were a good person, he would want to be connected to such a powerful and public man. But here the instinct to conceal his identity is strong.

'I'm Seppe.'

'Well, Seppe, it's good to meet you.' He sets off and Seppe follows, still clutching the knife. Renzo looks over his shoulder. 'That whittling knife's yours if you like. I'll show you what you can do with it.'

Seppe had carved hundreds, thousands of pieces in the decade or so since, but every single time he picked up a new piece of wood, carving erased his father's poisonous whispers and uncontrolled roars, erased his mother's futile, terrified attempts at mollification, erased the stamp stamp stamp of blackshirt troops on the move, even more terrifying when the Major led the way. And with every new piece of wood Seppe still considered what Renzo would guide him to do. Hydrated wood was harder to carve, easier to get wrong because the blade didn't run true, might snag on the denser material. Renzo had kept his carpentry materials as far from the waves as he could manage, building himself a trolley at the back end of the port to pull them from place to place as he, also warped with time, bent until he was almost doubled over.

THE BARRACK DOOR BANGED open and he jumped.

'So it's true! The Major's son got himself captured! Someone said there was a Seppe from Livorno sneaking around. I had to come and see this *stronzo* for myself.'

Seppe's whittling knife clattered to the floor.

No. *No.*

Fredo Neri was *here*, cronies jostling beside him. Fredo, who he hadn't seen since the desert, whose last move had been to swear vengeance. Fredo, already issued with the black armband marking him out as a dangerous POW and wearing it with swaggering pride. He stomped towards Seppe, menace clear in the clanging of his boots against the wooden struts of the bunk.

Seppe went cold. He kept his head down, but it didn't make any difference, never had. Fredo jabbed him hard.

'Oi, you! Move. I'm having this bunk; you need to take one of those spares by the latrine pot. There's no way I'm sleeping down there.'

Fredo had been one of the first from Livorno to go to war, delighted to enlist and fight for Il Duce. Seppe's father had reported this news with vicarious pride, then beaten Seppe for not demonstrating the same fervour. The Major's delight when Seppe finally enlisted had been undocumented, but Seppe couldn't help but see his hand in the posting he received, landing him straight after brutal training into Fredo's regiment in the African desert.

'Come on, move. Get near the shit where you belong.'

No! This was a new country, a new situation, the first time Seppe had ever felt truly safe. It didn't matter what had happened in the desert, where he'd finally exacted a drop of revenge and doubtless exacerbated things. Fredo couldn't touch him in here. Seppe stood firm, met Fredo's gaze.

It was short-lived; he couldn't stand to stare at him for long.

'Don't think I don't remember what you did, the choices you made. You might have been running from Daddy at the beginning but it's me you have to fear now.'

Fredo threw Seppe's pillow down the hut, aiming at the night soil buckets.

'If you're not going to do it yourself, scum, then we'll do it for you.' The two men either side of him, wiry and mean-looking, preened as if only too keen to follow Fredo's lead.

No!

But Fredo was already out to get him. What was the sense in giving him further reason? Seppe's actions in the desert had been hasty, borne of a long-held grudge. He would never have done it if he'd known he'd end up trapped here with the man. Better to give Fredo this small victory than to add to the already looming threat of retribution. Even as he watched, Fredo followed the pillow back to the front of the hut. He picked it up between forefinger and thumb and, making sure he had Seppe's attention, dropped it into the night soil bucket. It tipped over with the weight, the stench mushrooming, lacing the room.

This would only be the beginning. Seppe bent down for the whittling knife with numbed fingers and moved.

July, 1942

They are deep into the African desert when the trucks finally stop and the order comes to set up camp. Seppe had tried to listen out for where they must be, the continent so vast that this not knowing only adds to his disorientation, but the commanders are concealing this information for their own unexpressed reasons. He jumps out, rubbing the crimped ache in his left shoulder. The heat races at him and he flings an arm in front of his eyes. It's pointless; the swelter snakes under his clothing, coils around his bare arms, claims him as its own.

'Get a move on!' He's pushed forward by the mass of soldiers clambering out behind him, follows them to the supplies truck where tents are being doled out. Another endless, monochrome landscape with nothing to break the line of sight but constant, wind-rippled sand, each grain as uniform as the next. And the heat! Seppe's lips are parched and cracked, his water canteen dry since Fredo tipped it over in the burning sun just as they were due to climb into the truck. But there will be no water supplies until the tents are up.

He collects his pack supplies from the truck, his arms sagging under the weight of the tent. Fredo is somewhere in the mass of shouting northerners, delighted to be moving closer to the fighting. They are the same lowly rank, he and Fredo, but where Seppe sees only danger in such proximity to the firing line, Fredo revels in this enactment of duty to Il Duce. His zeal makes Seppe sick to his stomach; even in basic training Fredo delighted in learning the precise angles for maximum damage, not seeing that they themselves are the maximum damage. But for as long as Fredo is amongst kindred spirits, singing and marching their way to their designated spots, he is out of the way. Better that he's chanting about murdering the lily-livered Allies than that he's insinuating himself behind Seppe.

Last week, as they marched through the desert, Fredo had lengthened his stride so that the scraped tips of his hob-nailed boots bit into the back of Seppe's heels, step after step after step. Today the wound is red and weeping, sand slicing into it and each new move only intensifying the wound. Tomorrow Fredo will find another way to diminish Seppe. It has been like this since they arrived. It will only end, Seppe thinks, with death or capture. He is ashamed for how fervently he longs for the latter, and sometimes, secretly, for the former. How blissful would be the release, the escape from Fredo, from this senseless war. He draws himself in every time Fredo is nearby, tenses for the next slight. The very act of diminishing himself breeds self-loathing and resentment. Resentment of his father, whose sickening beliefs obscured care for his family; of his mother for compelling him into this senseless war; of Fredo. And disgust with himself for never standing up to them.

Seppe hobbles forward and finds his space in the platoon's line of sand-filmed tarpaulins. The war has been dragging on for years and the supplies are no longer complete. Perhaps those early conscripts had marched into battle with a full complement of gear, but those days seem as alien to Seppe's version of this war as they do to the hazy memories of peacetime. The incomplete supplies are a solace. It relieves the tedium of assembling the tiny triangle of tarpaulin into a tent, makes it a puzzle that changes every time.

It soothes him to build things even here in the punishing heat of the desert, his hands finding the rhythm that connects him to Renzo, to a time when he feared only his father, and was not marching in a platoon of zealots. It is as if his father has evoked the worst possible punishment.

When Seppe's hands are busy, his agonised thoughts of Alessa also fade.

He blinks hard, pushes the memory down, forcing it beneath the sand, and turns again to the bundle of tarpaulin, incomplete as usual. Behind him the noises of the battalion swirl and point, forming patterns in the sand-saturated air around them. The chaos recedes as Seppe bends towards his task.

He needs two tent pegs. Tent pegs are not a problem. He puts down his pack and scrabbles around in the bottom of it for the screws he'd picked up on their first, rattling journey. He takes a length of string from the ball tied to the outside of his pack and cuts it off with the rough spiral of the screw before winding it round the screws, a loop secured at the top, to form a tiny parcel.

'*Eccoli.*' The tiny points of the screws drive into the ground more easily than the military-issued tent pegs and will stay put in these shifting sands. He uses two of them at corners, then bends down to straighten up the groundsheet.

'Oi, master builder.'

Seppe turns around, stands to attention, sand gritting beneath his boots. Their commander often calls him in to fix things. It's all less time spent with a weapon in hand.

He's been fooled. It's Fredo, mimicking the commander. Fredo's eyes are gleaming. He has found a way to destroy this moment of peace. Fredo is determined to undo Seppe, picking away at his snatched moments of calm like the rats nibbling at their supplies until Seppe is hulled. Seppe is the easy target, the honourable target. If Fredo can defeat Seppe, he will please the Major back home, and it will be a win for fascism, even as the Regio Esercito is being pushed inexorably back by its real enemy.

Seppe understands without Fredo uttering a word. If only he had any idea how to stop it.

'My tent won't go up straight. Come and fix it. God only knows where the likes of you learned how to do this.' All around them, men are starting to line up for inspection, row upon row of shaven heads with caps crammed on despite the heat.

This sounds benign enough; many is the day that Seppe has fixed a tent for a fellow soldier. But his heel is sore, the infection hot and pulsing, and the shame froths in him like pus, spews out his answer before he has considered the implications of refusal.

'No.'

'What do you mean, no?' Fredo comes closer. From here Seppe can see the crooked tooth, the cowlick that even as a small child was more menacing than charming. He will not step backwards. He is steeled by this endless burning sun, by the dread thirst that chaps his lips and spits out his words, husked of caring. For weeks now they have been marching, driving, building camp, breaking down camp, crouching in the shadows of moonlight not knowing if an ambush is imminent. The days oscillate between trudging boredom and terror of death, meld together in this desiccating heat. Seppe's emotions are worn down, neutralised. None of it can matter any more.

'Sort out your own tent.'

'What did you just say?'

Seppe shrugs. Fredo leans forward, shakes him by the shoulder. The ache from the truck isn't fully gone and it twinges. 'You *will* help me.'

The physical touch prods awake in Seppe a memory of his father, shaking him as a child, demanding to know where he'd learned 'that filthy song' of resistance, a precursor to a beating. That was the end of Seppe's time with Renzo, of the peaceful time and the touch stirs everything to the surface. He didn't stand up to his father, but out here perhaps he can stand up to Fredo. Just once.

'I will not.' He twitches Fredo's hand away from his shoulder and glances pointedly at this own tent, inspection-ready and proud, then nods his head at the approaching commander.

'This is the third time my tent won't make inspection,' Fredo whispers, urgent now, barely containing his fury. 'The commander will punish me.'

This is true. The commander is cut from the same cloth as the Major, the same cloth that Fredo himself seems to be trying to fashion himself from. Painstaking care is taken in the desert to ensure a façade of organization and success amidst this pit of sweat and defeat. This manifested itself in regimented lines of tents even when half the equipment was faulty and dunes make neat quadrants near impossible. Last week the commander had ordered a man to run four miles in the beating sun for failing to present with properly starched collars, out here where sand snuck into the seams and rubbed weals into the tender scrag of your neck. The man had contracted sunstroke, had spent three days in the medical tent before being ordered to the front line, and did not return from it.

Fredo is almost on his knees, the panic palpable. Seppe shifts forward, acquiescing. He can't be someone who lets someone else suffer. But as he moves, the ridge on the heel of his boot scrapes against the open sore and he's frozen with pain, his mouth watery and metallic. *Fredo did that.* Seppe runs a tongue over his dry lips, Alessa's voice clear in his mind. *If he suffers, he suffers. It's not your problem.*

He shifts back, favours his good foot.

'You'd better get back to your post. It's nearly inspection time.'

As if to emphasise the point, the trumpet sounds. Fredo casts a look at Seppe, half-anguished, half-vengeful. 'You will pay for this.'

This is without doubt. Seppe will feel the ramifications later in some imperceptible but vicious way; a slit slashed in the back of his shirt to burn his skin in the sun, buttons missing from Seppe's jacket to trigger inspection ire. Fredo's tactics are devious. Seppe could almost admire the guile, the evidence of a long game. Right now all he has is this bitter moment of victory, and he will savour it. He looks out towards the makeshift armoury, where even now gun parts are being cleaned, weapons assembled, ready for their next miserable, tense march towards potential death. Tomorrow they might all be dead . . .

EVEN WITH THE DOOR to the carpentry workshop shut tight, Fredo's vitriol surged in volubly from the uniform store two huts away, although the usual hubbub as the men cleared the parade ground of debris barely seeped through. This screw Seppe had been battling wouldn't thread properly, the metal catching on his infected thumb.

Fredo stopped roaring. The screw found its way in the silence and wound easily up the groove. Seppe exhaled. Now to fit the other two screws and that would be another chair finished. He was staying on track, though he barely slept now. On his second night beside the night soil buckets, a bleary POW had apparently mistaken his bed for the latrine and now, since then he was constantly on guard for a warm stream of piss to splatter him again.

The door slammed open. Fredo marched in. 'I won't stand for it. It's all part of a conspiracy to wear us down!'

Fredo's Italian uniform had been taken from him, presumably to be burned with the others. Now he was in an old British uniform with black POW patches, the same as the rest of them. It happened each intake. The Italians were stripped of the uniforms they'd been in for months, deloused, and given these 'new' uniforms. Fredo's black armband was still in place, though – he was fiercely proud of his status as a 'real' enemy.

'It's clean,' Seppe offered. He had relished the relative softness of the new uniform against his skin, the absence of sand and lice and the stench of self. The lice didn't stay away for good, of course, but it helped for a few days.

The guards had been taciturn but kind. To Seppe, straight-forward behaviour from 'the enemy' brought more comfort than the convoluted machinations of his homeland.

Fredo stared. 'You're on their side! You are defending these English ways?' Had Seppe spoken out loud? Fredo loomed closer and Seppe crouched behind the chair he was crafting. 'You are worse than I thought! Not only a coward but a traitor too.'

Fredo kicked the chair. Seppe toppled back from the force, sprawled on the sawdust. Fredo laughed, but there was no mirth.

'I'll show you, traitor.' Was he going to beat him? Seppe's arms came up around his head. But Fredo simply laughed again, hurled the chair against the wall. The leg snapped as it landed.

'Like I'd waste being punished just for giving you what you deserved with one of your useless traitor chairs.' Fredo picked up another one, slammed it hard into the wall. The hut juddered again. Seppe should stop him; he had to stop him. The guards would penalise Seppe for this waste, rations cut and his cigarette tokens denied for a week or so. He cowered and watched Fredo pick up and destroy another chair, and another. If Seppe got in the way, it would be him thrown against the wall instead.

Outside, a bell rang. The mess bell. Fredo trod closer so that he was inches away from Seppe. He was panting, sweat dripping down red cheeks. Seppe backed up against the wall, the wood panels rough and unwelcoming as he pushed up against them. Fredo stepped forward, menacing, forcing Seppe into a corner.

'Oh, you've got it coming all right; don't you think you haven't. Nobody humiliates me and gets away with it, especially not a traitor like you. You should be ashamed to be your father's son.'

Fredo grabbed another chair leg and tore. Wood splintered, the smell flooding out like blood. Seppe tasted metal on his tongue and his ears rang with the urge to get away. But Fredo kept him trapped in the corner. One by one he snapped every chair. Fredo's aggression was festering in captivity, escalating; it would be Seppe himself next, he knew it. He pressed hard against the wall, needing to feel something.

'Tell anyone I did this and you'll be next sooner than you think. Don't think I'm done here, traitor. This is just the beginning.' Fredo stalked out.

Seppe pushed himself off the wall, legs shaking.

His teeth chattering, he forced himself to take stock of the damage. Treat it like a casualty of war, that's what he needed to do: triage it and work out how to fix it.

As he surveyed the scene, another part of his brain taunted him. Why could he still not stand up to Fredo? The scars of his youth, the memory of being tracked . . . they handcuffed him. They bit through the numbness that months of noise, of fighting in the desert, had provided and reduced him to that sixteen-year-old cowering beside the canal whilst Fredo loomed over him, gloating that he'd tell the Major that Seppe was trying to make it back to the docks and then there'd be another beating.

Shame ran through him, cold and liquid. He had thought the camp was sanctuary. But Fredo would certainly inform the Major that his cowardly, secret-holding only son was refusing to rail against the enemy. Fredo was barely literate but would doubtless consider this piece of vengeance worth the struggle with pen and paper. And the Major, with his connections to the Livorno *fascio* and beyond, would surely find a way to reach him even here. Seppe was trapped by more than just the wire fences of the camp.

Nine

Coventry, January, 1944

CONNIE STARES IN SILENT shock. She pulls the dress around her but the shivering won't stop.

Nothing of her home is left. It's buried behind a pile of rubble.

She looks back at the bus conductor. 'What's going on? You've put me off at the wrong stop!' The air is freezing, bits of dust hanging motionless in it, and she hacks, bending over.

The conductor puts a hand on her shoulder, fatherly. Not that her actual pa ever does any such thing, unless he wants to borrow a few bob for the club.

'Got hit last night, love. Thought you must have heard the news and stayed away deliberate.'

She clings still to the metal pole whilst she searches up and down the street. He's got it wrong; this isn't Hillview Road. Where's the club at the end, by the bingo hall? Come to that, where's the bingo hall?

'You've put me off at the wrong street, mister,' she insists, frantic now.

The conductor still looks at her, that expression unchanged. In answer he points at the crumpled metal plate on the ground beside her. It can't be the street sign. That is nailed to the side of Number One. This is only a pile of rubble.

'We need to get moving, love.'

Connie stares at the conductor. He gestures at the road. What else is there to do? She steps down onto ground that seems to shake beneath her. The conductor rings his bell and is swallowed into a cloud of ash. Bombs are nothing new in Coventry. In a couple more days this stop will be taken off the route.

Connie's tongue sticks to the roof of her mouth and she coughs again into this filled, frigid air. Brick dust is every-where, and a stink of burning. Beyond a pile of smoking rubble ARP wardens are calling to each other. She can't see them through the blanketing dust. She gags, her eyes streaming, and lifts her bag up to her mouth in a fruitless attempt to keep out the grime. Her mood has crumbled like the buildings either side of her, toppling sharply down into despair as she picks her way through. Corners of walls stand tall and protected like a grotesque forest of concrete, rubble forming the forest floor. She strains to listen out for Mam, for Linda and Barbara, even for Dad, but the ringing in her ears blocks anything that might be there to hear.

She'd marched down the middle of this street only last week, after yet another row with Mam about not being stuck in minding her damn sisters. She'll find them now, and she'll look after them all week – all year – whatever Mam wants. The dust layers thickly over her like fear, stifling all thoughts, the ringing in her ears louder and the wall-trees shrinking as her vision tunnels with panic. She's small again now, coiled up.

She'd give anything to scarper, to winkle out Don from

his cosy barracks and stay in their world of unknowing a little bit longer. But she can't.

Connie walks slowly, as slowly as she dares, making each step tiny. Shivers take her again and she wobbles off course. But eventually there she is. Number 27.

Connie sways. Her bag drops into the dust in front of her. Someone's having her on. This can't be Hillview Road, can't be home. There's nothing left of it. She wants to shriek, turns around in horror for someone to scoff, tell her she's seeing things, it's the lack of sleep and one too many gins last night. She clamps her hand over her mouth and bites down hard but nothing's working. She can't feel her teeth against her finger, can't trust her eyes.

Everything's gone.

No, that's not quite it. It's like someone's dropped a doll's house. Their front door is gone. The walls facing the street are gone. The roof, the window frames . . . She stares, and the more she takes in, the bigger and more unmanageable it gets. It looms in front of her and she can't grab it, can't make it make sense. Everything has shut down.

Where Mam and Pa's room should be, a wardrobe hangs open, grotesquely out of place, half over the gap at the front where the wall should be. Is that Mam's dress with the blue spots on? The one she's always saving for best?

Connie's legs go now and she plonks down on the road, pulls her knees tight up to her chest. The ground is cold, goosebumps appear straight away on her skin, and she looks at them as if they're nothing to do with her.

Her bag is open beside her, but who is there here to steal anything? The scavengers will be along soon, clambering up after Mam's dress and whatever else they can get their hands on, but even they haven't copped on yet. For now the only noises are the sharp scrape of shovels against brick. There are no cries from under the rubble, no sign at all that people have ever lived here.

Connie's hair droops into her eyes and she rests her head on her knees. Weariness cloaks her. She closes her eyes but when she opens them it's all still here. Now she does scream, again and again, sending signals out into the dust. Her family do not hear her.

'Constance Granger? Is that you?' Old Mrs Cole. Is that one of Mam's best teacups in her hand? Is she planning a tea party here in the middle of the street? Connie raises her head but doesn't get up.

But Mrs Cole is crouching down beside her, trying to get her arms round Connie. She isn't the hugging type; more likely to throw her prayer book at you than come for a cuddle. That's when Connie knows.

Mrs Cole stopped being an old baggage and showed the first kindness Connie ever knew from her. She'd been off visiting her sister when she'd heard the raid, knew from the searchlights where it must be. She'd raced back at the dawn's light to see what could be salvaged and found the whole street gone, wiped out. She'd stayed to see who they found.

Nobody.

Nobody was brought out alive from here. Got the lot, that raid.

Shards of brick bite into Connie and she welcomes them. Good. Let her feel something, let there be pain. It's better than this awful realisation. Anything to hold that off. She rocks backwards and forwards, arms hugging her knees tightly to her.

'Won't they have made it to the shelters?' She won't believe it. They'd have been fine. Mam would have got them out, would have come back from the boozer when she heard the sirens. They'll have a right cob on them but they'll be fine.

Mrs Cole picks at a nail sticking out at an angle from a bit of wood. 'The shelters flooded when the water main burst.'

Connie gags. She's seen those bodies be pulled out before, purple and swollen. Beside her, Mrs Cole waits, saying nothing for perhaps the first time since Connie has known her.

'Right sudden, that one was,' the warden tells them, joining them in their awkward mid-road huddle.

'Jerry was at us before we'd drawn breath, the first bombs down before we'd even got the sirens sounding. Weren't even supposed to be bombing up here as far as we can tell; word is that one of their lot lost their way and wanted shot of some leftover bombs before they got back across the water. Couldn't get a soul out alive. They were just too quick for us.'

Connie has to wait for an hour for a bus and, when it comes, she gets on without knowing where she's going, makes her way back to the factory with unseeing eyes. None of it's real. It can't be. She clocks herself in and rescues her overalls from the peg in the lavs where she'd left them. Once she's done her shift she'll try again, will go back to Hillview Road on a different bus and it will all be all right. It has to be. She won't go to the dance tonight and then, when she gets home, they will all be there. Maybe she'll even go via the chippy and surprise them – she can afford it with all this overtime she's been doing.

Connie reaches her place on the line and there's someone there. The other girl looks at her.

'What you up to?'

'Working.'

'We're halfway through a shift and you're not working

today, love.' The girl looks more closely. 'You're covered in dust. Are you right?'

She's taken into the foreman's office and given a cup of tea with four sugars. One for each member of her family, she thinks, and the sugar won't revive them any more than it will revive her. Eventually someone gets hold of Cass and she hurries in, takes Connie by the elbow as if she's feeble-minded and ushers her out. 'You can stop with us for a bit, Mam won't mind.'

Connie can't cry, not during any of those empty, merciless nights dossing in with Cass in her lumpy bed, and she can't make it stick. Night after night her eyes refuse to close and she stares up at the brown lampshade, that night playing out over and over again like a Pathé newsreel. Come dawn she drops off just before the bed creaks with Cass leaving to get to work. On her days off, she takes the bus back to Hillview Road. She stands outside number 27 in the hope that maybe someone's got out, got word to her about where they're kipping now. She keeps as still as she can and tries to hear Linda upstairs singing, Mam bawling at her to keep the bleeding racket down. Outside her home is the only place the tears will come and she returns over and again, tears falling into the dust, waiting for them to return.

One day she shows up and the looters have been. Mam's best dress has gone, the kids' clothes, even the drapes. The tears won't stop that day.

The factory sacks Connie in the end for never showing up; but she can't blame them. A few weeks later, Cass's mam makes it clear that she needs Connie gone too. Connie accepts it with none of her old fight; what is there to care about now? Cass's mam doesn't know her from Adam and can't find it in herself to worry about yet another homeless factory worker in a city full of them. Perhaps she'd have hung on to Connie for a couple more weeks, though, if the shock of it all hadn't caught up with Connie in quite such a nasty way. She can't stop being sick. Though Connie tries to brazen it out, Cass's mam is repulsed – and fair enough. 'Ain't you got no family you could stay with?' she asks one morning, watching Connie sluice the back steps as she stands in her headscarf, one elbow crooked to banish the fag smoke. But she doesn't; Mam and Dad kept themselves to themselves. She's on her own now.

Ten

May

S EPPE CLENCHED THE TOKENS. The edges bit into his hand, proof he was alive.

'Scum like you get nothing from this shop whilst I'm in charge, not with those traitors' discs.' Fredo's eyes narrowed, his arm barricading the doorway, the black armband crowing.

'I've earned these! They mean the same as money. You can't stop me using them.'

Fredo laughed and strode forward until his lips were an inch from Seppe's. 'I can do whatever I like.' It was and wasn't true. Fredo was so devious and these camp guards so trusting that many of his transgressions simply went unnoticed.

The stink of him rotted the air. This close, you could see the lice crusting around the black of the armband and crawling in the brown seams of his uniform. Fredo refused to wash because that would mean defeat, giving in to the evil Allies. To reduce this dyed British uniform to nothing more than a fetid, creeping bug repository was his way of showing who was boss, even, apparently, if it meant itching and stinking and being covered in weals.

Seppe fought his own impulse to scratch. Fredo had terrorised and repulsed Seppe for a decade now, his political fervour only increasing his own belief in his licence to bully. But now they were both living on enemy ground, a place that brought Seppe comfort Fredo could never imagine.

'What are you staring at?' Fredo took a pace back, hoicked and spat, hitting Seppe square in the face. A warm trickle insinuated its way from nose to chin, bitter to the taste. The urge to scrub it off, or even to lick it away, was overwhelming. *Don't react. You reacted in the desert and it didn't help.*

Seppe emptied the tokens onto the counter, pushing them off his palms where sweat had stuck them. 'Give me what I've paid for.'

Fredo was spiteful, but he wasn't stupid. If he didn't hand over the cigarettes, he'd be thrown off shop duty and given the job of incinerating the night soil.

Seppe exhaled as the cigarettes were slammed down. *There* they were. God knows, they wouldn't lessen the reek of living cheek-by-jowl with 700 other POWs, but they'd make it bearable. With one hand he reached out for the cigarettes, the other already fumbling in his pocket for matches.

'Not so fast, collaborator.' Eyes still arrowing hatred, Fredo fisted the contents of the carton, the cigarettes poking out from his fingers like so many beheaded flowers.

'Remind you of anything? Shame you make such flimsy chairs, wood pigeon. You're a useless carpenter. Worthless, chickenshit soldier, too, and no sense of loyalty. You aren't loyal to your fellow men, you dishonour Il Duce. You don't deserve these.' Slowly, deliberately, Fredo broke each cigarette in half, every muted crunch making Seppe sag with deflated hope. Today was going to be a struggle after all.

'What's the matter, soft boy?' Threads of precious tobacco unfurled onto the counter, the smell sparking in the dank forest air. Could he scoop them up before they wilted? No, with Fredo in this mood, the best thing to do was to accept the loss and get away.

Seppe stuffed the fragments into his coat pockets and shuffled down through the rows of Nissen huts. He turned right at the mess hut and paused at the chapel. Should he retreat in there? But God had forsaken Seppe before, and there was no guarantee of safety in an enclosed space. Better to stay out in the open.

Seppe slowed when he reached the parade ground, scrubby and muddy, but exposed. Fredo couldn't do much to him here, out in the open, couldn't try and attack him with a broken chair, kick his shin viciously or tip the night urine into his boots. He cupped his hands to get the stub of cigarette glowing. He wasn't going to waste these, whatever Fredo tried to do. The wind extinguished the spark. It was mild here, not like Egypt, where those whistling gusts had bulleted hot sand into every crack and crevice.

Seppe turned round out of the wind, sucked hard. *There* it was, the numbing bliss of the nicotine snaking down his throat even through those brutalised fag ends. It tasted better out here than it ever had in the desert, or back home in Livorno.

There was nobody else in sight, the air blown clear of the constant noise. The bulk of the men were out in the forest or working on the fields. He looked across at the darkness of the trees. After the forbidding expanse of the desert, no place to hide, the labyrinthine woods promised something that this camp, with Fredo in it, no longer could. Perhaps it would be better to be concealed in their depths than up here lathing endless pieces of furniture ready to be broken all over again. Fredo delighted in destroying each object, called it his 'resistance effort', and wore the ensuing restriction of privileges as a badge of pride.

This forest, the guards had told them, had been there for generations. Its history was vast enough that his concerns would be swallowed, concealed by everything they'd borne witness to. And to be amongst the trees, to listen to the symphony of their leaves, to inhale the rich scent of spruce and pine and yew intermingling . . . this was something that could nourish him, that Fredo could never take away from him. If only that were Seppe's world.

'Oi! *Coward*! You forgot these.'

Fredo strode across the parade ground towards him, a handful of papers clutched in his fist, in full sight of the perimeter guardhouse. *Don't react.* Fredo forced these on anyone entering the shop: rudimentary leaflets proclaiming the greatness of Il Duce that he and his cronies scribbled late at night. They rained down onto Seppe's head. He concentrated on the sweet path of the nicotine as it grated his lungs.

'Lily-livered disgrace.' Fredo's breath was so close now that it was forcing the words right down Seppe's ear canal, their poison dripping into his very core. He cringed, and Fredo hissed in satisfaction.

Don't reply. Don't give him the pleasure.

'What's the matter, mummy's boy? Can't speak now, is that it? I've been hearing things from home about your sister, you know. If I thought you were despicable before that's nothing on what I think now. You deserve everything that's coming to you.'

Seppe whirled round, fists raised. Fredo couldn't – mustn't – bring Alessa into this. The ever-present guilt beat his pulse faster, and his blood surged. 'You leave my sister out of it!'

Fredo laughed and idly sidestepped a jab. 'Ah, so it's not just a Livorno rumour. Think you're so clever, not writing home, don't you?'

Cleverer than you, you piece of shit. I saw you, tongue sticking out, frowning over every word.

'If you believe that'll keep you safe from Papa, you've got another think coming. No chance; no chance at all. I told my family you and I had been reunited here, two Livorno boys back together again to represent our esteemed city. I took extra care to express my great sorrow that you're a collaborator for the English now. My mother will be delighted to inform your father you're safe – what an honour, to take news to the Major! The Major has friends everywhere. There will be only too many campmates willing to make life that little bit harder for the disgraceful son of a northern dignitary, a founding member of the *fascio*. All your father has to do is send instructions.'

Fredo had got word to the Major? Seppe's fist shook; he jammed it into his pocket, feeling for his whittling knife. Fredo was right. There would be innumerable devotees of his father and his father's more powerful cronies. Would his father send word to Fredo and the like? Would he even bother? The Major's concerns were normally much more immediate. But Fredo was clearly determined not to let it lie, and that was enough.

Seppe turned and ran. He wove between the rows of latrines and hit the main passage between the accommodation blocks. His legs were pumping now, his heart dictating the pace. *Running away again, are you?* His father's voice, taunting. And now the Major knew how to reach him, after months of ignorance.

The boundary fence stopped his flight. '*Che cazzo è!*' Seppe bent double, panting, looked through the chain-link at the diamonds of the world beyond. How could he get out there? If he was out there, beyond Campo 61, he'd be safe, away from Fredo. The camp wasn't benign any more.

Fredo hadn't followed him. He hooked his fingers on to the wire and looked out. The spring drizzle caressed his face. The camp sat at the top of a hill, Wynols Hill, the guards called it. Those bushes a few feet from here must be marking a perimeter of some sort, though they were pretty straggly. There were a few houses beyond the hedge, away across the fields, black eyes staring in at them over here on the camp, the shrieks of children audible from time to time when the wind blew their merriment up towards them. Sometimes, before curfew, some of the older, more embittered captives would come here and jeer at the distant houses as if this lack of liberty were their fault.

Down there alongside the houses must be the road they'd come in on. The trucks weren't transporting new arrivals now as much as they were taking the campmates to their forest work placements. The trucks arrived back as he finished in the carpentry shop each day, the men jostling to wash before the meagre evening meal was doled out.

Off to the left lay the reason Campo 61 had been built here: the expanse of dense forest. It seemed like something out of those fairy tales Alessa had loved as a kid. *No, don't think of Alessa now.* The woods stretched as far as he could see, their verdant promise darkening as the light was lost to the density. He needed to get out there, in the forest. If he stayed up here with Fredo he might lose control and become his father. At the core of the shame and self-doubt that he whittled and smoothed to forget, was this most humiliating fear of all.

The guard on the gate of Campo 61 was asleep, his snores rumbling below the birdsong. Seppe tiptoed towards him, examined the lock. It would be easy enough to eke in the blade of his whittling knife and persuade the padlock open, but why would he? He wasn't escaping, not really. There was nowhere he could go. But the promise of a few hours in the forest was intoxicating. Could he get away with it?

Seppe rattled the lock, jangled it again until its clinks punctuated the guard's sleep; his head jolted forwards, cap in danger of tilting off.

'Where do you think you're off to?'

Seppe tilted his head in the direction of the forest. 'To the trees. To work.'

'Miss the truck, did you? Fair play to you for walking down there; there's plenty who wouldn't.' He unlocked the gate, waved Seppe through, shivered back down into his seat, chasing sleep.

The track and spiky emerald hedgerows behind the camp quickly gave way to trees. They rose in their hundreds, oak and beech, ash and yew, careless and lurching, twisting and turning him on the path. The walk wasn't a problem, not after all those miles in the desert, sand scissoring between his toes while the pack on his back sweated into him. Seppe delved in his pocket for the whittling knife and pulled out the little piece of wood that slowly, surely, was becoming a tiny owl like the one that perched on the fence of Campo 61 at night. A smile tugged at the corners of his mouth. He was outside. He strode more upright. So this is what freedom might feel like.

Eleven

'I'M NOT GOING, AND I'm not doing poxy brush clearing, and that's THAT!' The noise exploded out through the gap in the door of the hut into the woods and Seppe grabbed his hand back.

'I don't care if the others are all off. What's that got to do with it? It's only me I'm talking about, not the whole lot of us. You have to let me stay and help with the felling.'

Seppe pivoted so that he was beside the hinge of the door, peered through the gap at the commotion. The words weren't being spoken so much as fired and he understood them about as little as he had the bullets he'd faced in the desert, but their intent was equally clear. How many people were in there? He squinted. Only the two of them, by the looks of things. The way the girl was ranting, he'd expected to see a squadron's worth of men lined up. She was getting ready to go again, her arms bent like a boxer's. She was quite stocky, at least in that great big overcoat, and her face was suffused by a frown.

He had happened upon the hut almost by accident after

101

leaving the camp this morning, just needing to get out. As he made his way into the forest, leaves whispered above Seppe's head, crackled beneath his boots, the ground crunching despite this constant light rain. The world was *alive* out here, the scent of bud and blossom in every breath a stark contrast to the thud of bombs into sandbanks, or worse, the iron tang of blood and the screams when a shell hit a target. This was a place where you could hide, where you could start again. Hypothetically, this would be a place where he could also run, but for what purpose? No English town would harbour a foreign soldier in their midst, and he'd end up back in the Regio Esercito facing who knew what.

A thought germinated. *Could* he find work out here? The camp trucks discharged dozens of Italians every day to do the work of those British men away fighting. What a stupid, stupid world they all lived in, that sent men away from this tranquil place to die, only to replace them with their apparent enemies. Not for the first time, Seppe frowned at the senselessness of it all.

He stepped gently onto and over a fallen branch, unsure if it would take his weight. If his father could see him now, on his way to work for the enemy, there would be blows, and rows.

But his father seemed increasingly far away the further into the forest he walked. The trees whispered agreement, branches shifting. His shoulders relaxed, the music bubbled up inside him; he started to hum.

He clambered onto a moss-covered tree stump and stared downhill. Below him in a clearing was what looked like a worksite. An enormous pile of tree trunks was chained together. Two women wearing berets with headscarves underneath them squatted beside a trunk on the ground, beside the pile. They might know who was in charge of allocating the jobs. He scrambled down the bank into the clearing.

'Where did you spring from?' The woman at the near side of the trunk dropped her chain and strode forward, smiling. She was young, barely eighteen or nineteen. He pulled off his cap, welcoming the warmth through his fingers.

'I am looking for . . .' *Come on.* What was the English for what he was looking for? He pointed at the trunk on the ground, then spotted the badge on her beret. A fir tree at its centre glinted in low rays.

'I work with wood.'

'Fair enough.' The girl turned back to her partner, uninterested and seemingly too distracted to pick up on his foreignness. 'Let's try this again, shall we?'

Seppe skirted the edge of the clearing. A tin cup lay haphazardly on the floor beside a sawn-off oak stump. He righted it and placed it on the stump where its owner would more likely see it.

Across the clearing was a wooden shack. It would be interesting to see how it was put together. Was it someone's home? He moved cautiously towards it. It looked like it might fall over in a strong breeze.

The door was slightly ajar. It had been so long since he'd been inside a dwelling that wasn't an army barracks or a prison camp that the urge to look inside surprised him with its intensity. He glanced around but the girls were busy trying to move their errant tree trunk onto the pile.

Seppe put his hand to the door. It was damp, the grain saturated and bulging. Some kind of pine, not one he'd ever worked with in Livorno. It was splintery in this damp, but it didn't look like it had warped.

'I'm telling you, I don't want to go to Scotland. I'm staying put here, and I want proper work!' What was happening in Scotland? He couldn't hear the other side of the conversation, only a muttering that rose and fell like tragedy. The girl was in the same uniform as the ones dancing the trunk between the chains, but he couldn't tell if she'd got a fir tree on her hat, too, because it lay upside down beside her feet. Her long fair hair flew as she gesticulated. You didn't need much English to tell she wasn't winning the battle, but she wasn't giving up.

'Tell me why I can't get the hardwoods down. Go on. I know I'm a girl – do you think I don't? And how has that ever stopped me doing twice the job of your men? You need me for as long as this war's on, not that any of you yokels have noticed the war. You don't care about clothing, so the coupons don't bother you, and the only time the stupid paper mentions it is if a pig's gone missing and someone's agitating about what the War Ag will make of it. People are dying, you know. *Real* people.'

The girl raised her fists again and Seppe recoiled.

There was a shuffling from within. Were they coming out? The last thing Seppe wanted was to be caught spying. But he didn't dare move; they'd hear him.

He shuddered at the shrieking hinges, but the pair inside seemed too deep in their row to notice. The hut seemed even smaller from within, though maybe that had to do with the girl, who filled it with her wayward hair and stabbing arms. She appeared to be a little older than the others out in the yard. The man – what had the girl called him? Frank? – looked a good decade or two older than Seppe, his brown hair darker than the girl's but not as black as Seppe's own. He was leaning on the desk, looked worn out from the intensity of the girl's argument.

The air was thick with tobacco, a denser scent than that at the camp, though. It tickled down into his throat and he coughed.

'What the hell?'

If only he could retract the cough. But he couldn't, of course he couldn't; and now they were both staring at him. Frank put both palms flat on the table and pushed up, limping over to Seppe at the door.

'Who do you be and what do you be after, now?' His voice was guttural, seemed to fit the forest more than it fitted this slight, wiry man. What had he said, exactly?

'I am Giuseppe – Seppe. I am Italian.'

The girl laughed, a short bark. 'Here's the enemy, wandering around free as a bird and nobody down here seems to care. We'll all end up murdered in our beds at this rate.'

Frank glared across at the girl. 'That's enough from you, Constance Granger. Might seem odd to you with your city ways, but we have a need of them POWs down here, what with the planting and the felling and the rest of it. It wouldn't be enough to just have you twittering girls.' His words lilted and undulated like the leaves swaying in the breeze. Just when Seppe thought he had the shape of a sentence, it tipped away from him again.

'What do you want, boy?'

Seppe swallowed, lifted his head and forced himself to look Frank in the eye. 'I want to work with trees.' He sounded stupid, so stupid. His fingers went again to the whittling knife, stroked its blade. It was hot in here – was that embarrassment? No, over there, behind the girl, something was glowing. Must be a stove.

The girl snorted. 'Join the queue. Frank's not letting nobody except the inbreds do the interesting work on his damn trees.' She glared at the foreman, stuffed her hands in her pockets. Seppe watched Frank closely. What was he going to do? If his father had been cheeked like that, the belt or pan would come out, the one with the lead bottom

105

to it. But Frank had sat back down, was shaking his head. He didn't look like he was about to attack.

'You do know as well as I do, girl. You were sent down here for lumberjill training, not to stay for good; that's how it works. Be grateful I've kept you on at all.'

'But it's cockeyed, Frank, you know that! You don't have to start all over again every time; you should let me out there properly. I can get the oaks down, I bet I can. I'm flying through those softwoods and it can't be much harder.' The words danced past Seppe without meaning anything much. They had the rhythm of poetry but could have been another manifesto.

Frank sighed. 'Beats me why you didn't want to leave with the others, to be honest.'

It was as if he'd snuffed her out. The girl's arms dropped and she slumped. Seppe's own heart was beating faster, the anxiety rising for reasons he didn't understand.

When she spoke again, it was somebody else's voice, closed and quiet.

'I just didn't want to, all right? I came here, and I'm staying put here, and that's that. And you know I can do the job, Frank, you had me showing those rookies from Hull how to place the wedge earlier this week. Let me stay.'

'All my men work in pairs, you know that, and there's not a one of them as would step down to let a wench take their place. Aye, you're not bad for a girl, but that's not the same as doing the job day in, day out, like them who were born here. I'll give you that the blokes we've got left might be a bit old and creaky, but the forest's in 'em, ent nothing they need to be taught. Even if you know how to fell the stands, you couldn't tell your oak from your spruce without pointers, I saw you.'

'But *I* can – I know trees.' Need propelled the words

from Seppe. 'I work with wood. Look.' He offered up the whittling knife and the half-carved owl like a prayer. The girl and Frank stared at him as if he might be insane, or dangerous, or both.

Frank turned away first, dismissive. 'Making trinkets is nothing like getting trees down, lad.' No, no, Seppe understood that, but how to explain it? He ran a finger around his collar, shifted his feet.

'I not sure . . . yet . . . how is best way to cut the tree. But I know which is oak, which is spruce. On my way to you, I see beech and yew and oak and ash. I can show you, now, if you like?' What was he doing? There would be no point entering into a tree-spotting competition with this man who was created from the bark itself.

'Aye, well it's easy enough to tell 'em apart, don't need a Johnny Foreigner like you showing off.'

'But knowing the trees, it will help with the, the –' Seppe looked down again at the paperwork on the table, all stamped with the British crest. The word he needed was there in big letters underneath the coat of arms, and it was the same as the Italian for once '– the quotas. If I am knowing which tree to come down, then I can help to get quotas on time?'

'Them quotas are my business and mine alone, and I'll thank you not to go snooping at every blessed thing you see in here.' But Frank's voice slowed as the thought came in to land. 'What are you doing here in the first place, eh?'

'We are captured and kept in Africa, then –'

'No, not that. Why haven't you already been assigned a job?' The foreman's face darkened. 'Not one of them blackshirt fascists, are you? Thought they weren't allowed to leave the camp.'

Seppe felt sick at the idea and his answer came out more vehemently than he'd intended. '*No*. I am not them. I have job that keeps me in and I want to be out. I am carpenter for camp. Make things.'

Seppe waited. Even the girl had realised it was best to be quiet now.

Frank shook his head again and the room became smaller, hotter. 'Sorry, lad, I can't risk it. Too many of you Italians we've had out here, friendly enough, but more shirkers than workers. This ent just a place of work; you lads don't seem to be able to understand that. This is my home, and with so many of our kind gone to fight this faraway war –' Connie shot him a look and he held her off with a raised hand '– it's up to me to make sure our forest stays as intact as it can be despite them Home Timber Production demands. You lot treating it like a holiday camp don't help me one little bit.'

'But I . . .' Seppe's stomach dropped.

Frank shuffled the papers on his desk. The little finger on his left hand was missing, a scar barely visible. One of his feet stuck out at an angle from the desk; his boot was mosaicked with wood chippings.

'I am not *them*.' It was all there, pent up behind the words. Frank and the girl stared.

'Aren't you now?' The foreman looked like he might almost smile. 'And none so fond of them, neither, by the sounds of things.'

'No. I will work.' That was safe enough to say, surely.

'You ever driven a tractor, ridden a horse? Handled an axe?'

He knew the lie to choose, didn't hesitate. 'Yes. I can cut the trees.' He swallowed down the guilt that followed. How difficult could it be, if this man with the limp could do it?

'Look at that for a turn up, Frank! You've got yourself a new tree-felling team.' The girl was bouncing again, but she wasn't thumping any more. 'And if he knows his way around an axe you don't even need to train him; couldn't be simpler.' She flung out an arm to make her point and a sheaf of papers scattered around the hut like seed.

'Christ! Sorry, Frank.' She bent to pick them up, squatting wide, primitive, like Seppe had never seen a woman crouch before. He fought the urge to close his eyes against the confusion of emotion and instead bent down beside the table to help. It had been patched together from old cords of wood, and listed where someone hadn't planed off the left-hand leg. Wonky furniture made him all lopsided inside; next time he was here, he'd fix that.

'If I tell you to pair up with this sorry ha'porth here, Connie, will you leave me alone for a bit? Lord knows we needs all the help we can get.'

'Frank! Honest to God, I might hug you!'

Frank frowned at her, then turned it on Seppe.

'I'll sort it with the camp guard, but it'll likely take time to release you because he'll need to fill out endless paperwork.' Frank's face made it clear what he thought of this, if the stack of scrumpled papers on his desk hadn't already done the job.

'If you fail, if you two can't get them trees down on schedule, then you're back up at Wynols Hill and you won't be out again until this war's over, you mark my words. And you –' he picked up a piece of oak and pointed it at Connie '– you're on the next train to Scotland if you cock up, mind.'

She was already gathering up her things. 'You're a gem, Frank.' She winked at Seppe, waved on her way out. 'I'm off. I'll see you at the stand as soon as you're cleared for work, timber partner.'

Seppe thought he might collapse with relief. No more taunting. No more repairing endless bits of furniture after they'd been destroyed in a fit of 'we'll show them who's still boss' pique. Hidden out here, doing honest work. All he needed to do was get down the oaks. He stood up, his hands full of papers, ignoring their trembling.

'I will see you.'

Twelve

SEPPE KNEW. AS SOON as it dropped beside his plate, his moist hands and closed throat knew who was inside the envelope. He pushed away his toast and pulled the letter in front of him, sweating. He couldn't face breakfast now, though he'd needed it today of all days, his first shift out in the woods working for Frank. The hubbub of the breakfasting POWs receded; the world closed down around the envelope.

Could he destroy it? POWs had no such luxury of 'return to sender', but he could throw it away, simply not open it.

No.

To not read it would be to surrender, and he couldn't – wouldn't – surrender to his father again. Never again.

He eased the point of his whittling knife into the corner of the crease, then stopped. Not his whittling blade. He reached instead for the butter knife, his sleeve dragging through crumbs.

'Eh!' Gianni, opposite, threw up a hand in disgust. 'I needed that!' It was good-natured, though; Gianni didn't know any other way. He was from somewhere not far from Salerno and at night Seppe heard him sobbing for his family, the only hint that Gianni might not be as eternally sunny as he seemed. But by daytime he kept everyone laughing with his easy manner and way of treating the camp as if it were a choice. His parents and four younger siblings were safe in Allied-occupied territory and this was enough for him to trust the English. 'How can they be my enemy when they are feeding those I love?' It was a dangerous opinion to have around Fredo and his ilk, but Gianni's openness rendered him untouchable. Seppe envied him this, and was drawn to it.

'Sorry. Here you are.' Seppe offered the knife to Gianni, who waved him away.

'Don't worry about it. Your need is greater than mine.'

These spring mornings carried a chill to them in England, but it wasn't the cold that was causing his hands to shake. Seppe tore open the envelope. The spikes of his father's rancour were undimmed by the flimsy paper. A spiral of venom rose from the lines, the sheen of anger, pride and sheer vicious temper bitter in Seppe's mouth.

Along from Gianni, Fredo turned and leered.

'A letter, eh? The old man finally sending his love to see how his yellow son's getting on? Or maybe it's instructions for me about what to do with you.' Fredo reached forward to snatch it and Seppe jolted back, bashing the porridge vat, which tipped dangerously. He stuffed the letter back into its envelope and jammed it into his pocket, pushing up from the table.

A row had broken out about the heel of the bread and attention was thankfully diverted as Seppe made his escape. Every morning was the same: constant yelling, arguments;

everyone frightened about what was happening at home, stuck here and unable to do a thing about it. Every week a bunch of men would solicit news from letters home and from this attempt to make sense of their country's fate, posting a 'fact sheet' in the parade ground. The censor had, of course, eradicated any meaningful details by the time the letters reached camp, and the 'newsletter' struck Seppe as a work of fiction, internal self-generated propaganda to make the men feel they were still out there fighting. He didn't dare articulate this, of course. Such a view would only result in his shoes or bed sheets ending up stuffed in the latrines again, or worse. The atmosphere here worsened with every new arrival, the camp now divided into those who still fervently supported the beleaguered Axis troops and those whose relief that their families were alive surpassed any broader political views. The peace Seppe experienced when he first arrived had fractured, the edges sharp and tentative. The relief as he struggled into his greatcoat and stepped out was intense.

Walking out through those gates would never lose its novelty, its sense of illicit freedom. Seppe came down off the lane and turned into the forest, the trees welcoming him in. He turned a corner at the point where the path forked, his boots shivering dew off bearded ferns.

Fragments of his father's written words slithered through like the leaves underfoot. '*Your mother thought it would please me that you had joined the army. Your mother is feeble and knows nothing of the world. Your capture is a disgrace. That you are <u>collaborating</u>, working for these Allies, brings shame upon us all. You have betrayed the family name and you have done this deliberately. I will make it clear to your mother that your actions are those of a coward, and that her suggestion was misguided and false. Next time she is inclined to meddle with the work* *of men she will have cause to reconsider. You have never amounted to anything and this will continue to be the case.'* He knew what that meant; his mother would be in for a trouncing again, perhaps worse than that night. And it was Seppe's fault. The ever-present guilt rose again. How was she coping without himself or Alessa to stand beside her, to assume the weight of their father's wrath?

He walked, and walked, unseeing, until he was halted by someone in his path.

'Oi, dreamer! Time to start work, you know.'

The smell of earth, the sound of birdsong, and the woman's voice. Connie, planted right in front of him, her hair scattering loose from her beret and a curious half-scowl, half-grin. He smiled back.

Beside the timber pyramid, two women were doing battle with vast logs and chains. The newness of their Timber Corps badges glinted against too-clean uniforms as they twisted this way and that. They'd never get that log secured unless they straightened out the knot. His fingers curled.

Connie glanced across. 'Brand new lumberjill trainees; Frank'll have his work cut out with that lot, all right. Caught one of them asking Frank where the ladder was for measuring the beech trees. You'd have thought she'd asked him to drop his keks, the look on his face! I jumped in before he could have her guts for garters and showed her the tape. Thought measurers were supposed to be the bright ones. Not this lot.'

'Tape?' What was she talking about?

'You know how this works, don't you? Measurers go round the width of the tree, not up into the branches. The poor cow almost fainted with relief when I pointed it out.'

'Oh.' But then how did they know how tall it was? He pushed a shaking hand into his pocket.

'Here, let's get going. If you've done this before, it's going to be a cinch. You take the four-and-a-half pounder and follow me.'

The axe handle was oak, smooth from years of those who'd gone before him. Was it odd, to use oak to fell oak? Or was it the only natural way?

'Bit quiet, aren't you? Everything OK?' Connie peered at him and his stomach constricted. But she only shrugged and beckoned him along. 'Come on. One of the locals left a tree half-felled over here when he nipped off for a fag. Frank'd do his nut if he ever found a tree like that, so we can sneak in and pinch it for our tally; the poor sod won't have the balls to tattle on us.' She smiled and winked.

Seppe stared at her. When was he going to start understanding what she said, what any of them said? Her accent wasn't the same as Frank's: it was flatter, more nasal. She spoke so quickly, and with such certainty that her words slipped past him before he could gather and examine them. She seemed to do everything decisively, no time wasted pondering the consequences. Already he envied her this.

Connie tutted again, tugged at his sleeve with gloved fingers. 'Cat got your tongue today?' She looked at him more closely, nodded at something. 'You're not with me, are you? You're somewhere else. Well, do me a favour and come back here for the time being so that we can get this show on the road.' She led him a little way further into the trees and he turned back to see how the new lumberjills were managing with the chains. 'Don't you worry about them, they'll be at it all day.' Connie trampled down ferns, pushed away branches. Seppe shouldered his axe as if it were a rifle and fell in line behind her. The desert had been cold like this in the winter.

'Here we are.' He stumbled into her. 'Whoa – mind out there!'

Seppe snapped to attention as if on the parade ground and followed Connie's gaze. In front of them a giant oak tilted as if drunk, a deep wedge cleaved out of its trunk. All the way above, unaware of the tree's fate, little brown birds feathered branches that dipped towards Seppe then reeled back.

'Is that safe?'

Coward. He could hear the word forming, almost see it leaving Connie's lips. He braced for her explosion, but instead she grinned.

'No, not in the slightest. Which is why the silly buggers shouldn't have snuck off like that and left it. All the better for us though, eh?' She reached behind the tree, one hand to the small of her back. When she straightened up she was brandishing some kind of saw; a long, many-toothed beast with handles at either end. His mouth became sawdust. It was only a matter of minutes now before his lie was discovered, and he'd be back to the camp, perfect frustration fodder for the small and vicious band of *fasci*.

'They even left their fretsaw behind. Kind of them!'

Connie paced around the trunk, and peered at the incision. She bent down, her hand stretched as it continued to support her back. She must have strained it: unsurprising given the sheer physicality of the work. This was nothing like carpentry; it was so much more elemental. The oak towered above them. The birds called to each other from the branches as if the tree itself was singing. How were they ever going to bring it down? Its branches were as long as pews and thicker than his arm.

'This lot at least seemed to know what they were doing, which is more than you can say for half of Frank's men. Can't do without them, he reckons, but the only ones he's got left are so old or crook that they're no use in the Forces. And no use out here, either.' Connie was still eyeing the incision in the trunk. What was she looking for? He bit hard on his lip when she leaned into the fulcrum, ran her hand down the plane.

'Right!' Whatever she had seen, it had galvanised her. 'Need a few more blows with the four-and-a-half pounder and the six pounder, but I can hang on to that one if you like. Or do you prefer the bigger one?'

How should he know? But he had told them he could do this. He shrugged, outward insouciance in direct proportion to the anxiety that was building internally.

'You come this side; doesn't need much more taking out of it here before we switch to the saw. I'll get this wedge out of the way.' She darted forwards again with that odd half-bend and fiddled at the base of the trunk. It swayed like a drunk.

'There. Now the bugger will move.' She looked expectantly at Seppe. His heartbeat pounded in his temples.

Seppe heaved the axe to hip height, clenched it as firmly as he could in both fists and closed his eyes. Sweat was dripping out from under his hat even though the tip of his nose was freezing cold. The birds had become louder.

'What're you playing at?'

He opened his eyes again. His hands faltered and he thudded the axe back to the ground before it slipped from his grasp.

'Is this some special Italian trick, doing it blindfold? In this country, we keep our eyes open when we're chucking an axe around. We're in a bloody war. If you want to die there are plenty of other ways, in case you hadn't noticed.'

Seppe flushed, heat sweeping up him. He picked up the axe again. His hands were chafing already from the sweat against the grooves of the handle. Frustration blended with panic to chase out reason and his father's voice hissed into the vacuum. *Hopeless waste of space, taking orders from a woman, and an enemy woman to boot. Wouldn't know men's work if it came forward and slapped you.*

The axe was even heavier now. His fingers slipped on the wooden handle and it plummeted into the soft earth. He wrapped one hand over the other and hefted. It swung up unsteadily this time, thunked back down.

'For crying out loud!' Connie strode over to him and wrenched away the axe, pushed something into the tree trunk. 'You haven't got a clue.' Her look of angry disbelief was the most honest anyone had been with him since Alessa. 'You've never done this before, have you?'

He shook his head, and his toes curled inside his boots. 'Don't . . . please don't tell Frank. Please don't.'

Connie glared at him, tugging at her ponytail. 'Don't you worry about that. If I tell Frank that half his extra felling team hasn't got the foggiest, then I'm done for too. You heard him, he'll ship me off to who knows where to start all over again. And I'm not having that.'

She paced, one hand twisting her hair. Behind her scowl, the first shimmer of tears.

'I'm sorry.' The words wouldn't come. Hopelessness torpedoed them and he struggled to retrieve them. 'The forest – I must stay in the forest. Frank asks me I can cut tree, I say yes. Is wrong of me. But I need to stay here.' Had he conveyed what he needed to? He watched her.

'All right, no need to stare at me like that.' Connie's voice softened, but only marginally. 'You have no idea, absolutely no idea.'

She stood stock still for a moment and he held his breath, a child again waiting to see which way this would fall.

She snapped her fingers, smiled that unexpected smile again.

'We've got no choice, then, do we? Story of my life.' She thrust Seppe's axe at him. 'Come on, get in behind me and I'll show you what to do. Frank needs a felling team, so that's what we'll give him.'

Connie stood away from the tree and crouched as if going into battle, axe thrust out in front of her. Like this, her coat was stretched tautly across the swollen moon of her belly. His eyes widened. There was no mistaking what he saw.

Thirteen

Worcestershire, March, 1944

CONNIE DOESN'T CLOCK IT herself, not at first. She just knows that she has to get out of the city. After Cass's mum throws her out and the factory tells her they've given her job to someone who'll actually show up, she goes down to the recruiting office in the centre of town and signs up for the Women's Land Army, because it's a job that brings a billet with it. Maybe being away from Coventry will stop the sudden bursts of tears and the urge to yell at people for no reason. But the panic of it all still worms inside, twisting her belly and making her sick when she wakes up and remembers it.

To start with, she gets on all right at the farm and the farmer's wife even gives her a pile of cast-offs when she realises how little kit Connie's arrived with. Then one morning Connie yaks into a fresh ten-gallon vat of milk. The bile floats on the top of the milk, globs of orange and yellow lurid against the yielding froth, and the farmer, normally as soft as you like, yells at her, really yells, when she suggests skimming it off like cream.

She skedaddles for a bit, round the other side of the milking shed until he calms down. She's still a bit queasy, so she leans right over the gate just in case. The ground is all churned up here where the cows barge through twice a day for milking. It's the clay in the earth that turns the puddles that rich red-brown, the farmer told her. Tiny murky lakes of blood, that's what it looks like to her.

Blood. Hang on a minute. Connie straightens up. She's late, isn't she? *Really* late. She's never been the sort to pay that stuff a lot of attention, and since the – since what happened at Hillview Road, she's had bigger things on her plate than her monthlies. Though come to think of it, she can't remember dealing with that for a while.

Connie starts pacing, staying in close to the side of the cowshed for protection. What's she going to do? She doesn't have any real cronies to talk to, not for something like this. Neither she nor Cass has ever been what you'd call the pen-pal types and this isn't the sort of thing you can dump on someone you've only just met. And as for telling Don – well! Her lips curve despite the wave of panic swelling.

She might be able to get hold of him through the base, but what for? It was his glamour that had pulled her to him, the sense of danger and difference. He might want to play Daddy, and she doesn't want a version of her pa, down the club every night, stopping off to belt the kids. And – her pacing slows right down – *she* doesn't want to be Mammy, knee-deep in bottles and burdens. She doesn't want a baby.

She can't do this.

She can barely take care of herself; all that keeps her going are her dreams of leaving Coventry and getting down to London, finding a proper glamorous job like working as a cigarette girl in the picture houses and going to fancy dances every weekend and trying to put aside a couple of bob for her big escape down to London, whenever that might happen. She can't give up on that; she'll have nothing left. There had been a woman three doors down from them at Hillview Road when Connie was just a kid, still in school. She'd fallen pregnant and not a bloke in sight, and the whispers had started before she'd even got the babba home from the hospital, curtains twitching every time she came out with the pram and this in a street where half the men were in the pub by lunchtime on payday, and not out of it until Sunday dinner, neither. She'd kept her curtains closed day and night, poor cow, and before the baby was even walking properly she'd scarpered, fled to her mam's by all accounts. 'Good riddance,' Mrs Cole had hissed, as if the woman had brought her sin upon them all. Connie can't become that woman, not when she doesn't even have Mam there to take her in.

There are places, she thinks, people who know how to take care of this kind of thing. A couple of the girls at the factory had fallen, been to see a woman who'd sorted them out. Must be places in the countryside, too, if you know how to ask.

That night, after tea, she screws her courage to the sticking-post and asks the farmer's wife. But Mrs Prissy doesn't give her an answer, just clatters the saucepan into the sink louder than a Lancaster bomber going over. Connie gets the message. The next day neither the farmer nor his wife will look at her and there's no snap waiting for her to take out to the fields. Connie's toes curl and she swallows down the shame as she wraps her own tiny portion of bread and cheese and makes her way out to the yard, same as usual.

'Mucking out duty for you today.' The farmer won't come within ten paces of her. Anyone would think it was *his* baby she was trying to get rid of.

Connie bites her lips together so tight it looks like she's rouged them, and nearly doubles over from the effort of keeping it together, but the shed is as clean as a new napkin by the time she finishes.

The day after that the billeting officer arrives and tells her that her services are no longer required. Connie blinks hard and runs upstairs to ram everything into the kitbag they'd given her at training.

The billeting officer looks at her not unkindly; she obviously hasn't been told why Connie's being kicked out.

'They're looking for girls for the Women's Timber Corps, you know. Nice strong lass like you might take to it all right.'

It would matter less if she's sick on a tree, and the posting is down the other end of the country, where they won't have her pegged as the girl who ruined the milk and her reputation all in one. Who knows what the work will involve, but if she can milk cows and shift slurry with this great bosom of hers half on fire and rubbing up against the straps on her dungarees, she can manage a bit of wood. And if she can hack it to keep this to herself for a bit longer, there's bound to be a cottage out in the forest where she can put the baby, some kindly country woman who won't notice one more kid.

Connie can't bring up this baby, she really, honestly can't. It seems like she's going to have to have it, but if that's the case she needs to find somewhere for it to be brought up right so that she can leave as soon as it's born. War is a time of opportunities as well as despair, that's what the wireless keeps saying. She'd be a useless mother and it isn't where her life is going. She's got bigger plans than that. She's off to London, has been saving up for this. Once she's got the hang of being a cigarette girl she'll move on to some properly elegant job, maybe in one of their clubs, or maybe even overseas if she catches the right eye . . .

MOVING ACROSS TO THE WTC had been child's play; nobody gave a monkey's, really, since she'd already been part of the Women's Land Army. The recruiter had looked her up and down, checked her hands to make sure she really had been working and wasn't some soft-palmed do-gooder, given her the new uniform and signed her across. Things had settled down since she'd been here in the forest. She could make a fair fist of this. Her hands understood the timber jobs better than her Land Girl duties and her guts stayed put. When Connie woke up these days, it was with achy limbs and the sleep of the dead rather than with a desperate retch for the pail under the bed.

Every now and again, something fingernailed up a sliver of memory; and every single time, the chucking up returned, even though she had to be several months gone by now. No Mam and Dad. No littluns. No 27 Hillview Road. When this war was over she'd try and make sense of it. But that could be years away and they might all be dead by then. All she could do for now was manage this bitter loneliness as best she could, bury it all where it couldn't hurt her. And to do that she'd stay the hell away from the city until the baby's out, then hightail it back there and get on with her life.

Fourteen

SEPPE CAME AND STOOD next to Connie, careful not to get too close.

Was she married? Had he missed that? She certainly didn't act like any wife he'd met before, but things might be different in England. She hadn't mentioned a child, not once.

'Not there! How am I going to show you from the side? Get behind me. In close, so that you can feel what's going on.' He held himself upright.

'Come on! I'm not going to bite you.' She slotted herself in front of him with barely a breath between them. He made himself as small as he could, but he could smell her, a sharp, tart scent underneath the traces of leaf and bark. To be standing, unsupervised, nestled into a woman in her condition – what if one of the guardsmen wandered past, or one of Frank's men?

'For God's sake, relax a bit.' Connie shuffled back and bumped into him as she resumed the half-crouch. To his horror he felt himself stir. He tried to inch away.

'Keep still, will you? And pay attention.' Connie grabbed

his axe and pushed it forward. Apprehension at what she might do with it next swiftly resolved his ardour.

'Get your hands on here too; we'll swing it together.'

He mimicked Connie's stance, her scuffed boots tucked in alongside his, the sharp points of her elbows needling the crook of his arm. It had been months since he had been so close to another person, and he'd forgotten the comfort that could come from simple physical contact.

'Ready? Three, two, one –' The axe swung up, up, up above his head and came plummeting down. Seppe was barely conscious of the motion, his whole body focused on staying clear of Connie's. Her fair hair was escaping from under the beret and it tickled his nose, shivered away the forest smells and sounds until it was the only thing in his world. Her hair smelt different from the smells he was used to at Campo 61, different again from the whiff of her body. *Clean*. It smelled clean, the merest trace of sweat discernible. He'd missed such closeness, the sensation of someone else so visceral and real standing in such close proximity. He missed trusting someone enough that they allowed this almost careless nearness. He missed Alessa more with every passing day.

'Not bad, but we need to get it going higher and faster.' Again and again they swung the axe, each downward motion torture for Seppe as he contorted away from her. At last they stopped, the axe thumping to the ground beside them.

'Phew! You know what? You might yet crack this.' Connie swept the escaped strands of hair away from her face, grinned at Seppe. 'You got a fag?'

'Fag?'

'You know, a ciggie. Woodbines – God, or Players if we're lucky I've seen you smoking so you must have some.' Connie mimed holding a cigarette to her mouth, taking a puff.

'Ah, *sigaretta*. Yes, but only . . .' Seppe pulled out the

126

carton, held it out to his side so he didn't have to be confronted with her expression. Fredo was keeping up his campaign to make Seppe suffer in every possible tiny way, and had yet again snapped the tubes like so many beheaded flowers.

Connie stared at the cigarettes, then back at Seppe as if he'd temporarily lost his mind. 'What the hell happened here? A pretty daft thing to do to nicotine.' She scrabbled around, one hand in the box, until she found a stub which was slightly longer than the others. 'Still, waste not, want not, eh? Got a light there, have you?'

'No, but I –'

'No light? How were you going to smoke them?'

He hadn't given that much consideration, had been focusing only on getting out and away from the camp. Connie dug into her pockets for a match. 'That's better.'

She yawned and stretched and he glimpsed the bulge of her overalls before she curved back round. He had to acknowledge her condition – it was rude otherwise. But why hadn't she alluded to it? Or Frank?

He opted for a safer question.

'Your husband, is he at war?'

'What husband? If that's a pick-up line it's a pretty shoddy one.'

'No!' He whispered it. '*Scusi.*' If only he could fold up and disappear behind the trees. 'I thought only . . . with the baby . . .'

'What baby?' She faced him, eyes blazing, arms crossed against her chest, daring him. 'I've got no idea what you're talking about.'

He held her gaze. 'My sister – she was also – I think I see –'

'You want to watch that, thinking you're seeing things. They'll cart you off to the loony bin sooner than you can say "Mussolini".' She fixed him firmly with her gaze. 'No husband. No baby. Do you get me?'

Seppe nodded. What else was there to do? The curve of her stomach was unmistakable. But he knew about silence, about keeping quiet.

'I understand.'

She studied him, nodded. 'Now, are we going to get this tree down or shall we stand about all day creating fairy tales?'

She hefted the axe high and swept the blade into the side of the trunk, barely clearing the ground. The metal whistled through the bright air and changed tone as it greeted the wood. Connie's chopping possessed the speed and surety of all her actions, but it must be wearing her out. He leaned forward.

'Let me do this.'

'What?' Connie paused to swipe sweat from her forehead.

'This – this is big work. You will be tired.'

She rounded on him, a trapped animal, and he stepped back, fought the urge to bring his hands up to his face. 'Didn't I make myself clear? Keep your trap shut and your axe swinging.'

Connie helped herself to another cigarette from Seppe's packet and stood off to one side, the lit end flaring against the grey-brown of the shadowed trees.

After a couple of deep, satisfying drags, she ground out her cigarette and spat on the butt.

'Come on then. If you're so clever, show me you've been paying attention.'

He swung the axe up until his arms were at shoulder length, aching to feel the axe in motion. He hung on for grim death, like they'd practised. The head arced, the flat steel glinting. Then – 'whumpf'! – the axe bit, scattering needles of hardwood, tiny darts. He let them stick him.

'That's it.' The tree rocked above their heads, the timber moaning and creaking and Connie smiled in satisfaction.

'But the tree, it's not coming down.'

'No, of course not. We need to cross-cut now.' Connie darted off, came back with the two-handled saw he'd seen before. 'Come on then. Don't want to leave that trunk dancing about, do we?'

The cross-cutting should surely have been easier than the axe, but he couldn't make it work, not remotely. The only reason the saw moved at all was because of Connie on the far side of the tree evening out his futile attempts at any kind of regular rhythm. Seppe's hands were raw from the axe and he winced every time it was his turn to draw the saw through the resisting wood. The oak was determined not to be vanquished; with every tug he could feel the opposite force from the grain. *Stop being so sentimental.*

'Quick – skedaddle! It's going!' Connie scrambled to her feet and ran to the edge of the copse. From above came a sound like the rushing of water. Twig pummelled twig, tendril fought tendril, branch pushed against branch. It rushed on down, waiting for nobody, the whispering of branches at the top only matched by the creaking at the trunk as the weight forced its way free.

'Tim-BER!' Connie turned to Seppe and clapped him on the cheeks. 'You did it!'

Seppe, finding no words, thrust his hands deeper into his overalls. The mighty oak barrelled its way downward, two saplings folding in its wake. *All this because I took an axe to it.* Tears prickled his nose, his eyes, and he pressed hard on the comfort of the whittling knife in his pocket. Ridiculous, to mind a tree coming down, but so much had shattered over these past months: Alessa, his home life, the endless and futile battles in Africa. He had seen men topple with less grace than the tree, night after night, thudding dully

129

beside him on the desert floor. To inflict damage to this tree in the middle of the most peaceful place he'd ever known: it united all the grief and rage of what had gone before.

As the tree hit the ground with a shattering thud, a cloud of dust and twigs swirled up like a spell. Connie wrinkled her nose and peered through the chaos at Seppe. His cap was between his hands as he stood silently looking at the felled oak.

'What're you doing? It's not a funeral, it's our job. Get that hat back on before you catch your death and I have to start planning *your* funeral next.' She slumped down on a moss-coated tree trunk and stared beyond the trunk. 'Well, you can handle an axe now, so that's something. But Frank'd suss you in a heartbeat if he saw how cack-handed you are with that saw.'

'Sorry. I am wrong; I shouldn't have –'

'Too true. You shouldn't have, should you?' She yawned, lounging beside the tree, and looked at him with her head tilted to one side. 'How easy is it for you to get out of that camp of yours?'

'It is easy enough.' Was this a lie? The guards seemed to care less than he'd imagined they might. Regardless of its truth, he would do whatever this woman required of him.

'We'll meet in the mornings before shift starts – can you do that without any grief? Get out here when it's quiet and start practising? If we get a few extra trees down while we're at it, that only helps Frank's quota. Can't see him kicking off about that.'

'I will do this.' There was no other answer.

'Good. And we need to get it sorted out sharpish. If Frank saw you in this state, even once, that'd be the end of it.'

The end of it. But this needed to be the beginning. He nodded. 'I understand.' Connie would keep his secret, and he would pretend not to know hers.

'Hopeful sign' as Sunday School Treats Return

Application was made for a half-holiday at Drybrook and Steam Mills schools for a united schools' treat on Thursday, July 13, and this was gladly granted as 'a hopeful sign' (as the Chairman said).

Dean Forest Mercury,
Friday 9th June, 1944

OUR BIGGEST ARMY EVER

At last they will go in and finish the job.

Dean Forest Mercury,
Friday 9th June, 1944

Summer, 1944

Fifteen

June

CONNIE STRETCHED OVER FOR the alarm clock – no point trying to roll in bed any more, not with the size of the bump these days. Five o'clock! But she wasn't tired, not really. Outside it would already be bright sunshine, the whole forest busy, and she wanted to be a part of that. A city woke up all grimy, the sun's rays just casting unwanted light on what was broken or gone. Out here, now they'd hit summer, the days sprang awake and everything looked so hopeful.

This was the fourth day in a row she'd been woken up by the little blighter inside her kicking fit to burst. It wasn't the only thing that might burst, either – if she didn't get out to the lav soon she'd be in all sorts of trouble.

The floorboards were cold on her toes even though the rest of her was an oven.

Best to leave the blackout where it was for the moment, no point risking waking Amos with its clatter. Connie padded downstairs and along the corridor. It'd be smarter to go straight out the back to the lav than round the front and, knowing her luck, bump into the milkman on his rounds as she trotted around in her scanties. This nightie was so worn that it didn't leave much to the imagination and it wouldn't take a baker to figure out the bun in this oven. Connie giggled despite herself and Bess, asleep beside the memory of a fire that hadn't needed to be lit for weeks now, stirred and nosed against Connie's legs. Even bending down to stroke Bess needed thinking about these days, with this great bulk setting her off balance.

The grass was wet beneath her bare feet, sparkling with what must be dew, and she giggled again at it all squishy between her toes. She couldn't remember ever having seen dew in Coventry. There wasn't anywhere for dew to land in the city, especially not once Jerry got going and everywhere was permanently clouded in dust and grit.

Here the dew spangled her way like a miniature red carpet, the grass tickling, buttercups shiny golden coins between her toes. Bess meandered out too and, next door, Joyce's chickens got wind of the dog and started squawking like a bunch of newsboys.

Connie made it to the lav and pulled up her nightie, relaxing as the pressure came off her belly. Everyone knew babies kept you awake at all hours, but she'd never realised she'd be woken up by it even before it was due out. Maybe her time was nearer than she thought. But even if she'd got her dates wrong – and she might have, if she was honest – surely she hadn't got them wrong by this much?

She sat for a minute. The chickens were still mithering away and the birds were still hard at it. That was something people never told you. The countryside wasn't quiet at all. There was never a moment when something wasn't squawking or chirping, or the trees were hushing each other or the bees were humming away. She'd had no idea that things made so much noise, just things that were part and parcel of the world, not machines, not people. They'd given her the willies those first few weeks, these night-time noises, but after a week of dawn loo runs she was getting used to them.

Connie stepped out of the privy and stood there for a minute, one hand in the small of her back, arching into the streaky dawn. The baby shifted too – was she stretching as well? Connie put her other hand on her belly so that the baby knew she was there. The sun was right up now. Not much warmth in it yet, but it had cast a shadow image of the cottage down as far as the apple trees. Seemed hard to fathom that those little white flowers were going to become apples, but that's what Joyce insisted, and there was no arguing with her.

Connie stretched again, in no hurry to go inside. She wasn't getting back to sleep now; the baby's energy had got into her bones and she was itching for the day to start. She'd sit on the bench underneath the kitchen window for a bit, take a load off. It must be coming on for quarter past five by now and she'd arranged to meet Seppe for felling practice at half past six. He was coming on all right, Seppe. Not much of a talker, and he looked like he wanted to run a mile if she got behind him to show him a move. But he was copping on. Yesterday he'd told her off when she'd started to explain about the wedge; had produced one from his trouser pocket of his as if he were a magician rather than an Eyetie Prisoner of War and placed it in such the right place that it ended up being the quickest tree they got down.

Seppe's face!

She found the memory of it warmed her insides like the sun gleaming down through the orchard now. That made two things she was good at; she could get the trees down, and she could teach how to do it. Not long and they'd be able to stop with these early mornings. Though to be honest, since this little one was waking her up anyway, it wasn't such a hardship.

The bench was digging into her bum, which was surprising given just how big it had got recently. She shifted around a bit, looked down the garden to where the old stone wall had gone from night-grey to dawn-amber with the light. Look at her! Sitting on a bench at daybreak, a baby almost ready to pop and responsible for teaching a prisoner a secret. She was having an adventure in spite of it all. She just didn't know what kind of adventure it would turn out to be.

Sixteen

Amos whistled for Bess, who'd been lapping at the brook. Time to get back home, have a bit of bread and cheese, maybe look at his Billy's latest letter again. That was something all right, news from the lad, a lick of happiness at least.

Amos had tried a few times now to sit down and reply, but the words soured between his head and his pen. Give it time, his May would have said. It had tilted things, Billy being away had, like leaning against a branch and finding it couldn't bear your weight. But now there was a new letter, and summer was here. Good news might be round the corner.

Amos pushed on up the ridge where there was a decent breeze. It hadn't taken long to find the sheep today; they'd trampled the cow parsley right down on their way through to the shade of the oaks. The new lambs were sizing up well, soon be time to have them dealt with. Amos sighed. Lord knows why they'd had to go and make it all so darned complicated these last few years, all them forms to fill in and prove that you weren't hanging on to the meat yourself, even though that was how it had worked for years, how it always worked. War or no war, people needed feeding. He'd see if Joyce would give him a hand with them bits of paper again this year.

Not long after the peak the wind blew up a noise that seemed all out of place. What was down there? He stopped and caught his breath, considering. If you went straight through from here, you'd be at old growth. That was the stand of oaks Frank reckoned they'd lose next time those know-it-all Ministry men came from London, them with their clipboards and their grabby need for wood. Bit odd that anybody'd be out that way on a Sunday. May as well go and have a look. The house rattled with Billy's absence, and that lumberjill – Connie, it was – could be pricklier than the gorse.

It was easy enough to follow the noise down the valley ridge; halfway down, it came into focus. Felling – that's what it was, and on a Sunday morning? Wasn't like Frank to work people seven days a week, not unless there was a big push on that he couldn't ignore.

It was the saw Amos could hear, not the axe, and it was out of kilter. A blade went through timber like a drumbeat: one-two, one-two. Whoever was at the saw right now was making it hop, missing on the downbeat. Like a thrush singing backwards, it was; this racket might sound fine if you didn't know better, but when you did, it grated. No real forester would make a hash of it like this, he knew that for sure. This was the trouble with these incomers. Ten minutes' training and they were swanning round the forest like they owned it, cutting down English oak that had stood there for hundreds of years. Like ivy on a trunk, swarming all over and changing the shape of things. But Frank did say it was for war work, for masts and the like. If it might keep his Billy safe in some way, it stood to reason that the forest would have to be involved too. Amos didn't rightly know what to make of the whole sorry mess.

'Well, I'll be blessed.'

It was Connie, fretting the saw like it owed her something. But who the dickens was that on the other end of it? Not a forester, he could tell you that for nothing. Nobody born to the job would hold the saw like that, as if it might bite him. Long way from Sunday best, his uniform was, and patchworked with great black patches. Not like his Billy, all spick and span, creases pressed into his uniform by Amos the night before he left. However much he hadn't wanted Billy to go, he'd sent the boy off smart.

Amos looked again at the fellow with the saw and shook his head. Had to be one of those Italian prisoners from that camp over at Wynols Hill. Look at the state of him. How long had they been there now – since last thaw? And yet this one opposite Connie was still all skin and bones, even from this distance. He had eyes as dark as midnight and sunken cheeks that'd worry Amos on a winter ewe, never mind a grown man. Looked nearly as done for as those schoolkids they'd sent here from Birmingham earlier in the war, before Billy was called away. They'd all scarpered back off home, said they couldn't stand the quiet and they'd take their chances with the bombing. Now the schools were full with evacuees down from London, so Joyce had told him, filling the local kids' heads full of nonsense about burned-out Jerry planes and spending whole nights underground on railway station platforms. The sooner they all went back home, the better.

Amos looked back over at the lumberjill. Fair play to her, she was pulling smoothly enough. In fact, if it weren't for her they'd be all over the shop. She didn't keep her trap shut even when sawing, mind. Couldn't be too much of an earful, though; the Italian laughed, shoulders shaking, his features more open even from this distance.

Amos wasn't interested in words. He'd watch the two of them for a bit longer, though – make sure they weren't ruining that old oak. He pulled the peak of his cap down tightly on his forehead. Connie looked dead set on getting it down. Her chin jutted as she stabbed across at the Eyetie, getting him to move over a bit, change his grip. Even from this distance there was something a bit off about the way she stood, even if her grip was all right. Never mind worrying about anyone else's. But the Italian trusted her, you could tell by the way he leaned in, listened to her with a soft smile curling his lips even from this distance. They had that easy partnership you couldn't learn, that either came or didn't and was vital for the sort of work Frank's men did do.

The girl stopped talking, clapped him on the shoulder and he nodded, leaned into the saw as if it was his sweet-heart, and the rhythm sorted itself out straightaway. The one-two was so crisp now that Amos started tapping his hand on his crook along with it.

Amos wouldn't believe it if he hadn't seen it with his own eyes, but they'd got that oak down. Next time he saw Frank, he'd tell him. The wench weren't so useless after all, it turned out.

Connie squeaked open the door to the house and tiptoed in. A shadow lurched forward and she clutched at the wall. 'You scared me half to death there!'

'Come here a minute.' Amos beckoned her down the hallway. She'd been out at the site with Seppe all of today, in the end, and she was desperate for a kip. Getting trees down wore her out more than anything she'd ever done at the factory; all her muscles ached at once. But it was the old bloke's house, and she couldn't risk being chucked out, not now, so she threw her shoulders back and followed him down to the kitchen.

Amos pulled out a chair for her and she sat down, uneasy. This wasn't like Amos; it seemed like he was up to something. Perhaps he was going to throw her out. Her gut twisted again.

'Thought you might be hungry.' On the table in front of them was what looked like half a chicken in some kind of gravy. Her gut stopped twisting and her mouth watered.

'What's this about?' She grabbed the fork in case he changed his mind.

Amos pulled out the chair beside hers and sat down at his own empty place. He didn't look at her 'Came from Joyce. She wants to make sure we're not starving whilst she's still teaching you to cook.'

Connie looked at him sideways then back down at her plate. The food was good, but that made sense now. She'd been over to Joyce's three times now, each time learning a different dish but mostly just enjoying the company of the older woman, who asked no questions and simply got on with kneading dough.

She bit into a carrot so orange it looked like a warning sign. It was sweeter than she knew carrots could be and she shovelled it in.

'Good grub.'

'Aye, Joyce is a dab hand in the kitchen. Smart with her book learning, too – she keeps all of Frank's papers in order. Don't know how he'd cope without her. Got a tongue on her, though.' Amos smiled and it was so unexpected that Connie coughed down a lump of carrot.

'Settling in all right, are you?'

Connie raised her head and looked at Amos. The most he'd ever said before was 'Ta' when she'd passed him the salt. 'I – yeah, I suppose so.'

'Not like your big cities, we aren't, not like Gloucester; but you can keep yourself entertained all right out here.

My Billy was always out and about with his pals.'

Where did they go? Connie wouldn't mind knowing what the locals did for fun, especially after making a show of herself at that last lumberjill dance. But Amos had tailed off, was staring down at the empty plate.

Connie had been about to ask if she could put the wireless on and see what was out there in the world, but the beginning of that sentence had stopped her in her tracks. Thoughts of her get-out plan, pushed to the back of her mind recently, reappeared urgently. Whatever had caused Amos's unexpected friendliness might vanish as quickly as it came. She'd better get the information she needed whilst she could.

'How far is it to the train station?' This forest was so vast, she had no idea how to ever find the place she'd arrived at.

'Nearest one is Cinderford, 'bout six mile away. Best thing to do from here would be to head up towards Soudley, pick the road up there. You could cut across Staple's Edge but it's a bit of a climb, mind.' She could taste his question: *why?* But he couldn't know why. Nobody else could get involved.

'Trains don't run that often though, not these days.' Amos picked up her empty plate and went over to the sink. She followed him, her own question pulling her.

'But what happens if you need to go somewhere?'

'Where would we need to go?'

There was no answer to that, so Connie stood and watched Amos scrape the gravy off his plate. She shouldn't have wolfed down that dinner.

She yawned. 'I'm off up now. Thanks again for that.'

Amos nodded, concentrating on the plate, and something in her twinged. The talk of trains not running had scared her, though. First chance she had, she needed to go and check she could still get away.

Seventeen

SEPPE PULSED HIS HANDS, shaking out the aches of the axe into the warm afternoon air. He'd conquered it. Today he had felt the rhythm that Connie was always insisting was there to obey. The raw soreness of his hands was forgotten and the oak had fallen cleanly and in half the time. Connie had beamed and for once hadn't said anything. Now that Frank couldn't banish them from timberwork for incompetence, they were safe; it was too monumental even for Connie's words.

He paused at the fork in the path that took him back up to Campo 61 and the parade ground. Nobody would miss him for a few more hours, not on a Sunday. Seppe looked around – but of course there were no sentries, no workers, just the high grasses amidst the trees rustling with the busyness of summer. You'd never know there was a war still raging on in countries miles from here. It unsettled Seppe. The guards were proud of their forest, seemed more than happy to let the POWs wander as long as they were back by curfew, with the exception of the small band of 'sympathisers' still deemed likely to try and spread fascist propaganda. Seppe had quietly welcomed this uncharacteristic strictness, especially when it led to all the sympathisers being moved to one 'higher security' barrack. He'd reclaimed his bunk from Fredo and was now back beside Gianni and far from the night soil.

He passed a stand of spruce, ringed with white chalk where the Pole Cats had marked it for a telegraph pole. Connie had explained these Pole Cats to him the first time he'd spotted the chalk. Apparently they were specially trained to select the straightest, tallest trunks to be used as the poles that gave them their nickname. Pole Cats went out ahead of the felling teams, roaming forests all over the country, and daubed the coppices with different colours to show the axemen what to cut down for each quota. Every time Seppe saw a chalk ring he marvelled at the skill of these unseen women, the confidence they must possess to look at a tree and decide its fate: this one a telegraph pole, that one a ship's mast, those over there to be pit props.

And now he was a tiny part of this same system, had the beginnings of an understanding of forest husbandry and could be of use. Something in Seppe lifted and he followed the second path, the ubiquitous beech and oaks thinning as it steepened. The path hitched over a hump and gave way to a platform of flat, white stones which dropped sharply into the river-ribboned valley far below. The trees below were all but indiscernible from each other from this distance, the forest on either side of the brown waters a viridescent blanket hugging the contours of the hills.

Seppe settled himself on the biggest of the rocks. It was smooth and warm against his skin and he closed his eyes, his breath slow and calm. Peregrine falcons, their beaks sharp flashes of yellow in the vastness of the vista, soared on the currents, dipping out of sight behind the cliff edge before reappearing, effortless.

There was a tickle at his neck. He turned and pinched off the offending grass poking from a crevice in the rock. He pursed his lips and brought the grass to it. He blew and the grass vibrated between his lips, high and sharp like the calls of the birds of prey. The corners of his mouth crinkled. The tune eked out, flew over the cliff with the birds. Seppe closed his eyes again, gave in to the music and the warmth and the peace. He finished the melody, began another, his toes tapping now on the rock. Falcons swooped through the sky as the sun moved round and the warmth leached from the stone, but he played on. Nobody was pursuing him. Nobody was making demands of him. He had secured his job. All was well.

Eighteen

July

'OH, FOR THE LOVE of God!'

It had been a month since Amos had mentioned the train station and until today she'd been too whacked every night to face that walk. She'd only popped home to change her socks before heading up to Cinderford, and what was this on the doorstep? A parcel wrapped in newspaper. It reeked of fresh death, just like all the others had.

Eating dead things straight from the hedge seemed to be a countryside special, and she'd never cop on. In her world, meat came from the butcher if it came at all. Still, if Mam were here now she'd probably give her a clip round the ear for being such a spoilt brat in the face of all this grub.

Connie swallowed hard, banishing the memory, and bent down for the parcel. If she got this over with, she'd still have time to get to the station. Frank hadn't sussed how close Seppe had been to not hacking the job, so he was pleased with their work rate and seemed to keep doubling the amount they had to do. It was great for overtime, meant she was able to put away a little bit extra every week so that she could leave a few bits for the baby, make it less of a burden for whoever took the babba in. But time was moving on and she was feeling the baby move around more and more, reminding her it was coming. This was supposed to be one of the exciting parts, she knew that much. But the strain of keeping the bump obscured from view all day and the nervousness of what, exactly, she was going to do after the birth just gave Connie the heebie-jeebies.

She couldn't have the baby actually in the woods; she'd need to push it out when Amos was off wandering the forest with Bess, looking for his sheep. When Mam had had Barbara and Linda, both times the noise she'd made could have been heard in London, never mind the rest of their street. Seemed to go on for ever and a day, too – but Connie couldn't think about that or she'd lose her nerve and it wasn't like she could do anything but get on with it, was it?

She heaved a sigh and picked up the parcel with the tips of her fingers, pushing open the back door with her knee. May as well make the most of things and put the dinner on before she went out to check the trains. She dumped the package on the kitchen table and peeled away the sheets of *Mercury*. The inner layers were soaked through with cold, sour-smelling blood; it had glooped together in the sharp pockets of the parcel as if relieved to find a place to rest.

'For the love of –!'

The skinned, headless creature under the paper was about the size of a doll, but a doll from the horror pictures, all dark-red flesh and squishy-looking bits of white stuff. Rabbit – wasn't that what Joyce said they were when they were doll-sized? She pushed it into the pot then opened the back door and pulled up a great handful of parsley from the beds, taking a huge breath of fresh air at the same time.

Joyce seemed less set against newcomers than Amos. She'd found her the billet, after all, and was showing her what to do with all this mad food that seemed so alive. Maybe she got a kick out of helping people.

Connie stuffed the parsley on top of the meat with a handful of parsnips and a couple of potatoes she'd found in the scullery. She splashed a jug of water over the lot of it – there! That'd stop it from scorching and clean off the veg at the same time. She was getting the hang of this dinner lark. Nearest she'd got to cooking in Coventry was being sent down the road for a bag of chips on payday.

She wasn't quite sure how she'd ended up being in charge of the dinners here, but Amos was a decent sort and cooking was a simple enough way to stay in his good books. It'd only be a matter of time now until he found out about the baby – her dungarees were about to burst and she must look like a total nutcase, wearing her great big overcoat now they were finally getting some warmer weather. If Seppe had twigged it, Amos couldn't be far off. She'd be out of his hair as soon as the baby was born, but until then she couldn't risk him throwing her out, not now.

The doctor would have to stay out of it, too; that would cost money she'd need for rent in the city and it was always better to avoid people who'd ask questions. Have the baby, tidy up, then find somewhere to leave it to be looked after on her way to the station. It was hardly the stuff of dreams, but it was the best plan she had.

Did that make her selfish? Mam had called her selfish the last time she'd stayed out instead of coming home to mind the little ones. Who wanted to be brought up by a selfish mother? The baby would be so much better off with a mam who wasn't always cocking an ear elsewhere, wondering what else was going on.

She pushed the pan over to the side, where it wouldn't burn. Enough fannying around here, thinking about things. She needed to find those clean socks and be off. It was a hell of a walk up to Cinderford, but if she started now she'd make it back before Amos was home from that final check of the sheep.

Connie stopped and lit a cigarette to get her up what must be, God willing, the last hill, her feet rubbed raw even in these dry socks.

When the straggly houses on the outskirts of Cinderford finally appeared – gardens lined with rows of vegetables, blackouts still up in some of the upstairs windows like rotting teeth against the whitewashed walls – they were as welcome a sight as that first glass of gin at the end of a shift.

Connie peered down the weary main street. There was a church just over there with a big porch. That would be the place to put the baby, where some charitable type would be bound to take pity on it. And there was the train station, up the top there, beyond the row of shops and the little white houses. Nothing was signposted any more, but you'd have to be a bit daft not to be able to recognise a railway station.

She stopped halfway up to get her breath, leaning against a shop window. There was a display of tiny baby clothes in it, all laid out as if the babies themselves had disappeared in a puff of smoke. She wasn't too worried about clothes for the baby; she could use one of her sweaters to keep the little blighter cosy for the short time it'd be with her. That'd be all right, wouldn't it? As long as it was warm? Everybody here was proper able to make do and mend;

the baby would be kitted out before she'd even opened her eyes.

Connie peered more closely into the window, sizing up the baby gear as if it was an oak and she had to place the first cut. What did her sisters wear when they were that small? She balled her fists against the remembered smell of tattered socks and plump little iodiney grazed knees, but she couldn't picture what size they'd been when they'd been born. Bigger or smaller than that rabbit she'd shoved into the pot earlier?

Maybe she should go in and pick up something for the baby, so that it didn't grow up to think its mother was a heartless sort. Connie jangled open the door and kept her head down. In and out, that's what she needed to be.

Hanging off a display in the corner was the perfect thing – a pink twill bonnet with a ribbon. Connie rifled through her pockets and found her battered coupons. There! That'd do the trick; whoever found the baby would know that Connie had thought about her. And the baby would realise later that her mam was a glamorous, adventuring type who couldn't stick around here in the trees wasting her life.

The forest would be a great place for a baby to be raised, she'd been right about that, certainly if you were a bustling homey type like Joyce. But Connie wasn't set up that way, and she had enough gumption to know that what was best for her wouldn't be what was best for the baby.

She'd barely got up to the counter when the bell jangled the door open. It was Joyce. Joyce! Of all the people! She needed to keep her job, and she needed to keep her digs, and if Joyce knew she was in the family way she was bound to tell and Frank and Amos would give her her marching orders, not a shadow of a doubt. And she couldn't have that, not yet.

Connie pushed her way through to the door.

'Forgot my coupons.' As the door swung shut behind

Connie she heard the shop assistant: 'Forgot her manners an' all.' She probably thought Connie had been trying to pinch something. The cheek of it! She hadn't lifted a thing since rationing had started. It wouldn't be right.

Connie got safely round the corner off the high street and leaned against a wall beside some enormous white-flowered plant that made her sneeze and sneeze. Probably going to be the next thing to end up in the dinner pot, and now she'd got snot all over it.

'Well, you made a right dog's dinner of that, didn't you?' Could she still get up to the train station, or would Joyce spot her and wonder what she was up to? Surely there was some excuse she could make up? Connie badly needed to at least get her mitts on a timetable so that she could work out what time of day would be best in terms of finding somewhere for the baby and then getting out before she lost her nerve. Maybe if she couldn't get as far as London straight away, she could get over to Bristol – that wasn't supposed to be all that far from here.

But she simply couldn't face risking the train station, not now. Maybe Joyce wouldn't say anything, or would believe Connie's story, but what if she didn't? She half wondered if Amos knew, had noticed how she was filling out, but he kept shtum about everything. Joyce would have an opinion, and Connie would hear it whether she wanted to or not. Joyce had been good to her and she felt sick at the idea of letting her down because Joyce reminded her of Mam, and she knew Mam would be disappointed to see what had become of Connie.

Tears, unexpected and unwanted, began to flow. Connie scrubbed at her eyes with the back of her hand. There was no hope now of checking out the trains, but at least she'd found the churchyard, got a bit further along with the plan. And the baby would do fine without its bonnet.

153

Connie bit her lip and set back off down the hill, slower now. It had been a stupid idea, anyway. She'd simply have to wait for a train to take her away when the time came. She'd always flown by the seat of her pants and she had to trust it would work out. She sniffed slightly, looked up at the sun dipping down below the treeline. Make do and mend, that's what she'd have to do.

Nineteen

'LET'S GET THIS BEAST back to wherever he came from, shall we?' Connie pushed herself up off the log they'd been sitting on to eat their bread and cheese. 'I'm full to bursting with the extra snap Joyce sent up with Frank today.'

She frowned at the horse standing placidly roped to a log. 'Don't see why we couldn't have stuck with the tractors. This dirty great animal gives me the shivers.'

Seppe pointed at the churn beneath their boots. 'Even a tractor can't move through this mud.' Frank had been bitter about it when he'd assigned them the task. 'Don't normally get like this in July. We've been working the land too hard. Never mind destroying the enemy, we're destroying our own country.'

'What about the roads the Yanks are building out here?'

'This is for their war work and not for ours. The horse is the best way.' He patted the horse's flank affectionately.

Connie eyes narrowed. 'Farmer's boy, are you? I'm surprised you don't know your way around an axe better.'

155

'No, I come from a big city. Big for Italy, anyway. Important in the north. But my father . . . sometimes it was better to be away from the house. Since a child, I have spent much time in stables. He does not think to find me there.'

The smell of the horse had Seppe half back in the stable, crouched in fear, the straw quivering as he trembled at the thought of being discovered.

Connie considered him thoughtfully. 'Sometimes it's better for us all to be out. My dad wasn't scary, but he liked a drink, and there was no knowing what mood he might come home in.'

If they continued this line of discussion he might tell her things he'd regret later.

'Come here – let me show you something.'

Connie frowned at Seppe but she moved forwards gingerly. She was brave under that tough exterior. *Don't bite her,* he prayed in the horse's direction.

Seppe took her hand. It was soft, softer than he could have imagined given the hours they spent felling. He pressed it up against Prince's neck and together they stroked the horse. Connie's shoulders dropped a little and she flashed him a smile – one he saw too infrequently these days. On the whole she'd been quieter recently, more thoughtful. She didn't think he noticed when she stood off to one side sometimes, her gaze elsewhere, her thoughts with people or places he couldn't access, couldn't even imagine. They barely discussed their pasts, though now that her accent slid away from him less often, they were better able to talk from time to time. She was a hard worker, and kind, and he found himself seeking out ways to make her smile. Connie was someone you wanted to see smile; when she was happy, the glow captured everyone around her, too.

It made it easier to forget Fredo's continued assault, the

sting of his father's letters. '*Alfredo's mother gossips about your sister; claims her son heard it from you in that coward's camp. Your mother is very worried and has been provoking my mood, which is fragile after such concerning news.*'

But the forest was where he came to escape these thoughts, and he mustn't let them invade now. Seppe smiled at Connie.

'Shall we get this horse home?'

Seppe set the pace, one hand on the bridle. He looked back as they met the first slope. Connie was pushing up the hill, flinching each time Prince's tail swished, one hand supporting the weight of her belly.

Steam rose off the horse's withers, mingling with Seppe's breath as he clucked at Prince, slowed him to a halt. Connie pushed past the horse to his side, her breathing laboured. Despite the exertion she was milky pale against the sheen of glistening ferns. He caught a glimpse of her teeth, clenched tighter than a clamp, and an urge to protect her rose like sap. He had never seen her chatting to the other lumberjills; nothing beyond the superficial banter she loved almost as much as Gianni did. It was up to him to keep her safe, and her determination that she had to manage alone only made him want to help her more, not less.

How could she still be pretending this wasn't happening to her? Why hadn't Frank detected anything yet? Joyce had, he was certain of it; that's surely why she'd sent the extra food. Had Connie confided in Joyce but not in him?

When he got back to camp he'd talk to Gianni, who knew how to find everything. He could barter his camp-issued postcards home. Gianni was always desperate to write to his family whereas Seppe never used his allocation. Then he, too, could bring Connie some eggs, perhaps a hunk of cheese. That would be something to be proud of.

But this wasn't about him and his growing inclination to watch out for this maddening, caring young woman. Where would she live with the baby? What would Frank do?

How did Connie think she was going to raise a baby out here, away from her home, wherever that was, and without any obvious family, let alone a husband? She'd never mentioned a sweetheart killed in the war, so clearly whoever the father was, he was useless and not worth the time of day to leave someone as resourceful and funny as Connie to have to deal with this on her own. *I would never have done it*, the little voice in his head whispered.

Seppe opened his mouth, then shut it again. He'd broach the subject after they'd chopped down a few trees; that always calmed her. They were working on spruce today, which was always preferable. It stained your hands less than the crazy bluish tinge you got from cutting down oak, and it made him less guilty. Felling oaks that had stood for generations felt like the ultimate betrayal of these under-stated foresters who were nothing but kind to him. It wasn't the kind of thing he would ever dare say in camp, where Fredo or one of the other black-armbanders would find a way to punish him for sympathising with the enemy.

'What's up with this weather? Don't it know it's summer?'

As they stabled the horse the first drops were falling. Before they knew it they were in the middle of a deluge. Plump raindrops bowled down, in a hurry to join the mud at their ankles. Connie's hair plastered to her face and she stuck out her tongue to catch the drops, laughing, released by the downpour. But she was going to get drenched; they needed to get inside.

Seppe looked around him. Had Gianni and his gang left up a tarpaulin by some miracle? No, only trees as far as the eye could see, even their burgeoning summer canopies not enough to withstand this downpour. He cursed, softly this time. But wait – that would work, over there.

'*Vieni.* We shelter here.'

The rain was thundering onto the boughs now; even if he yelled she'd never hear him over this. Instead he pointed at a huge yew whose trunk had split open years ago, probably even before the last war, to look at the regrowth. Branches criss-crossed in barbed arches above the splintered trunk, a cathedral of a tree.

Connie came up so close he could feel her body outlining his, the heat coming off it, his arm against hers prickly with awareness of her warm flesh. She bellowed into his ear and with difficulty he pulled his attention to her words. 'Under that? It won't give much cover.'

'No – inside. Come.' Seppe squeezed past the florets of tiny twigs and leaves forming an archway into the ruined centre of the yew.

'Here.' He bent an errant sprig out of the way, flattened himself against the inner wall of the tree to make room for her. Here, inside the trunk, it was as if the rain had stopped, save for the pounding outside. Near the top, new branches had sprung up and across the split trunk, forming a vast protective canopy. Shiny emerald needles interwove above them to provide shelter.

Connie slid down the inside of the trunk, knees bent, hands clasped low on her stomach. He sped down beside her, eyes wide.

'Are you OK?' There was no mistaking what he meant. Connie rested her head against the yew and met his eye. 'I'm fine. Honest.'

She wasn't going to confess; it was up to him to persuade her to talk. She mattered, that's what it came down to. She mattered, and he couldn't let her struggle on alone any more. Seppe hadn't realised he could feel like this about someone, that winning her trust would occupy him to such a great extent despite his own struggles in the camp. To care about someone only led to danger. On the surface Connie seemed exactly the sort of person who didn't need anyone's help. But Seppe recognised a carapace when he saw one, had spent too long constructing his own, and he longed to reach out. The prickliness concealed vulnerability and his heart ached for her whilst at the same time he admired her, this girl he had known only a few months now. He minded very much what happened to her.

Seppe sat down beside Connie, the knowledge of what he must do next making him shiver. He put one palm on the clammy wood.

'You know how I find this tree?'

Connie blinked at the change of subject and shook her head. 'No idea how anyone tells any of these trees apart.'

'It isn't to do with the tree.' His mouth was gluey, not wanting to relinquish the words. 'It is because of me. I can find hiding places.'

'What are you, some kind of spy?' Connie leaned her head against the damp wires of the internal roots. They smelled of earth and mould, a warm, oddly welcoming scent.

'No, not spy.'

Could he dare to say it aloud? The hissing of the rain outside the trunk was a thousand secrets being told. He pressed his finger against the soothing blade of the whittling knife. She needed a secret before she could tell a secret. He understood. He caught her gaze, held it, quelling the urge to look down, to focus on the knife.

'My father – he is not a nice man. Very much not. He does bad things. All my life, since I can walk, I hide. Now it's automatic to me. You, when you see a tree, you know this one is ready to fell, that one not yet. I look at the same trees, I can tell you which ones are good for hiding, which ones not.'

'But your pa's not going to get you out here, is he?'

'In Campo 61 is a man from Livorno, he knows – he knows a bad thing my father has done, and he wants to make my life as hard as he can because this man, he is seeking vengeance on me. My father thinks me a coward, a collaborator; this is impermissible to him. And now he thinks I will spread bad words about him, so he will tell this man to make my life as bad as possible. He has done it before.'

July, 1939

The week after Seppe's fifteenth birthday, he returns home from the Livorno city docks humming 'Bella Ciao', Renzo's song of hope and resistance. The tune comforts him, keeps Renzo with him when he's back in the Major's house.

Seppe has barely shut the front door behind him, is lifting the bolt back into place, when his father is by his side, eyes narrowed, boring into Seppe.

'What is that you're singing?'

Seppe knows there's no need to answer this question, unless to quell the anger. His father's mood, already volatile, has worsened these past weeks, brought down by Ciano's death and the increasing possibility of war. But before he can decide, his father speaks again. 'Where did you learn this filth?'

'At school.' A lie, and a stupid one. His father takes a step away and undoes his belt. Seppe tenses, looks at the belt.

'Keep your eyes on me when I'm addressing you!' He snaps back to attention. 'Don't think you're too old to feel the leather. Now tell me again – where did you hear this?'

Seppe is mute, cannot give away Renzo. He pictures Renzo, humming as he oils the stable latch, planing down the half-door in the heat so that the horses can stick their heads over for the breeze, and he gulps. The Major notices, snaps the belt in Seppe's face, daring him to move away.

'You tell me now or we use the buckle.'

Could he do this without betraying Renzo? 'The docks.'

'The docks! To consort with that scum. You little –'

There is no escaping the beating.

And worse than that, the next week the Major enlists Fredo, son of his closest ally in the *fascio*, to tail Seppe, ensure he never gets back to the port. Fredo, already long bedded-in as a bully and in awe of the Major, delights in this new opportunity to humiliate Seppe at every turn.

Seppe never sees Renzo again. All he retains from this period of safety is the whittling knife.

THE RAIN POURED ON outside, the sound of a thousand buckets being emptied over and over. Seppe tasted dank centuries of moss on his tongue, oblivious to the battles being fought, the war raging as fiercely as the rain. Connie looked away, touched her fingertips to the damp base of the yew. He pushed harder on the steady knife in his pocket. *Stay brave.* He waited. Had he said enough?

When she spoke it was as if she'd aged a generation.

'When I said I'm fine – the baby's fine, too.' She leaned towards him, spoke with more measure than he'd heard from her before.

'There's nobody in the entire world knows about this but you and me and that's how it has to stay. I think Joyce may have twigged, but I'm saying nothing until she asks. Do you understand, Seppe?'

'But your family – the baby's father –'

'Dead and gone. One lot's dead, the other one's gone. This is my problem, and I'm going to deal with it my way. That's all there is to know.'

Her eyes on his were fierce but underneath the rain he could hear her breathing, ragged and desperate. He nodded into the space between the two.

Gloucestershire Regiment
2nd Battalion
27th June, 1944

Dear Father,

I hope this letter finds you well. It would be good to hear a word or two, know you were getting on all right back home. There isn't a day – an hour, really – that goes by that I'm not thinking of you and our Bess and the forest. I did think I might have heard word, Father, especially now that the dipping and the shearing's long since done. I'm right sorry if I've upset you so much by going against your wishes.

I'm on the continent now, not too far from ▮▮▮▮ apparently. You haven't seen anything like it, our Dad. The roads are lined with sandbags and the villagers all gone, who knows where. Gives you the willies, it does, to see the ghost of a place like this and know the enemy's lurking.

Hopefully now the Yanks are involved we'll be able to push on and see a difference, get this job finished. Joyce tells me there are even Yanks in the forest now; is that right? Seems funny to think of them sprawling all over the place with their big trucks and their chewing gum whilst I'm stuck out here.

I'll be honest, Father, it's lonely out here at times. I know it's my duty, and it's the right thing to have done. But it's so different from home, where everyone knew everybody and the rhythm of things stayed the same no matter what. There's no rhythm here, no rhyme nor reason. The land smells different, the sun casts different shadows, and I feel right exposed without our oaks around. Makes it harder to stay steady when the countryside itself don't do what you expect it to.

This isn't how a soldier's supposed to feel, is it? But I don't know how a soldier's supposed to feel. I'm a miner, and a forest boy, and I'm here because of both those things, to fight for King and Country. I just hadn't reckoned on it getting under my skin so much.

Writing to you, putting the address on them letters; it makes me feel like I'm nearly back there with you. And that's the thing that keeps me going, if I'm straight about it.

Please write, our Dad.
Your affectionate son,
Billy

Twenty

CONNIE SLOUCHED, SWELTERING, ON the bench outside Amos's back door and flicked again through the *Dean Forest Mercury* in the vain hope she'd missed something interesting in it. Nope, not a sausage. From the apple trees at the bottom of the garden, a blackbird cheeped at her as if to say, well, what did you expect?

Loneliness and thoughts of home, never as far away as she wanted, skulked at the edges, threatening, and she shrank from them. She could write to Hetty again, but what was she going to say? 'The trees are coming down, the new trainee lumberjills are making a right pig's ear of things, oh, and I'm having a baby in a few weeks but none of them know about it here except that Italian I work with who's turning out to be a real pal.'

Seppe, though. He *was* a proper friend these days; she felt her fidgety worries melt every morning when he smiled at her and picked up that axe. He didn't say much but the things he did say were like being stroked; she rose and stretched and felt better for him. And he had this odd knack of listening that made you want to say something worthwhile.

He couldn't be up to much in that camp of his on a Sunday. From what he'd said it had a church he didn't go into, a theatre he avoided like the plague and a football pitch that gave him the willies. Connie rose from the bench.

Connie slowed down to catch her breath as she saw the fence up on the brow of the hill. She'd been so excited about the idea of company that she'd more or less galloped up the lane and now it seemed like she'd been spat out at the top of the forest, surrounded by the sort of open space she hadn't seen since she'd got here. The trees proper changed the way you looked at things and it had been weeks since she'd seen further than a few feet.

The camp was so much bigger than she'd imagined, more like a village. From where she stood, pressed up not far from the gates, she could see straight down a big open area, full of raggedy-looking blokes playing football and too busy to have noticed her yet. Round the edges different groups of men were intent on cards. As she watched, someone threw their hands in the air in disgust and the cards went flying. Connie snorted; she'd seen her pa do that more times than she could count.

Off the square led what almost looked like a proper road with a couple of black-faced square huts side by side – were those the lavs? – and either side of the path, six or seven long thin buildings with corrugated tin roofs and little windows like bad teeth. And at the bottom of the road, just as Seppe had described, was the chapel. He'd helped make that cross, had described the palaver of clambering up there with it, while below him a dozen Eyeties recited Hail Marys and he had been unmoved, more concerned with the angle. She'd tried to ask him why he didn't care about the religious stuff – it was one of the things the Eyeties were known for – but he'd clammed right up.

Connie concentrated again and discovered what looked like a vegetable garden just off the parade ground, and yet more buildings off to the right, beside a noticeboard that bristled with paper. It was going to be harder than she'd thought to find Seppe.

Still, nothing ventured, nothing gained. Loneliness shoved her forward to the gatehouse.

'Can I go in and call for someone?'

The guard languidly pushed back his hat, which had been shading his face, and looked at her, his head cocked.

'No civilians allowed in, love.'

Her heart sank. She couldn't spend another rest day on her tod – she'd end up bawling. 'Can I walk round the edge and see if I can spot him?'

The guard shrugged. 'Don't see any harm in that.'

She'd made it almost halfway round before she spotted him leaning against a fence post, his head tilted against the sun. He was carving something as usual. Connie picked up a stick from the ground and prodded him through the chink in the fence.

Seppe rose to greet her, a frown forming. 'Connie! There is a problem?'

'No, you goof. Just . . . I wondered if you could use some company.'

He beamed, an unexpected light in his face, and she beamed back, happy he was so pleased to see her. They walked together round the perimeter fence to the guard hut, Connie on the outside, Seppe on the inside. When Seppe bent down to talk to the guard he just nodded, tipped his hand back. She exhaled. No grief about fraternising with the POWs then. There was an official line on such matters, but out here nobody seemed to pay much attention to directives sent down from the cities, except Frank.

Seppe joined her the other side of the fence. 'This way.' He headed them away from the lane she'd walked up.

'Do you know a shortcut?'

He glanced at her. 'Shortcut for what? This is our rest day, no? Nobody is telling us what we must do. So I want to see what is over this way.'

More trees, seemed to be the answer to that. But what did it matter? Now that she had company, the empty space lost its teeth and began to feel like freedom. Doing anything was better than doing nothing, and Seppe wasn't just company; he was Seppe. He was her friend, she realised, mad as it seemed.

Seppe's stride was familiar to Connie now; she matched him step for step and that was enough to stretch away the nag of loneliness and grief that had hollowed out her footsteps towards the camp. Thoughts of Mam and Linda and Babs were never far off, but with Seppe around the edges of those thoughts softened and she could manage them. Without him, she struggled still.

'What's that? More POWs?' Connie stopped outside a set of big metal gates that loomed out of the trees.

'No – it's where the Americans are.'

'Huh.' Made sense they had their own camp, given how chocka Joyce was always saying the Forest houses were these days.

They veered off the path and pushed through bracken until the whistle of the ferns turned into something else.

'A stream!'

Seppe turned and smiled at her as if he'd put the water there himself. 'Gianni has been talking of this water, and

I wanted to know myself what it is like. Livorno, my city, it is beside the sea and I miss that sometimes. Today, I can pretend I am there again, at the port.'

'Must be a tiny ocean if this stream brings it back to you.'

He poked her with one finger, teasing. 'It's the Mediterranean Sea! Do they teach you nothing in these English schools? Livorno is a famous port in history, and we have not only the sea but canals too, to rival Venezia. One day we will go and I will show you.'

'Yeah, and how will we manage that, exactly, with you stuck in a prison camp, and me being skint and working?' But the thought of it tickled her and she bounced along, her belly jiggling. The world seemed open now, full of possibilities, not shrunken and spiky like it so often did. Funny that it took a prisoner to make her feel like this. 'It makes me think of donkey rides and ice creams, and paddling in the sea. And if we can't have the donkeys or the ice cream, we can at least have the paddling.' Connie sat down on the moss and pulled off her boots and socks. 'I'm going in – coming?'

Seppe flashed a rare smile. 'It will be cleaner than the water I wash in at camp.'

'Better hose you down, then!' She bent down and scooped up handfuls of the brook water. It wasn't too cold at all. 'Here you go!' Seppe gasped as the water hit him, and she ducked and laughed, anticipating the comeback.

Before too long they were both soaked, laughing and breathless. Seppe was right, it was like being at the seaside. Not that she could remember the last time she'd been at the seaside, if she was being honest.

'All right, all right – enough!' Connie tiptoed across the pebbles back to the bank and lay out flat. 'I'm worn out after that!'

The wet clothes clung to her body, her belly rising up like a blimp. But this was Seppe. She wanted to cry with relief at the perfection of spending a day being herself, no needing to prove anything or pretend not to be lugging around heartburn and needing to pee in the bushes every ten minutes.

Connie propped herself up on her elbows and gazed down into the water. Seppe splashed out and sat beside her in silence. The grass tickled the inside of their arms, soft and friendly. The water sang to itself as it gurgled past them, fluid curling over the pebbles, rounding them as they nestled beside each other.

Seppe leaned forward. 'Look! Fish. What do you call them here? Minnows, no?'

'Don't ask me – never seen a fish outside the chippy.' She leaned forward and looked where he looked. Those must be the fish, the silver licks and bends amidst the pebbles.

'Can we catch one?'

'We can try.' Seppe cupped his hands, thumbs overlapping, then lowered them slowly into the water.

They waited, agonising moments passing. Connie's nose itched and she swallowed back a sneeze.

'There's one!' Steadier than a heartbeat, Seppe clapped together the heels of his hands and trapped his wriggling catch inside.

He pulled his hands out of the brook.

'Connie – quick! Something to put him in!'

She pulled off her hat and scooped it into the water, then passed it on to Seppe. He opened his hands above it, as if passing judgement on a miracle, and the fish dropped into the hat.

'There! Dinner!' Seppe's whole body was a smile. Connie peered in.

'Won't make much of a mouthful.'

He punched her arm, as gently as a kiss. 'I am making a joke. Perhaps not a good one.'

She punched him back less tenderly. 'I don't think Tommy Handley need worry just yet. But it's a good start.'

'Yes, and this fish is a good start. Now we know that we can live in the woods and find our dinner.'

Connie glanced at Seppe. But she didn't want to think beyond now, not for either of them, not today. She dug her heels in and stood up.

'Don't know about you, but I'm feeling like it's high time for my actual dinner.'

The look he gave her was full of something she couldn't quite translate. For a moment, a mad moment, she imagined them going home together. He'd have to make the grub – there was no way they'd survive on her cooking. She laughed out loud at the thought and Seppe eyed her quizzically.

'A penny for the joke?' She loved how he'd almost got the English saying, but not really.

With an effort she jettisoned the idea. What was happening to her, going all soft as the time for the baby got closer, daydreaming of shacking up with any old Tom Dick or Harry? She blushed, pushed him gently to cover her embarrassment.

'Not worth a penny, mate. Don't you worry about my nonsense. Time to go home.'

Twenty-One

August

SHE HADN'T GOT ANY rest worth its name; the baby had been doing somersaults all night long. Was that normal, or was it sending out a distress signal? Mam would have known.

Connie shut the thought firmly away and picked up the pace, trying to march away that empty feeling that came when she first woke and remembered. The early mornings were light these days, the path into the woods buttery with sun. The baby was quiet now after her night-time acrobatics and Connie had a full day of hardwoods ahead. Every Monday she wondered privately if this might be the week she needed to fake an illness before anyone found out about the baby, but either the men of the forest were paying her no mind at all or she was doing a better job than it felt of arranging her clothes as best she could and carrying on regardless.

'Off to work early, aren't you? My Frank's still polishing off his bacon and eggs.'

Connie looked round as Joyce strode up the path,

headscarf firmly in place, an empty basket over her arm.

'You're not exactly dawdling yourself.' She did like Joyce; there was a solid certainty about her and she'd taught Connie a lot when she'd given her those cooking lessons.

'Tuesday's the day they stock back up at the grocer's. Need to get there and get queuing by eight if you want half a chance.'

'I'd have thought you got everything you needed from the garden.'

Joyce winked. 'Aye, but we use our coupons like you city folk so that the government don't cop on to how much we're growing and send someone down to dig our own gardens for victory.' Joyce looked across at Connie as they kept pace up the hill towards the ridge. 'Our Frank give you that bit of bread and cheese, did he?'

Connie dropped back a pace or two so that she faced the back of Joyce's coat. Was this going to be the talk she thought it was? She couldn't bear to look at Joyce if so, was suddenly small and worried. *Deep breaths.* 'He did, ta very much. That was good of you, Joyce.'

'Aye, well. Thought you might need the extra for a bit.' Joyce didn't make any attempt to turn round and Connie's step missed a beat. Did Joyce mean what Connie thought she did?

'If there's anything else you need, you get word to me, all right? Surrounded by them men up there all day, you are; they may as well be blind, but you can always come and find me if you need me.'

Joyce turned and Connie held her look. 'Thanks, Joyce.' And she meant it. A load lifted.

Joyce nodded, and was gone.

Twenty-Two

SEPPE WAS STANDING IN Frank's doorway, the smallest hint of a draught cooling on the gap between his collar and his cap on this baking August day. Beside him, Connie shifted, wedged her elbow against the jamb. She was quiet this morning. Maybe it was the heat. It must be worse for her than it was for him, especially since she was still wearing that big coat even though it must be drawing more attention than it was diverting these days.

'Here we are, then,' said Frank. 'More demands from London. If they carry on like this we'll have no forest left. Seem to want them faster and faster, they do, as if they hadn't taken our best men for the war, and damned near our best trees already, too. Whatever the dickens they're doing out there, I wish they'd get on with it. This ent forestry work, it's only timber production, and it'll kill off our forest for good if they don't stop playing silly devils, to say nothing of them buggers who keep pinching the cordwood.'

Frank paused for breath and Seppe glanced at Connie.

But she didn't seem to have even heard him. Frank looked at her too, as if expecting some wisecrack in response, shrugged when none came and pointed a sweaty finger at the quota list.

'Norwegian spruce this week, up near Brierley. There's a stand of 'em up there should be about ready. It'll fit this lot's need for softwoods.' He shook the paper again, this time as if trying to dislodge its demands, and Seppe nodded, steered the silent Connie back outside. The tang of the undergrowth in full burst was thick these August days and he coughed as they moved back into its clutches.

It didn't take long to reach the coppice, and the spruce were just as Frank said. Seppe placed the wedge beside the first trunk, ready for a quick insert when the time came, then hefted his axe.

'I start now.' No answer, so Connie probably thought he'd got the angle right for once. She'd never lose the habit of correcting his swing, he knew that now. He set the axe in motion, the worn handle gliding through his fingers as he built up a rhythm.

A shriek rent the air.

Had he hit Connie?

Across the clearing, Connie clamped a hand across her mouth. Craven relief ran through him. She was too far away – there was no way he'd have hurt her from here. But he glanced down just in case, gripped the now-leaden axe more tightly.

Connie had dropped her own axe and was grappling blindly for support. The half-chopped spruce swayed wildly as her fingertips scrabbled at its bark.

And again Connie keened, bent double.

Seppe's blade thudded to the ground.

'Connie – what is it?' He raced over to her and unclasped her hands from the spruce, folded his fingers over hers.

They had matching calluses along the inside ridges of their thumbs, sandpapery bumps.

Connie's eyes were full of fear; she didn't see him.

Oh.

Of course.

Seppe leaned away from Connie reached for the comfort of the whittling knife. His forehead was slick with sweat. *Be brave.* But his mind was crowded with images of Alessa, her belly curving through her nightdress; Alessa, marching down those stairs with a bravado he'd never be able to match. He had let down his sister, hadn't helped her when she'd needed him most. He knew, now, there was no way he would let Connie down.

'Connie. I find doctor. All right? You wait here, I go find doctor.'

'No!' Her breath was tinny, sour.

She straightened up, still gripping his fingers, which had started to go white beneath her grip.

'No doctor! You promised!'

What did she mean? They hadn't ever mentioned the doctor.

'Connie, please, you need doctor. I go quickly, bring him straight back.'

'No!'

Was it the pain or the prospect of the doctor causing such anguish?

'Do you worry about payment? I will help.' He'd find a way.

'No! No doctor!' Her face screwed up.

This couldn't happen. He refused to be responsible for the death of two infants. He bit his nails into his palms, counted to ten.

'Then Joyce? I find Joyce.' Joyce had sent the extra food most days these past weeks, Frank handing it over in a silence that indicated he didn't know what was behind Joyce's generosity. Seppe didn't understand how Frank hadn't twigged but was relieved and grateful all over again to the compassion and understanding shown by Joyce. It was as if the two of them were joined in a tacit battle to protect Connie – and who knows what would happen now the truth would have to come out with the baby?

'No.' Connie was panting; she glared, sweat-glossed.

'Connie, listen to me. We need someone who can help.'

'Nobody must know.' Her eyes filled with tears and he put a shaking arm around her shoulders. 'Too early. It's all happening too early.'

Was it? He had never asked her about dates. Stupid, stupid, stupid.

'Not like that. Well, maybe like that too but I can't be too sure.'

She convulsed, whether from pain or fear he wasn't sure. 'I mean I'm not ready, still haven't figured out what I'm going to do. I should have sorted it ages ago but it was too big and I just couldn't, Seppe, I couldn't. It wasn't supposed to happen like this.' Connie sank to her knees and he descended with her. She was so young, and her fear was emanating off her.

'The baby will be all right.' He had nothing to base this on, but women had babies all the time. It didn't always end like it had for Alessa. *It almost never ended like it had for Alessa.*

But there was no time for that now. The stand would fill soon with loppers and measurers and transport for the timber; the very least she needed was somewhere more private. Could he get her home?

'Can you make it to Amos's house?' But Connie turned wide, frightened eyes on him.

'I can't go there. He'll do his nut.'

It was up to him, then. Seppe straightened. This forest was the safest place he knew. He looked at the trees, green canopies bobbing, providing shade, solace, and his breathing slowed. The Forest would help. He kept his arm around Connie and took hold of her elbow. They stumbled down the slope into a dell. The trees grew thick and straight here, overlapping rows sheltering Connie from sight and masking any noise. This would have to do.

Seppe released his grip on Connie's elbow and she dropped to all fours, rocking backwards and forwards in an attempt to escape the pain, her head hanging low and heavy between her shoulder blades. She arched her back, dipped it, arched again, dipped again, desperate to find a safe spot. Seppe knelt down beside her and she clawed at his hands, drawing blood.

Connie couldn't think. All there was was pain, a pain right inside her where she couldn't get at it. All she could do was try to get away from the pain. She arched back again, fleeing it, but it sank upon her, dug in and wouldn't let her go.

It was gone. She panted, drawing in air, gulping it down before the pain came back. She couldn't do this. She wasn't ready.

'I can't do this.' It came out as a plea.

'You can.' Seppe's voice was soft in her ear and his hand was firm and steady on her back. Perhaps it wasn't too late. Seppe was her friend even though she was a bad person. He'd help her get the baby to the church, find someone who'd give it a good home. Seppe would understand – he'd know she was the wrong mother for this baby.

Another wave rose and she choked, clawed by pain. She could see Seppe's lips moving but she couldn't hear him. Everything was inside now. She grabbed for his hand, dug in.

Mam. Mam would know what to do, know how to make this pain stop and how to deal with the baby. She needed Mam more than she'd ever needed anything.

'I can't do this on my own.' It barely came out, and Seppe bent closer to hear her.

'You don't have to. I am here.' She couldn't explain what she'd meant. The agony roared back and she pressed down on Seppe's hand. The sensation took her over and she couldn't get upright again, leaned against him, panting and wheezing.

Her whole body seemed united in punishing her for thinking she could pull this off. There was no telling what was front, what was back, what was top, what was lower down. It was all unbearable.

It swamped her again and she sucked in air. She needed to get down. She rocked on all fours, Seppe kneeling again beside her. This was better, but only just. She fell into it, rocked and rocked and rocked. Everything was shifting, aching, searing and there was nothing she could do to escape it. She was completely overtaken by the pressure, the rhythm. She had no control over this, none at all. She shrieked, terrified.

'Can you get up? This ground is not so comfortable.' He was right beside her.

'Can't move.'

'You can, *cara*. Please. You are strong. I know this.'

Then a rolling voice that wasn't Seppe.

'How far along do her be?'

Amos!

'Since this morning.' What time was it now? But another wave took over and rendered the thought irrelevant.

'Come onto this, girl, save your knees.' It was soft, smelled like Amos. She wept.

Through a momentary lull in the pain she concentrated

on Amos talking to Seppe in that way he had that you couldn't refuse.

'Do you know where Frank's house is? Mine is next to him. Get there now, boy. Bring a blanket, a pail. A washcloth. The barrow.'

'But it is against regulations. Prisoners aren't allowed –'

'Does this look like the time to be worriting about regulations? Nobody here cares about them rules. Go *on*, lad!'

He was sending Seppe away? She needed Seppe, he was her calm centre. But she had no breath, no space to say this before her body took over again. This endless fire – this couldn't be right! Connie put her head down and arched her back, yelling as loud as she knew, but the pain pushed after her. Amos followed her down. He didn't touch her, but he stayed close.

'That's it, lean into it. Don't you worry like, it'll stop soon enough.'

'Not your normal lambing. Sorry.' She tried to smile, gasped again with the pain and Amos patted her shoulder.

'Don't you be fretting, now.'

The ache ate her up again. She shut her eyes and wailed.

Seppe heard Connie's moans when he was still a way from the dell, his arms full of sheets, balancing a sloshing bucket of water. She was surely dying; this couldn't be normal pain. He stumbled, righted himself against the nearest trunk.

He scrambled down the sheer sides of the dell, desperately trying to hold the water upright. Connie was down on her hands and knees, overalls discarded to one side, sweat-covered and wailing, Amos squatting at her head, talking to her by the looks of things. *She was alive.* The old dog lay off beside the overalls. Seppe couldn't look, couldn't stop looking. This was human life at its most visceral. No battle scene had been more primal.

'Make it stop! Make it stop now! In the name of God, Amos, make it stop!'

'Come on, girl, nice and steady does it. Won't be long now. That's it, you keep going there, just like you are.'

The sun faded slowly away, the last optimistic sparkle on the foliage fading as the shadows crept forward. They overlapped tentatively at the fulcrum of pain, enfolding Connie as she swayed and wept. Perhaps the cooler dusk air would help her, though she seemed beyond all time and place.

Dusk. Seppe swore softly.

'Amos. My curfew.'

The old man's response was feather-light, his murmuring tone never faltering, his eyes not leaving the girl.

'Rightio. Off you go, then.'

He lingered, moved towards Connie. 'I can't leave her.'

Now Amos looked up. 'Sounds like you have to if you want to be coming back.' Amos's skin creased around the memory of the body it used to fit, but there was steel in him that made you do his bidding.

And he was right. Seppe had been cutting it too fine already, slipping out for the extra sessions. Did the old man know about those, somehow, the secret somehow murmuring through the density of the trees?

'I can't leave her. I promised her.' Alessa flashed through his mind again, shadowy against these trees.

'She'll be needing all the help she can get these next few weeks, son. You won't be any good to her stuck in that camp.'

Amos was right. No more Connie. No more Frank. No more freedom. But nothing mattered in this moment more than Connie.

Connie groaned again and Amos turned back to her, one hand waving dismissal. '*Go*. I'll get word to you.'

Frank was waiting for Seppe at the Forestry Commission hut.

'I don't know what it is you've been up to, and I don't want to. But I'll tell you summat for nothing: you don't leave an axe out in the open like that. Anyone could've come along and pinched it, got up to Lord knows what. Stashing it in the coppice is one thing, but to leave him out in plain sight . . .'

The axe. He'd forgotten all about the axe, to say nothing of that half-felled spruce.

'Frank, I –' Connie's agony ricocheted still in his ears and his words blazed.

'It's done now. But you leave them tools out like that again and you'll be back in that camp.' Frank took his pipe out of his mouth, his forehead creasing.

'Where's that felling partner of yours?'

In the nick of time, the camp truck rolled up. As it set off, bumping its way down the track, there was a new rhythm for Seppe to the jouncing of the wheels.

Connie. Connie. Connie.

Twenty-Three

S EPPE SLEPT UNEASILY THAT night, tossing and turning to the sounds of his campmates' snores and grunts. Alessa's dying cries dripped from the rosary, mingled with Connie's moans, turned into the roar of soldiers in the desert, parched and desperate, crescendoed into his father, a beating for each fresh rumour that reached his ears. Seppe tasted blood in his sleep, woke up hollow, shaken, reached for his carving to steady the pulse pounding in his temples. Connie. How was Connie?

The oatmeal made him gag this morning; he pushed the tin bowl across to Gianni, left the mess hall and set out into the forest.

Seppe jabbed his way through the throng of local men lined up for their orders, ignoring the complaints and shoves.

But as he strode into the clearing, Frank was leaning in the doorway of his hut, looking out for him.

Waiting.

She's gone.

I failed her.

He had no breath to ask the only thing that mattered. Frank met his gaze with a questioning one of his own. Had Amos really not said anything to Frank?

'Amos dropped this off for you.' 'This' was a thin white envelope, neatly addressed in a careful copperplate.

Seppe tore it open and reached for the flimsy sheet of notepaper inside. Why wouldn't it unfold? He wrestled with it, grabbed the edge as it took flight.

One line.

Relief unfurled like a leaf in spring.

'Boy!' He thrust the paper at Frank. 'Connie – the baby. It's a boy!' *Connie's alive.*

'Baby?' Frank retreated as if the paper itself was a squalling newborn.

'Well, I'll be –'

He glared at Seppe.

'Tell me it's not yours, lad. That'd be a right mess we've got ourselves into.'

Seppe watched the cogs turning, the calculations almost visible in the air between them.

'No – no, can't be yours. Well, that's a blessing, at least.' This seemed to decide it for Frank. A smile spread.

'A baby! I'll be damned. That girl – never a dull moment, eh?' Frank limped across to the door of the hut, pulled it shut behind them to mutters of outrage from the waiting men.

'Why isn't she with her family? Or her husband?'

Seppe remembered Connie's phrase. 'Dead and gone. One or the other.'

'It's up to us, then. She's a damn good worker, for all her chopsiness.'

Up to us. Frank saw an 'us' which included himself and also Connie. The acceptance, the simple sense of belonging, sideswiped him. Seppe leaned against the edge of the table, his legs unable to hold him. The table teetered, and the top layer of papers wafted to the ground.

'Watch it, Seppe lad. Bad as blimming Connie you're getting now.' But Frank was smiling. 'A baby! And she did bring it here to the Forest to be born. Least we can do is help out a bit. I'll talk to my Joyce, see what the best thing would be.'

Amos poked at the stew on the range. The blessed thing was taking forever to heat up, and the stink from the napkins in the pot beside it was stronger than you'd give a newborn credit for creating. By the time this stew was ready, all he'd be able to taste would be napkins and Borax.

There was a rap on the panes of the kitchen window and Frank saw himself in. His nose wrinkled and he came forward to peer into the pan. 'Crikey Moses! What are you brewing up there, old butt?'

'Shh!' Amos used the stew fork to point at the ceiling. Globs of fat dolloped down into the bubbling napkins. 'They're sleeping up there.'

'Those napkins don't go on the range next to your vittals. Saves them for wash day, you do.'

As if Amos needed Frank to tell him that. Frank and Joyce who'd never been blessed with kids. Brought his Billy up on his own, hadn't he? Knew more about napkins than most men round here. He'd wash them when and how he pleased. First Billy had told him he didn't know how the war worked, now Frank was barging into his kitchen to lay down the law about childrearing. Amos stabbed the fork right into the napkins' water. Drops of something hot and brown splashed out.

Frank took a pace back, a look of revulsion on his face. 'How is she?'

186

'Aye, all right.' Amos bent over the stew, close enough to block out the napkin stench, and sniffed hard. The food still smelt of nothing like tea.

'What a turn up, eh?' Frank picked up the stew fork, poked it into the pot. 'Our Joyce reckoned she'd had a notion. Slow to catch on, I was. Joyce had got into the habit of giving me extra dinner for the girl, to feed her up, like. I thought she was simply looking out for her. You know Joyce. Wish she'd have told me.'

'Aye, well, wouldn't want to be caught gossiping, would she? Your Joyce keeps her nose out of other people's business, and you should be glad.'

'Don't go telling me you knew and all? Right dozy sod I must be.'

'Didn't know nothing for sure, like. And she ent never mentioned a fellow, nor a family come to that. Get the sense she's on her own down here. But that time I told you about, when she and the POW were out there sawing? There was something off about the way she was bent over. I put it down mostly to cack-handedness, tell you the truth. But when I came across her yesterday, I had half an idea what I was looking at, put it that way.' Amos had told his suspicions to May's picture, and all, but he wasn't going to tell Frank that.

Frank took off his cap and twisted the brim through his fingers. Amos waited. Let him spit it out.

'She's a solid little worker. The way her and Seppe get down them oaks – hard to teach that, it is.'

Amos nodded, sniffed again. That was better; you could smell the carrot and onion now, blocking out the napkins.

'I'm not going to kick her out, if that's what you're wondering. What do you take me for, Frank Watkins?'

The relief shook off Frank like dew off a ewe's fleece. 'Cheers, Amos. Appreciate that.' He rocked back on his

187

heels. 'What's your Billy going to make of this, then? Always one for the newborn lambs, weren't him? This is even better'n that!'

'Aye, well, he'd have to know about the girl first.'

'You mean you haven't told him about Connie being here? You still haven't written to your Billy?' Frank came closer and Amos moved to the other side of the pot. 'Cripes, Amos, the lad's not out there on his holidays. How long you going to keep this up?'

'I do know it's not a holiday.' Fragments of Billy's letters floated into Amos's head, gritted any sense of contentment with guilt. 'What goes on between me and our Billy is up to me and him, nowt to do with anyone else.'

Amos speared a likely looking chunk of meat. Nice and hot it was now. Bit gristly, but that wasn't to be helped.

'Was that it? Girl's got a bed here as long as her do want it, and that babby too.'

He waved the fork at Frank and plunged it again into the stew pan. 'Tea's ready. This baby, he's Forest-born. And Foresters stay here in the Forest, you know that.'

Twenty-Four

CONNIE YAWNED, THEN WINCED. Every morning the same robin trilled her awake from the tree outside her window, which might be all right if it wasn't usually ten minutes after she'd finally got the baby off. Her breasts were like barrage balloons again, but cement ones, hard and lumpy. The baby had wailed half the night, jerking his head away every time she heaved him on to an aching nipple, his face scrunched up whatever she'd tried to do. Had the milk in them curdled because the baby wouldn't take it? He was a week old – shouldn't he know how to do this by now? And shouldn't she? Honest to God, next time he cried she was going to join in, she was sure of it, and then she'd never stop.

She sagged against the pillow.

Mam would know.

As clearly as if it had happened, she saw Mam on the train down here, her best hat hastily shoved over that ruffled dark hair. She had tried so hard not to think of Mam, but only Mam could help.

It took a minute to get the tears under control.

'Come on, then.' Lying around in bed wasn't helping anything, and however early it was, if the robin was shouting then Amos would be out dealing with the sheep.

Amos. You'd go a thousand years and never meet someone like Amos. When she thought how he'd pushed that barrow through the shadows of the oaks the night the baby was born, Bess up ahead as if guiding the way and her bundled inside in a pile of blankets, clutching at the baby in case Amos tipped them out. But Amos was silent and steady and got them home without either fuss or jibe, had made no mentioned of it since. Sometimes she wondered if she'd dreamed the whole thing, but there was no way she'd walked home and when she'd held the blanket to her face, it smelled of old wood and sheep's wool.

Connie padded downstairs and creaked open the door into the parlour. The blackouts stayed up in here all the time and the room was thick and musty. She fumbled her way to the heavy bureau in the corner and pulled down its slanty top. Right at the back, behind an ancient bottle of God only knows what, she found it – a pencil and a wodge of paper and envelopes. Years of dust swirled up and caught in her throat as she pulled them out, and the noise of her coughing barked back at her in the gloom. Connie shivered and hotfooted it back up the stairs to the still-warm bed where she pulled the pencil and paper to her.

She hurtled to the end of her letter and stuffed the paper into the envelope before second thoughts crept up on her like those Messerschmitts. No point in reading it back. Her breasts were killing her now, really killing her, and the baby's grunts had turned into proper squawks. She really ought to give him a name; she knew the looks Amos and Joyce shot her when she called him 'the babba' were code for 'name your child, you useless baggage', and she didn't blame them. But she wasn't going to call him after his own father, nor hers, and she was so wiped out all the time and so close to tears that it just felt too overwhelming.

Fierce little tyke, the babba was; got to like him for that. Just as well, too, given that he was a boy, not a girl after all, and likely to end up fighting for his life in some foreign country the way this war was going. Connie scooched forward on the bed and got hold of the baby under both armpits, hauling him out of the cot. He stopped screeching for a minute to scowl at her and she stuffed her swollen breast towards his mouth. For once it worked and he chomped down, pain splintering her nipple even as the throbbing eased off a bit. She looked down at him, attached like that, just as the babba lost his grip on her. A jet of milk squirted out and by the time he snuffled back into place her hand was drenched.

'Oh, baby!' After a few minutes she plonked him back in the cot and got out of bed. On the chair beside her bed, crisp and useless, her dungarees reeked of starch and carbolic where Joyce had pinched them to wash. They should smell like the outside, of sawdust and sweat.

The baby caught a fist on the wooden slats and yowled, then arched, heels and head on the mattress, his body twisting like he was trying out the jitterbug. What was going on? Was he choking? In the dead of night – and Lord knows she was greeting the dead of night often enough – she knew it was all her fault, that he knew she hadn't meant to keep him and was punishing her for it. She hadn't been out of the house yet, let alone made it back up to that church with him to put him there safely and scarper. And lately, tell the truth, she felt like crying (again! What had happened to her?) if she thought of leaving him, just as much as she did if she thought of being stuck here with him forever. Her plan was in tatters and there was nobody, nobody at all, she could talk it through with because they'd all think she was round the bend to want to leave the forest in the first place. Even Seppe, steadfast and understanding, but the gentlest person she knew would turn against her if he knew the plans for survival that went through her head. She was on her own with this one and she was scared something rotten.

Twenty-Five

'*SCALCO*! YOU COMING?'

Seppe's thumb caught against the scratch of his sleeve as he jumped and his mouth watered tinnily. Where had Gianni sprung from? The camp was usually half-empty on a Sunday these days, the guards laxer and laxer because they knew the prisoners would come 'home'. Gianni was spending more and more time with his sweetheart, Mary, a good-natured girl whose father owned the pub in the next village. Word in the camp was that Gianni had fallen on his feet. Nobody was surprised by this and nobody begrudged him it, either. Relationships between campmates and civilians were strongly forbidden, but somehow none of the usual rules – however few they were – ever applied to Gianni, who was simply too charismatic to be bound by these things. Even those guards with relatives in the war, who hated the 'foreigner' prisoners and what they stood for with a fervour that matched Fredo's reverse enmity, were won over. 'We don't mean foreigners like *you*,' they'd say, opening the gate for him as he squeaked in a shade after curfew. It was a gift.

Blood dripped down the handle of Seppe's knife onto the wood no matter how tightly he pressed his thumb into the wad of his sleeve. What a stupid thing to do, and after he'd worked on it for hours, too, as night slipped into beckoning dawn day after day. He'd had to hide it from Fredo. But despite the sick feeling in his stomach at the thought of what Fredo would do if he discovered such evidence of friendship with the enemy, the urge to please Connie pervaded. At least the stain was on the underside of the carving. Connie would never notice, not once it was screwed into place.

Gianni plonked down next to Seppe. He smelled of pomade – how on earth had he procured that? Would Connie like it if he, Seppe, smelled like this? Seppe frowned at such base thoughts. Connie had a child to care for now. This was the important thing.

'My *cara* Mary says the Bell has new cider now the apples are coming off the trees. We're off to see if this apple drink is as good as the *inglese* claim.'

The bleeding had stopped. 'Not me.' Seppe's mouth watered at the thought of the fruit. August was the ripest month in England, no question. But now his thumb was staunched, the end was there for the taking. This last carving to finish then he could deliver it. No resting now.

'What? It's Sunday afternoon. Come with us, play a little football, have a little fun.' Gianni moved closer, peered. 'What are you up to this time? Carving a feather?'

Gianni must be at an odd angle; Seppe turned it so that the latticing was more obvious.

Gianni peered.

'*Oh yes*! Now I see; it's more like a hand than a feather.'

'Eh, *idiota*!' Seppe scrabbled on bone-dry earth, thrust a handful of last year's treefall and the smell of almost-gone summer in front of Gianni. 'Look, it's an oak leaf, like these.'

'Well, up to you, my friend. If you'd rather stay here there's nothing I can do. But you're crazy; there are enough leaves in this place without you carving wooden ones.'

'You have a good afternoon, OK? Tell me about this cider stuff.'

Gianni winked. 'Don't worry. If it's good, I'll be working out how to make it tomorrow.' He picked up his pace to catch up the others as they neared the far gate.

Seppe pulled the sandpaper from his pocket and drove it firmly against the carving. Tiny filaments whistled and he swallowed hard.

Another twenty, twenty-five pushes and the leaf was acorn-smooth. He craned his neck to see the parade ground clock. It was listing again; must have got knocked by the football training, but he wasn't fixing it today. It was time to get going. He took a deep breath and stood up.

Seppe pulled his fingers through his hair, shifting from foot to foot as the echo of the door knocker coursed from fingertip to toe. His boots were filthy and his hair stank where it straggled into his eyes. He should have scrubbed his boots, at the very least. It had been too long since he'd been to visit anyone in an actual house; where were his manners?

'What are you doing here?' The air coming through the crack in the door was dense, domestic, full of memory. Seppe's voice seized up.

'What you got there, then?' Amos pushed the door wider, and crouched down. 'A cot?'

Amos lifted the end closest to him and the cot creaked. Seppe stiffened, but there was no attendant crack.

'Crikey-oh, lad, there's some weight to this, isn't there? Let's get him inside.'

All of a sudden the cot looked so big, so polished here

in the gloom of the tiny stairwell. Trepidation bittered Seppe's throat, sludged his thoughts. Would he even be able to get it up the stairs? But Amos was at one end of it already, knuckles swollen around wooden slats, steps creaking as he crabbed his way up, the cot making its steady way behind him like a hearse on a cart. Seppe lifted the other end and heaved up the stairs.

As soon as Amos backed open the bedroom door, Seppe was cocooned in the smells emanating from it. It was far from the opera of the bark, worlds apart from the guttural notes of Campo 61. It was a lullaby. Seppe blinked it away and looked into the room.

'What're you doing here?' Connie was in the bed, covers tucked under her arms. She didn't sound any different. He craned further, saw only a bed, a rickety closet and a packing crate. No baby. What had happened to the baby?

'If you've come to see me rather than prowling the landing, come in, why don't you?'

Seppe's pulse beat in his fingertips, already sore from heaving the cot through the forest. Amos tutted at Connie, moved to the end of the bed and picked up the crate. Seppe edged into the room, lifting the cot in the middle so that it didn't scrape the floor.

Amos, crate cradled under one arm, stopped and spoke, apparently into the crate. 'This is Seppe. Have a looksee at what he's made for you.'

Seppe looked again at the crate. *In* the crate. A fist barrelled out at him and he flinched. Connie laughed from her throne of a bed. He smiled up at her, but she was looking past him, past the baby, towards the door, as if planning an escape.

'*He*'s not going to get you, not yet, anyway.'

'This is him?' There was a baby in there. The one he'd helped survive.

'That's the one.'

Amos placed the crate down on the end of the bed. Connie edged up the pillows, fisting the covers tighter around her.

'Don't give him to me, he'll start bawling.'

Amos eased out the baby as if he were birthing him again, smiling down at him with a gentleness Seppe recognised from that day in the dell. Seppe could barely watch, couldn't look away.

'Here, take him a minute.'

Did Amos mean him? Seppe put out his arms, elbows bending to meet the weight of the child. The baby was heavier than he'd have thought; and warm; really warm. He was the epicentre of this new scent, too. The newborn smell radiated milkily as Seppe pulled him against his chest. The baby squirmed into the crook of his arm, curled up against him like the first shoot of a germinating acorn. Seppe gazed down. He was so new, so untainted.

'What in the name of God is that?' Connie stared at the cot, which Amos had placed where the crate had been. Her voice was shrill, but tears brimmed. Had he upset her? Seppe reached for the comfort of the knife.

Amos gave Connie another of his looks and stamped off down the stairs. The urge to beg him to stay nearly overwhelmed Seppe. He couldn't do this alone!

'It's a – a *culla*.' He tensed, and looked at Connie. She met his gaze with a thousand spikes.

'A what?'

'A . . .' Oh, come on, what had Amos called it? 'A bed, for the baby. A-a cot.'

'I can see that. What's it doing here, I mean?'

She hated it; he'd got it all wrong. He needed to leave.

But the baby snuffled and squeaked in his arms and he couldn't move his feet. This wasn't about Connie.

'It is for him. To say welcome.' The cot loomed over the foot of the bed, looking much bigger in this cramped room so full of Connie. He'd tried to make it as much like an Italian cradle as possible, like the one that he had been sanding again in preparation for Alessa's child. But it was a misfire, a palm tree amidst the old-growth.

'The baby's already got a bed.' Connie gestured at the crate. 'Don't hear him complaining. What would he want with something that posh?'

'I –' The silence between them stretched, arced, sucked the air from him. The baby shifted in Seppe's arms, snuggled back down. The movement triggered a new wave of the baby smell, fresh and so hopeful.

The door opened and Amos slipped back into the room.

'Budge up then, Amos, let me see it.'

Joyce too. Oh, thank heavens. Seppe's grasp on the whittling knife eased. Joyce read people the way Frank read trees. The little room full of newborn smelt again of the outside coming in, of bark and mulch, sharp and comforting. He could breathe now.

'This it?' She bent over, peered at the crib with its four pillars. 'Them's Forest of Dean leaves on each of the corners, aren't they?'

She looked at Seppe and he nodded, careful not to dislodge the squirming baby. The air came back to his lungs but he still couldn't meet Connie's eye.

'Ash, beech, oak and yew. I omitted the softwoods because Frank says they are new, not so much from our Forest.'

'Frank's right.' Joyce straightened up and came over to Seppe, right up close. He tensed, ready to jump out of the firing line. She stroked the back of the baby's head, her fingers cracked and red, smelling of carbolic. 'This is a real nice bed you do have here, my poppet; you'll know the names of our leaves before you can walk under them.' Joyce straightened up and addressed Connie, one hand still on the baby's head. 'Proper heirloom, this is; do you well for however many more you go on to have.'

'Heirloom? What does the likes of me want with an heirloom?' Connie's voice quavered the tough words and her fingers plucked at the covers. Did she not like it? Seppe scrutinised the cot again for the source of this fear, but could only see what he'd always seen. Joyce and Amos were clustered at it now, lifting bedding from the crate and fussing it into the cot.

Joyce ran her fingers over each of the carved leaves. Thank goodness he'd spent that extra time with the sand-paper. At Connie's words, Joyce lifted her head.

'You pack that in, Connie Granger. Bit of gratitude wouldn't kill you; this much workmanship didn't get done in a day.'

Could he make Connie understand? 'I wanted to bring something for you.' He looked steadily at her.

'This isn't much use to me, is it?' She dropped his gaze. 'It's for the baby, not me.'

'It is for you both. Joyce is right, it can last you for another time, another baby maybe.'

Her eyes flashed. 'Is that what you think of me? That I'm going to stay here, popping out sprogs?'

Joyce came to the rescue.

'Rightio, then, let's see what the baby thinks of it. Come on, Seppe, you put him in it.'

Him? Really? But he couldn't resist the honour. He lifted the baby gingerly and hovered with him over the crib. 'Here is your new bed, little – what is his name?'

Amos grunted.

'Hasn't got a name yet.'

Connie sat forward. 'I know you think I can't do anything

right with the baby, Amos, but I've got this bit sorted.' She darted a smile at Seppe, missile-quick but wavering. 'What was it you said your name was in English? Joseph?'

Seppe nodded. His heartbeat drummed so hard the baby must be about to vibrate.

'Well, then. He's going to be Joe. Maybe he'll build someone a swanky cot one day, too.'

There was a pause. Seppe blinked hard and handed the baby – Joe – to Joyce before the infant slipped through his hands. Had Connie been planning to name the baby for him, or had that been an impulse? Did it matter? She must think something of him to entrust her child's name to him. He approached the bed, but words thinned and wilted away.

'Connie – I –' Dust motes danced in glistening rays. 'I will take care of him. Of Joe. This is a distinction for me. If he needs something, you let me know and I will help.'

'What're you on about? Needed a name, didn't he?'

'Does he need something now? To be made clean? To go for a walk?'

'He's fine, Seppe. Don't take it all so seriously.' She couldn't look at him again. Joyce threw a worried glance at Connie, but said nothing.

Every time Seppe looked at Joe he would know his responsibility. He wanted the weight of him in his arms again, but Joyce had placed him in the cradle where he seemed more than happy. It would be better not to disturb him, no? He had so much to learn.

'Forest baby in a forest cot; born inside the Hundred and now sleeping surrounded by our trees. Not bad, is he, eh, Amos?' Joyce beamed into the cot.

'Now that you've all rearranged my room d'you think I could get a bit of kip?'

Joyce stepped over to Connie, put a hand on her forehead as if checking her temperature. 'You need anything, our Con?' Connie shook her head, spoke so quietly that Seppe had to crane to hear her.

'Just to kip. Honest, Joycie.'

Seppe's heart ached. She was going to cry the moment the door shut, he was certain of it. He had upset her, and there was nothing he could do to comfort her . . .

Amos peered at Seppe as if he'd never properly considered him before.

'This lad here needs a haircut, Joyce.' He took Seppe by the shoulders and steered him out of the room before he'd had a final chance to see Joe – Joe! – in the cot again, or to work out Connie's reaction. Was the baby going to be all right, alone there at the end of the bed? Seppe would constantly be on the alert now. He listened hard as Amos led him downstairs, straining for every last gurgle. Maybe Connie had picked Joe up again, was singing to him? But there were no songs amidst the baby noises.

Seppe was so caught up that he barely registered being sat down onto one of Amos's kitchen chairs, a dishtowel draped round his neck. Joyce prowled behind him.

'Need to make this quick, like. I've got the washing half hung out and all the darned pegs keep falling apart. Don't they have barbers up at that camp?'

They did, but all his tokens had been used on extra food for Connie recently. Chocolate was expensive, and the inevitable 'tax' Fredo levied cost him more, too. Seppe hadn't visited the barber for weeks.

Amos swatted at Joyce.

'You saw that cot; it must have taken hours to build. How's the lad had a chance to worry about his grooming? He needs a quick tidy up same as you always give our Billy.'

'All right, all right, keep your hair on.' Joyce laughed and there was a tug on the back of Seppe's head as she ran the comb through his hair. 'Get me a jug of water, Amos, there's a love? Tangled as a ewe in gorse, this is.'

When had Seppe last washed his hair? He'd avoided the ablutions huts as much as he could since last week, when Fredo had jammed his uniforms into the drain. Please God let there be no lice crawling white and blind over the silver of Joyce's blade.

The scissors tickled his neck and he tensed. With his hair gone, Joyce would see how filthy his collar was. Seppe willed himself not to cough, to be still. The silence was thick like leaf sediment, but soft as it, too, no threat pending. Fear of lice, shame about his collar, worry about Connie's reaction; they were all clipped away with his hair, for now at least. How long since he'd been taken care of like this? He closed his eyes and let himself be seven again, sun streaming in through the kitchen window in Livorno, his mother relaxed for once, singing *Rigoletto* as she cut his hair ready for communion. The tune came up his throat; he hummed along *sotto voce* with its memory. The heat warmed his face and he could smell the polish on the hard back of the chair, hear Alessa chattering in the background about all the curls she'd have to keep once her hair was cut. If things could only have stayed like that. If he could preserve seven for ever – but it didn't work like that. A sadness settled around him.

'There!' Joyce broke the moment just in time, stepped in front of him to admire her own handiwork, her expression his mirror. 'Not bad, if I do say so myself.'

Amos joined her. 'You've sheared the lad as if he's a sheep. Bit late in the season for that, mind.' He smiled at Seppe, tentative.

'You do be welcome here any time, lad, you hear that? No matter what them guards say about POWs not being allowed in people's homes; if you want to see that babby, you come here and you see him.' Amos patted Seppe on the shoulder and for a moment he almost believed it was achievable. To see the baby again, to be near all that possibility, the newness and cleanness of him. A bead of optimism pooled.

Then he remembered Connie, arms folded tight across her body, a deep frown as she considered the crib.

'But Connie –'

'Connie gave the baby your name, didn't she?' Amos jerked his hand. 'Yours, nobody else's. Looks like she could do with all the hands she can get, tell you the truth. Don't you go worrying about her.'

Seppe was too choked up to speak the words if he'd known them, so he nodded, almost a bow. He would make them things; a crook for Amos, perhaps a scoop for Joyce's chicken feed to replace that jaggedy old can she used.

'Goodbye, Amos, Joyce. And thank you.'

The distance to the camp was shorter on the way back.

The baby and his mother were both fast asleep and the kitchen was clean enough to suit the king – or his May, more like – so there was nothing left but to get on with it. Amos sat down at the table and smoothed the notepaper over the grain of the oak. Could you use normal paper to write to soldiers? Soon find out, he would.

The light hadn't faded yet from the bottom of the garden. That bit of wall still needed fixing where a branch had fallen onto it in the last of the spring storms. How was he supposed to start this letter? 'Dear son, Sorry I haven't been in touch. There's a baby living in your bedroom . . .'

He sighed and rested the pen on the table. The look on Seppe's face when the girl had named the baby for him. It was spur of the moment, any fool could see that, but that hadn't bothered the lad. He was a loner by Frank's account, kept himself to himself, and now he had something that mattered to him. Must be hard being away from home, and being a prisoner and all. Didn't seem the type to have ended up in the war – there must be a story behind that, just like there was with his Billy.

Billy wouldn't mind the baby. Frank was right: Billy had always loved lambing time, insisted on bringing home any orphaned lambs and bottle-feeding them. He'd probably missed hearing about them. If Amos wrote to Billy about the goings-on here, it would give him something to hold on to. You needed that if you couldn't be at home, even if you'd chosen to go, Amos saw that now. His Billy hadn't had a crib nearly as fancy as that, but he'd been a right bonny baby, and it wasn't just Amos and May as did say so. Happy little chap, he'd always been; terrible to think that he might be feeling lonesome and fearing that Amos had all but abandoned him.

Foresters didn't bear grudges; living with the trees showed you how it all kept moving on whether you wanted it to or not. He picked up the pen again.

Twenty-Six

Joe let out a burp Cass in the factory would've been proud of and chundered a stream of milk over them both and the bed.

'Not again, babba!' She couldn't lose the habit, even though he'd had a name for a week now.

Connie grabbed an edge of the bedspread and daubed at him. Even her fingers felt exhausted, and she couldn't remember the last time her eyes hadn't felt salty from being open all night. And from the tears, if she was being honest. Nobody had told her she'd turn into a leaky tap when she gave birth. One of the dozens of things she'd found out on the job.

Downstairs, a door opened and shut. 'Coo-ee! You up there, Con?'

Thank God.

'We'll come down, Joyce!' Connie clambered out of the bed, lying the baby on the counterpane. Joyce had taken to popping in, had simply turned up one morning not long after Joe had been born. 'Right messy job it can be, looking after a newborn. I'll take them clothes for you, save Amos the trouble.' Connie had come to rely on these visits. She could say what she wanted to Joyce; nothing seemed to faze her.

Joyce had the kettle on the range already. 'Looks like you were up half the night again.'

'He doesn't believe in sleep and I can't leave him to cry, got to do my best by him.' She looked down at Joe, tied to her in the counterpane. His yelling had turned to whimpers. She stroked his head, looped one of his curls over her little finger, his big blue eyes spearing her with a trust she didn't deserve. She wondered if his eyes would stay blue. Joyce said all babies came with blue eyes, but they didn't always stay that way. Shamefully, secretly, she couldn't remember the colour of Don's eyes so she'd just have to sit tight and see how things turned out, she supposed. Just like she'd have to do with this whole big mess. Connie resisted the urge to put her own head down on the kitchen table and wail for a week.

'Poor little sod, saddled with a mam who can't get even the basics right. Wish he could see me cutting down the big oaks. He'd know I was actually good at something, then.'

Joyce tutted. 'You're better at this than you're giving yourself credit for. It's just darned hard work, that's the truth of it. As for the trees – there's nothing stopping you showing him, is there?'

'What are you on about?'

Joyce blew a raspberry on Joe's cheek and he giggled, settled down right away. That never worked when Connie tried it.

'You haven't been farther than the back garden for days. I'm not saying you should get out there and start felling again yet, but there'd be no harm in you taking our Joe out to the felling sites, show him where he was born. Do you both the world of good.'

Connie didn't need telling twice. She paced down the corridor and stuffed her feet into her boots, Joe tilting in the counterpane pouch. 'I'll have that tea another time, Joyce.' Joyce had made her see sense, more than she knew. Why *shouldn't* she be out there felling again? All she had to do was persuade Frank.

Everything had gone berserk since Connie had last been in the forest. The trees were greener than she'd known anything could be, and the birds were having an enormous shouting match. The ferns – that's what they were called, weren't they, those big flat leaves that waved at you? – were gangly and bloody giant. For the sheer hell of it she took Joe off the path and marched through the centre of them for a bit. They brushed her waist, giving way easily, and she giggled, free again. It was like being in a *Tom and Jerry* cartoon, bounding through the grass.

It took ages to get to Frank's hut, and she wasn't as fit as she had been, either. By the time she got there she was all puffed out.

Connie pushed at the door to Frank's hut with moist hands. A corner of the bedspread was caught on an old stump and as she tried to yank it free it pulled tight over the baby's mouth, setting him off again. Connie bit down hard on the inside of her cheek and refused to give in to the urge to scream. Or cry, which would be worse.

'Connie! That you, girl?' Frank came to the door of the hut, his arms outstretched. 'I swear our Joe grows a bit bigger every day. I've been telling Seppe all about him.'

Oh! Was Seppe there too? Yes, there he was, behind Frank. He smiled at her in that sorry-I'm-alive way that made her want to sigh in frustration and protect him all at once and she waved, a bit shy all of a sudden.

'Taking the little one out for some fresh air, are you? Sure you're not overdoing it?'

She took a deep breath. 'I'm here to get going again. Thought I could start with that stand of oak up at Mitcheldean.'

Frank shook his head. 'You're not back on duty yet, Connie.'

Her toes clenched in her boots. 'What do you mean? I was never *off*-duty. Did you see me sign off, Frank? I had a baby not an illness – and to be straight with you, it was a lot harder work than getting down a few poxy trees.'

Frank put up a hand. 'Connie. You've just had a littlun and –'

She rubbed her eyes. Frank meant well. 'I know, and he's wearing me out. I'm up half the night whilst he screams at me. What's that got to do with getting trees down?'

Frank crossed his arms, his boots blocking either side of the doorway.

'That baby's but weeks old and you need to be resting inside with him.'

Connie bit down hard on the inside of her cheek, but the words came anyway.

'Resting from what? From having my bits torn apart like someone shoved a bomb up there? From ending up with a belly like a blimp and breasts rubbed raw?' Frank was looking every which way but at her. She needed to calm down, but the words wouldn't stop pouring out. 'Who do you think I am, Frank? Did you stop when your finger got lopped off, when you did your leg in?'

'This isn't the same as that.' But he shifted his weight off his bad leg.

'Course it is! You don't stop because things are a bit sore, and nor do I.'

'If you want something to do, our Joyce has been taking in sewing for the POWs. It's not much, money-wise, but it's better than nothing.'

'But I don't want sewing. I'm as useless at that as I am with the baby. I want to be out here, as soon as I can be, doing proper work.' Her eyes were dry with the tears she didn't dare shed, and her throat was lumpy with panic. 'Come *on*, Frank. I'm going mad stuck inside with him yelling at me all the time. If I don't do something I'll lose my mind.'

'What about Joe?' Frank's arms dropped to his side. Was he going to give in?

'What about him? I've told you, I'm doing my best by him.'

Frank sighed. Didn't he believe her?

'Not that. Who'll be minding him when you're out here?' He stopped her before the words were out. 'Don't go saying our Joyce – got enough to do already, she has.'

'Amos could take him out with the sheep.' When Connie had woken up yesterday Amos was out in the garden singing some old hymn to the baby, holding him up to the blossom as if showing him what was what. 'They get on well.'

But Frank was shaking his head and her guts collapsed again with the weight of it. 'That baby's yours, and yours alone. We're here to help, you know that, but to my mind, giving you an axe and a saw when you've got that babby there to mind isn't help, it's hindrance.'

'Excuse me?'

Connie jumped and the baby jumped too, whacking her in the face. Why did Seppe have to skulk everywhere? She rubbed her cheek.

'What?'

'Joe could come out with us.'

Frank's face furrowed and Connie couldn't blame him. What was Seppe on about?

'Out with you where, lad?'

'Out here, to the felling sites.' Seppe squeezed past Frank and came right up to stand close to Connie. He picked up one of the baby's hands and stroked it. Joe gurned at him in that way he had and Connie almost smiled.

'He could come here with Connie and I can help. Perhaps they both take two, the trees *and* the baby. The baby is my responsibility too, and it will mean Connie doesn't have to do it so much.'

It was a good plan, even though Seppe was more or less agreeing that she was no good at dealing with the baby. Connie's cheeks grew hot but she forced herself past the humiliation.

'That's a good idea, Frank. Look!'

She tugged at one end of the counterpane. Good job she'd brought it. That proved she thought about what the baby needed – right? 'Joe can lie on this under a tree and when he's older he can help.'

The counterpane wouldn't budge where it was tied round her waist. She yanked again and it gave way in a *whoosh*. The baby tipped sideways and she lost a grip on him.

'Don't worry! I've got him.'

How did Seppe make it look so easy? Connie turned to Frank.

'You know it makes sense. I'm one of the best wood-cutters you've got, and if I'm out here with Seppe again, it'll improve his work rate too, you know it always does.' She smiled at Seppe, suddenly unsure. 'No offence – you know what I mean.' He nodded and smiled, and her heart relaxed its grip on concern.

Would Frank go for it? She could hardly get the words out round the great big rock of longing that was stuck in her throat.

'Aye, all right then. But one bit of harm comes to that baby and you're done, do you hear me? And you'll not be on softer targets, mind. If you're out there you'll do what the rest are doing.'

The rock shifted. Not very far, but enough to let her breathe again.

'Frank, I could kiss you!' Frank's face was a picture. For the first time in weeks, she laughed. She'd had a plan, and that plan had had to change. But now she had another one, and people to pull it off with. Life was starting to make sense again.

The Aylburton Marrow

A great marrow weighing 73 lbs. has been grown by Mr A. Hayden of Aylburton. Mr Hayden, who is a keen gardener, is an expert on marrow growing and has devoted considerable time to it.

Dean Forest Mercury, Friday, 29th September, 1944

Autumn, 1944

Twenty-Seven

September

THE FOREST IN AUTUMN was a shock after those months of desert monochrome and even the singing green of these last few months. Already in September it was a symphony of colour; high yellows and reds melding with ochre and amber, providing a richness and depth from sky to earth. 'Too early,' Amos had muttered, clearly viewing this sudden kaleidoscope of nature as more proof that the world was in chaos, but Seppe revelled in its unexpected harmony. Even the ground added bass notes of multi-faceted auburn as the winds turned with the leaves and whispered them down to foot level. Seppe hadn't known a landscape could be so full of colour, that colour could be so soothing. Renzo's tune, 'Bella Ciao', sprang to his throat every time he trod deep into the opus that the forest was creating all around him. Any flash of scarlet he'd seen in the desert had meant destruction, uncertainty; here it was a salve.

But even the splendour of the woods couldn't insulate Seppe from the baby's distress. Joe's plaintive cries ripped into Seppe like a saw's teeth greeting metal. They'd been out here all morning and Joe must have been crying for half of it. How could Connie concentrate? But there she was, lining up the axe again – the six-pounder as usual. Ever since she'd been back out here with Joe these last few days, she had insisted on the bigger axe.

There was only one way to grab her attention when she was like this. Seppe got between Connie and the oak and she dropped the axe, rested her weight on it like a gatepost.

'What are you up to? We're almost there. I was about to get the wedge in.' She one-handed the axe handle and rummaged in her pockets, smiling as she appraised the oak.

'Not the tree. Joe.' Seppe had to shout to make himself heard. Connie glanced round, one hand still delving for the wedge.

'I can't make him stop. I'm sorry, Seppe, I'm at my wits' end with him and nothing I do works, so I'm trying to come to terms with the noise.'

'But he cries now for a long, long time. I think we must check him.' The baby had been preparing for this even as they'd been getting the tree ready. His brow had folded, the angry fists clenched. Now the tree had several deep incisions in it and Joe's face was the colour of fury, the birds scared away by his screams.

'I've fed him. I thought it might be that, but it isn't. I don't know what he wants. I've tried, honest, but he cries all the time, no matter what I do.' Connie drooped. She looked like she might cry, too.

'Stop for a minute.' Seppe balanced the axe onto jigsawed mulch and went over to Joe.

'I pick him up?'

'Help yourself.'

The baby was all rigid misery. How best to hold him? Maybe if he stiffened one arm and rested Joe along it belly-first?

That seemed to work. Now to check the rest. 'Is he clean?'

Another shrug. 'He was when we left the cottage this morning.'

'Do you have the thing – the – for changing him?' Joe's wailing had turned to despair. Seppe tucked the baby closer to him.

'The what?'

What a stupid word to forget. He mimed it.

'The napkins? No. Didn't remember to pack them this morning.'

Seppe closed his eyes. Today, Connie had plundered Frank's hut, made sure they had the fretsaw as well as the circular saw, that the axe she preferred was properly ground. But she'd wiped the baby's face with the rough of her sleeve after she'd fed him, and now she was giving up as if Joe was a tricky clue in a crossword and she couldn't find a pencil.

'You remember the wedge but you forget for the baby?'

'I know what we need for felling, that's why. It all makes sense; my brain knows without me telling it. But him – I don't have the first notion.' She poked at the ground with the axe head and a clump of brown sediment heaved loose. 'I don't think I'm cut out for this, to be honest.'

Her voice was fragile, the bark peeled away. He trod carefully.

'Did you – your home – were there brothers, sisters, small children?'

When she spoke it was barely a whisper. Seppe rocked Joe so that his whimpers didn't drown her out. 'Two littluns – Babs and Linda. But that was different.' Her

219

eyes beseeched him. 'At the end of the day it was up to Mam to keep them fed and watered, not me. I played with them, but I didn't have any of the work of it. I know that now.'

She nodded at Joe, fidgeting in Seppe's arms. 'Don't tell him, will you? It's not his fault. It was easier to think of it before, when I didn't know him. But I was going to sort it so that he had a decent chance in life. I knew it couldn't be me who looked after him. I was scared, Seppe. So scared.'

She looked at him, her eyes huge, so desperate that he had to look down. 'You're all being so kind and helping, and I know I have to give it a go, I do. But most days I still don't know how I'm going to cope.' She swallowed. 'If you weren't here, I don't know what I'd do, to tell you the truth.'

Connie would have given Joe away? Bile rose in the place of the words he didn't trust himself to speak. The thought that she might have forsaken Joe lay chasm-like between them and he couldn't bridge it to comfort her.

He wanted to shout at her, demand to know how she could treat another human being like that, but then the words jammed. This was Connie. She was terrified, and more to the point she was telling him so; Connie, who didn't confide in anybody, who lived inside that shell of defiance where she thought nobody could reach her.

Seppe didn't know what to do with such conflict. His hands were trembling – surely she would notice? Seppe laid the baby back down on the bedspread, and Joe started bellowing again. With an effort he refocused. The conversation with Connie would have to wait. A core of pride smouldered. *She trusts you enough to be vulnerable.*

'Let's see what's up with you, shall we, little man?'

The napkin was lurid, the stench billowing into Seppe's

face as he undid the pins. No wonder Joe had been yelling. Seppe cast around.

'Get me some leaves.' Connie picked up the clump of mulch she'd dislodged with the axe and he tutted, actually tutted at her, before he could help himself.

'No – *leaves*. The ferns, under the oak.' She offered him a fistful and he pulled them from her. They were cool to the touch, but at least there were no prickles. They'd have to do.

'How can you do that and not mind the stink of it?' Connie, a hand clamped over her nose and mouth, was surveying him in horror. He laughed, despite his lingering revulsion at her revelation.

'When you live with hundreds of Italian prisoners you stop noticing bad smells.' Joe was nearly clean now, his face uncreasing and the howls slowing into sobs. Seppe pointed.

'My bread.'

'How can you be hungry now, after that?'

'Not for eating!' He took out the food and shook the cloth clean of crumbs. Then he folded it and pelted it on to Joe. The cloth was soft enough and should keep the rest of him dry.

'There!' He admired his handiwork. He must look like Connie did when she'd made a good first cut into an oak. Joe was quieter already.

'That's you all clean and tidy now, *caro*.' He did up the last of the buttons on Joe's overalls and handed him to Connie, but she recoiled, gave him another beseeching look.

'I've got trees to get down. Can't be standing around holding a baby all day.' She looked down at Joe. 'Nothing personal.'

She was so formal with the baby, so careful. Maybe it was fear? Connie would reconcile herself to motherhood

221

eventually. In the meantime, Seppe realised he needed to make sure he took as many shifts as he could, spent as much time with Connie and Joe as possible. He needed to make sure Connie had help, that the concept of disowning Joe never returned.

Seppe placed Joe back on the bedspread, angled so that the sun was out of his eyes, and picked up the axe, heavy again.

'Where is the best place for me to stand?'

Twenty-Eight

CONNIE YAWNED AND GLARED at the clock on her bedside table. Six o'clock already? And on a Sunday, too. This time of day wasn't even supposed to exist, in her book, unless it was a shift she was getting overtime for. She picked the clock up and turned it face down with more of a bang than was strictly necessary. Better to take it out on the clock than on Joe, after all. Wasn't he supposed to be sleeping better than this now, though? Six weeks old; surely he'd had time to get his days and nights sorted by now. He'd been awake for what felt like every hour last night and she'd paced every inch of the room a hundred times over, all the while thinking there must be some trick she was missing that was making him unable to sleep. She'd checked for loose napkin pins, bicycled his legs the way Joyce had shown her to get rid of any wind, tried singing to him like Amos (but softly, since Amos wouldn't welcome being woken up by her mangling his songs in the dead of night). What was she missing? It couldn't possibly be this hard for everyone, could it? 'I've half a mind to put you in Bess's basket for the night, let her mind you like the sheep,' she'd muttered to Joe around 2 a.m. He snuggled into the crook of her arm and gurgled, and she dropped her head so that her cheek rested against the soft matting of his hair, the smell of talc and baby enveloping her so that he was the only thing in the room. When he wasn't scaring the living daylights out of her the baby could be not half bad. But the good moments were fleeting and the hard bits, especially in this endless stretch of grey night, they seemed to go on and on without hope. She'd sighed and shifted him onto the other shoulder to see if that helped him get some kip.

It didn't, but you'd have thought that when he did eventually drop off he'd have granted her more than four hours' grace. Her eyes ached in their sockets the way her shoulders ached after a morning on the hardwoods, and she hadn't even known it was possible for eyes to hurt like this.

Joe gurgled again in his crib and she turned from the clock, her arms tensing at the thought of reaching in there and pulling him back out. 'Stay there just a bit longer, babba.' She turned away from him and grabbed her overalls from the back of the chair.

When she got downstairs with Joe, Amos was already in the kitchen, wireless burbling away, something about a big push on the front. The front of what? Her world was shrunk right down these days, barely reached further than the felling site.

Amos handed her a cup of tea, wordlessly spooned baby milk into a bottle and put it into an already bubbling pot of water on the pan. Amos did most things wordlessly, but at this time of morning she was grateful for it. He must be listening out for news of his son's regiment. She should say something, but talking about big things wasn't her style. Push them down, bury them. She and Amos had that in common.

The wireless moved on from the news and Amos clicked it off. Connie shifted Joe in her arms. 'Can you take him for a minute?'

Amos collected the baby and wandered outside, Bess at his heels. Frank and Joyce had worried about how Bess would take to a baby in the house, it turned out – 'She's not a pet, you know, however our Amos do treat her,' but Bess had apparently decided the infant was a lamb, and herded him endlessly. Connie spooned three precious sugars into her tea and wandered outside to the bench with it. A cup of tea and a cigarette and she'd manage the rest.

'Bad night again, were it?' Amos was talking to Joe rather than to her. 'You'll get there, don't you be fretting about it.' He walked back up the garden. 'I'll give you your bottle now, shall I? That'll see you right.'

Joe was at his best in the morning, perky after a night of sending her spare, and so happy to see the bottle there was no messing around with the feed. Giving up on the idea of feeding him herself had been the right thing in the end. Maybe it was easier if you could get your Mam or your mate to hold the baby's head whilst you hoicked your tits into place, but she could hardly ask Amos, good as he'd been, and nor could she pop over to Joyce in the dead of night. It had been so painful, too, and she'd never figured out if that bleeding was normal or not. When her milk had dried right up, it had been a relief, to be honest.

Amos sat down beside Connie on the bench, Joe already guzzling. She shifted her tea to the other hand so that she didn't scald the baby and lifted her face to the sun.

'Can't believe it's so warm still.'

'Aye.'

The edges of Connie's exhaustion softened, smoothed away by the sun, Joe's sucking sounds as he demolished the bottle, and the steadiness of Amos's company. She wouldn't go so far as to say that they were friends, but if she'd ever known her grandad she'd have done well if he'd been like Amos. The old man's bone-deep love for Joe warmed her, though surely she shouldn't have to watch him to learn how to care about her own child? Connie pushed the thought away and gazed at the apple tree. Those white flowers had turned into apples all right, tons of them.

Amos followed her gaze. 'Probably need to get those down now.'

'What, the trees?' Is this what happened? Was it like a factory line? You used up the apples and planted more trees? But a tree took years to grow, she knew that now. She looked more closely. Maybe there were sapling apple trees planted amongst the ripe ones.

'No, you daftie.' This was new too, Amos teasing her. She was still a bit thrown every time, but she thought she liked it. He'd seemed quieter than usual recently, even for Amos, so it was a relief to hear him saying anything.

'The apples. The trees stay there; we prune 'em, give 'em a bit of a pollard if they need it, and off they go again. Those trees must be nigh on twenty years old.'

Joe pulled off the teat of the bottle and started to squeal. Amos tilted the bottle, handed it to Connie. He hoisted Joe up onto his shoulder and immediately Joe gave out a burp loud enough to shame a navvie.

Amos considered the trees again. 'What's today – Sunday? Tell you what, why don't we do the trees today?'

'Do what?'

'Get the apples down. Take a few of us, though. Why don't you ask that Italian of yours – the one our Joe's named for?'

'He's not "my Italian"!'

The look Amos gave her said everything and nothing. She tried a different tack.

'Anyway, I thought the POWs weren't allowed into civilian houses.'

Amos snorted. 'Have you noticed that stopping that Seppe? When it comes to you and our Joe he don't see the rules, though Frank do say he's a decent one otherwise. We aren't asking him into the house, any road; it's the orchard we need him in.'

'All right, all right. I'll go and get him.'

Amos handed Joe to Connie and clapped her on the shoulder. She fumbled with the baby, righted him again.

'I'm off to see to them sheep. I'll knock for Frank on my way back and then we'll get cracking.'

Joe bounced on Connie's knee, making babbling sounds and trying to poke her in the eye. He wasn't tired at all. How could that be, when everything in her body was begging for sleep? An urge to poke him, to do something just to make him suffer like she was suffering flashed into her and then straight back out. She shuddered. What kind of a monster was she to even be able to have those thoughts?

She needed to move. Things never worked out when she sat still. They'd go and get Seppe, that's what they'd do.

Her route up to the camp took her past that big gate to the compound that housed the American troops. Before the baby she'd often lingered, the accent still making her smile, the idea of all the men out here on an adventure giving her hope. She'd never met a miserable GI – must mean the country was worth something. To be fair, she'd never seen a GI anywhere but at a dance, where everyone was either hoping to get lucky or three sheets to the wind, and often both. But it seemed a pretty good way to live.

She hadn't got up here for a while though, and today, the GI gate hung open, no cheery guards at their gate. 'Let's go and see, shall we?' Connie hoisted Joe up a bit and wandered in through the gates, looking around for challengers. An owl hooted – wasn't it the wrong time of day for that? She shivered despite the sunshine.

The camp was deserted – not a single Yank sitting around, and those big trucks of theirs had gone, too. Where on earth could they all be? What was it on the wireless this morning? God, she'd been at such sixes and sevens recently. Joyce had told her something a month or so ago that made sense of this, she was sure of it. But her brain was fogged and reaching for it was like looking for the bus stop in the murk. You knew it was there, but you'd be buggered if you could get to it. Things had been better since she'd been out working again. Work was a tonic. It was as if the only place she ever thought straight was in front of an oak with the six-pounder chafing her palms.

A breeze shook the trees above them and Joe whimpered.

'Sorry, baby. You're right – time to move on.' Something was up, though. An entire camp's worth of American troops didn't just disappear into thin air, surely.

Connie made her way on up the hill that led to the POW camp. There'd been renewed fighting on the continent, she was sure she could remember that from before Joe arrived. That must have been where they all shot off to. An image of the remains of her home in Hillview Road flashed unbidden in front of her and she shivered again.

It was a new guard at the POW camp, not one that knew her, and he wouldn't let her past the gate.

'Have a heart! What do you think I'm going to do? I just want to get Seppe for apple picking.'

The guard leered at the baby and Connie scowled and turned aside. 'Apple picking? Is that how he got here?'

'Don't be disgusting!' If she'd had a clear shot she'd have spat at him, but she might end up gobbing on Joe's head, and that wouldn't do. 'If you won't let me in, can you at least send someone to find him?'

'What do you think this is – the social club?' But the guard put his fingers in the corner of his mouth and whistled. A couple of lads playing football nearby with a half-deflated ball ran over. They seemed more interested in Joe than in her.

'Go and find Seppe, the woodcutter, will you? Tell him he's got company.'

The lads headed off. They couldn't have been much older than Connie. She yawned. The sun was warm still and she was baking now after the hike up that hill. Was Joe too hot in his sling? She peered at him but it was impossible to tell.

A crowd of blokes had gathered the other side of the fence now. You wouldn't think they were Mussolini's bad boys, not to look at them all scruffy and crumpled. Some of them must have been in camps for years now. That one at the back was a dead ringer, twenty years younger, for a school-teacher Connie had once. Couldn't imagine a less likely looking man of war. Though probably even Mr Purdoe had ended up in the war, or the Home Guard at the very least.

Still, it was nice to have a moment or two of the company of men who weren't old enough to be her dad or her grandad. Connie unpacked Joe from the sling, smoothed down her coat a bit so that they could see her. She smiled at the nearest POW, a young-ish-looking lad, but he failed to notice. Connie followed his gaze. He was trying to catch Joe's eye. Joe's! Not hers!

She looked at them all again, this raggle-taggle bunch of men the other side of a chain-link fence, and it plummeted at her. They were all fascinated by Joe, waving and cooing.

Her eyes prickled with tears. Look at the poor bastards. How long had it been since they'd seen a baby? Maybe some of them had kids at home, and here she was being all mardy about lugging this one up here. Bet half of them would kill for a chance to carry their little tykes around. Connie moved closer to the fence and a dozen fingers reached through the chain-link at Joe. She smiled at them, eased Joe's hand forward and put it within reach. Joe giggled at these men who were making funny faces at him, crooning to him in what must be Italian.

She looked again, more closely. They weren't all cooing. There were a few at the back staring coldly, black armbands pulled over their jacket sleeves.

The gate clanked. A baker's van pulled through, two young lads hanging on to the back of it on ramshackle bikes. They let go as the van met the gates and turned back down the hill, waving their caps at the men and pointing at the fatter of the two boys. The men waved back, cheered them.

'Every day, the boys race each other down the hill. The men have bets on who reaches the bottom first.'

'Seppe!' It was such a relief to hear his voice, to see him in front of her and know that he, at least, didn't have to be sad. 'Here – do you want Joe?' She got it now. Connie lifted Joe away from the fence and waved his hand at the men. 'Can you tell them I'll bring him back soon?'

Seppe looked from Joe, to his campmates and back to Connie. He looked like he wanted to hug her.

But if he did that she might cry and this life of hers had no room for tears, so she looked away.

'Of course.' She stroked Joe's cheek.

They set off away from the camp.

'Where are we going?' Seppe was funny. He'd been following her on, no idea where she was taking him but no complaints, neither.

'Amos has decided it's time to get the apples in, reckons we need a man to help us.' Seppe's grin lifted her and she smiled too. 'I know, I know, but I wasn't about to tell him that I was better than most men he knew, was I?'

'To be honest' – hark at him, starting to sound like one of the locals – 'I am surprised you did not tell him this.'

'Oi!' She sideswiped him and he kinked out of her way, laughing.

'Careful! I nearly went into that branch.'

'You're a big boy now – you'd have lived.'

'But Joe . . .'

'You wouldn't have dropped him. Not a chance you'd let go of that baby.' It was one of her surest facts in all the mist of motherhood, rising through as sharply as that branch that had nearly spiked Seppe. Seppe would no more let harm come to Joe than Amos would.

There was a ladder in the nearest tree by the time they made it back to the cottages. Connie hopped over the wall. 'Here, give me Joe and watch out for that loose bit.' She knew that look of Seppe's. 'If you can figure out a way to fix this wall without the whole damn thing falling down, I bet Frank and Amos will be all ears.'

Joyce was laying out a rug on the grass beside a tower of crates lined with old *Mercury*s. Did anybody ever read that damn paper, or was it only printed so that the Foresters had packing material?

'Is that my Joe back from his walk?' Joyce reached out her arms in a movement so like the Italians up at the camp that a cloud passed over Connie as she remembered what they didn't have. She leaned down with Joe, gentler perhaps than usual.

'He can lie here and mind the food.' Joyce straightened up. 'Right. Seppe, will you go round ours and give Frank a hand with the other ladder? You can help me move these crates under the trees, our Con.'

It was good work, apple picking. Frank told Seppe to

go with Connie – 'You're used to the wench's cheek' – and sure enough they found a rhythm quickly, familiar with each other's pace. Amos didn't seem to mind how many apples she snuck a bite from since the crates were filling fast.

Connie watched Frank and Joyce, stretching with one hand, dipping with the other to place the harvested fruit onto the newspaper, years of practice showing in their movements.

'Reckon we can outpace Darby and Joan there?' She mock rolled her eyes at Seppe's confusion. 'Frank and Joyce. Let's show them we can get the apples down fast, too.'

She lifted round the ladder, looking for the fullest part of the tree. The ladder swayed and she stepped back to get her balance. Seppe put a hand on her arm.

'There's no rush. This is not a contest. To be honest, I am happy for this to take all day.'

'You what?'

'This is not a job with a quota, Connie. This is Sunday in the sunshine, with a picnic and a baby.'

The image of the POWs at the camp fence hit her again. *They have nowhere to go.* But Seppe *did* have somewhere to go. Why hadn't she seen this before? Her insides shrivelled with the shame of not having thought beyond her own nose.

'You're right.' He stepped back in mock surprise so she walloped him. 'There's no rush.' The idea of not going fast made her head hurt. Life was always fast – wasn't that the point? But Seppe was right. This here, this Sunday, with grub and company, this wasn't something to be sped through.

She grinned, warmed by more than just the sunshine.

'Hold the ladder. I want to see how high I can get.'

Twenty-Nine

October

CONNIE BENT DOWN BESIDE Joe on the forest floor, copper-brown with autumn, and scuffed at the goo on his overalls. She was doing better at looking after him in these last few weeks, she reckoned. She'd finally got the hang of giving him the bottle, and the napkins were less likely to make her gag. He was a funny little thing too, Joe, which helped. She liked him, liked his refusal to do what was expected of him, hadn't known he'd be a person so quickly.

'What are you up to, little one?' The baby didn't answer her. Of course he didn't. Too busy gazing up at the wavy leaves and cooing.

Seppe looked up from picking woodchips out of the fretsaw. He'd been humming his tunes all day, making Joe giggle.

'Just wait until he's trying to move properly.' As if he'd heard, Joe grasped towards a pine cone and squawked at her, delighted with himself.

'Crawling? The last thing I need is a crawling baby.' Connie waved at the baby as she sneezed again. 'This stupid cold. Can't seem to shake it.'

'It's not a cold. It's from the grasses, the harvest.'

'You what?'

'All the men in camp who help the farmers in the fields, they are sneezing and coughing and complaining when they come back at night after cutting down the hay all day. Perhaps it reaches you here in woods, even late in the year. In Italian we call it the *febbre da fieno*.'

'It's a right royal pain in the bum, whatever you call it.' She sneezed again. 'When will it stop, can you tell me that much?'

'Later in the autumn. When the rains come.'

'Well, that's peachy.' Joe was stretching out an arm towards the shine of Seppe's saw. 'Come here, you little magpie.' She hooked an arm under his gut and pulled him away, shutting her ears to his yells. 'Oof! Right little lump you've turned into.'

Connie pulled the tarp from under the splayed branches of that last oak they'd got down. It snagged on an offcut and bit into her fingers. This lot needed pollarding, but she had to leave it and just concentrate on the felling. Frank would send someone else to sort it out. The sloppy new girls hadn't got as far as yesterday's pollarding yet.

'Where are the lumberjills?' So Seppe had noticed it too.

'Sulking, I reckon.'

'Sulking?'

'You know. Got a right face on them.' She prodded Seppe and laughed. 'Have you learned nothing working with me? Thought that'd be a word you had down pat. Sulking. Like this.' She pouted and he laughed too.

'But you don't do so much of that, actually. With you, it is more *così* –' He mimed an explosion.

'Cheeky sod!' Connie poked him again, pulling her scariest face. Now they were both laughing. Right on cue, Joe blew a huge raspberry. He could be funny, that one.

'I see. But why are they sulking?'

'Cos all their fancy men have been moved out. The GIs. Given their marching orders, weren't they? Not a Yank to be seen. Remember I told you I saw that empty barracks? Turns out they were all sent away again a couple of months ago. Wasn't this huge news in the camp? Thought the lot of you must be like bulls let loose in a field of cows now that the competition's shipped out to be shot at.'

'The Americans went away? To war?'

'No, out dancing.' She pulled another face and he pulled one back. Since they'd been bringing Joe out to work with them, Seppe stood up for himself more, she'd noticed. Shame Joe's presence made her more unsure of herself, not less.

'Where d'you think they went? Buggered off, trucks packed full of that explosive they've been stashing in the mine shafts for months.' She was a bit sketchy about that last bit, to be honest. She'd got it from Joyce, who still popped round most mornings to help out with Joe after Amos went off with the sheep. Connie had been busy checking out her reflection in the kitchen window now she'd got Joe on the bottle and her body had a chance of getting more back to normal. She'd only half paid attention, and it had been niggling her since she saw those gates wide open.

'Lucky bastards.'

Seppe reeled round on her. 'No, not lucky, not lucky at all.' His fists were clenched, his jaw jutting.

'What? At least they're *going* somewhere, getting out of this place.' She'd seen those Pathé newsreels, great squares of them marching in formation, off to face their future.

Seppe shook his head and muttered something in Italian. 'You must never, ever think like that about war.'

'What? You can't tell me it wasn't exciting, getting

235

dressed up in that uniform, all those girls lining up to kiss you goodbye.' She started humming Vera Lynn and he glared so fiercely she took a step back.

'That is not war. That is the pictures. War is not sleeping for four nights because when you sleep, you know the enemy will sneak up from the other side and decimate you. War is living in your clothes for weeks until they rub your body so red you wish you could continue the battle naked. War is not knowing where you are, not really, not knowing any of the smells, the sounds in the night, having no idea when it will ever end and if the only ending will be your death. War is not exciting. Not ever. War is fighting against your will for causes you've seen bring misery to those you love, and being forced to watch your comrades being torn apart right next to you.'

She hadn't seen him so upset, and part of her was ashamed for having made light of it. But she knew what she'd seen, and the GIs she'd met had always been cheery, ready for an adventure.

'It can't all be like that, can it? Some of it must be fun.'

Seppe threw her a look of complete contempt and she shrank back. Seppe *never* treated her like that. He was the one she could always rely on to be on her side.

'I cannot listen to this. Come on, *caro*.' He scooped up the baby and marched down the path, back towards the hut.

'Seppe! Wait!' She sighed, bent down to roll up the tarpaulin. 'I wasn't trying to upset you! Don't get your knickers in a twist!' But he refused to turn round, pretended he couldn't hear her when he was barely five feet away.

Connie heaved up the tarpaulin and kicked at the ferns ahead of her until the cheerfulness of the green gave way to manky brown. It was all very well for Seppe; he'd had his turn out in the wider world. Now she could start to see through the fog and terror of those early baby days, the itch to do something bigger was crawling back and the GIs going off only served to remind her that she was stuck here. She hadn't meant anything by it.

Connie turned abruptly down the hill, the saws clanging and clattering in the tarpaulin, and bumped slap bang into Frank.

'Frank! What's so important that you've left the hut at clocking-off time?'

Frank nodded behind him. There were two of them, a man and a woman, in suits on a Wednesday, and fancy shoes that wouldn't stand a chance against the forest floor.

'What's up with them – lost their way?'

'They're from the Home Timber Production Unit. Here to check on the old-growth quotas, see the oak stands. Some big cheese from the navy demanding more wood to fix ships, and fines if we don't meet their demands.'

Her conversation with Seppe about the GIs was still fresh. This was a chance to use that information to cheer up Frank. 'This is good, isn't it? If they need more ships it must be to stop Jerry from swarming in here. We're helping to keep the trees safe, Frank.' Connie grinned despite herself. Even to her ears she sounded like Amos. It must be rubbing off on her. But Frank didn't respond, not even with a glimmer of a smile.

Frank's silences weren't like Amos's or Seppe's. Connie knew what was in them, and this silence dried her eyes, put her up on her toes. She peered at the officials who'd come to try and tell Frank how to do his job. The woman was holding up her clipboard near her chest like armour. She'd get every last bit of woodchip down her blouse if she hugged the board like that up at the stands.

'I'll come with you.' She lifted down the tarpaulin and peered down the path.

'Did you see Seppe on your way up?'

'Just got to the hut, he had, chatting away to our Joe.'

So she *was* allowed to accompany him. Pride fluttered.

She barrelled on through the ferns until she could see them.

'Seppe!' He didn't move; still got a cob on. Please himself. She'd chivvy him out of it later, when there was time.

Connie covered the last few steps and dropped the tarpaulin at his feet.

'Put these back in the hut for me? I'm off to go and help Frank sort out this quota nonsense.' Frank had followed her back down the path, was tapping his foot waiting for her.

'Hut's unlocked, lad. You'll get 'em in all right.'

'And Joe? I wait with him at the hut, or take him home?'

Joe hadn't even crossed her mind. The familiar guilt washed in.

'Stay here.' Amos might tut if Seppe brought Joe home, think she was neglecting her duties. Amos had come through for her, fair play. She owed it to him to not let him down.

'What about your curfew, lad?'

Didn't Frank know anything about Seppe? If he had a chance to spend extra time with that baby, he'd grab at it.

The suits were catching them up. 'Come on, Frank. We need to get up there before them, check it's all tidied off.' Oh, that was a point. She pulled the tarp away from Seppe again and tugged out the fretting blade. 'Might need to smooth off some of those stumps where the lazy buggers leave them unfinished.'

'Good idea.'

Her heart plummeted. Frank must be dead worried. He never, ever let her decide which job they should do, even when she was right. She scrambled to catch him up; dodgy leg or no dodgy leg, he could put a move on when he wanted to.

'What's the matter? You know those oaks off by heart, and the quotas.' She'd seen him at the end of every shift, blackened fingernails checking down the ledger, making sure the day's tally matched what needed to be sent. And when Frank looked at those numbers, he saw what Connie was only barely starting to cop on to: the parts of the Forest he'd need to bring down in order to hit the numbers. Thirty oaks wasn't a line on an account book: it was that patch up beyond here, where the trees thinned out towards Ruardean. That's what made even the stroppiest wood-cutter heed Frank: he had the whole thing sussed.

'Aye, well. Might not be enough, might it?'

He sighed, and in that sigh she heard the forest, relying on Frank to protect it.

Frank went straight home after the meeting with the bigwigs, sloping off like Amos's Bess if she'd missed a ewe. He'd held himself small and glanced anywhere but at those interferers in their fancy suits. His limp was worse than ever this evening, seemed he'd scarcely make it over the ridge to the cottages.

'See you in the morning then.'

Frank flicked a hand in her direction and was gone. She'd better hurry and get back to Seppe and the baby. It had been strange not to have been around either of them – her time in the forest was entirely circled by their joint presence and she'd felt lopped off but – how could she even think this? – brilliantly free. For an hour or so she'd just been Connie, not Connie who needed to keep Seppe on track with the felling, or Connie the girl who'd had the surprise baby, just Connie, like the Connie who used to sag off at the end of the shift to drink gin and gossip. She missed that Connie. But – and this shocked her to even realise – she'd missed being with Joe and Seppe too, even though it had been only so brief. She rolled her eyes. *Make your mind up, Granger.*

Dusk was creeping in around the trees. Connie wasn't bothered by the dark, not exactly, but the woods still spooked her at night, crackles and hoots and stuff slithering and shifting. It wasn't like home, where you knew what was down each alley.

Seppe and Joe were where she'd left them, sprawled out beside the hut. Seppe stood up as she panted closer, put one finger to his lips as if her breathing might wake Joe. He didn't seem furious with her any more, at least. Seppe was lovely; whenever she saw him with Joe she remembered it and it made her want to be a better person, to match him.

'It's a right pig's ear; the quotas are bigger than we thought. Due sooner, too. Frank's going to need our help, and sharpish.'

'But how? We are flat already.' He was whispering as if he was a spy in the pictures, not a prisoner on the dirt beside a curled-up baby. Seppe had thrown his jacket over Joe as a blanket and the baby looked good enough to eat, like those tots you see in the Pears Soap magazine adverts. Maybe she could enter him for one of those ads . . . if she couldn't have the life she'd hoped she could, at least Joe could have a better one.

'Flat? Flat out, do you mean? We'll have to get flatter, then. Frank's in a right state; those London busybodies made out he was hopeless. I nearly lamped them.'

When the suits had started in on Frank about 'war effort' and 'surpassing demand', Frank's grazed knuckles had driven into the bark with the effort of not biting back.

Connie had sent daggers of fury at the officials and their clean-fingered interfering. You couldn't just plant another sapling and expect it to be ready in a year or two. Frank had shown her the regeneration plots, the way you needed to cross-plant to ensure the right foliage cover, the trees that would grow best in shade and those that didn't need such deep taproot so could afford to be planted on less rich soil. Connie had wanted to drag these busybodies to the sawmill and feed them into the chipper, clipboards first, one by one until they packed it in.

'They're insisting on the new numbers by the end of the month. I can fix that. I can get down as many as we need, you know I can. If it was spruce I'd get on with it on my own. But the oaks take two of us, and it's the oaks he needs.' She flopped down beside him, bashed her knees on a root, sneezed again.

'Connie, we can't. We have too much to manage already. Frank won't allow it.'

'Course we can. I wasn't going to *ask* Frank; I was going to *tell* him. There's extra dosh in it too; piecework, isn't it?'

'Not for me.' Oh, that was right – not for the POWs.

'Well, then, do it for Frank. Do it for me.' He was so close she grabbed at his lapel to make her point and he didn't jump like he used to.

A quiver came where she hadn't had one for months. She paused, then looked at him again. He met her eyes, unflinching, and reached down for her hand. His touch was feather-light, then gone.

She broke the gaze first.

'I would help you, Connie. You know I would. But I worry about bringing Joe out for such long days.'

'What are you on about? He's happy as Larry out here, you know he is.' The baby was snuggled into that bedspread, soft enough to make your heart break.

241

'We've got to help Frank; look at all the chances he's given us both.' She yanked on Seppe's lapel again but he was surprisingly strong and she ended up nearly rolling onto him. He smelt different, this close, less of the woods and more – more like a man. She could practically taste him.

Pull yourself together, Connie. She needed to get a grip, convince Seppe to do the extra felling.

And what a disaster it'd be, too, to have her end away with Seppe. He wasn't the love 'em and leave 'em type; he'd probably end up thinking they needed to get wed.

She drew away until she could concentrate again.

'Don't you see? If the quota people send someone down here to keep an eye on things, make sure Frank's hitting the quotas, Joe and me'll be sent back to the cottage out of the way. I've had it up to here with this war, Seppe, and these blokes in suits who are telling us what to do. Frank's the only decent gaffer I've ever had.' She'd forgotten all about keeping quiet now.

'And there's no way some officials from the capital are going to let you and Gianni and the rest of you wander round the forest the way you do now. You'll be stuck back in that camp and you won't see Joe nearly as often as you do now.'

'You are right.'

'What?'

'I'll do it with you.' Even his voice was different today. Huskier. When had he turned into Humphrey Bogart?

She was so close, and so relieved. Before she could think it through, she leaned forward and kissed him.

Seppe tasted of the woods, of hard graft and capability; her lips curved against his in recognition. But he pulled away.

'Connie! What are you –'

242

'Shush.' She brushed her lips against his, closed her eyes and rolled close into him, her arms up around his neck to pull him nearer. His breathing was raggedy too, now, and he didn't pull away. It was so good to be doing something for her again, not something she *had* to do. She wriggled with the sheer joy of it, and he gasped and shifted underneath her so that she was practically on top of him, his arm firm against her back, holding her to him, his legs tangling with hers. *That's it.* How to rid herself of these overalls? Not as easy as a skirt, that was for sure.

She sat up, and he sat up with her, misunderstanding.

'Yes. Yes, you're right. We must stop. Joe . . .'

'What? He's sleeping.' She tugged at Seppe's sweater but he gently took her hands in his. Good grief, even his hands were sexy right now. He'd be sandpaper-rough against her skin. She leaned forward and kissed him again, properly kissed him. She'd missed this. Connie moaned slightly and reached forward to undo her dungarees, but he pulled away.

'No – we can't.'

'What the hell do you mean we can't? Of course we can. It's only a bit of fun, for heaven's sake.'

These dungaree buckles were refusing to cooperate with her shaky fingers. 'Give me a hand, would you?'

They were lying facing each other, so close she could feel his breath hot and fast on her cheek.

'Connie, no. We must stop. We can't do this unless –' Seppe refused to meet her gaze.

'Unless what?' The penny dropped. 'Don't get all hot under the collar – we don't need anything. You can't fall again when the baby's still so young, everyone knows that.' Beside her, Seppe flinched. Had she got it wrong, or was he horrified she was being so blunt? She *had* got it right, hadn't she? Oh, who cared?

She squirmed forwards into Seppe, her overalls working their way down her body and her flesh sparking as it met the roughness of his clothes. Seppe sighed deeply, took her by the shoulders, gently touched her cheek. He was surprisingly sinewy under that uniform, the skinniness of him hiding muscles she hadn't given two thoughts to before.

'Are you sure?'

'Yes, I'm sure! Is that enough for you now?'

She didn't wait to hear his answer or check his reaction. Joe might wake up any minute and there was no more time to waste.

Thirty

The War Office
Whitehall
SW1

Date: **October 14th, 1944**

Mr A. W. Jenkins
Briar Cottage
Lower Yorkley
Glos

Sir,

I regret to have to inform you that a report has been received from the War Office to the effect that No. **973442** (Rank) **Pte** (Name) **William Reginald Jenkins** (Regiment) **Infantry: Gloucestershire 2nd Battalion** was posted as missing on the

date unknown. The report that he is missing does not necessarily mean he has been killed, as he may be a prisoner of war or temporarily separated from his regiment. Official reports that men are prisoners of war take some time to reach this country, and if he has been captured by the enemy it is probable that unofficial news will reach you first. In that case I am to ask you to forward any postcard or letter received at once to this office and it will be returned to you as soon as possible. Should any further official information be received it will be at once communicated to you.

Thirty-One

AMOS HAD ONLY COME back to pick up a longer bit of twine, tie back some of the gorse. The damp was properly in the woods now and the sheep liked to take shelter in it, kept getting hooked up in it.

The envelope sat there at the door, and he knew. Weren't they supposed to hand deliver that kind of thing? Just as well the sheep had needed him.

He whistled quietly for Bess and turned back into the forest, the letter stuffed into his pocket along with the twine. The ewes could wait.

Amos pushed past a holly bush, brushed off its spikes. Droplets splattered him, tiny woodland tears. Nobody came down this way, not any more. Nobody could remember it how it was thirty-odd years ago when he'd first been here with his May, when they were courting.

He slowed his pace, peering around. It was here somewhere – used to be beside an old stump. That could be the stump, there, covered in moss now, rotting a bit. He prodded his crook at it and an edge clumped off. Beetles scuttled and a woodlouse curled up against the exposure.

Amos took another couple of steps forward. This had to be the right tree.

He hadn't been down here much these past years. Used to bring Billy at first, after – when Billy was out of the hospital and well enough to be carried around. The house had been full and topsy-turvy. The aroma of the wrong cooking, where it should have been May's, the clamour of the wrong voices. Well-meaning enough, they all were, but the house shouted of her being gone. Down here by the tree it was still just him and May, so Amos brought the boy down to feel that for himself. Fanciful nonsense it had been, Amos knew that, but who's to say it didn't work, blanketing the boy in memories of his mother the same way Amos would shroud an orphaned lamb with the fleece of a stillborn one to make sure it bonded with the mother and thrived. But he'd stopped that as soon as the boy came old enough to go about on his own.

Amos pushed in amongst the branches until they almost held him in an embrace. The boughs dipped down in places, almost to the ground, their weight nearly too much to bear.

This was the spot, right here, where he'd asked May to marry him. Down on his knees amongst the rich arrows of the fallen yew leaves, air full of the spice of the prickles; and May, he could see her now, pushing her hair out of her face, eyes saying everything he needed to know. They'd brought Billy down here when he was a nipper, let him crawl around on the leaves. Billy's giggles used to set May off; she'd lean against Amos, finding it hard to catch her breath. May should be here with him now, not all these years dead. He'd think he'd got used to it and then it would trip him up like a crook round the ankles.

'Oh, May. Billy's gone.'

He groaned, anguish spearing him, and leaned his head

against the bark, the furrows of his skin mapping to its grooves. Why hadn't he written sooner? Now Billy was gone, most likely dead, and Amos had been stupid and stubborn. He'd been all alone out there. Amos had failed him.

Thirty-Two

November

'THREE MONTHS OLD ALREADY!' Joyce hoisted a beaming Joe onto one hip. 'Hard to credit, ent it?'

Connie followed Joyce into the kitchen, shoving her hair into a ponytail.

'Right, let's make a brew, shall we, little man?' Joyce brandished the pan at Joe and he giggled, grabbing for the handle.

'Um – not to be rude or anything, Joycie, but I need to get a move on. Seppe and I are pulling these extra shifts and it'll only get done if we work all the daylight hours.' The rain was rattling against the windows, which meant it was going to be wet and blowy out there today and the clouds would be shifting, the woods extra gloomy. Better to get cracking. If Connie had her way, they'd have worked during dusk and dawn too, but Frank had put his foot down. 'Them Timber Production chaps might be daft enough to up the quotas just as we move into the shorter days, but I ent daft enough to have you working in the dark.'

'I know that, my love.' Joyce made a big show of putting a bib on Joe, reaching behind him to tie the bow. 'You've made the world of difference to my Frank this last week. He's lighter on his feet and I even heard him whistling again yesterday. I reckon I can take care of our Joe for a bit whilst you're helping Frank, especially in this downpour. Seems only fair.' She joggled Joe and he giggled again.

Connie just needed her boots and her coat. Her hands were chafed to buggery with all this wet weather, but what did it matter?

'Cheers, Joyce. I didn't know how I was going to get it all done this week. I thought Amos might be around a bit more, but he's been out at all hours, muttering to those sheep of his, I suppose.'

Joyce busied herself with Joe again. 'You're doing fine, Connie. I wouldn't worry about Amos.'

'But I am, Joyce. He's barely here, and when he is he hardly gives me the time of day, just stares out the window at the oaks. I was awake half the night trying to work out what we'd do if he kicked us out.'

Joyce looked off into the distance as if weighing the truth against loyalty. The rain hammered into the silence, insistent.

'Amos would never kick you out, and you know he's dotty about our Joe. But he's got a lot on his plate right now.'

The cuckoo clock on the chimney breast sang the half hour. Seppe was going to start wondering where on earth she was. Connie twisted her hands together, chilblains stinging.

'What do you mean? What's happened to Amos? Joyce, tell me!'

Were those tears in Joyce's eyes? Connie's hands were sticky with sweat.

'What is it, Joycie? You're scaring me now.'

Joyce took a big sigh and Joe's hair fluttered. 'It's Billy. Amos got a telegram a few weeks ago and there hasn't been a peep since. We can only imagine that Billy's done for.'

Connie's eyes prickled. 'Oh, blimey. Poor, poor Amos. He should have said something.'

'You know Amos, love.'

Connie tussled with whether to say it, but this wasn't a time for shirking the truth, not if they'd got a telegram. 'Where was Amos's boy – Germany? The fighting seems to have got worse, not better, since the Yanks did that big push.'

She put a hand on Joyce's arm. 'You must be worried sick too. I know you've always had a soft spot for him.'

Joyce dabbed her eyes with the corner of Joe's cardi.

'It's just not knowing what's happened to him. And you're right, love. It's not looking good. It'll do for Amos if his Billy doesn't come back neither. You didn't want to see him after his May died; enough to break your heart, that was.'

Connie was stricken. 'I'm sorry, Joyce. I wouldn't have said a word if –'

'I know that, lovie. But careful with Amos, all right?'

Connie nodded, looked Joyce in the eye. 'I'll keep an eye out for him, Joyce. And no news is good news, right?'

Joyce's smile was more subdued than usual, but it came. 'I suppose you're right.'

Connie shrugged on her coat and bent to give Joe a kiss. Impulsively she hugged Joyce, too. 'I'm sorry, Joyce. It's bloody horrible, this war, isn't it?'

Seppe had started clearing the brush when she arrived at the stand of oak, out of breath.

'Sorry!' She pushed straggles of hair back under her hat, reached up and kissed him on the nose, and looked around for her axe. Whacking the axe at something was just what she needed now to shake off this bloody nasty war. She imagined Amos, tramping through the bracken, his mind veering down the path of his missing son, like it or not. Christ, it just wasn't fair.

'Where's Joe?'

Connie blinked hard and got Seppe into sight. Enough of this.

'Joyce has got him, said she'll help out while we do this. Kind of her, wasn't it?'

Seppe came in closer to her and put one arm around her waist, a question mark. 'Very kind. So this means we have time without Joe?'

Those brown eyes were doing a number on Connie again. With an effort she pulled away, splashed one boot at him. 'Look at the state of this bog! You've got to be joking. And we've got work to be getting on with!'

Work was the only salvation she knew. And right now she needed to work hard enough to forget for the lot of them.

Thirty-Three

SEPPE SHIFTED THE WICKER basket to the crook of his arm and pushed down on the door handle, warmed by this low sun. Joyce had said he should go right on in when he'd knocked next door to enlist her help.

As he placed the basket in a shaft of sunlight on Amos's table, there was a clatter of footsteps down the stairs and Connie appeared in the kitchen doorway, Joe pinned up against her shoulder.

'Oh, it's you! I thought I heard the door go.'

He turned down the corners of his mouth and faked sorrow. 'Were you expecting someone else?'

Connie bounced forward and reached up to kiss him. His cheek tingled.

'You know what I mean. Joyce usually stops by at this time of day.'

'Today, instead of Joyce you have me – and this.' He brandished the basket. Connie peered at the cloth covering its contents, then back at him.

'What's that?'

'It's a picnic. Joe is nearly four months old now and it's time we took him on a Sunday trip. It is time. And this sunshine makes it perfect for a picnic, no more rain for now.' It was weather to make your heart swell, low November light glistening off the muted rainbow of browns and yellows, bringing hope even as the days grew shorter and the nights darker.

'Seppe! You've made my day!' She leaned forward and kissed him again, smack on the lips. At times like this Connie was a child again and his heart melted.

She handed him the baby and clapped her hands. 'I'll get our things.'

They stood at the back door and the woods beckoned them in.

'Where shall we go?'

Connie shrugged, arms out wide. 'I don't mind at all. It's just good to be out and doing this. Let's just find somewhere nearby, shall we?'

Seppe looked down at Connie as they walked along. She was wearing her lumberjill dungarees – he wasn't sure he'd recognise her out of them – and matching him stride for stride, her ponytail bouncing along. On impulse he reached out and tweaked it and Connie poked him in the side.

'Oi! What are you up to?'

'I couldn't resist.' It was true in so many ways. He couldn't resist her, found every chance he could to spend with her. It was unimaginable, really, that life had turned into this. All around them was peace, auburn light casting soft optimism. Something rustled in the leaves – one of Amos's sheep, maybe, or just a gust of wind – and then was gone. Seppe's heart was full of all the sights and sounds, the sheer audacity of something as straightforward as a woodland walk. They could be any other family out for a picnic, no need to consider his threadbare uniform proclaiming him the enemy, no need to think that Joe was so fair he barely credibly belonged to either of them. Seppe hoisted Joe up in his arms, the fabric of his little overalls scratchy against Seppe's cheek. For as long as today lasted, he could live in this fantasy of a real life that felt like this. It couldn't endure, but this wasn't a day for dwelling on the reasons why not. Today was for enjoying.

He took Connie's hand. She looked up at him, but said nothing. He smiled.

It didn't take long to find a spot, a clearing of springy grass beside a stand of saplings. Seppe laid out the rug and placed Joe in the middle. He rolled to one side, contented, and started to pull at a loose tuft. Seppe opened up the wicker basket and handed Connie parcel after parcel to lay on the rug.

'Blimey, Joyce doesn't do things by halves, does she?'

'She is still feeding you as if Joe is yet to be born.' Seppe reached the bottom and lifted out a glass bottle with still-warm tea sloshing inside it. 'And as if it is winter, thank goodness.'

They sat in companionable silence and ate, hardboiled eggs leaving saffron smears around their lips and chins, juice from the meat pie glazing them.

'Food has never tasted as good, has it?' Connie stretched and looked regretfully at the empty cloth. 'Must be something to do with eating outside.' She laughed. 'You'd never try that where I grew up – for starters, there was never anything around half the time with all the rationing, and if the grub was half decent it'd be nicked off you before you'd got any of it into your gob.'

'It's delicious, especially after camp food.' Seppe found a patch of yielding moss and set to work pushing it aside, idling into the sand beneath it with a stick. There might be a loose piece of oak here, useful for a trinket. Connie sat up on the rug, angling herself into the sun's rays and began to make a daisy chain with the last remaining flowers of the autumn.

'I've missed this, you know.' She concentrated on the daisies. Her smile was as broad as that river you saw from the top of the hill, her crown of daisies a halo in the sluiced light. She was as happy as Seppe had ever seen her and it was contagious. He got up on both knees and bowed to her, kissing her hand. 'Beautiful, *principessa*.'

She pulled him back down towards her, one hand under his chin, and brought her lips to his so softly he wondered if he'd imagined it. 'Thank you.' She snuggled in beside him and together they watched Joe, still doing valiant battle with the tufts on the rug. He seemed to be convinced that he could pull them off if he just tried hard enough.

Connie giggled. 'D'you reckon he's going to win?'

'Oh, I think so. They are quite stubborn but he is stubborner still. He gets it from his mother.'

Seppe pulled her closer, touched his fingertips very gently to her cheek. It was as soft as the figs that grew in his mother's garden in Livorno. His thoughts were a jungle, tendrils reaching out. Sometimes he allowed himself to think about this being his life – their life – always, after the war ended – if the war ever ended. Often he couldn't bear to think about something so tentative and unlikely; it was the height of audacity for him, a foreign prisoner, to be even privately imagining a life as a free citizen with a British family. For now, for today, this was enough. This was more than enough.

Thirty-Four

THE CINEMA SCREEN LIT up. 'This is Europe,' pronounced a disembodied narrator, filling the room like the voice of God. Fredo had contrived to sit beside Seppe, no doubt to inflict whatever unseen injury he could while they were amongst civilians and Seppe couldn't escape. Seppe glanced down. Did Fredo have a blade with him? He felt sick. It had been months now and Fredo had never let up his petty vengeances.

The screen filled with a flickering black-and-white shot of Allied troops, and Fredo hissed.

'The British and American armies have done what Hitler and his cronies didn't manage and crossed the English Channel to fight on enemy soil,' intoned the narrator. It was a shock to hear the news backwards, to witness the English perspective of the war rather than the Chinese-whispers version of 'truth' put out by the fascist sympathisers within the camp. Fredo hissed again, half rose, and Seppe prodded him.

'*Sta'zitto*! You'll give us away.' There was no way they

should be in this cinema in the first place. Seppe had refused to come on the trip when Gianni brought it up – an evening in Campo 61 without Fredo would be its own version of solace – but Gianni had persisted because Seppe was the only Italian who really knew his way through the woods.

'Think of your Connie's face when you tell her what an adventure you've had!' Gianni had exhorted. It was the 'your' that did it. After that, Seppe would have agreed to anything.

Getting to the cinema had indeed been an adventure, largely due to the sheer amazement of his campmates at being out in the forest at night. 'Eh, *scalco*!' Gianni's voice quavered somewhere ahead, but the whiff of whatever he'd put on his hair carried back to Seppe on this stiffening November breeze. 'We need you up here at the front. I'm afraid we'll get stuck forever in this sinister forest and miss the pictures.'

'It's not so dark.' But Seppe stitched his way through the other men. Gianni shook his shoulder lightly in welcome.

'These damn tree roots! And the branches keep attacking me.'

You couldn't help but smile at Gianni. To Seppe, navigating by the pinch of the yew needles, the brush of the fir, these touches were his saviours. He loved the forest at night, when the trees melted into the darkness and lost their solidity. The woods became instead a textured landscape of whispers and caresses, everything less certain and more possible.

'Look, this way.' Seppe trod them down the path. 'There. The cinema is just over here.'

Fredo slid up alongside him and shinned him, teeth bared and glinting like a fox, then shook his head and disappeared on into the depth of the shadows.

Seppe shivered despite himself, thought instead of Connie's hair as it had gleamed in this same moon only a few days ago. Thoughts of Connie and Joe made him braver. He had a new life that Fredo didn't; a child depended on him, after all. There was less room for dread. After the war, who knew what would happen – but this war was part of the very fabric of Europe these days, would surely never end. He wished he could write to his mother and tell her of his happiness, his safety – but he never, ever wanted to be in contact with his father again. His mother was too quiescent, would be honour-bound to share anything with her husband. He knew he should resent this less, but the months and years had done nothing to diminish his deep-seated regret that, bar one rare incident, his mother had done nothing to protect him and Alessa as children.

It was bad enough that Fredo clearly relished passing back snippets of Seppe's collaboration with the enemy to their Livorno cronies. Seppe could tolerate – just about – the treatment meted out by the northern fascists in camp. He knew better than to confront Fredo; he just needed to keep his head down and not give them the satisfaction of his response. He hated it, carved a tiny series of revenge fantasies. But he could withstand it. There was no sense at all in incurring his father's wrath from afar.

Seppe turned back to Gianni. 'This film had better be worth the risk.'

'You wait until you see the leading lady, you'll be glad I persuaded you to join us.' Gianni grabbed Seppe's bad hand and squeezed it. The gesture was friendly, but Seppe sucked in air fast, pulled it away.

'Hey, what's the matter?'

'My palm, the skin's all gone from it.' Seppe splayed his hand and Gianni jumped back in mock horror at the oozing red patches.

'Rubbed your palm raw, eh?' Gianni elbowed him.

Seppe grinned. 'How did I know you'd say that? It's from working double felling shifts, nothing like what you're imagining.' But he couldn't mind the teasing. You only teased someone if they belonged, after all. And his hand was a war wound, but one he was proud of. They'd spent three weeks working round the clock to fulfil the extra quotas. At the end of it the London people had sent special notice to Frank to congratulate him on a job well done. Frank was overjoyed, had been bragging about their success to anyone who'd listen. The war was one step closer, perhaps, to being over, and Frank was maintaining the forest as it needed him to, concentrating not just on timber production but on husbandry.

They were heading towards the main street in Coleford now, the moon slanting down on their unfamiliar shirts and trousers.

'Don't ask,' Gianni had warned when he'd handed out the clothes. 'Let's simply say there's a washing line that's lighter tonight. And don't anyone think of making a break for it. You know you'll never find your way out unless you have Seppe with you.'

Wherever they'd sprung from, they were softer than the uniform, didn't make Seppe scratch. What would Connie think if she saw him like this? Although it didn't seem to be his clothes that Connie was interested in, quite the opposite. She'd undone his shirt with haste only a few days ago, flinging it to the ground and pressing herself up to him with scant regard for the actual garments. Not that he had raised any objection; when she was so close to him, her breath hard in his ear, he lost all sense of where he was and whether he'd even been wearing clothes in the first place.

He preened in the dark, then caught himself. He'd need

to mind his manners if they were to raise Joe nicely. Not that Connie showed any signs of acknowledging the significance of their liaisons, or that there might be a future for them. But he dared to hope that she felt how he felt. Surely such intensity of emotion was only possible when it was reciprocal?

'Speaking of sore palms: you and the *inglesa*, huh?' Gianni made a gesture that was unmistakenly filthy even in this darkness. Seppe's skin prickled in the good way and the bad way all at once.

'I don't know what you mean.'

'You expect me to believe that? For weeks now you're barely making it back to the truck before we're off, and that grin – it's like you've seen a pineapple! Or the Pope. Some kind of miracle. But one thing's for sure, it's got nothing to do with the Virgin Mary. Or your precious quotas.' Gianni leaned in. 'I can smell it on you, you know. When you slide in next to me, despite all those exhaust fumes, I can smell it.' He mimicked sticking his nose up into the air and sniffing blissfully. Gianni was impossible, but it was also unthinkable not to smile at him.

'There's that grin again! Do you know how often I've seen you smile, eh, *scalco*? Maybe three times, in months. And now – now you're an artillery gun of smiles. Are you actually doing any woodcutting?'

'We're back on normal quotas, but running slightly ahead of schedule. Connie would kill me if Frank thought we were falling behind.' He couldn't even say her name without grinning. It was a relief – no, a joy – to talk to someone about Connie.

'But there is time for other activity too, no?' Gianni roared and from behind them, one of the others snickered back. He leaned in. 'But tell me, where do you go?'

Seppe had never been so conspiratorial before. For now,

knowing the densest thickets was proving to be a huge advantage. But it was getting colder, and the novelty would wear off soon enough.

He may as well test his plan on Gianni, see how it sounded out loud. 'I am thinking of building a hut.'

Gianni whistled. 'A whole hut simply for fucking in? She must know some tricks, to be worth that! It'll take you ages.'

'Not only for that.' *For living in.* But he couldn't share his plan, not yet.

'Where will you build this remarkable Hut of Fucking? Can we all have a key?'

Gianni winked and bounded across the road towards the cinema. Seppe hadn't had a chance yet to ask Amos about the land, or Frank about the offcuts he'd need to build it. But they wouldn't say no; how could they? They'd see the sense of him building shelter for Joe. *And for Connie.*

Seppe waited outside, apart from the others, whilst Gianni performed whatever black market magic was necessary to procure them the tickets, smiling and joking with the locals as if he, too, had been born here. The stars were crowding above in the inky night sky, like yesterday. That strip of tarpaulin he'd found stashed in the back of the woodworking shop had been a godsend, but Connie hadn't seen it like that. 'It's too cold and damp out here now for stripping off and lying on that! And it stinks of linseed oil – Amos'll cotton on right away if I go home smelling like a pit prop.'

'But the stars were beautiful, back there in the clearing.' He'd never seen so many in Livorno, even since the blackouts brightened the night sky. Everything was sharper these days.

Connie shuddered, pulled the tarpaulin about her like a

blanket. 'The only reason we're seeing so many tonight is because all the clouds have rained themselves out. I can't help but think that Jerry could have a field day with such a good view over our cities. And that ain't no good for anyone, believe you me. Last time I saw a night like this was the last time I saw my family.' It was the closest she'd come to even hinting at what she'd left behind. His heart had swollen as it broke for her. Connie usually turned any talk of their relationship into a joke, reminding him it was 'only a bit of fun'. But now she was confiding in him, ever so slightly. Could things change?

'Do you think of them often?' What a stupid question. The dead were with you even more than the living, he of all people knew that.

Connie had pulled into herself, head down. 'Let's talk about something else, shall we? Nothing gained by going over lost ground.'

He'd covered each part of her with kisses, all the bits he could reach, pushing cold sweater up against warm, pliant flesh until the tiny stars of his kisses had smoothed away her frown. Stars tasted salty, of sweat and joy and primal desire . . .

'I've got them! Come on!' Gianni hissed from the doorway, pulling Seppe out of his reverie, his eyes gleaming as he waved the tickets.

They filed in and Seppe sank down into the chair in the gloom of the cinema. What was the name of the main picture they were here to see? Actually, who cared? He was warm and safe in the most comfortable chair in the world, the forest was over the road for cover, and tomorrow, if they could find a copse thick enough, Connie would drag him into it and do things with her hands and her tongue that even here, in the dark, he couldn't name to himself. For those minutes when he held her head in his hands, kissed her, saw her eyes gleam with knowing and longing, he would be truly alive.

On the screen now, scenes of war reeled past in grotesque, blown-up Pathé vision. It wasn't Seppe's war. This war was sanitised, presided over by a Brit with a booming voice who was talking across scenes of GIs in enormous tanks pushing triumphantly through swathes of countryside. 'On this mission are the battle-hardened veterans of our Sicilian and North African campaigns.' So this was the Fifth Army again, that sworn enemy of the Regio Esercito throughout those endless desert nights. He might have fought against some of those men marching across the screen. Was it wrong to almost want to thank them? Without that defeat, he wouldn't be here, where there was not a grain of sand, no bodies ripening in unforgiving desert heat, maggots blistering in fetid wounds. This war was happening else-where.

Seppe settled back in this miracle of a chair, letting the waves of battle flow over him, the modulated tones of the narrator almost soothing as a map of Europe dominated the space. His eyelids drooped and on their insides was Connie, twisting beneath him, silent for once, her hands gripping him, urging him . . .

'Eh! *No!*'

He sprang back to attention. Fredo was up from his seat now, fists pummelling towards the screen, his face in the beam of the projector, twisted and awful. What did he expect the British newsreels to show? If he couldn't cope with this, he should never have come. Already the people in front of them were turning and tutting. If they were kicked out now they would surely have their camp privi-leges revoked.

Gianni grabbed Fredo by the shirt tails and tried to pull him into his seat, whispering frantically. Seppe looked at the screen and goosebumps marched along his arms and down his neck. That wasn't some anonymous landscape, not any more. They had moved down the narrator's map and that was – now Seppe was out of his seat too, staring at the screen – that was Italy. It was Livorno! What was going on?

The images were spiralling past faster than he could recognise them and he gripped the seat arm to stay upright. There were the familiar docks, the ships at their anchors out in deeper water, soldiers weighed down by rifles lining the pier. And there were the stables; he craned his neck, ridiculously, to check for the horses but they'd moved on already, the camera showing – *santo cielo*, could that really be right? Seppe leaned forward, the thudding in his ears drowning out the narrator.

That was Churchill! It was barely credible, but there was no mistaking him. He was on some kind of launcher, taking off from Livorno dock, and all around him the caps of the navy, the peaked hats of the British Army. Churchill in Seppe's city. What had happened? The old man sat splay-legged on the outermost edge of the boat, wide-brimmed hat making him look almost like Amos sitting out on the bench in summertime. The images on the screen scrambled his brain. What was this man, who sat like Amos, watching the world unfurl in front of him, doing in Seppe's city?

The images were blurred, only Churchill really clear in the centre of the screen. It was impossible to tell how many buildings had been damaged. The port looked largely intact, but what had happened in the battle for the city? Seppe's heart beat as if he, himself, had taken up his weapon.

Who has survived?

The camera panned back to endless vistas of rubble, Churchill peering at some kind of plan that a British officer was explaining to him. Churchill in a jeep, cigar in mouth, driving through the streets past house frames snapped like twigs. It reeled past faster than Seppe could keep up with it, the strain of understanding what he was seeing compounded by the speed with which it whipped along. The camera remained resolutely on Churchill and Seppe wanted to reach up, ridiculously, pull aside the curtain at the side of the screen and see the rest of Livorno, just out of shot.

Churchill in the jeep again, out on the road to the vineyards. The dust kicked up through the screen, stuck in his throat. Seppe knew that Livorno dust; it cloyed. The sun beat down and rendered it sharp and sticky on your lungs, not like here, where sunlight filtered through the leaves, green and warming.

Churchill peering at a pile of brushwood as if he were here with them in the forest, not a thousand miles away inspecting the destruction of Seppe's homeland.

Fredo groaned, a pain that pierced, and Seppe saw what Fredo saw: the neck of an enormous cannon poking through the brush, the soldiers taking aim and the great gun juddering under the weight of its discharge. The film was silent now, the clouds of destruction speaking for themselves. *They're shooting at your home. This man is the enemy.*

There was nothing left of Livorno. No menace, no memories, just swathes of rubble. If any of Livorno had survived, it was hard to tell. Something lifted in Seppe and tears sprang. He had never dared hope for this. He could never have wished for destruction – that would be contemptible beyond all comprehension, make him no better than the men who had made his life untenable for months now. But in this moment all he could feel was relief. If there was no home to go to, his obligations to home were discharged.

Then the map was back on the screen, showing the

next point in the Allies' move further across the north of
Italy.

Seppe risked a look at Fredo. Tears streamed down his
cheeks, his fist opening and closing in desperation. He
stared at the screen with eyes that saw who knows what.
That's how Seppe should be feeling, surely, not as if a
weight had been removed? Guilt at his own reaction
softened his usual antipathy towards Fredo. For all his
bitterness, his antagonising of Seppe, the man clearly cared
deeply about their mutual home town. Seppe should be
ashamed of himself. But he wasn't. His sense of relief was
tinged now with an equally unattractive emotion: he was
pleased to see Fredo suffer. After all these months of slow-
burning aggressions, he couldn't help but revel, even just
momentarily, in Fredo's distress.

Seppe prodded Gianni. Gianni was a southerner, but
he was passionate about home and would find Seppe's
reaction despicable if he ever caught a glimpse of it.
Perhaps he could atone, however slightly, and at the same
time get out of the cinema before Gianni noticed his lack
of distress.

'There's no way Fredo can stay here in this state. I'll
take him back to camp.'

Gianni's face was a question in the gloom. *You? Take
him back, alone? Are you sure?* But then he nodded, waved
at the screen in explanation. 'I'll stay here with Lauren
Bacall.'

Fredo glowered when Seppe pushed him forward slightly
more forcefully than the situation required, but his eyes
were glazed, not really registering who ushered him out of
the cinema. They'd barely woven their way through the
grumbling rows and outside when Fredo's legs gave way.
Seppe shoved his shoulder under Fredo's arm moments
before his campmate's head cracked against the brick of

the cinema wall and heaved him across the street. The shops on either side were quiet and shuttered. Seppe nudged Fredo along the top of the hill, away from the town square at the bottom of the row of buildings, and shoved him through the bite of the hawthorn with more aggression than he possibly needed. A cobweb brushed his face and the drops of moisture transferred to his cheeks, substitute tears for the ones he couldn't cry.

'Keep quiet! If anyone hears you wailing they'll report us both.'

Fredo collapsed, his face contorted, his legs twitching their grief. Seppe's gut twisted with the memory of their compatriots out in the desert, sand crusting the blood – and then of Alessa, legs and arms curled over her stomach, the stain spreading.

Fredo would be so easy to kick like this, vulnerable, not expecting it. Seppe's boot jerked and he curled away his toes with the force of the urge. He pulled his mind back to those scenes on the screen, but it was sterile, grey.

He knelt beside Fredo, who was writhing still. 'Perhaps some survived. We can't know.' But even as he said it the voice in his head grew louder and louder until it blocked out other words. *Perhaps your father is dead. Perhaps it is all over for you now.*

'Fredo – the council offices. They were in ruins, no?' He needed confirmation that he'd seen it and not just wished it.

Fredo turned anguished eyes on him. 'Wreckage. Everywhere only wreckage.'

Conscience brushed Seppe. *Hope for the Major's death and you are no better than him.* An owl hooted behind them in the copse that led back to Campo 61. The grass was dew-cool and soft against his cheek. He breathed, slow and steady, the whittling knife untouched in his pocket.

Fredo's torment washed over him, none of his own rising to meet it, not even, yet, worries about his mother. Only the realisation: *I'm free.*

Old Tree Crashes across Road
in Yorkley

Last weekend brought wild, wet weather and one 'casualty' was an old beech tree near Oaken Hill Lodge, Yorkley, which crashed across the road on Sunday morning.

Dean Forest Mercury, Friday, 1st December, 1944

THE GROWING FAMILY
A Mother's Joy

. . . A woman who is (. . .) constantly below-par, cannot possibly look after the home, her husband and children in an efficient manner. Suffer she may herself, but the greatest sufferers are those who are dependent upon her ministrations.

Dean Forest Mercury, advertisement, 8th December, 1944

Winter, 1944

Thirty-Five

December

'SHUT THE DOOR, FRANK love, will you? It's blowing a gale out there tonight. If December carries on like this, them trees'll be bare before we know it.'

Connie looked up from the dough she was kneading on Joyce's kitchen table and grinned at Frank, stamping off the cold in the doorway. 'He knows that, don't you, boss? It won't stop your husband, Joycie.'

'Aye, well nobody can live here and mind the seasons changing, but that's not to say I want winter in my kitchen. Bad enough keeping the fire stoked these days as it is.' Joyce walked over to Frank and placed a careful kiss on his cheek, her floury hands held aloft either side of him like warning signs.

'Get it all done, did you?' Frank smiled at her.

'As much as I needed to.'

'What were you up to, anyway?'

Connie bashed the dough with sullen knuckles, broke off a chunk and gave it to Joe. He'd probably stuff it straight in his gob, same as everything these days, but it couldn't harm him; it was only uncooked bread.

Frank wasn't supposed to be out in the forest without her. He'd packed her off at lunchtime, same as usual on a Saturday. It'd been proper brass monkeys out there, but he'd better not have sent her home because it was cold. He must know she was made of sterner stuff than that.

'You could have told me you were staying on; I'd have given you a hand.'

Frank braced his palm against the lintel and heeled off his work boots. The smell of trees and sweat rose up and mingled with the pies already in the range. He roasted his hands on its lid, the cold coming off him like bombing raids.

'I knew our Joyce was showing you how to make a game pie this afternoon. I wasn't going to get in the way of that.'

Connie glowered at the dough. It looked like it had given up all hope. She could have been out in the trees with Seppe instead of stuck in here, realising yet again what a rubbish housewife she'd make.

'Give that here a minute.' Joyce bustled over, removed the dulled scrap of misery from Connie's hands and stretched it, one two three. Now it wasn't a battered bit of shrapnel; it was a tarpaulin like the ones the army used on those trucks. Joyce was a bloody marvel.

'What were you up to out there all this time?'

'Planting new-growth. Spruce saplings needed going in now before the ground's any harder. There's been a wicked frost up there these last few nights.'

'Wrong time of year for new-growth, ent it?'

Frank shrugged out of his jacket, unwound his scarf and stuffed it into the pocket beside his cap. 'It's all topsy-turvy this year, love. Them quotas keep flooding in and after all that work this one here did with our Seppe, there's new trees to plant.'

'Already?'

Frank came and sat beside Connie at the table, his elbows instantly dusted with flour.

'Well, even spruce do take their time to get to felling size, and who knows how long this war will go on. Best to keep planting in the new ones now, even out of season, hope they'll bed in some roots in time for the proper cold weather.' Frank's words were empty, like a wall that had been left standing with nothing behind it worth protecting.

Joyce put a mug of tea in front of Frank and took Joe from Connie, hugged him to her. 'I don't know, Frank. It's a right pickle this year, one way or another.' She looked down, brushed a hand across her face. Connie shivered.

Frank had noticed too. 'What's the matter, love? This isn't like you.'

'Oh, I'm being silly. It's just – well, the trees going in at the wrong time of the year, and still no word from our Billy. It can't be good, can it, Frank? I feel right at sixes and sevens today.'

Connie's cheeks were hot. Here she was mithering to herself about pastry and being allowed out to work when Joyce was worrying herself sick about Billy. Let's face it, the odds were the poor sod wasn't coming back. These forest folk kept their opinions close like nobody she'd ever met before, but that didn't mean they weren't feeling things. The forest itself warned them of loss even as they chopped it down. Bloody great gaps staring at them in the very woods that had sheltered them all their lives, and people pulled from this life into a new world that swallowed them up.

'The trees will sort themselves out, Frank, won't they?' It came out imploringly.

She turned to Joyce. 'And Billy – listen, Joyce. No news is good news in this war, that's what I've come to believe.' She'd come to believe no such thing, but she could give Joyce this.

Joyce sat up straight, stroked Joe's head. 'You're right, Con, of course you're right. It's just – well, sometimes it do strike you, you know? Even the sight of you sitting there, where I taught our Billy to make them pies when he weren't that much younger than you –'

Connie reached her hand across. 'I know.' She swallowed hard. 'You'll get through, Joyce. I don't know how, but you will. We all will.'

Thirty-Six

'SEPPE! THERE YOU ARE.' Gianni was haloed by blurry cold, but rather than barrelling in to the sleeping hut as usual, he stood in the entrance as if he'd forgotten what he was doing. Without his smile he was faded.

Seppe sat forward on his bunk and put down the knife and the wood, tugging the blanket closer around his shoulders against the night air.

'What's the matter? Aren't you supposed to be at rehearsals for *Seven Sweethearts*?'

There was the smile, albeit a diminished version. 'There may not be a camp show this Christmas. Nobody will play a woman except me. We will need to rename it *One Sweetheart*.' Gianni seemed to remember where he was, let the door go and came further in. Seppe heaved him up onto the bunk. The wooden frame, missing so many of its slats for use as benches in the theatre, creaked, swayed, held, and Seppe exhaled.

'But I am not here to talk about my show-stopping brilliance, even if I will be stealing your sheets for my

279

"wedding dress" before long.' The joke had no weight behind it. He was really out of sorts; was he sick? Had he got ill? The chill had set in now, the nights colder than maybe Gianni knew from the south.

Gianni shifted so that he was facing Seppe head on and Seppe stilled at the seriousness in the movement. 'It's Fredo. Have you seen him?'

'What, today? No, but I have been felling, and then after dinner I came in here out of the way of the football and the theatricals.' The images of Livorno still played across Seppe's mind in every moment of solitude, and he craved them, sifted obsessively through their debris to discover the reason for his deadened response. He knew himself to be capable of emotion, had even tested this out by conjuring up an image of Joe snuggling up in the crook of his arm, warm and trusting, of Connie, head back, laughing, her fingers entwined in his. But when it came to Livorno, it was as if a connection had been severed, never to return. Once or twice he had considered sneaking back out to the cinema in the hopes that they'd show the same reel and maybe he'd be moved this time to a more human reaction to the images. What was wrong with him, that he was so callous?

Gianni put a hand on Seppe's knee. 'I know you have had problems with Fredo before. I understand that. At the beginning – no. This would be too much. But now you are more, are stronger from this crazy place. And you and Fredo – you know each other from a long time ago, no? I think this is what he needs right now, someone who knows him. Someone who understands.'

How to tell Gianni, who cried every time a letter arrived from home, that Seppe didn't understand how anyone could feel attached to home, that he himself was even now poking at the wound of his destroyed city in an effort to make himself feel something other than unburdened?

He couldn't. Seppe patted Gianni on the leg and jumped down from the bunk. 'I'll go and talk to him. Where is he?'

'Oh, thank you.' Gianni had tears in his eyes. Seppe almost envied him this. 'He is in the chapel.'

'The chapel?' Seppe hadn't set foot in it since he had arrived, except to build benches before God and the rest of the prisoners had arrived. And last time he had seen a padre – well. Last time he had seen a padre had been when he enlisted.

The camp was shrouded in cool dusk as he headed out from his barrack and across the parade ground towards the chapel. His mind looped back, thoughts of the padre and thoughts of Livorno colliding, bringing him back to the evening his father had lost the council vote.

But now his father wouldn't ever threaten him again. Yet it wouldn't sink in; he couldn't trust it yet.

There was a way to try to believe it, something he'd been avoiding, though Gianni had confirmed it for him, tears streaming with a sorrow Seppe knew he should be experiencing himself. The camp guards, not without some sympathy, had allowed the POWs to post up on the parade ground a list of casualties from the northern push, compiled haphazardly from accounts sent in from those few survivors.

Men had congregated in front of it ever since it appeared, some unable to tear themselves away from the awful beauty of seeing their mothers', their wives', their children's names in front of them in this foreign land, even as their presence confirmed the one thing they dreaded above all other. Those whose loved ones didn't appear on the list rejoiced; but as time went on with no word from home they knew this rejoicing to be futile. Seppe had stayed away, not out of stubbornness or dread, but because to stand in front of the board and remain unmoved would be not only unforgivably insensitive but potentially also rashly dangerous. He hated himself for this instinct for self-preservation that kicked in even now, was deeply ashamed.

In the bleak hollowness of impending frost, the crowd had dissipated. Seppe stepped away from the chapel and approached the board. It didn't take long to find his parents' names. Seppe stared at them, willing the emotion through. He noted the careful slant to the writing, the place in his mother's name where the ink must have run dry and the scribe dipped the pen again in ink. He couldn't make the words in front of him pierce to the emotion he knew he should feel.

Seppe looked one last time. His father was not top of the list; this would displease him. Seppe smiled despite himself, then felt a stab of self-loathing, and made his way back to the chapel. Perhaps he could help Fredo even if he himself was condemned to damnation for being so callous.

Seppe pushed open the chapel door. The chapel was at the far end of the camp, looking over the barracks. It had been mostly built by the time he'd arrived and he'd never fully understood where the POWs had got the materials from. He'd asked Frank once and Frank had just shrugged. 'People need to build things, don't 'em?' Foresters didn't worry about resources the way people did in the city or in the desert. If it was there, and you had a use for it, it was yours.

Candles flickered inside the chapel and illuminated the 'stained-glass' windows, shining ruby and emerald and sapphire with paint 'borrowed' from the same benign sources. Seppe had largely avoided the structure until now but every morning and evening it was full with those more devout than him.

Sometimes the camp choir practised in here, tenor versions of 'Ave Maria' feathering out across the barracks, but tonight it was quiet. The space commanded quiet. Seppe walked automatically to the front of the altar, genuflected to the crucifix, then looked around for Fredo. There he was, huddled into a corner against a wall, all edges and defences gone. Still Seppe couldn't help it: his breath caught and he had to force himself towards Fredo. What if this was just another ruse?

'Seppe.' Fredo half rose, then crumpled again. 'It is all gone. All gone.'

'Perhaps people got out before the bombs fell.' He forced himself into the sentence, at the same time praying the sentence could never be true. He pulled himself in, away from his own words.

Fredo's face was buried in his knees and Seppe had to lean forward to hear him at all. 'My war was to protect Livorno. I have failed. Failed my city, failed my family.' His voice tailed off and Seppe took a deep breath. Nothing was making sense any more, none of it at all. Fredo was in sure danger of bringing him to tears, this man who had been his nemesis for years now. And the real threat was gone. The certainties that had walled his life for as long as he could remember were toppling, one by one, and he was vertiginous with the changes expected of him.

Seppe raised his hand to pat Fredo on the back, couldn't make himself do it. 'You will be OK, you'll see. You're a survivor.' Seppe couldn't come into God's house and tell lies, no matter how great the provocation and small his religious belief. But he could cite facts.

Fredo was sobbing now, really sobbing. Seppe sat down beside him, the bench glacial and knowing. He folded his hands into his lap and waited. The bench grew harder. There was nothing he could do here; this initial virus of grief would rampage and later, when Fredo needed to talk about Livorno, Seppe would find a way to neutralise his feelings, to find the response that sat between fear and joy and which the majority of his campmates surely experienced. All he needed was to find someone to sit with him, to hear him out as he was doing for Fredo.

It jolted him with the same precision that those Allied shells had hit the port stables. He patted Fredo on the back, forgiving himself the wincing, and left, pulling the doors shut behind him. Would he get out of the camp at this time of night? It wasn't quite curfew, but the sky was a dark hood over the perimeter, had been for hours. He would try it.

Ern was the duty guard. Seppe quickened his pace. Ern wouldn't mind him leaving the camp briefly.

'What are you up to, this time of night?' Seppe heard the echo from his early days of illicit training and his heart lifted enough for the response that would ease his passage.

'I am going to see a girl about a tree.'

Ern laughed in recognition, pushed open the gate. 'Go on, then, but make sure you're back by ten. My shift finishes at half past and that surly bugger Alf Green might not take so kindly to the likes of you gallivanting around.'

'What blessed time do you call this, lad?'

Amos, rumpled and heavy with sleep.

'I need – I need to talk to Connie.'

'What, now?' Amos read Seppe's face. 'Wait here.'

The door clicked shut. Seppe stamped his feet, fists tucked up into armpits.

When it opened, it was to Connie.

'Seppe! What's up?' She shivered, reached up behind her and lifted her greatcoat off the peg, slipped outside, a shadow. 'We'll have to talk out here – Joe's only just got off.'

Seppe looked at Connie, shadows on her face changing its planes, now softening, now strengthening it. A deep ache pulled words into his mouth. But not the real ones, the important ones; those he couldn't bear yet. 'Walk with me?'

He didn't know what she saw in his face but she frowned, anxious, then nodded, took his hand.

The forest was a different place in moonlight; enchanted. Mercury beams of light caught and twisted silver limbs as Connie and Seppe ducked under the oaks. Seppe, not daring to speak yet, led Connie down tracks that sparkled in the moonlight as its beams refracted the stones glistening amongst the leaves.

They pushed through a thicket and stumbled down a grassy bank. There in front of them was a lake. Its surface, flat as death, reflected the trees that lined its shores, upside-down branches sweeping into the water as if to scoop it up, feather it out.

In the centre of the lake, as if by accident, was a tiny island. Illuminated by the moonlight, moss clung to rocks, softening them. Trees grew here too, their roots twisting and curling back onto the outcropping, forming its topography through decades of stubbornness.

Connie gazed around her, the moon an alchemist, rendering the quotidian unrecognisable. Seppe found a pebble, no bigger than a button, and threw it in. The ripples circled outwards from where they sat, backs up against a tree, the bark buttered with rime. Connie hadn't asked him anything yet. For all her talking, she knew when to be silent, something that the other timbermen often missed about her. Even though she felt things deeply, she simply wore life lightly, didn't need to interrogate every last little element. Maybe that was it. *And I wear life as if it were a lead overcoat.*

'Connie, I have a question.'

He stopped again, gathered a scattering of pebbles this time and lifted them high, arcing them into the lake. The water responded like wood to gunshot, splintering and dividing. The mood was broken, the shimmer of before sharded by the scattershot outbursts.

'So.' He bit down hard on his lower lip. Blood filled the gap like sap in a broken twig; bitter, inevitable. He sucked down hard, kept his face open and bright. The bitter night air found the wound, pierced it with every inhalation. The night shadows cast freckles on what he could see of Connie's face, her brow furrowed, calloused fingers making a stick dance. He counted the twig through her fingers, watching it roll from little finger to ring finger, from ring to middle, and onwards, ad infinitum.

When it gets to the end of the final ten, I'll say something. But he couldn't.

Another ten.

Halfway through, she fumbled the twig. It dropped between her middle and fourth fingers, joining the others on the damp ground. *Talk, Seppe. Say something.*

'My city. It is bombed.'

Connie turned away from Seppe, looking out towards the island.

He waited. There was nothing else to do.

'Where your family were?' Connie twisted back towards him, eyes bright with tears. 'I'm sorry, Seppe.' She sniffed and he foraged in his pockets for a handkerchief.

He concentrated on the trees clinging on to the rocks. They had flourished where nothing should flourish, branches spreading out over the water, claiming the space where no tree had ever before entered.

That's what you need to do, now there is nothing to stop you.

286

He handed her the handkerchief. 'But this is the problem. *I* am not sorry.'

His words curled white in the night sky, visible, irrefutable. He felt sick, but his truth was out.

Connie was quiet for a moment.

Then: 'Nobody can tell you how to feel. Your dad was rotten, wasn't he? I'm not surprised you're happy to be shot of him.'

Across the lake, a scuffle in the copse. They listened. A fox after a rabbit by the sound of those squeals.

'In Campo 61 there is another prisoner, from my city, and he is broken by this. But not me. Italy is not my home now. Italy has not been my home for a long time. I wish that it was, but it cannot be so. I think – I think maybe I am a monster for not behaving as Fredo does, for not caring about my home.'

'But your home wasn't happy – you've told me that. We can't help how we feel about home, none of us can. You cared about your sister, didn't you? And your mam, from what you've said. It was only your pa.'

'This is true. He was not a good man. But I am a coward, and that is worse.'

Seppe shuddered, but the memory flooded in, and this time there was no evading it. The cold of this English night shrank people to the core of themselves; all that remained was the crystallised truth.

Thirty-Seven

Livorno, 1942

THE MAJOR, FULL OF righteous indignation and red wine tonight, roars into the house after the meeting. Seppe, woken by the noise, comes to the banister, looks down through the gloom.

'What is it this time – she's a useless whore who betrayed him, or she's the passive martyr preventing him from greatness?'

Seppe doesn't want to smile, but Alessa, arriving beside him in her white nightgown, has hit the nail on the head. It's like being a kid again, standing here with his little sister whilst they eavesdrop on their father's tirades. He looks down at her and this time can't help but smile. Standing there with her toes pointing towards each other, long black hair falling into her eyes, she looks very like she did ten years ago. But Alessa is married, newly pregnant; has moved back to the family home only for company when her husband returned to the front to fight this war of Il Duce's.

'This time it's about me. He's insisting I join the Regio

Esercito, to stop waiting to be called up and to volunteer instead, be a proper man. He only pulls the strings to keep me out because it's his peculiar way of making amends to Mamma. But now the war is dragging on, and I'm doing his chances no good, he says, by not being a man. Mamma is panicked about it, all those "whores and diseases". The fighting seems secondary to her. It's the first time I've known her stand up to him.'

Alessa glances up at him.

'This isn't your fault, Seppe. You know anything could have tipped him over, anything at all.'

There's a ferocious rattle of pans, then a dull thud as the pan connects with something. Their mother is quiet: a good sign. The blows aren't unmanageable, she isn't fuelling the Major's ire by reacting to it.

Alessa sits down on the floor, face pale and sickened, still peering through the slats at the glimmer of the kitchen. 'I wish Bruno was here. He'd go down there and stop him, wouldn't stand for it.'

Seppe slides down next to her, grips his knees with sweaty hands. Alessa is right: her husband is what even their father would call a 'proper man'. Bruno wouldn't be cowering behind a newel post, willing the noise to stop. What's wrong with Seppe that he can't save his own mother? His innards fold in on themselves. Interfering will only make it worse for their mother; she's always insisted on that. He opts to believe her.

There's a hefty *crack* from downstairs and a pinched scream. He fights the urge to clamp his hands over his ears as if he were five again. And then Alessa is up, tipping forward on to hands and knees, reaching for Seppe's hand to pull her upright.

'What are you doing?' But he knows. The thuds and thumps are accelerating, an intolerable opera.

'I can't stand by and listen to this, Seppe. Not any more.' Tears run down Alessa's cheeks, glistening on her dark hair. She is wonderful, this sister of his, fierce and shining with determination.

Alessa is halfway down the stairs, one hand holding fast to the banister, one supporting the barely perceptible swell of her stomach.

'Stop that! Stop, you brute!' Her voice pierces the vacuum created by their mother's own silence. 'Hold on, Mamma! I'm coming; I'll make him stop.'

Seppe can't bear it. He wants to go back to his bedroom, to pretend none of it is happening, to put his head under the pillow as he did so many years before and wait for dawn to bleach away the horror. And he wants to run downstairs, stop his father once and for all. But he's glued to the landing, watching Alessa disappear into the gloom of the kitchen. Now the Major's voice lifts in pace with the beatings, and Alessa's is raised too. He can't work out the words over the banging of the pan, the noise of his mother shrieking and Alessa and his father bellowing, but the pace is faster and faster and there seems to be nothing that could bring this to an end. He has to go down there, has to wrestle the pan away from his father and banish him, stand up to him at last. But he can't, he simply can't move. His body is frozen with memories of the years of beatings it's endured and his feet won't carry him.

The banging stops. And with it the yelling and the shrieking. In their place comes an unearthly sound.

Seppe races down, limbs freed by the need to discover the source of this wild keening and make it stop. He skids into the kitchen, halting when his bare feet meet warm stickiness. His mother kneels on the floor, Alessa's head cradled in her lap, one hand working the rosary beads

290

faster than Seppe has ever seen her do them before. Blood pools beneath his sister's head. *Blood.*

The Major stands at Alessa's feet, the iron pan still dangling from his hand. He looks up as Seppe steps closer, trying to avoid the blood, unable to check.

The Major raises the pan in warning.

The Major's eyes are flinty but his breathing is ragged. 'It will be an accident, do you hear me?'

Seppe kneels beside Alessa, puts a hand on her cheek. Enough is enough. She's made her point, now she needs to wake up. 'Lessa. You're frightening me now. Come on, *cara*. Time to stop playing.' She has to wake up, has to. He gets up and pulls the water jug from the table, splashes water on her face where it mixes with the blood and sends streaks of salmon pink towards that black hair.

'Lessa, come on. It's me. He's stopped now. Time to stop pretending.' His voice isn't his own; it's as unearthly as the scene before him.

The water trickles futilely down from her forehead into her hairline, for all the world like a benediction.

Perhaps that's what's needed.

'Shall I go for the padre?' But his mother's eyes widen and fright gleams. She glances towards the Major and shakes her head. She's quiet now, her lips moving in pace with the rosary beads.

'No priest is entering this house.' His father's eyes are steel. He looks at the pan in his hands and back to Seppe. 'Do I need to make this clear?'

'At some point the priest will need to see her.' He can't believe this to be true, even as he says it. Seppe's voice cannons around the walls. Never before has he challenged the Major.

His father slams the pan down on the tiles. How Seppe longs to take his father's face and smash it with the same force, but years of conditioning leaves him impotent. He hates himself for it, loathes himself with a passion he didn't know he was capable of accessing after all these careful years of subjugating his feelings, being only the person his father – and thus his mother – needed him to be. What sort of man lets his sister fight their battles for him? And what sort of man then can't avenge himself against their father? A weak one. A pathetic one. That's what kind.

Seppe looks down again at Alessa. She is so peaceful. But her cheek is cooling beneath his palm. Surely their father can't actually have killed her? The word looms, scarlet and torrid, in front of Seppe's eyes. His head spins and he puts his other hand on the floor to steady himself. Things like this don't happen. Alessa is the happiest person anyone knows. She isn't lying broken on the tile, one hand still protecting the child that now will never live.

'Not under my roof!'

Seppe covers his mother's hand with his own.

'We will call the undertaker in the morning, make the situation clear to him. If any priest comes, it will be to the funeral parlour.'

The Major glances at Alessa. Does Seppe imagine the flash of tenderness, of regret? Then he's gone.

Seppe has marched the memory of this night a thousand miles, through the grit and heat of the desert, up and down the parade ground, and he can't exhaust it. With every pinch of his blade, every stroke of the plane, the memory remains as raw and fresh as the night it happened.

Seppe and his mother half drag Alessa to the parlour, where his mother arranges a crucifix and a statue of the Holy Mother at her head. Her head . . . He finds a bowl, dabs at her hair until it's trace-free, until she's as peaceful as she can look. That blood is between his fingertips now, will never come away. Alessa is dead, and it's because he hadn't done anything to help her. Alessa is dead, and the unborn child with her. Mamma is moving mechanically, her thoughts inaccessible, each movement determined only by the one that precedes it. Perhaps she is seeking comfort in religion; perhaps, like Seppe, this is so unreal as to be beyond discussion. Upstairs, Mamma plucks a dress from Alessa's wardrobe and Seppe helps her remove the blood-stained nightgown. They dress Alessa as if she's still alive in a vibrant red dress and hat. Mamma takes her own best shoes from the cupboard, places one on Alessa's right foot and Seppe's breath catches in his throat. Alessa had coveted those shoes since she was in school, had begged to borrow them, but had always been denied. He takes the other shoe, tries to ease it on. But Alessa is cooling beneath his touch and he is afraid to continue.

Seppe wants to gag at this most lively of people being turned into a statue before his eyes. His sister. His sister, who used to wake him before dawn by jumping onto his bed. Who mocked him for being so quiet, for not wanting to play with the other boys, but was always there to offer him a game of her own instead. Who stood up for their mother whenever he despaired at her cowedness, reminding Seppe that their mother had always known her place to be beside her husband. He pulls out his knife and the little piece of wood lodged in his pocket and starts to carve a miniature Alessa, but his tears on the blade make it too slippery to hold. Nothing works now that Alessa is dead.

That night in the parlour, his mother rubbing her fingers raw on the rosary beads, he realises she is doing more than reciting the Hail Marys. Between the bouts there are other words. 'Join up,' she keeps saying. 'Enlist.'

'Enlist where?'

Mamma doesn't take her eyes off Alessa. Is she waiting for Alessa to rise? 'Join up. The Regio Esercito.'

'The Regio Esercito? Join the army?' Is he hearing her all wrong? 'You want both your children dead?' The only favour his mother has ever asked his father is to keep Seppe out of the war, and she has paid for it with every month that the war has continued. But now she wants him far away from her too. He has failed her, failed them all.

Seppe doubles over, can't look at her. He barely hears her through the ringing in his ears. 'It will keep you safe. It will keep *me* safe.'

Rage surges, the rage that belongs to his father's actions. 'You want me out there as cannon fodder and this will secure our safety?' He stares at her now, but she won't meet his gaze. 'Fascism has ruined our family and you want me out there, fighting to make it stronger?' She hates him. She's a madwoman. It's the grief talking. It has to be.

'Safe from your father.'

The knot in his stomach unwinds slightly, becomes a rescue line. 'But you will still be here.' The Major is right; Seppe is a coward. How could he leave his mother here? And yet . . . how could he stay, now his mother has thrown him the rope?

'With you in the army, he can be proud. It will help with his council election, help him to forget any rumours that might spread about this.' She reaches for Alessa's hand, gathers up the rosary in the other.

'No, Mamma. Come with me. Let us go away. Leave him.'

She smiles up at him, sadness permutating everything. 'You know I cannot. But you alone – *you* can.'

Is this true? Possibly. Can Seppe believe it? Enough. For a while – if even for a short while – this will save his mother from more beatings. That was the way to look at it. All the options are bad options.

The day after they bury Alessa, Seppe makes his way to the Livorno town square and enlists. Days later he stands shivering with the others against the stone walls of the station, waiting for the train that will consign them to basic training. There are maybe fifty of them, some Seppe recognises from church and, before that, from school. Plenty for his father to move through, clasping hands and accepting condolences. Seppe presses himself as far into the wall as he can, the cold of the stone not suitable penance. Nothing, nothing will be penance enough for not protecting Alessa. He can barely stand to voice her name, even in his head; it spikes him, an accusation. At least like this he is protecting his mother. *Believe it, you have to believe it.* Nobody tries to talk to him. Their curious looks make him twelve again, alone in a corner of the playground, not understanding why nobody would play marbles with him. He had always been different; opposed to his father's views and isolated from his classmates perhaps as a result. Now he must insinuate himself amongst them and fight their battle even as he has lost the only battle that can ever matter.

The padre approaches them, pausing at each recruit. He is a fraction taller than Seppe, his halitosis perfectly positioned to hit Seppe's nostrils. *Surely God could do something about that breath?* Seppe raises his head slightly and looks the priest in the eye as he delivers his benediction.

How much does this man know? Seppe had paused outside the church two days previously, drawn by the confessional. How easy it would be to rest in the dark with the smell of polish filling your nose and to say, 'This is what my father did, this is what I failed to do, this is

the man he is, I am, save me, save him, save us, oh Father.'
But he wasn't man enough for that . . .

The recruiting officer pushes them onto the train.
Amongst the throng of the frantic wavers, Seppe spots the
Major, striding firmly away, Mamma scuttling behind him.
Seppe looks away, his love for her threatening to bring
him to tears. He should stay, should stand up to the Major
and protect his mother, his home. But even as he articulates
this, another thought engrains itself. This isn't home any
longer. This can't be home. Home exists no more.

AS SEPPE FINISHED SPEAKING, a gust blew up over the lake.
Connie shivered. 'This is your home, Seppe, here with me,
and Joe, and Frank and Amos.'

He gazed again at the island-clinging trees. The roots
gave him solace; moss-covered, entirely misplaced, but
tenacious.

She reached for his hand, leaned into him.

He inched closer to her, took off his greatcoat and draped
it over Connie's shoulders.

Thirty-Eight

THE WHOLE FOREST HISSED with icy rain; even the birds were drowned out, and they must be half-frozen. Here they all were, almost at Christmas, and Connie's boots squeaked each time she jammed her chilblains into them, the laces sopping and refusing to budge when she fumbled at them with stiff fingers. She was trying to move as little as possible, to keep the cold from sneaking through her coat and under her overalls, but there was no way of felling that didn't involve proper moving around. She could only hope it'd keep her a bit warmer, but already she couldn't feel her toes.

Seppe was driving her batty today, nagging on and on about keeping Joe warm and dry, as if that wasn't playing on her mind.

'Connie, *cara*. Please take Joe inside.'

'Don't *cara* me when you're telling me what to do. How am I going to stop mid-spruce?' She should be nicer to him; she wanted to be. But she was bone-weary and the forest wasn't helping, all the leaves off the trees now and

297

the trunks standing bare and upright like a field full of silent soldiers. `

'The spruce was not "mid" when I first asked you to take Joe home. You started felling it on purpose.'

She almost missed the old, scared-of-his-shadow Seppe. He'd been a different person these last few weeks, now the shock of his city being destroyed had abated. If anything, it seemed to have given him energy. She understood that; she'd got herself out to the farm and then down here under the same conditions, after all. It made a difference knowing there was nobody else you could fall back on – in his case, because they'd only make it worse, from what he'd said. Either it ate you up, swallowed you whole, or it made you ready to tackle anything.

Now Seppe took the six-pounder every day without looking to her for approval on the first incision, spent handover times chatting to Frank about 'when the war was over' as if he planned to stay put in the Forest if the war did ever end. Seppe talking about staying made Connie nervous in ways she couldn't make sense of. He seemed settled now, ever since they'd had that night-time walk. She'd been trying to make him feel better that night since he'd seemed so cut up about his town, and God knows she could understand how that felt. And it seemed to have worked, because he'd been so much more chipper ever since. But now, just as he felt better, she'd started to feel worse. Maybe it was seeing just how happy Seppe would be with a life in the Forest forever and ever that made her realise quite how trapped she felt when she imagined it for herself? She'd had plans once, too, had imagined a new life for herself the way Seppe was doing now.

Connie was happy enough, honest she was, but she wanted to cry whenever she thought about the fact that she could never plan anything again now. That was it.

She'd had her chance, she'd cocked it up, and now life would just unfold the way it did for everyone else. This was her life now, stuck here where, every spring, the trees would turn the world green, every summer the blossom would come and the streams would run warm. In autumn she'd be expected to help pick the apples and the nuts and God knows what else, then the rains would set in and they'd be getting down trees with fingers so cold that they'd probably barely feel it if the saw nicked them. Thinking of life in the forest was like turning a coin over and over. If she considered summer picnics by the brook and juicy apples, and slumping on the bench of a morning with Amos and a brew whilst Joe ran starkers in the garden . . . well, that was pretty sweet. But, if she flipped the coin, she was stuck with a life where the same thing happened year after year, as predictable as Dad putting two bob on the horses on a Saturday afternoon. The trees would plod on, varying nothing in the routine until they died or were cut down, and she'd be the same. The same as a bloody tree, for God's sake! And not even a decent dance or caff to pass the time, and everyone knowing everyone else's business with not a chance to turn yourself into something new if it suited you.

The city was just a pipe dream now. Her coin was flipped. She'd come to terms with that, or at least had thought she had, but seeing Seppe starting to make even pie-in-the-sky plans made her miss the very possibility of it. She liked Seppe, of course she did, probably loved him, even, on a good day. She smirked. She especially liked him when he unclipped the bib of her dungarees and slid one hand down into her shirt. The roughness of those fingers as they caressed her warm, ready skin – it was something she could never get enough of. But, whether or not that was the case, he was a POW, here at the pleasure of the King. So how come even Seppe had more choices than her? Connie longed to wrestle the six-pounder back off him and lose herself in the force of its blade against an oak.

'Look, I'll finish off this last bit with the fretsaw then I'll take him in, OK?' Connie blinked away ratty hair and looked across at Joe, or the bit of him she could see. 'He's fine in that tree trunk.' He was, too. Those little gnome holes at the bottom were exactly the right size for him to sit up in and at four months he was desperate to explore whenever he could. Ever since she'd relaxed and let him start nosing around in the tree holes he'd been right as rain out here. When she pulled Joe out he'd smell wetly of moss and twigs, his fists full of worms and tiny weeny woodlice, his hair damp under his cap. She loved to cuddle him best of all when he was like this; all cold and mellow from playing around. But he stayed put – couldn't get enough of grubbing around in there – and that gave her time to change to the cross-cutter and get a half-decent rhythm going on some of those bigger boughs.

'Arrgh!' Seppe had snuck up behind her and put his arms around her. As if getting all nuzzly would change her mind about Joe. 'You made me drop the saw! Frank'll do his nut if I knacker that one.'

'There are better things we can do if Joe can't see.'

'Not right now, there aren't.' She bent down and picked up the saw and he stroked her bum as it stuck out. She bit down hard on the inside of her cheek and concentrated on not clobbering him with the axe handle. The rest of the lumberjills had been 'borrowed' by the Women's Land Army to get in the harvest, and were never sent back to forestry work. Frank had more sense than to suggest that Connie go with them, had simply told her they needed to do their own pollarding and lopping from now on, once they got the trees down. She was done in. Frozen. Permanently wet. Trapped.

'But we are losing the light, my little worker. Come with me to see the hut. I have a question.'

Connie's toes clenched in her damp socks. She knew he was trying to be nice, and she wished she could enjoy it, but instead it made her long to crawl into the tree trunk with Joe too.

'What question? It's a wooden hut – no point getting too fancy. I don't know why you've got these grand ideas about living in it. There's still a war on, you know. The camp guards could call you back inside at any moment.'

He put a hand to her waist. This nearly always made her soften, but today it felt like shackles. She gritted her teeth and lost the rhythm of the saw.

'I need to know where to put the sink. Beside the window?'

The sink? Was he setting her up in the kitchen now? She almost turned on him with the saw. Instead, her hands dropped and the saw snagged on a knot in the wood. 'You decide. Make it without one, for all I care.' They hadn't talked about what might happen after the war but it was clear where Seppe's thoughts were leading.

Better not to think at all, if you asked Connie; it would only lead to grief and her letting more people down. She set the saw against the fur of the bark again. It was proper old-growth timber; you could tell from the fungi growing up in its higher branches. She checked the teeth against her finger, exasperated. Sharpened last week; should get through it well enough.

The saw shuddered to a halt again. Seppe was the other side of it, holding it from underneath like they never, ever should, so that she couldn't even saw on through without risking his fingers.

'Connie. There are things we need to check about the hut. We are ahead of quota again; Frank won't mind. And Joe must get out of the rain; I insist.'

301

His words ignited everything she'd been trying to dampen down. She dropped the saw, not caring when it splashed into a puddle.

'You can't insist anything, Seppe. Joe is mine, however much you and Amos think I'm cocking it up. I'm doing my best.' The rain pelted down, each droplet a burst of shrapnel filleting the sky. Her hair dripped into her eyes and made her blink.

'Every day his cough is getting worse.'

Seppe wasn't going to let it go, was he? 'All right, all right. I'll take him now if it means you'll shut up about it. And get off my case about the hut, will you? It's a glorified shed you're building with bits of old scrap, not some fancy frigging stately home.'

Seppe dropped his end of the saw too and it twanged against the trunk. The look on his face! It was as if she'd slapped him, not just said it like it was. Oh God. She couldn't take it, not now. She wished she could be kinder to him, but she just couldn't. She was a heartless cow, but every time he talked about the hut, the heebie-jeebies got worse.

'It will be a home. And Gianni – Gianni has a friend from Salerno in a camp up in Scotland. He works on a farm, and Gianni swears that he lives in the – in a building outside the farmhouse. So it is possible, you see?' His voice was soft, as if she'd just trodden on something in him and he was trying to bring it back to life with his words.

Connie needed to get out before more words escaped. The rain was really stair-rodding it now, blocking her view. She yanked Joe out of the tree and he yelped as he scraped his cheek against the side.

'Come on, little man.' She scrubbed at Joe's cheek with a soaking wet glove and he bawled louder, blood seeping into her glove. Was the cut deep? Seppe would notice in a minute that she'd damaged Joe, and she couldn't bear it if he told her off about something else this morning. Time to scarper.

'We're off now, satisfied? I've got a good mind to get all the way out of this poxy forest. I never meant to stay here in the first place and enough's enough.' Connie knew that little-boy-lost look of Seppe's, but she wasn't falling for it today. 'You can do all the pollarding on your own tonight. If you miss the truck back to camp, it'll serve you right for interfering.'

Absolutely typical that today they were at the further-most reaches of the softwoods. By the time she sloshed down through the apple trees with Joe towards the cottages, a river was raging down Joe's overcoat and he was coughing like a navvy with a pipe. They were both shivering and though she pulled Joe close, it didn't seem to make a difference to either of them. The leaves were bulleting down off the trees; she had to twist to duck past them. And there was Joyce, sou'wester pinching her face into a frown, fisting drenched ovals of grain at grumpy-looking chickens from a wooden scoop. For a desperate moment Connie wished she could swap places with the chickens. At least they were content, pecking round out here, being fed their grub come rain or shine.

'Not been out in this with him, have you? The two of you must be frozen. Come in for a cup of tea, a minute.' Joyce upended the grain dish on her way back to the cottage door, and the chickens clustered at her toes, their feathers flat with rain and shiny as the autumn leaves. Connie hesitated. She was fit to drop, and Joe needed drying off before he proved Seppe right by getting pneumonia. But Joyce was smiling and a cup of tea sounded good.

'You're both drenched.'

'I know, I know. I've had Seppe banging on about that

303

already.' The tea scalded her throat and held the tears away.

'Here, love – put him into this while you have your drink. Got a bun here too, I do have. Bet our Joe would like a bun, eh, poppet?'

Joyce put a fat rock cake into Joe's hands and handed Connie what looked like a sheet made out of wool. It smelt of Frank, of wood and Woodbines and loyalty.

'Good grief, Joyce, this big enough? Do you and Frank wear it at the same time?'

'Oi! Enough of your cheek, thank you, madam. It's warm and dry, that's what matters.' Joyce was smiling, though, and Connie couldn't argue with that, though Joe apparently could. He screamed when she pulled the wet things off over that graze on his cheek. He was soaked down through to his vest, poor little sod. Would he calm down if she jiggled him a bit?

She bounced him once, twice, and the shrieks got worse, mixed in with that hacking, old-man cough of his. 'I'm sorry, babba. You got dealt the wrong hand when it came to your mother.'

'Ah, c'mon now, Con, that's not true.' Joyce had taken off the sou'wester and her hair was perfect, all tight curls but no rollers in.

Joe had calmed down a bit. 'This simply isn't my thing, Joyce.'

Joyce nodded. 'My Aunt Maud were the same after my cousin were born. But she came round to the baby in no time. You'll see.'

The tea wasn't so hot now. Connie took a big gulp, swallowed it down. 'I dunno, Joyce. I know people get the baby blues, but this is different from that. God knows I try, honest I do, but I'm really not born to it, not like some people are. The bigger he gets, the harder it is. I reckoned

I might get the hang of it once he was crawling and sleeping and stuff. But he never sleeps, and the moving around will be nothing but a pain, I see that now. I can't be watching him and the trunks at the same time; and I'm good at the felling, really good. One day one of them trunks'll land right on top of Joe and then Seppe'll give me a right what-for.'

'Aye, Seppe does love that boy, doesn't he? Mind, that's a good thing. It wouldn't be every bloke'd be glad to take on someone else's son.'

'I didn't ask him, you know, if that's what you mean. And it's not what it looks like between us.' Before she could help it, Connie had finished the sentence. 'I worry he wants me to become a little wifey, Joyce. How did I get myself into this?'

'Careful now, me darling.' Joyce lifted Joe's fist out of the way of the teapot, and he grizzled at her. 'I can see that.'

'What do you mean? It's not like I go round spouting on about it.'

'Nor do you need to. I see what I see. Here, you, come to your Auntie Joyce a minute.' Joyce stood up briskly, hoisting Joe on one hip. He was silent now, grinning at being bobbed up and down. Connie needed to remember that trick. It might work better than the jiggling.

'Look, girl. It's obvious you're not happy here. Frank do say you're all right when you're out felling, and I can believe that, but it seems to me that this life of mother and baby isn't your cup of tea. Doesn't suit everyone, but we didn't use to get any choice.'

Connie stared.

'Well, it's the truth. Me now, I'm happy enough down here; got everything I need and I get proper satisfaction of a well-kept house. But you wouldn't be the first wench to try something new in wartime and not want to go back to the old ways.'

'You're talking like having a baby's a stint in the WRENS. I can't just pack it in – you know I can't. Though I think about it sometimes, even though I shouldn't.' The tea was comforting, a reminder of the thousands of cups that had gone before, and she clenched it closer to her.

'I can't leave the baby, not now he's here. And if I took him away with me, how would I ever work? I only manage that out here because of Seppe, we all know that. I'd hardly be able to tote along a baby to some fancy job in London, would I? It's not Joe's fault I messed it up, is it? All I can do is stay here and make the best of a bad job.

'And Seppe – he only makes it worse. He knows how to deal with Joe without even seeming to try.'

'Doesn't mean you're no good at it; simply means he is. Some men are like that. Look at Amos.'

Connie snorted; she couldn't help it. 'Amos thinks Joe's another lost lamb.'

'Aye, that's as maybe, but don't forget that he's done this all before. You should have seen him raising his Billy.' Joyce turned away for a moment, gazed at the fire flickering in the grate.

'Handled the whole lot, he did, and wouldn't hear a word from May's parents, who wanted to take the baby off to live with them.'

There was comfort in listening to Joyce telling tales of the past, the baby gurgling. And Joyce seemed to understand how confused Connie was about her lost dreams. It was such a relief not to have to put a brave face on it, even for just a few moments.

'I was going to get away, Joyce. Go off to London and be a cigarette girl, something that got me into the pictures, or the dances. Then later I'd find a way to move to America

– maybe even marry a GI if they were still around! Go somewhere, see something different. Instead of that I'm stuck in this endless damn wood – no offence. Not exactly what I had in mind.'

'It's not too late, Connie. You girls today, you get these new chances opening up all the time. Not like it was in my day. Maybe when this war is over –'

'The war'll never be over!' Connie scrunched up her eyes to stop the terror overtaking her. 'It's been going five years. This war started before I'd even finished school and at this rate I'll be dead by the time it's done.' Or Seppe would want them to get married and have thousands of Italian babies. 'Seppe's great, he is, but I want to be Connie again before I'm someone else's wife. I'm too selfish, I know, but that's how it is.' She sighed. Did Joyce understand? It mattered so much that somebody did.

Joyce sat down again, picked up her knitting from the basket by the chair and deftly added another row. How was she balancing the baby and the knitting without dropping one of them? Joe watched, transfixed by the clicks, and Connie watched with him. Maybe she could get Joyce to teach her, knit something for Seppe to say thank you. A pouch for that knife of his, perhaps. As if that would make up for her behaviour.

'I don't mean to be bad, honest I don't. I wish I didn't feel like this.'

Joyce was nodding. 'I know, love. You're not bad.' She held out the baby like a prize. Consolation prize, more like.

Thirty-Nine

THE RAIN WAS SHEETING down so hard between the oaks that Amos heard Seppe bashing away at the hut before he saw him. The blessed lad was going to break his neck up there in this downpour. Even the ewes had had the sense to get out of it; they were all bunched together in the beeches up near Drybrook when he'd left them today. He'd need to start thinking about winter shelters for them if it carried on like this, but they were hardy enough, just needed persuading to move to the old-growth now the weather had turned.

'Watchoo up to, boy?'

Seppe replied through a mouthful of nails, the rain drumming at his words.

'Getting the roof on. Frank told us to stop felling because of this rain. This is a good chance for me before the light fades completely today.'

The lad was getting there all right with this hut of his; quite the handy carpenter, he was. But that centre purlin wasn't going on right, you could see that even from here, and he'd risk the whole lot toppling. And he was right about the light; the days were drawing faster than ever now with all this rain making it so gloomy.

'Hang on there a minute.'

Amos fetched the ladder from the shed and climbed up alongside Seppe.

'I've tried everything. This one won't line up properly.' Seppe bashed his fist on the stubborn cross-beam and it bounced slightly.

Not like the lad to be worked up like that. Amos went down a step on the ladder and squinted along the length of the roof.

'There's your problem: look here.' Halfway along the roofline one of the uprights jutted out, getting in the way of the ash beam. 'We can sort that out easy enough. You got the plane handy? Give it here a minute.'

It had been a while since Amos had used a plane, but it wasn't something you forgot. The boy was hunched up next to him like his Billy used to be and Amos swallowed hard. Must be the rain, getting in his throat.

Amos lined up the plane with the wood and pushed down.

'There.' Nothing like a job done well, even in this weather.

Weather. That was a point.

'Where's Connie with our Joe, if you're rained off?'

Seppe was halfway back up the roof. Amos had to strain for the answer over the blessed rain. 'They left before me, before Frank came past.'

'Why aren't they home, then?'

Seppe closed right in, like he was a pheasant who knew the goshawk had spotted him. 'I think – sometimes she would wish for a different home. A different life.'

That was the problem! The boy had forgotten the nails;

small wonder the damn thing wasn't staying put. Amos filled his palm with nails from the jam jar and Seppe lined one up. Amos had wondered, he had, about Connie and Seppe. Odd pair, to his mind, but there was no knowing what went on beneath the surface.

'Well, she's here, isn't she? And our Joe, too. Doesn't matter what you think she thinks. Proof of the pudding and all that.'

Seppe's next sentence was a mumble

'I'm not sure how much longer for.'

'She wants to leave here? That's what she said?' Seppe nodded and knocked a nail into the dead centre of the wood, steady as you like.

'But what about the baby?' Amos gripped the roof ledge extra tight.

'Him as well, I suppose.'

'And you think she means it?' The boy moved the next nail, positioned it just so. As he lifted his hammer, he gave a tiny shrug of his shoulders.

The rain drove on down into the earth, the leaves drove off the oaks and the nails drove down into the wood. This little hut might turn into something after all. A home for Seppe, away from that camp he was always so keen to avoid.

The sky was filling in behind the rain, darkness drawing down on them. The weight of it all pulled Amos down. Billy, out there underneath a different sky. If he was still out there at all. But he couldn't – wouldn't – think of a landscape that didn't hold his Billy.

Amos swallowed out the thought.

'My son – Billy.' The words were sharp as splinters but they sounded all feeble against the caw of the jackdaw, calling them home now the night was cloaking in. 'Chance is he might be a prisoner of war now too, like. It's a slim chance all right, but it's all I've got. Either that or he's . . .' He couldn't finish it.

Seppe paused, nail halfway down. He turned on his ladder and nodded, almost formally, then moved back to the nail. *Tap tap tap.* The lad was concentrating so hard you could taste it. Amos's mouth was metal, sour.

Seppe picked up the next nail, his thumb to the wood again.

Amos looked at it.

'I thought I'd send him a parcel. In case he do still be alive. Through the Red Cross, like. Turns out you can send all manner of things; food and cards and whatnot. Christmas is coming up and it's what our May would have done. I don't know which camp he might be in, but them officials, they'll know that, won't 'em?'

Seppe looked at Amos, didn't say a word. Amos couldn't read that expression. It wasn't mocking, and it wasn't pity, but it was sad all right.

After a moment, Seppe nodded.

'Many of my campmates have received these parcels. But . . . You know which country he was sent to?'

'The last letter I got, he was in that Germany from what I could make out.' This was what pinched at Amos as he pushed through the hawthorn and the gorse of a morning. If you didn't know the smell of a place, the angle of the light on the ground, the camber beneath your feet, how could you ever say you understood? Him and his Billy had never been further apart.

'And you – sorry, but I must ask this to understand – you have heard no news. Nothing from the British government?'

'Not a sausage. But that's a good sign, son, right?' He scanned Seppe's face, anxious. Those within war bore it differently, could understand things the likes of him never would.

311

Seppe climbed down his ladder, waited at the bottom for Amos. 'I am very sorry, Amos. I think without news of where he is, even Red Cross will not be able to deliver this parcel.' His face had lost its rage now, was soft with concern. Amos looked away.

'You're right.' Of course the lad was right. He'd been a fool.

'I'm sorry.'

All he'd wanted to do was get a piece of the forest to his Billy. If his Billy – but Amos shut it down and his throat tightened. He nodded, and made his way indoors.

Forty

THEY SIMPLY COULDN'T GET a rhythm going today.

'Have you got the wedge?'

Connie delved into her pocket, handed him two. He'd need the smaller one for these spruce, but he should know that by now. She couldn't be Seppe's mother as well as Joe's; there was already too much to remember. She'd lain the tarpaulin underneath the blanket and brought along an old tin cup Joyce used for the chicken feed so that Joe had something to bang with a stick. That scrape on his cheek was healing all right; he'd soon be good as new. Maybe she wasn't a natural, but that didn't make her a bad person. She just needed to concentrate on Joe and she'd work out how this life could be her life forever. But her chat with Joyce lay like a splinter in this determination, opening up the possibility of another way like a wound that, untended, would start to fester.

Seppe slotted in the wedge and Connie moved the axe to the other side of the copse, well away from Joe, picked up the saw. She still couldn't look at Seppe. He probably hadn't meant to treat her like the little wifey, but she couldn't find it in her to apologise for flying off the handle.

She wasn't concentrating and the wood knew it. Connie got up and dislodged the saw where the teeth had got stuck again. Every single time this morning. They hadn't been this off-kilter since those spring days when everything smelled fresh and they'd sneak out to practise. She pulled off her beret and tugged her hand through her hair, looking at the empty mouth they'd carved into the pine. It shouldn't be taking so long, not such a narrow trunk; must be going for a mast rather than a pit prop or rebuilding. The angle looked all right, but the line they'd pulled through it so far was zigzagging. If they didn't figure it out soon, it'd be a hell of a job to sort this out ready to send on.

Seppe lifted Joe off the blanket and came to stand beside her. The baby gurgled and reached out for her and she cupped his hand in her curled fingers.

'You don't want to bring him so close to this. What if it goes?'

'It's not going anywhere, that's the trouble.'

'Well, it has to.' What was the matter with her?

Seppe stared for a moment and she met his gaze.

'All right.' He walked back over to the blanket, put him down and handed Joe his stick and cup again.

'You start, and I'll follow.'

Seppe looked across at this. 'You don't want to start?'

'It's not working today, is it, me leading? And we need to get this tree down. So you set the rhythm and I'll find my way into it.'

This time it worked better. She swallowed it all down, let her mind focus only on the rocking of the saw, kept her hands slack to begin with and tilted into the motion Seppe was setting. Then one-two-three – NOW she had it.

It wasn't the best timberwork ever, but it would get the tree down.

They got three more down, the rhythm coming to them more easily now, but she couldn't make herself care. Maybe this was how it would always feel? Perhaps her work wouldn't feel so important now she was trying to focus better on being Joe's mam? But at the back of her mind she knew that couldn't be true. When the saw gripped the grain was usually when she came alive. She couldn't shake off the last argument, couldn't help but feel that she'd said too much that last time.

'Can we stop again? I should check Joe's napkin.'

If Seppe thought anything, he wasn't saying it. He tipped back his head for a swig of tea from the billycan and then looked at her for a long moment.

'What?'

'Will you come with me?'

'Where? We're in the middle of getting down this stand, in case you hadn't noticed.' And she was in the middle of changing yet another filthy napkin. When did babies start going on the pot? Surely it couldn't be long now.

'I think you will like this.'

It wasn't like Seppe to insist. That in itself was enough to get Connie on her feet, lugging Joe with her. He didn't seem mardy with her, though God knows she wouldn't have blamed him.

'I hope it's not far, then. Frank'll do his nut if we don't get this lot down.' It wasn't true. Frank never did his nut with them; they were always faster than the other crews. But it suited the cloud she was under right now.

'No, not far. *Vieni*. You'll see.'

They made their way up the hill, further away from Frank's headquarters but away from the camp, too. It was hard going, carrying Joe in this sludge of leaves and her

315

boots skidded once or twice. Her feet were rubbed raw and soaked through again, had been for weeks now. Seppe held out his arms for Joe, but she shook her head and he seemed to know not to push it. If she couldn't even manage to carry the bab, she was no kind of mam at all.

Someone was cooking bacon; the smell of it wafted out of a window and Connie's mouth watered. Bit late for breakfast, wasn't it? Typical forester, though, to have their windows open even in this sunken grey cold. She stopped, shunting Joe up a bit on her shoulder, and looked around her.

'Where are we? Didn't know there were any houses up here.'

Seppe looked down the path at her and half-smiled. 'There aren't.'

'What are you talking about? Can't you smell that?'

He pointed ahead. 'You'll see.'

She trudged on up to where he stood and looked to where he pointed. The trees were all but bare and on beyond them, in a clearing, was what looked for all the world like a makeshift caff, a tarpaulin slung between branches, sawn-off logs arranged in a circle around a fire, half a dozen Italians and a couple of girls sitting around as if it were a social, not the middle of the working day in a freezing cold forest. Gianni crouched at its centre – where else? – holding a pan over the flames.

'Eh, *scalco*! You bring us the baby? And *la bellissima* Connie?' Gianni made an elaborate bow and the bacon nearly slid off the pan into the fire. An Italian Connie hadn't seen before yelped and grabbed the pan off him.

They rolled a log closer to the fire and sat down.

'You are hungry?' Gianni didn't wait for an answer. Everyone was always hungry in Gianni's book; their desert days had never left him. He thrust a fork into the pan,

316

handed the bacon to Connie as if it were a lollipop. It was going to be a right palaver trying to eat this with Joe on her lap.

'Here, let me take the babby.' Connie hadn't noticed the other English girl and jumped at the voice. 'I'm Mary. I'm here with Gianni, make sure he don't burn down our forest.' The girl was a local and she was clearly batty about that chopsy mate of Seppe's, the way she was beaming up at him.

'Ta – that'd help a lot, actually.' Not having Joe was a proper weight off. She slumped back on the log and took a great big bite of the bacon, swigging it down with a mug of tea someone had handed her.

'What are you all doing here? Is it break time?' There was a roar of laughter from the other men. Beside her, Seppe stopped chewing to put a hand on her arm.

'Work? This lot don't believe in helping the enemy. Prefer to help themselves, as you can see.' But he grinned at his campmates as he said it, and they grinned back.

'But your foreman –'

'In the pub.' Gianni shrugged. 'If we are not trouble to him, he is not trouble to us.'

Connie moved closer to Seppe, leaned against the warmth coming from his greatcoat. These blokes wouldn't last a minute on Frank's watch, that was for sure. But what did that matter right now?

'So, Christmas, eh? We are talking about what we do for Christmas, it is not so far away now. Me, I go to Mary's house. And you?' Gianni stopped, peered pointedly at Connie as if it had anything to do with her. Before she'd had a chance to answer, Seppe jumped in.

'We're prisoners, had you forgotten? We're in camp for Christmas.'

Gianni laughed. 'The guards don't care. As long as we

are back by the night roll call . . . More food for the others.'

The talk moved to the camp football team's victory against Bream that past weekend. Gianni, needless to say, had scored a miracle goal that had saved the day. Mary, rocking Joe by the fire, rolled her eyes at Connie. It was all right, this.

Seppe finished his bacon and stood up, offered his hand to pull her off the log. This time she took it.

The winter sun had found a way through the clouds. Their shadows glided before them through empty trees and their boots crunched in step through frozen leaves. She didn't know if it was the bacon, or the cheery English girl, or just the chance to chat and not fret about everything all the time, but Connie's gut had untwisted. She'd find a way through. And she could start by being kinder to Seppe.

'You could come to us, you know.'

Seppe kept pace with Connie, one of his strides to two of hers.

'To you?'

'For Christmas.'

Forty-One

AMOS PUT BILLY'S PICTURE back down on the mantelpiece and looked at Bess, who'd raced across the crowded kitchen. What had she seen? Amos walked over to the kitchen door. The panes were all fogged up, only a uniformed shape shining through, and for a missed breath it was his Billy out there in the garden, found after all and home for Christmas like some dopey story on the wireless.

'Come on in, lad.' Amos swallowed down the bitter disappointment and cracked open the door so that Seppe could squeeze in. 'Chaos in here, it is; still a couple of hours till we're ready for our dinner, Joyce says.'

As if summoned by her name, Joyce bustled forward. She grabbed the poor lad by the wrist and shut out the hooting of the owl.

'Don't leave him standing on the doorstop like that! Merry Christmas, Seppe, love.'

On the range, the pot lid rattled out of time with the wireless and Joyce warbling away to it. Amos still didn't know why Joyce and Frank had come here for their

Christmas dinner, but Connie had insisted, said it would save him from her cooking. She had a point.

Amos fetched Joe. He was sitting up at the table banging a carrot whilst Connie stirred at something in May's big old mixing bowl with a frown deep enough to swallow up the Severn.

'Let's show our Seppe the tree, shall we?' Connie and Frank had dragged it in one night, giggling like a pair of kids, but Amos hadn't bothered with them; didn't need to be worrying about their hijinks, not with his Billy still gone and any last hope he had seeming more and more like the daydreams of a foolish old man.

He looked now at the tree. Joyce had come over to decorate it, and she hadn't done a bad job, considering. She'd painted eggshells red and green and hung them from the tree's branches; a string of paper chains wound round the boughs.

'Amos –' The lad had followed him in and was shifting from foot to foot like a ewe that needed worming.

'This is one of those new pines from Parkend. We planted these only in October. It's part of the quota.'

So that's what they'd been in cahoots about, Connie and Frank. The things that girl could persuade Frank to do! Proper fond of her, he was.

Joe reached for the nearest paper chain and Amos swung him across to his other arm, away from the tree. He'd have the whole lot over if he grabbed that.

'You don't need to be worrying about them quotas today, boy.'

'But these pines, they were designated by the Home Production Unit. If Frank has uprooted one, the quota is out and this is a criminal offence.' Seppe was out of breath. Seemed he'd learned nothing about how the forest worked.

'Calm down, boy, nothing's going to happen. Been the same every year for as long as I can remember – this war

320

won't stop Foresters borrowing a tree for Christmas from their own forest. You go up past them new pines on the way home tonight and you'll see. Gaps big enough to drive one of them Yankee trucks through up there tonight.'

Joe was wriggling away, chirping at something only he could see. Amos set him down at a safe distance from the presents round the base of the tree, wrapped up in old copies of the *Mercury*.

'But why are the people not being fined?'

Amos laughed at this despite himself.

'Who you going to fine, boy? Can't hardly come down on the whole blessed forest, can 'em? And them pines'll be back in place day after tomorrow.'

Frank joined them, golden liquid splashing around inside the tankards he carried.

'You tried our cider yet, lad?'

Seppe accepted the tankard, kept it at a safe distance from Joe. He sniffed at the golden liquid splashing around inside the tankards Frank brought over.

'No, not yet. Apples?'

Frank laughed. 'Apples, aye, and a bit of a kick, too. Been making this out back ready for Christmas.'

Amos wasn't a drinker, never had been, but he always made an exception for Frank's cider at Christmas. He took a healthy swig and spluttered.

'Crikey Moses, Frank! What did you put in it this year?'

'Need to drink it year round, mun; get used to it that way, you will.'

'The sheep would be needing to sort themselves out if I drank this every night.' It was good stuff, tart, and packed a punch. Might need another glass after this one. A toast to Billy. Amos shook his head. The cider was making him as mushy as the windfalls that went into it. He caught Billy's eye in the picture on the mantel.

321

With an effort he turned back to Frank and Seppe.

'Don't they feed you your Christmas dinner up at Wynols Hill, then?' Frank, suspicious.

'What? Yes, yes of course. We cook it ourselves. Many festivities in the camp for Christmas. But I wanted to be here today with – with family.'

It lingered. The boy never spoke of his Italian family, though he must have one. Amos caught sight of Connie framed in the doorway, looked from her to his Billy again.

Family.

Amos looked in the boy's direction. Seppe had one hand in his pocket, staring over at Connie as if he was trying to answer a hard question. Well, they always said you couldn't choose your family, but this war had upended so much that evidently you could, now. Good luck to them.

Amos nodded at Seppe, raised his tankard. 'Aye, well here's a toast – to families.' He tilted the drink again in Connie's direction, but she was gone.

'Well, Joycie girl, that Mr Hitler hasn't made a scrap of difference to your cooking.' Frank scraped his chair back from the table. 'Never knew rabbit to taste so much like turkey.'

'You're having me on! Real gamey flavour, that did have. You must have had a plate full of stuffing.' Joyce winked at Connie, but it wasn't funny. Connie's fingers were raw from the hours she'd spent chopping onions and shredding the never-ending parsley. If Frank could taste anything in the stuffing, it was probably bits of her skin where the blade had kept missing.

Frank did the rounds again with the cider, filling up Amos and Seppe's tankards. Connie's mouth watered. She could kill for some of that action, especially after that toast

322

of Amos's. Seppe kept giving her little half-smiles, as if he knew something she didn't and he couldn't wait to tell her and it wasn't sitting easy with her dinner.

Seppe sneaked up behind Connie at the sink and seized her round the waist, sending the water gushing down her only half-decent dress since she'd ripped up the yellow one.

'Hey, watch it! Look what a state I'm in now!'

'You are beautiful anyway.'

'And you're full of bull.'

He smiled, and heaved a stack of empty plates into the sink.

'You had disappeared so I told Joyce I find you, help you with these, give her a rest. Amos is taking care of Joe.'

'Help me with them? What makes you think I've got any intention of doing them?' She smiled, but she kept her eyes firmly on the plates in the sink, wouldn't meet his gaze.

'Next year we will make Christmas over there. It will be a home by then.' He nodded across the garden to the shack.

She leaned against the sink and closed her eyes. 'Yeah, maybe.'

'Connie.' The shake in his voice sprang her eyes open. Seppe was down on one knee.

'What have you lost?

'Not lost. Found.'

Oh, hell.

'We don't know how much longer the war will be. But I have seen, you are sad recently. I think maybe it is because life cannot move forward. So I wanted to move forward at least the bit we can.'

He opened his hand.

On his palm lay a thick silvery ring. Her gut twisted and she bent over slightly. He reached for her but she shrugged him away, took the ring and examined it to buy some time. What was she going to do? She felt sick to her stomach.

He was watching her now, holding his breath so tight that there was no air left in the room for her to swallow, let alone speak.

'It's – thank you. It's – it's a beaut.' She pushed it onto her fourth finger before it fell down the plug. Her fingers jittered and she clamped her other hand on her arm to stop them. There were gems in it – not real rubies and emeralds, couldn't be, but it was pretty, she'd give him that. The gems sat at the centre of little carved leaves. It was exactly the ring she could see Seppe making. It must have taken him hours. And what had he bartered or sold to get those gems? She closed her eyes and took a long, juddery breath. All that time he'd spent on this and she couldn't even be excited. This was just more proof she was a bit wrong in the head.

Seppe was up off his knees now, moving in, but she tensed past him, ducked under his armpit.

'I'll be back in a second. Just need to freshen up.'

'But shall we tell the others first?'

Tell the others? He just assumed she'd say yes.

Her heart was lead; shame licked at the edges. She was soiled goods now, with Joe as proof. When the war ended she'd be on her tod with the baby to feed, no prospects, no house. She could see why he'd think she'd be grateful for the chance.

How dare he! What on earth was she supposed to say to this? On Christmas Day, with a houseful of people?

Seppe was staring at her now, shaking his head as if to stop her line of thought.

She needed something stronger than cider now. Connie pushed through the kitchen, undoing her apron and dropping it on the floor as she fought for air. Seppe followed her, but she couldn't look at him. She caught Joyce's eye and as she moved down the corridor, she heard Joyce behind her: 'Here, Seppe, give us a hand with the rest of these plates, will you? Don't mind our Con; she'll be back in a mo.' Joyce was a peach.

Connie sneaked open the parlour door and made a beeline for the bureau. Where was that bottle of God-knows-what she'd seen before? Her fingers met something hard and she breathed out. The bottle was dusty as hell, even grappling out the cork made her sneeze, but it pulled clean without too much trouble.

Connie lifted the bottle to her lips, sighed as the first cool drops met her mouth. That was better. She wiped her mouth, then the neck of the bottle, and stuffed it back down into the back of the bureau.

She still couldn't face the music yet, though, not until she knew what she wanted to do with the tune. Joe would be all right in there.

Nobody noticed her grabbing her cigarettes and creeping round into the garden. Through the window she thought she saw Seppe, peering out into the darkness, and she cringed back into the shadow. She was the worst person in the world. Who tried to hide from someone who had just proposed to them, especially when he was one of your only allies?

Seppe's voice floated out of the front door, worry lacing his words.

'Connie? Connie, are you out there?'

He must have gone out the front so that the others didn't notice him looking for her. Her heart tipped a bit, but she couldn't say anything yet, just couldn't, in case she said the wrong thing. She closed her eyes.

Forty-Two

CONNIE LIT A FAG and smoked three in a row, lighting one off the other, her hands less jittery each time, despite the cold. The tobacco did its thing and she relaxed into the twilight, head tilted back.

'*Here* you are; been looking for you, I have.' A beam of light shone into the garden as Joyce stepped through the kitchen door, then all was murky again as the door clicked shut.

Connie offered her the fag packet. 'Want one?'

'You're all right, love; I want to hang on to the taste of cider. We'll get back inside when you're done with that. It's about time to open the presents.'

'Dunno if I can cope with any more presents, not after this.' She tilted her hand in Joyce's direction, the ring heavier than the axe ever was.

'Oh cripes, Connie.' Joyce had her hand now, was holding it up to inspect the ring in the gloom. 'And you're not over the moon?' The little stones glittered for a second then disappeared as the moon went behind a cloud.

'It's a beautiful ring. And to think of him, working on this all alone up there in that camp. He must really want this, Con.'

'I know. You should have seen his face, Joyce. So hopeful. A normal girl would be happy, wouldn't she?'

Joyce took a cigarette and didn't say anything for the length of the smoke. She must think Connie was being a selfish baggage, too.

The wind changed direction and Connie got an eyeful of Joyce's ash.

'Ow!' Her eyes streamed and she blinked hard, the moisture cold on her cheeks.

'Oh, Connie, love.' Joyce pulled her in and hugged her, warm and firm, and the shock of it brought the tears for real. When was the last time anyone had hugged her? Seppe didn't count. She was properly bawling now, as if she were the baby. Poor Joe! She was such a terrible mother and it wasn't getting any better, and now she'd be trapped here forever, living in that dismal hut and burning dinner every night.

The tears came and came without end.

'It's all hopeless. I can't do any of it, Joyce, I really can't.' Connie daubed at her face with a hanky Joyce pulled from her apron.

It would have been quicker if she'd been had by that bomb after all. She was worse than anyone she'd ever mocked back in Coventry, trapped out here with a baby by a one-night stand and a prisoner who wanted a home so badly he'd mistaken her for it.

The hanky Joyce had given her was sopping wet. She looked at it and cried harder.

'Here, use this.' Joyce pulled the apron over her neck and gave it to Connie. Connie scrunched it to her face, scrubbing away the tears. The apron smelt of all those

327

meals Joyce had cooked in it, all the cupboards she'd scrubbed and the jumpers she'd knitted, and now it was covered in snot and rouge where Connie's face had run all over it.

'Oh Joyce, I've ruined your pinny.'

'What it's there for, isn't it? More concerned about what we're going to do about you, to be honest.'

'What kind of monster hides and blubs when her feller brings her a ring, Joyce?'

'Ah now, Connie, you stop that, all right? We've been over this before. We both know you're no monster.' It was dark out here now, the twist of smoke from the cigarette the only tang of inside. What she wouldn't do for another one, but the carton was empty.

Joyce put a hand on her shoulder. 'You feeling a bit better now?' Connie nodded. Joyce always made her feel better.

'That's my girl. Ready to come on in, then? They'll start to miss you if you stay out here much longer. I know it's a shock, but it's the nice kind of shock.'

'You're right, Joyce.'

She was. That's what made it all so much worse.

Connie risked a smile in Joyce's direction. Joyce wouldn't notice her faking it in this dark. 'You go on in, fill up those glasses. I'll be right behind you.'

But when Joyce closed the kitchen door, Connie headed in the other direction, out over the stones and into the wood. She didn't have to go far, just far enough away so that Seppe's hut wasn't looming over her. It was pitch black out here, the noises filling in for lack of sight. Six months ago the rustling and shifting of the leaves would have put the frighteners on her but these days they brought her comfort. It's where she'd had Joe, after all: if nothing bad could come of her in that situation, nothing ever could. The woods wanted nothing of her, just her company.

She sobbed into the gaps between the trees, filling the lacunae with misery. How had her life come so off track? There was nobody here who knew who she'd been for most of her life, who could give her advice based on who she'd always be. She missed them so much, was sick of pretending that everything was OK. Connie yelled out, the anger and pain hitting an echo against a trunk and refracting the solid wall of her despair. Almost a year – a whole year – and her family were still dead. They'd never feel the weight of Joe wriggling in their arms, hadn't even known he was on the way, couldn't shine him a copper or spin him a top or give him a Vimto-soaked finger to suck on. They'd stay dead forever, however much she wished it to change. There was nothing, nothing she could do.

All the tears came now. There was no stopping them. The months of heartache, of uncertainty, of having to look after herself. She cried and cried until there was nothing left, then leaned back, panting, against the nearest tree. She cried for the child she'd been, for her sisters who would never grow older; for Mam, cut off before life had had a chance to get easier. She cried for her younger, more optimistic self and for the future she might have had but now never could. This war, this endless war that had stolen her youth, her family, had driven her to reckless mistakes she'd be paying for now for the rest of her life. No proper mother would think of her baby as a mistake, but let's be honest, there was no better word for it. She'd cocked up everything.

She laid a hand against the trunk of the tree. The bark was mosaicked and lichen-covered – oak. Connie smiled ruefully in the dark at herself. The things she knew now!

Her family was gone and there was no getting them back; but she had a new family in front of her. Now there was nothing to do but move forward, even if the view didn't look as she'd hoped. She could do worse than Seppe. And anyway, the war might never end and they'd never be able to get wed. She eased her way through the whispering forest, her heart in her mouth and her will in her steps. Her future lay inside that cottage, and now it was time to go and face it.

Re-Housing of Southern England

The re-homing of Southern England has been
a subject on which Miss Raeburn, in vividly
descriptive speeches in which she gave
graphic details of the horrors endured by
the London people during the flying bomb
menace, has been talking to Forest audi-
ences, principally WVS and WIs, in the past
week or two.

Dean Forest Mercury,
Friday 26th January, 1945

1945

Forty-Three

January

CONNIE PULLED THE BEDROOM door shut behind Joe and tiptoed out. They'd been felling old-growth at the furthermost edge of the forest this week, and she was dead on her feet. Christmas seemed like months ago, not a fortnight.

Her sleep was shot at the moment, which didn't help. Disloyal thoughts of her lost chance at a better life poked up through her dreams like the pea in the old fairy tale. The trees were closing in on her in this never-ending winter, the spaces between them darker and the way through less and less obvious with every step. Sometimes she had to blink hard and touch Seppe or Joe, feel the realness of the soft flesh of their necks beneath their thick coats.

There was a knock on the door. Connie skidded down the rest of the steps and eased it open before it woke Joe back up. All her movements had got so gentle now Joe was here; nobody had told her that about babies.

'Oh!'

It was Mary, that local girl who was sweet on the chatty

335

mate of Seppe's. 'Are you looking for Joyce? She's next door.'

Mary stepped from foot to foot. It was brass-monkey weather out there today; Connie's hands had only just stopped stinging. 'I'm here for you, actually.'

'Oh! Um – right. Well, look, come on in out of the cold.' She was whispering. She stepped away from the door and ushered Mary in.

'Thank you.' Now Mary was whispering, too. She was a pretty little thing; Connie could see why that Gianni had fallen for her.

They stood facing each other in the narrow hallway as if preparing for a quickstep. Connie wasn't sure what to do, it'd been so long since she'd spent time with any of the girls.

'Are you all right to talk out here? Amos is in the kitchen – I don't . . .'

Mary shook her head quickly. 'I won't keep you long, like.' She had the sort of smile that pulled a smile out of you in return.

'Seppe told Gianni your news.' Mary rummaged around in her handbag. 'I wanted to – hang on a minute . . .' She pulled out a battered lippy and a ball of string and passed them over to Connie.

'My dad's right; I could hide half the forest in here and be none the wiser. No – wait – here they are.' Mary pulled a fat parcel of newspaper from her bag. 'Have a look.'

Connie unwrapped the parcel. At least it wasn't some sodding dead animal. But this was almost more baffling.

'Clothing coupons?'

Mary's smile this time had an underskirt of trepidation.

'The thing is, Gianni and me, we're hoping to get married too. My dad loves him and he'd be great behind the bar at the Bell.' Mary straightened up against the wall.

'What I was thinking was, we're about the same size and shape, aren't we? And a wedding dress – it's going to cost a fair few bob. Gianni and me, we're still a fair way off setting a date –'

'So are we. The war's not over yet.' And there was the big question. Connie swallowed, forced herself to listen to Mary.

'Right enough, but from what Seppe's told Gianni – ' (what, exactly, had Seppe told Gianni?) '– you two will be first down the aisle. When the war's over Gianni will want to try and get his mamma over and we'll need to save for that. So we could pool our coupons, buy the one dress for more than maybe either of us could manage on our own?'

Mary was all lit up; even in the gloom, her eyes were sparkling. Connie swallowed. That's how she should be feeling about getting wed.

'We could even take a trip to Gloucester or to Cheltenham, see if one of them big stores had something a bit fancier? But I want you to hold on to the coupons.' That beam again. She was so happy, this girl. Connie had almost forgotten you could be this kind of carefree.

Mary leaned in and palmed the coupons to Connie.

'Here – you take 'em for now so you do know I mean it. No big rush, but when you're ready you let me know and we'll get travel permits sorted out, have a trip to the big city.' She looked ready to explode with happiness. Connie's heart sank, but she stuffed them in her overall pockets.

'Dad'll be needing me behind the bar. I'll see you soon, shall I? It's so nice to have someone to share all this with!'

The front door shut behind Mary and Connie leaned against it, eyes closed. That's how she should be, like Mary, all thrilled about marrying her Italian sweetheart. But all Connie could think of when Mary was babbling on about 'big cities' was her grand plans, now in tatters.

Seppe must know she wasn't sure, even if only by talking to Gianni and seeing how excited Mary was. She kicked one heel against the door, hard. Poor Seppe, knowing and not knowing. What was wrong with her that she couldn't be keener?

The coupons were lies in her pocket . . .

She leaned her head on the door, trying to make sense of it all. She couldn't go on like this. She'd make Seppe miserable as well as herself, to say nothing of Joe.

The knocker banged again and she jumped a foot. What was that now? Connie cracked it open.

'Joyce! What are you doing here? It's like Piccadilly Circus round here this evening.'

'Shh!' Joyce had pressed herself up against the house wall as if she was a spy. The thought made Connie giggle.

'Didn't want to come round the back, give Amos cause to know something's up.'

'What is up, Joycie? I'm none the wiser myself, to be honest with you.'

'I've been thinking and thinking about Christmas Day and what you said.' Joyce palmed something small into Connie's hand. But it wasn't coupons this time.

'What the hell's this?' Connie squinted. A piece of the *Mercury*. '"No lights on bicycles"? Joyce, that's hardly cloak-and-dagger stuff. And I've told you, I don't ever take that old boneshaker out; they ain't going to get me.'

Joyce shook her head and turned over Connie's hand. 'Not that, you ha'porth. *This*.' She jabbed at something scrawled in the margin. 'Didn't have time to find a bit of paper. Just saw it in Frank's papers now. He doesn't know I've seen it, much less that I've shown it you. He'd do his nut.'

'This' was an address in London.

'What you playing at, Joyce?'

338

'Shh, keep your voice down! Look what it is.'

'It's some fancy war department in London, I can see that. So what?'

'They're looking for workers to help rebuild the big cities after all that bombing they've had. Seems a bit daft to be doing it in the middle of the war, but I suppose the people in the cities need somewhere to live and they can't wait until the war's stopped.'

'What's that got to do with me?' But Connie stood upright, peered again at the paper through the murk.

'They need people who know heavy work, fitting joists and that, rebuilding houses. Wouldn't be so different from timberwork, that's why they sent it to Frank.' Joyce rolled her eyes. 'I expect they were after men, the dozy ha'porths, but you work harder than half the men out there, Frank do tell me so.' Joyce reached down and pulled a fag from her packet, staring straight ahead as she cupped her hands to light it.

'Bloody hell, Joyce.' Connie clenched the bit of paper so hard it almost ripped. She stuffed it in her pocket out of harm's way and it rustled beside the coupons, one secret almost betraying another.

Joyce tugged her sweater closer round her. 'I'd better be off. Frank thought I was only popping out to the lav; he'll be after me with the cod liver oil if I stay out here any longer.'

'See you, Joycie. And Joyce . . .'

Joyce laid a quick hand on Connie's arm. 'I know, lovie.' And then she was gone, too.

Connie belted up the stairs, her heart racing. The bedroom door swung open and she fell to her knees as if the air-raid siren had gone off. She stretched under the bed and groped around in the dark for her suitcase to hide the coupons and advert in, one eye on the cot to make sure Joe didn't wake.

She eased up the lid of the suitcase. *That smell.*

Hillview Road was inside the case still, Mam's Yardley and the talc from the littluns, even Dad's brew. The only place they were left now.

She slammed the suitcase shut, Joe momentarily forgotten, and gulped back some sense. *Come on, Connie.*

She sat down on the edge of the bed, head pillowed on the battered leather of the suitcase. Through the floorboards rose the smell of the ash in the grate, the noise of Amos tapping his foot on the floor. Life would go on without her.

Forty-Four

'THIS NEW YEAR ISN'T bringing us any new food, then. 1945 will be the year of slop, just like 1944.' Gianni pushed away his plate in mock disgust, but Seppe paid no attention. Gianni barely ever ate the camp food these days. He seemed to have most of his meals at Mary's father's pub, where rationing somehow didn't come into things.

'Don't agitate yourself about your precious trees!' he'd scoffed when Seppe had mentioned the risk of a blaze (there was no point asking where the bacon came from). 'It's so damp here you should be building us all an ark. My bacon is safe.'

'If you're not going to eat that, hand it over.'

It was still odd to hear Fredo's voice and not have the urge to cower. Fredo nodded at Seppe as he lifted Gianni's food over Seppe's head. Fredo without Livorno to fight for was a hawk whose wings had been clipped. These days he sought out Seppe, desperate to talk to someone from home, to keep home alive through conversation now that it existed only in his memory. Seppe could have these conversations only if the whittling knife and wood were firm and warm in his hand, acting as a conduit back to happier times with Renzo and a reminder that not every memory of Livorno was unbearable. Fredo, Seppe noted wryly, seemed oblivious to what it cost Seppe to have these conversations.

Everything was changing, little by little. If only Connie seemed happier, he could say he'd found peace. Surely she was happy, now they knew for certain what their future would look like? He ignored the whispers in his head that encroached late at night, reminded him she'd never said this was the future she wanted.

'This came for you.' One of the kitchen team dropped something on Seppe's plate and Gianni craned to look at it too.

'A letter! Haven't seen you with a letter for months – who's writing to you?'

'No idea.' Seppe's hands were steady as he opened it. His parents were dead. They had been well enough known for several residents of Livorno to make note; there had never been any possibility of doubt. For a month he had grieved for his mother, for the peace she had never known. But whatever else it contained, this letter held no terror.

The paper rustled as he unfolded it, scanned to the end. 'It's from the padre.'

'Ha! He's found out about you and the *inglesa*,' Gianni teased. 'Hell will be upon you.'

'Even the padre doesn't have that much power!' The words skittered as Seppe sped through the letter. He sagged back on the bench.

'He has met with my brother-in-law. With Bruno.'

'You have a sister? All these months and you've never told me that?'

'She died.' His breath remained steady. 'Her husband's been discharged; wounded. Bruno doesn't manage his letters

342

very well, so he's been to see the padre, asked him to make contact.' That wasn't all the padre was saying, but Gianni didn't need the rest. '*I have noted that your father died in the bombings. I have explained to Bruno about Alessa. We prayed together,*' wrote the priest in a sentence that held a thousand stories. And towards the end, '*Bruno sends his love, asks me to tell you that terrible things happen not only in war.*'

Seppe put the letter down and stared at it. He reached into his pocket for a handkerchief, bumped his knuckles on the whittling knife.

'Eh, *scalco*! You all right?'

'It's OK. It's good news.' The padre had shared his father's terrible secret with Bruno. It was no longer only his to carry. These tears were of relief. Of release.

Tiny nodding snowbells signalled hope. Seppe kept his voice light.

'No ring?'

Connie concentrated on her lump of cheese. 'No, not today. Must have taken it off to bath Joe last night and forgotten to put it back on.'

She hadn't worn it any day this week. He changed tack.

'Is there a problem with the ring? It's perhaps too big? You don't like the trees?'

'No, it's fine.' She glanced up at him. 'It's gorgeous, honest. I just . . .' Her sentence faded off and she tore a piece from her bread, offered it to Joe.

'It's because we're working on the spruce today?'

Now Connie was looking fully at him, puzzled.

'They are so full of sap, the spruce. It's sensible to not wear the ring.'

'Yeah, it would be. It is. Don't want to damage it.'

He leaned back against the recently felled pine.

'Have you thought any more about the wedding? We will do it here, I think, no? I can ask Frank about good churches; unless you have asked Joyce already?'

Connie shrugged. 'Nothing to think about, is there? Not 'til this war's over and you're no longer the enemy. We can't get married yet, can we? Could be years still. No point in bothering Frank and Joyce about churches and all that malarkey.'

'You're right, perhaps. But I like to think about it, like to consider our life. As a family. And I know you love to dance, or used to at least. I thought you might have ideas for our celebration.' He cupped her face in his hands and Connie stood up abruptly, brushing the crumbs off her greatcoat.

'No time for daydreams, me. Too much to be getting on with.' She looked over at Joe, trying and failing to scale the lumber. 'Does he need a change? I can't remember.'

Seppe got up too. 'The last change was before this tree came down. I'll do him now.'

'Cheers, Seppe. I'll get checking, see which tree's next to get down.' So they were back on familiar territory. He heard Amos's voice in his head. 'Don't go fretting about it.' But he did.

Forty-Five

February

HER SUITCASE WAS ALL ready on the bed; she'd packed most of it when the jumpers were boiling earlier. Time to get her skates on if she wanted to be gone before anyone arrived home. It might be mid February, but the days didn't seem to be getting any longer, the trees sucking up what passed for light. Everyone would knock off work once this winter gloom got too much.

Connie pulled a face at the tiny woollies draped over the range and the fireplace with bits of Amos's twine that she'd found on the mantelpiece. How did Joyce do the wash for them all, week in week out, and stay so cheerful? Felling was a piece of cake compared to this. Connie's gut had been right all along; she'd be hopeless at this kind of life. Her knuckles were bright pink from bashing the big wooden spoon against Joe's clothes and frozen from the shock of the February cold after the boiling water. Her eyes streamed from the viciousness of the carbolic. There was nothing on the box to say how much to use, so she'd chucked in a good dollop to be safe. She hadn't been totally sure it was even the right box but she was trying her best. The clothes would end up all ashy, but she couldn't risk anyone seeing them out on the line all at once.

Connie grabbed a pullover and held it to her cheek. Dry enough. She carried it over to the kitchen table and laid it down, sleeves tucked underneath, then went back for another one. Soon there was a tidy pile on the table. Connie stepped back and looked at it for a moment. The smell of the carbolic wasn't so bad now it was hidden a bit by the smoke of the range.

Connie carried the pile upstairs. Joe was still asleep in his cot. She gently lowered the piles, flattening them so that they didn't tip over. 'Your clothes have never been this smart, isn't that right, baby?' she murmured in his direction. He threw up an arm, chasing rainbows in his sleep, and she smiled. 'That's a yes, then.'

Connie looked back over at Joe and stepped towards the crib but then thought better of it. Amos and Seppe might have the golden touch with the baby, but she was the opposite. One last stroke from her and he'd be awake and screaming blue murder. She sniffed, but the blockage in her throat didn't shift.

She pulled another of Joe's woollies from the drawer and shunted it shut with her hip. Thank God Joyce had knitted him so many. Connie laid it on top of the rest of the belongings already in the case, then snapped it shut and swung it to the ground. It was lighter than when she'd arrived months earlier.

One last thing to do. She pulled the letter from the pocket of her overalls. It had got damp from the laundry and bits of woodchip had stuck to it. The ink had run a bit but you could still make out the curve of the S.

She propped it up next to Joe's bottle. It slid down so

she propped it back up with fingers that had started to tremble and grabbed her suitcase.

The baby grunted and snuffled, finding his way into his dreams and her arms ached to pick him back up and give him one more cuddle. If only she didn't love him as much as she did. If only she could close off the bit of her that loved him, the way she could with Mam and them, find a way to get through life without the loss swallowing her. But this was the best way. They'd all come round, given time.

Connie left the room, took the stairs as quickly as she could. Her socks were all wet from the washing; she slipped, grabbing the banister before she came a cropper. The suitcase crashed down into the hall, banging against the wall as it went.

Behind Connie, Joe began to wail. She sat down on the stair and rested her head on the newel post. He'd calm down in a minute and then she could go.

But he didn't stop. The noise must have really scared him. She pushed her hands on her thighs and heaved her way back up the stairs. The baby frowned at her through his wails and she swallowed hard as she picked him up.

'Come on, babba. It was just a bit of noise. Not as loud as the trees coming down, was it?' She rocked him and the crying became less panicked. *Come on, baby, come on.* How was it possible to so badly want to make it all better for him and at the same time want to scream in frustration? Connie placed Joe gently back in the cot and tiptoed towards the door. She didn't dare look back this time.

Before she'd got halfway there, he was roaring again. She didn't know whether to cry or scream. How many times – how many, many times had he done this? She loved him so, so much but right now it was taking all she had to unclench her fists and not shriek at him, the guilt sharpening every emotion, slicing through her.

'Oh, little one, it'll be all right, you'll see.' What if she walked him round a bit? 'Look out there – see all the birds on the trees? You'll know all their names soon enough if Amos has his way. He'll look after you, you know that, babba, don't you? And Seppe. Seppe's a good man. Don't you ever think me leaving like this has anything to do with him. Or with you – you mustn't ever think that. But I have to try. I have to find out what my life could be like, and we're both better off in our own place. This is where you belong, with the trees and the sheep and the people you've known all your life. Me, I need noise and strangers and situations that change. Those are terrible things for a kid, I know that much, and when you're bigger you'll know it too. London's no place for a baby, not even in peacetime, and you've never known peacetime, my little man. You're in good hands here – the best. There's nobody kinder than Amos, don't let him fool you. And Seppe . . .'

Connie stopped, dug in her coat pocket for her handkerchief. Just as well she'd kept it close by. She scrubbed at her eyes and sniffed. Joe batted at her wet cheeks and she clasped his hand in hers.

'Mam would have understood – your nanny – she always told me I was a wanderer. Maybe you'll grow up to be a wanderer too, my little Forest baby, eh? Then you'll understand.'

He'd quietened right down as if he was listening to her. She should put him back in the crib now and get on with it, but how could she? These were the good times, the times it all seemed almost worth it, when he was warm and snuggly and gazing up at her as if she was the only person in the world who cared about him. When he was quiet and she had him to herself and she could allow herself to think, *I made him. He's mine, the only person who will ever really know me now.* In these moments, nothing else mattered.

'You're a fierce little thing too, aren't you, my love? You'll understand better than most, once you're old enough. But don't you ever think it was because of you, or because of any of them. It's because of *me*. I'm just not any good at this and I need to get out of here before I wreck things for you and for Seppe too.

'I've got to go now, my love, or I'll miss my train. But I love you.' She'd never said that to anyone before. She never would again, now she knew how much it hurt.

Joe was properly calm again now, gurgling, his thumb firmly in his mouth, three fingers curled over his little button nose. As Connie bent down and placed him back in the crib, the envelope with its laundry-soaked writing caught her eye. She stretched across and grabbed it, stuffed it back into her pocket. What could a letter possibly explain? It would only make things worse. Writing would be a cop out. It might make her feel better in the short term, but it would hardly do poor Seppe much good to read the damn thing. She was going to break his heart and that was a terrible, terrible thing; she couldn't draw it out with any hope a letter might bring. She needed to shoulder this guilt as if it was the trunk of an oak, not try to lop bits off it and wait for Seppe to let her off the hook. In time, when she was settled, she could write to the baby and explain it all to him.

She was careful on the stairs this time, hanging on to the rail the whole way down. She stuffed her feet into her boots, picked up the case and eased the door shut behind her. Upstairs, Joe slept on.

Forty-Six

A MOS HAD SPENT A good two hours hunting for the ewes in the frost, bitter even for February. The daffs were pushing up valiantly through mostly frozen ground but he'd lose a couple of ewes in this cold snap, no doubt about it.

By the time he came upon them huddled beside the bridge arch near Soudley Ponds, his fingers stung with cold and he had to stamp his feet to feel them again.

'May as well go home for our bread, eh, Bess?'

When they reached the edge of the oaks, Amos stopped and examined the garden wall. The old stones had finally slipped completely in this cold snap. Might not be a bad idea to do away with a few of them instead of repairing it, maybe put in a gate out to that hut of Seppe's, now that it was almost ready to live in. Be easier than hauling the baby over the drystones every time.

Bess had gone on ahead and was barking at the kitchen door like she was fit to burst, throwing herself at it in her efforts to get in.

'What's the matter, old girl?' Had Connie left the door

open when she went off to work this morning and a fox slipped in or summat? But if the door was open, Bess would have no trouble getting in herself. Better get up there and find out.

He wasn't more than halfway past the apple trees when he heard the racket over Bess's yelps. It was Joe, wailing worse than a trapped lamb. Amos was in the house and up the stairs as fast as he could manage, following the commotion into Connie's room.

'All right, my boy, all right. I've got you.' Joe was wriggling in his arms, pink and raging, his pullover soaked. That wasn't the only part of him that was soaked and more too, judging by the stink.

Where was Connie?

'Don't you worry, old butt. It ent the work of a minute to sort you out. Then we'll get you downstairs, give you some milk. You must be starving.'

Joe settled down all right as soon as he'd had a bottle. Where had Connie got to? Had she gone noseying around in the parlour again, passed out after one too many sneaky swigs from May's bottle?

Amos pushed open the parlour door. This room still bore traces of absences, of May and of the things he'd sold to try and save her. Even now he couldn't step foot into it without the gaps of loneliness hitting him. The bottle of liquor wasn't all the way empty, but it wasn't far off. And there was something glinting beside it.

It was a ring: silvery, with gemstones of some kind, and trees etched into the silver.

Amos stood where he was and considered the ring. Foreboding drifted onto the sorrow he felt constantly about his Billy. This didn't augar well, not at all well. And it would fall to him to break it to Seppe, looks of things.

'Come on, little one.' He hoisted Joe onto his shoulder.

The babby was all snuggly and heavy, felt like he might drop off. 'Time to go and find Seppe.'

Seppe saw Amos crunching his way towards him on the frozen leaves, Joe drooped over his shoulder, and dropped the axe.

'What's the matter with him?'

'Nowt, he's just dropped off, that's all. It's our Con I'm out here for. She left him at home and that ent like her.'

Oh, *Connie*. Seppe's body relaxed in shameful relief. 'She didn't arrive this morning. She said yesterday that she might be a bit late, but she didn't say why. Sometimes with Connie I do not ask.'

But she should be here by now, and she hadn't mentioned leaving Joe at the cottage. Worry was icing his blood again, along with shame. Seppe wrapped the blade in the tarpaulin, wiped his hands on his overalls to get rid of the sap from the softwoods, which had oozed through his gloves. Something had happened to Connie and he hadn't even noticed.

'How's she been with you these last few weeks?'

'You know. Like Connie.' But quieter and crosser. Like Connie with the sap leached out. Seppe fiddled with the tarpaulin. Two evenings ago he'd run his finger along the down on her neck as she twisted her hair into her beret and she'd pushed his hand away, stared at him as if she was about to say something but then hadn't. It was this that had struck him the most keenly. He'd tried to put it out of his mind since then.

'Actually, not so much like Connie. But I thought, perhaps it is her getting used to marrying.' She had turned away, shaking her head when he'd asked what the matter was.

'Aye; she's been a darn sight less chopsy in the house, too. You know anything about this, then?' Seppe leaned forward. Amos was holding out a ring. Connie's ring. *His ring.*

He scrambled, pulse instantly racing.

'Perhaps she took it off to do the dishes, forgot to put it back on?'

Amos half laughed. 'Our Con, do the dishes?'

Amos paused. This was never good news. Seppe saw doubt and his worry amplified.

'I'll find Joyce. She must know where Connie's gone.'

'I'll come with you.'

'Suit yourself.' But Amos's tone was gentle, and Amos waited until Seppe had stuffed the bundle of tools under his arm before setting off back down the path. Why was he being so solicitous? What did Amos suspect? Seppe's heart hammered faster than the woodpecker in spring.

Over Amos's shoulder, Joe beamed at Seppe, stretched out his fingers. Seppe hoisted the tools more securely and reached out for Joe's hand. Surely nothing bad could come of today. He couldn't let himself think it.

'No sign of Joyce, nor Connie.' Amos rounded the corner from Joyce's front door and came back to them in the garden, stamping his feet.

'Maybe they are somewhere together? They have gone to the cinema, perhaps?' Seppe's heart banged against his ribs. Behind them, a buzzard called, the sound hooping and looping.

'Do you think that girl would nip off to the pictures when she had trees to get down?' Amos smiled, but there was nothing to smile about. 'And it do be Thursday, don't it? Joyce'll be up the butchers no doubt, gassing for hours. Nowt for it then but to check our Con's room.'

'But you have done this already, no?'

'Not to look for her. To see what's gone.' Amos held Seppe's gaze. 'I don't think she's just popped out to the shops, lad, and I don't think you do either, not really.'

Amos wouldn't dream of going anywhere near Connie's

belongings unless he had real cause for concern. Seppe's feet were leaden on the stairs.

Upstairs in Connie's – Billy's – room, Amos pushed open the window, seemingly oblivious to the temperature – 'better get some fresh air on us' – and Seppe smiled despite himself. Connie always complained about Amos's habit of letting air into every room. 'Even when it's freezing out there! How can he think it actually does you any good?' But she wasn't here to protest now, that much was clear.

Amos put Joe down and bent down to look under the bed, hands on knees. 'Have a look in the closet, will you, boy? Soon find out what's what.'

'We should wait and see if she is back at teatime?' It was hollow. He felt sick with the impending truth.

'Look, if she do show up for her vittals, we'll tell her we was worried about her. She'll see the sense in that. But standing around doing nowt only gets us nowhere fast.'

There was no hiding from Amos's frankness. Seppe pulled open the closet door, bracing one hand on the frame to tug it open. How had Connie put up with that all these months? His fingers clenched for the plane, lying downstairs in the roll of tools.

The closet was confusing, the single rail within barely bothered by clothes. An old navy sweater, worried away at the cuffs, a pair of working trousers, clean and pressed but faded still. A man's clothes.

'I'm – I . . . ' He pointed.

Amos, bent down to check under the bed, glanced up. 'Billy's.'

'Then there is nothing of Connie's in here.'

Amos pushed back upright, leaning on the bed. 'Her suitcase has gone, too. But there's letters or summat stuck under here that might give us a clue. Give us a hand with the bed, lad.'

Seppe's mouth was sour, hollow panic creeping in, but

he stepped forward and heaved at a corner of the mattress. Connie must have written him a note to explain where she was, and it had slipped under here. She wouldn't leave him, not in the middle of their plans, however ambivalent about them she might be. He knew her better than that. She'd have said something. The thoughts flurried, a chaos of autumn leaves. The mattress slipped as his hand shook and his thumb got trapped against the bedstead. '*Cazzo!*' He sucked on it, furiously, but the pain only intensified. He had to try again. There must be a clue here somewhere that they were missing. What Amos wasn't saying pulsed in Seppe and he needed proof, needed it right now, needed to know that Connie was somewhere safe and coming back later. Needed proof that she loved him and she hadn't left him. *Needed proof that he was worthwhile.*

The mattress was heavier than it looked, and thicker than any Seppe had seen for years. Even the weight of this against his shoulder made his back twinge with the memory of the hard slats of his bunk through the breath-thin matting. He peered from under it, the weight and the worry building.

'You're all right there, Seppe, you can drop that now. I've got 'em.' Amos backed out and showed Seppe the blue envelopes, crumpled and grimy. Seppe subsided onto the bed, anchoring Joe in his lap.

Outside, the buzzard called again, boasting, and was answered by the naked rustle of the branches. A twig tapped on the window as if it knew the answer.

Amos perched on the edge of the bed. Joe cooed at him and Amos put a hand out and ruffled his hair without looking, distracted. He placed the letters down as if they were unexploded bombs. The whittling blade was cool and reassuring against the ball of Seppe's thumb, his breath coming hard and fast. One of those envelopes would be for him; a clarification of her absence, a reminder of a

355

forgotten conversation that explained her going away temporarily.

'Best get on with it, then.' The envelope shivered in Amos's papery fingers. Seppe flicked through them one by one, his shoulders hunching as he progressed. Three different names, all going to the same address in Coventry.

And one to a Don someone. He passed the last one back to Amos, head down, ashamed. He was stupid to think she'd written to him. Joe shifted in his lap.

'I can't open them.' He couldn't bear it. She hadn't left him any note, but she had written to those little sisters of hers, and the smallest one couldn't even read. She had been desperate to talk to someone – anyone – but not to him. And he'd thought they were becoming intimate.

Jealousy stabbed Seppe, chased away by humiliation. Whatever those envelopes held, they would only make things worse now.

'You can still open them, son.' Amos held it out to Seppe but he shook his head, turned away.

'You do it.'

'Summat she meant to send, by the looks of it.' So that was what Connie's writing looked like – a careful hand, but slanted as if written by someone in a tearing hurry. He smiled before being drawn into the words themselves.

73 Hillview Road
Coventry
25ᵗʰ August, 1944

Dear Mam,

Congratulations – you're a granny! Baby Joseph William was born right in the middle of August. Don't have a go at me, will you?

After that night when I told you I'd be home and then wasn't – after that and then a bit – I joined this thing called the Women's Timber Corps. I'm in the middle of a forest down near Bristol. It's the arse end of nowhere but it's safe. No doodle bugs, no sirens. Too safe, tell you the truth. Nothing going on.

The work's top notch. I took to it right away and I'm good at it. Damn good at it, actually, and nobody's more surprised than me to hear me saying that.

It's more than I can say about my baby-raising skills. I wish I'd known how hard it was. I'd have helped you out more, mithered less about minding the littluns.

I miss you, Mam. I miss you all so much. Even Pa, sometimes. And Babs and Linda – I miss them kicking and squirming around in the bed at night. Just as well Joe don't leave me much time for kip, eh?

I wish I could know you've forgiven me for not coming home that night and leaving you in a bind. I wish you were here to tell me how to do this. I'm sorry, Mam.

Give those ragamuffins a hug and a kiss from their big sister,
TTFN,
Connie

'Well, I'll be blowed.' Amos balled his hands.

Seppe pulled Joe closer to him. The baby smelled of warm oblivion.

'I think this is written after her family is killed.' He'd tried again to talk to Connie about her family after they'd agreed to get married (had that really been what they'd agreed? Already it seemed so improbable). Connie had withdrawn, arms crossed over her body, and he had left it alone. Families weren't always good news.

'Killed?'

Amos peered again at the letter, muttering the words under his breath. After he finished it the second time he sat with it open on his lap, staring at Billy's clothes where they hung in the wardrobe. The window rattled in the breeze and the letter lifted slightly. Amos steadied it with a gnarled hand, turned to Seppe.

'Reckon you do be right, lad. Well.'

He scored open the second letter and the faintest waft of scent came into the room. Before Seppe could check himself, he looked around for Connie, even in this room so full of her.

'Cripes.' Amos tilted the letter slightly to one side and gave Seppe a look. What was the problem? Seppe twisted, grasping Joe more firmly, until he could read it.

USAF Station Grafton Underwood
Warwickshire
25th August, 1944

Dear Don,

I'm sending this to the barracks but for all I know you're out and fighting by now. Got no other way of contacting you so this seemed worth a shot.

Struggling to put a face to the name, are you? If I've got your measure, there will have been plenty of girls since me. And time has passed since we last saw each other.

Plenty of time for things to come clear. That's right, Yankee, you're a daddy. Father to a son and heir, as it turns out – master Joseph William.

Sorry to spring this on you, Don. It was a hell of a shock for me, too, to be honest. I suppose it was asking too much for those chances we took to come to nothing. But no use crying over spilt milk, eh? Better to make the most of the hand we're dealt. Don't worry, I want nothing from you. I've got everything sorted out – well, sort of.

I just thought a man deserved to know about his son. Give you something to fight for maybe, when you're out there. And if you don't want to know him, well, just pretend this letter never reached you. Nobody will be any the wiser.

Hope you're well. We had a good time, didn't we?
Connie

Who was this Yankee, who blasted through women faster than munitions and remembered none of them? This was Joe's father, here in the letter. Joe's actual father, and Joe – this warm, funny baby who beamed every time he saw Seppe, who would reach out his arms and bounce to be picked up – had never known his real father. *His real father.* Seppe swallowed hard but the thought wouldn't clear.

He couldn't sit down, not any more; the thought was too much. Seppe moved Joe onto Amos's lap and stood up.

'Do you think she has gone to meet this American?'

'Don't be daft. She didn't even post the letter, did she?'

'But maybe she has gone to find him, to tell him about Joe.' Perhaps Connie would rather marry this – this Yank – than him. Perhaps she thought that if Joe needed any father at all, he needed his real one. Perhaps he, Seppe, had made this happen, by bringing up the idea of marriage. Self-loathing rushed back and tears threatened at the back of his eyes. It was all too much, too much. He had taken what they had and destroyed it. His heart pounded and he had to sit down again.

Amos folded the letter back into the envelope. 'Well, maybe she has and maybe she hasn't. We don't know where she is. Perhaps Joyce'll know, when she's back from the shops. But far as I see it right now, Connie's done a flit and the bab's been left here with us. So it's up to us to look after him. Simple as that.'

'Done a flit?' Seppe stared at Amos. He could understand most things Amos said these days, but that couldn't be the right phrase.

'Gone, lad.'

Something tipped in Seppe's brain and he reached out a hand to steady himself against the dizziness. It was like losing Alessa all over again. But this time he'd done everything he could and still he had lost Connie.

'No. No. She isn't gone. She can't be gone.' His disbelief racketed around the room and Joe whimpered. 'She isn't gone. You mustn't say such things. The baby will be upset.'

Why was Amos looking at him like that, so soft and sympathetic? He didn't need pity; he needed Amos to stop saying things that weren't true. He swallowed hard.

'She's gone, Seppe. Facts is facts. You can see that, lad. But our Joe's right as rain. Look at him.'

Seppe couldn't look; wouldn't look. Anger was pulsing in after the disbelief, his cheeks growing hot. How could she leave him? They were planning a future together. This was to be his home – *their* home. His family. Amos was wrong.

'She will return tonight.' But nobody took a suitcase on a day trip. He stuffed his fist in his pocket but the point of the knife stabbed him and he pulled his hand out again. She didn't care for him. Didn't care about him. But he loved her. Loved Joe. Loved the promise of their future. He had scared her away.

Seppe sat down on the floor before his legs gave way, and pulled Joe into his lap.

'But how can she have gone? Joe's still here. She must have not meant to go.' She wouldn't leave him behind.

But what did he know – what did any of them know – about what Connie would or wouldn't do?

'She'd planned it, all right. Look.' Amos pulled open a drawer on Connie's nightstand and Seppe stared.

'Joe's clothes. I see that. But what? She'll collect these when she comes back for him.'

'Look closer.'

Seppe lifted Joe into the crib and went over to Amos.

'What?' The anger rose again. Who cared about clothes when Connie had gone who knows where? Amos was wasting time, distracting him like he was the baby when all he could feel was the white-hot dread searing through him.

'You know our Connie. Good girl, but not the tidiest. See here, though.'

Amos wasn't going to quieten down about the clothes until Seppe looked. He went over to the chest of drawers, looked inside again. Now he saw it, though he wished he didn't. The clothes all looked clean – and they were so neat! Arranged in careful stacks in the drawers, not thrown in higgledy-piggledy. Ordered. She had put everything in order.

He pressed down hard on the whittling knife and it dug into his thigh. The pain was a throbbing relief. *Good.* Anything was better than this.

'But how can she leave Joe?' *How can she leave me?*

Amos shook his head as he closed up the drawer again. 'The babby'll be all right. You can trust me on this. You and me look after him most of the time anyways, don't us?'

'She left us, Amos. She left me.'

'Aye, looks that way all right.'

'But for how long? What if she decides in one week, one month, one year that she is coming back? What if this American –' Seppe looked again at the letter – 'Don, what if Don decides that he will be Daddy and take Joe back to America?'

He hurled out the questions, but his head swarmed with more. Amos put a hand on his arm.

'Can't know any of that, can we? You look here. There's them as wants the sheep pen and them as wants the field. Our Con, she's a law unto herself. You know that.'

'She'll come back for Joe. And when she does, I can ask her where she's going.'

'No, lad,' Amos sighed.

'I can! She's my – I – she has to tell me where she's going. Where she's taking Joe.' He was pacing now, the floorboards creaking, dust pushing up. Amos came and stood at the end of the bed.

'No, lad. That's not what I meant.'

It glimmered through this time. 'Joe stays with *us*?'

'This is his home.'

The baby had dozed off in the crib, one arm outflung. Seppe stroked the hair that fell across Joe's forehead, and he snuffled against Seppe's cupped hand in the manner of a newborn lamb. Connie had left them. He wasn't enough for her, his dreams too small. Amos was right. She wasn't coming back. He needed to say it, no matter how little he wanted it.

'She's gone.'

Forty-Seven

Stalag VI-G Bonn-Duisdorf*
Germany
2nd February, 1945

Dear Father,

I'm not sure if you'll have got official word before this gets to you, but if you haven't, I'm awful sorry for the dreadful shock and that it's taken me so long between letters. The good news is that I'm alive. Thought I'd better say that because a fair few of our boys copped it in that last big push, and I dare say their dads (and mams) will be getting letters from them too, only they'll be from beyond the grave, or beyond life, at least. Don't know what happens in terms of a grave when you've been involved in a blast like we saw, if I'm honest. There was a long time there I knew you wouldn't be sure if I was alive or dead and the only thing that kept me going was thinking that you wouldn't have my death letter so there was a chance for a tiny sprig of hope.

Now if I know you, the minute you're over the shock of me still being on this mortal coil, you'll be worrying about me being a prisoner. The first thing I need to say is this: it isn't too terrible, not one bit. Weren't they building POW camps up on Wynols Hill and down at Naas when I left? I'll be honest with you, this is no Wynols Hill, but it's a darn sight better than it could be. Some of the lads are griping about it being primitive, but I don't know about that. We've got a roof over our heads, and if you've never had an inside privy you don't know to miss it. It's bitter cold out here – didn't know that Germany got so frosty. Tell you the truth, I hadn't never really thought about it until a few months ago.

There's rationing here, or some form of it, but Jerry's treating us kriegies fairly – 'kriegies' is what they call us over here, something to do with the war we're in. Hard to think of them as the enemy close up, truth be told. Makes me wonder about the Jerries over in the forest, in the Wynols Hill camp. Or was it Italians you said?

I know you're not one for sentiment, but it meant the world to hear from you. I got your letter right before they captured us and it made all the difference to know you're not angry with me any more. Joyce wrote from time to time to keep me from fretting too badly, but that's nothing like hearing from you myself. I can tell you this, Father, though you might think me soppy: I took your letter back to my bunk and held it up to my nose to see if I could smell the forest still in it, hear that robin that used to keep me company outside my bedroom window. Is he still there, Father, chirping away?

Speaking of company, it sounds like you've got some with a vengeance now. A baby in the house! Joyce hadn't said anything about a lodger. And now there are two of them in there! A bit of new life about the house sounds just the ticket. That Connie must be a dab hand at felling if Frank's bending over backwards to keep her and anyone who can see their way around the trees is worth hanging on to if you ask me.

Remember how you used to pretend it was me that liked to bring them orphaned lambs home? We both know that really you loved them too. Soft as anything, you are.

I hope this finds you well, Father. I don't know how long they'll keep me here – seems like this war could go on for years yet – but I'm safe now. Never thought, when I set off, that I'd be glad to be captured by the Hun, but it turns out it's probably the best thing that could happen right now. And the Forest will be there for me when I get back, that's for certain sure.

Your affectionate son,

Billy

Forty-Eight

SEPPE CREPT UP BEHIND the hut, the snow whispering his footprints onto frozen soil. He rounded the corner and, as usual, fought the urge to close his eyes. As long as he didn't know if she was back or not, there was still hope.

Two weeks, she'd been gone. Two weeks, and not a word. The snow had come down hard, her absence loud in the silence of this shrouded landscape. Everything had changed overnight. Even the trees betrayed him now, their branches heaped with snow that disguised their contours and discharged with a muffled 'whumpf' if you got too close. Getting too close was never advisable.

Two more sets of footsteps had appeared since this morning. He *knew* she'd come back.

Seppe's steps were lighter now as he drew closer, careful not to dislodge snow into the new prints.

No – he was wrong. It was only one set. Up to the door, then back away, criss-crossing his own in a frigid dance. So she'd been here looking for him and then gone elsewhere.

But it had been recent; these prints weren't yet laced with icy borders.

Seppe followed the tracks towards the wall at the end of Amos's garden. Were these the footsteps of someone in a hurry? The length of their stride alone would tell him what sort of a mood Connie was in. He aligned himself with the indentations in the snow and matched their pace without stretching.

As Seppe's foot descended into untouched snow, something else became obvious. His footprints, in these boots, were the same length and breadth as those of his visitor. They couldn't be Connie's.

He kicked at the snow and his toes connected with yet another rock that had fallen off the wall. Stupid wall! Stupid snow. Stupid footprints. And stupid him, for daring to believe it. This had never been what he thought it was. Connie was his friend, he saw that now . . . if only he'd had the sense to slow things down. He'd got it wrong, so wrong, that night at the lake, confused by his feelings about his father's death, Fredo's volte-face and the intensity of sharing Alessa's story. Connie was being a true friend to him and he had misinterpreted and messed it all up. When would he learn that people never cared for him the way he cared for them? Since Connie had left, shame cloaked Seppe, weighed down his shoulders, softened his responses to Frank, to Amos. His felling rate had dropped and he'd done no new work on the hut.

Those footprints belonged to Amos. Seppe looked again, saw paw prints interleaving the footsteps. Of course it was Amos. How could he have been so naïf?

Amos must have been watching out for him; he was at the door almost as Seppe arrived.

'What is it? Was I supposed to be with Joe?' It was difficult to remember sometimes when Amos needed him to have the baby and when Amos himself was caring for Joe. Last week they had both fed him a bottle. Joyce had suggested they work out a rota, but Seppe had refused. What was the point of a system when Connie would be back soon?

'Want to take extra fodder up to the ewes. No chance of them grazing, not in this, and they're in lamb. Need to eat, they do.'

'You want me to take it up, this fodder?'

Amos pulled his coat off the fireguard and shrugged it on. It steamed still where it hadn't fully dried out from before.

'No, you stay here with our Joe. He's asleep up there now, napkin's fresh. If you hear him, just go and deal with him. Everything's in the usual place.' Amos fizzed with energy that seemed out of place in such bitter, endless times. Seppe understood that Billy being safe was a wonderful thing for Amos, but the knot in his stomach wound itself into resentment. The Foresters all seemed certain that when the war ended, it would end in victory for the Allies. He wanted to tell them tales of the war, of the British men he'd seen up close, noses harshed with desert burn, eyes wide and desperate. This wasn't a war with a big strategy on any side, not that he'd seen. It was a war of one man fighting one man, man after man after man until the side that was the most depleted was vanquished, could give no more even though he cared no less. This, he wanted to say, this is what war is. It's petty and it's dirty and it's uncertain, even when the enemy is pointing his rifle at you and shrieking at you in a language so distorted by fear that you don't know if it's an order or a warning.

Let's say the Foresters were right, though. This is where the resentment really kicked in, and Seppe despised himself for it. When this war was finally done, Billy would come back here, to all this and a father who loved him. He had nothing of the sort and now it would seem that he wouldn't even have Connie. There had still been no word for him, no indication that she had any intention of returning soon.

Amos stamped into his boots, oblivious to Seppe's bitterness, or misunderstanding its roots. He pulled his cap down tight over his ears and whistled for Bess. 'Come on, girl. You and me've got a job to do.' He paused, one hand on the door latch. 'You'll miss dinner up at Wynols Hill again. There's a bit of pie keeping warm in the range.'

'Thank you.' Joyce kept nagging him to let the camp guards know he was helping here, relaxed as they were about curfews. But he didn't see the point for just a few weeks. Frank had been telling the camp boss Seppe was needed for heavy felling duties; after all, it had been true once before.

'Least I could do.' Amos opened the door, half glanced in Seppe's direction.

'And.'

Amos often paused, weighed out his words before continuing. Seppe waited. Amos shuffled his feet. The ball of resentment reconfigured, serpents winding anxiety up into Seppe's throat.

'Amos.' But he couldn't ask either, couldn't dare to hear something he couldn't bear.

Amos looked at Seppe, swallowed, then opened his mouth again. Seppe had seen him take this approach when lambing; one sharp shock then it was all over. He braced himself without meaning to.

'There's a letter. Joyce heard from her.'

'From *Connie?*' The serpents writhed.

Amos shuffled again. 'She's fine.'

He slipped out of the door, his boots crunching on compacted snow. As he eased the door into place, he breathed the final words into the closing gap between indoors and outdoors. 'She sent our Joe her love but she's not coming back, seems like.'

The words hung there, hot in the cold breath of the hallway. Seppe slid down the wall, past the pictures of Billy and May in the wooden frames he'd made for Amos at Christmas.

'She's fine.' That was it? He opened the door, slammed it again for the sheer wilfulness of the movement. The pictures rattled in their frames.

Fine? He wasn't fine. Fine was not an admissible word here. It wasn't even the truth. Seppe paced up and down, the emotion that had evaded him when Livorno burned roaring in now, hot and all-consuming. 'Fine' was not abandoning your child and telling nobody where you were going. 'Fine' was not leaving your betrothed with no word and no clue. 'Fine' was *not* writing to Joyce but not even bothering to write to the person who had offered you everything.

He stiffened against the wall and resisted the urge to kick it. If Connie had wanted to be in touch with him, she could have done it. If he didn't even merit correspondence of his own, then she couldn't expect him to go begging to Joyce to pore over a second-hand letter. It wasn't for him to chase after her. He had more backbone than that, whatever she apparently believed.

That was it, then. He narrowed his eyes. He had no choice, but he'd been in that situation before. All he could do was what was in front of him. And that meant building the hut, continuing out on the felling sites with whichever partner Frank found him, and making sure Joe had everything he needed.

Except a mother.

He reached for the whittling knife, found a nub of wood, and dug in hard.

THE STARS ARE COMING TO CINDERFORD GRAND
CONCERT

Specially in aid of Returned P.O.W.s
TOWN HALL, CINDERFORD, SATURDAY, JUNE
16TH
Presentation during show to a number of
Cinderford lads home from prison. Roll up
and give them the Forest Welcome.
ADMISSION 2d / Get your tickets now
Dean Forest Mercury, Friday,
6th June, 1945

June 1945

Forty-Nine

'COME ON, YOU! HAVEN'T you heard? They've posted the demob orders in the parade ground. The first convoys leave for Italy next month!' The door to the barrack clanged behind Gianni as it raced back on its hinges.

'Demob?'

Gianni cuffed Seppe lightly on the back of the head and ducked around him as he bounded down the steps.

'What kind of a soldier are you? Demobilisation orders! We could be kissing Italian soil again within weeks! Me, I am taking a photograph of Mary to show Mamma and then she will love her as much as I do, and Mary and I can be married!' He ducked between two of the ablutions huts and was out of range.

Four weeks today since the war was over. Victory in Europe. Seppe still hadn't established how he felt about this. The war was at an end, and in theory this was good. But what would happen to him now? Every night since 8th May he'd lain awake chasing his thoughts until the blackbird switched places with the owl.

Seppe stared at the clothes peg in his hand. It was one of a set he was making for Joyce, the divide down its centre still jagged and unfinished. In the warm June wind, dead leaves scuttled at the steps to the hut. How could demobilisation be so soon? It wasn't possible. He couldn't – wouldn't – leave, couldn't go back to Livorno. He was never going back. But would the powers that be make him? How did this work in practice? Gianni's plans to marry his English girl could be pie in the sky for all they knew. Seppe's hand grew sweaty on the smooth metal of the whittling knife. Could he stay now anyway, without Connie? She was in every swing of the axe, every fret of the saw. He missed the most trivial things about her – that little 'ah!' of satisfaction when a tree started to fall in the direction she'd meant it to, the brush of her eyelashes up against his cheek. Staying here without her was to be abraded by memories, a thousand dropped needles of pain in every pace. To leave here, though, would be to walk away from the thread that bound them.

And what about Joe? Since Connie had left, Seppe's days had been too full to think of the future, his mind too empty. Getting to Amos's cottage after the day's felling, handing Joe back over, helping to feed him or change him, getting back to camp without arousing questions from Gianni or Fredo – this took time, and energy. Until VE Day he had had no time for thought, had welcomed even the break from it, the way his mind shut down with sheer physical activity. After VE Day, all action had slowed as if the forest were waiting to see what came of it next.

Another pair of campmates pushed past him on the step, hell-bent to the parade ground from the looks of things. Already the noise levels were rising, the chatter drumming like thunder. He should go and check, see if his name was on a list along with the others. Seppe scooped up the finished clothes pegs and carried them back into the bunk-house.

'You're going the wrong way!' someone shouted, the joy of homecoming already in their voices. He turned and joined the tide surging towards the parade ground, the shove and sweat of these men as familiar to him as his own breathing.

The noticeboard itself was obscured, the clock above it knocked askew again by the throng of men jostling to find their names. The crowd carried him forward. The camp-mate to his side, a southerner he'd never really talked to before, grabbed Seppe by the scruff of the neck and embraced him on both cheeks. 'We're going home!' Tears streamed down his cheeks. He looked at Seppe's face, recoiled. 'You don't care! How can you not care? We are going home, man!' The southerner's expression turned to disgust and he pushed Seppe roughly to one side. 'What kind of an Italian are you?'

Seppe didn't belong here. Whatever that list said, he certainly didn't belong in Italy, never really had. Finding out the details wasn't going to change that. He needed to think, but here in the middle of this departure party wasn't going to be the place for it. If he stayed here, things might erupt, just as he'd almost made it through.

He needed to talk to Frank and Amos.

Seppe heard them before he'd rounded the hut. They must be out in Amos's garden. Sure enough, as he stepped over the wall he could see them. Joyce sat on the bench, tickling a giggling Joe, with Amos and Frank bookending her. As they saw Seppe, they waved as if seeing him off for the journey of his life (and how true that might end up being). Was the good mood from the camp infectious? They were obviously delighted to be regaining their forest. His head ached.

'Seppe lad!' Frank strode through the trees towards him,

apple blossom dusting his shoulders. 'Just the person! Come and have a drink with us. We're celebrating.'

'Celebrating?'

'That's right.' Frank filled a heavy tankard with the apple-smelling substance Seppe remembered from Christmas. 'Amos got a telegram today. His Billy's coming home!'

Amos was beaming. Had he ever seen Amos even smile before? He must have done, but any memory of it was eclipsed by the sight of this: Amos's face creased into lines that must have been there all along, just never put to use these past years.

'He'll be home even before autumn dipping time, by the sounds of things. Not long at all, now.' Amos's voice was even different. Rounder, warmer.

Joyce got up too, walked over to Seppe, Joe hitched on her hip, the same smile on her face. Joe wriggled to get down and Seppe smiled despite himself. Joe had recently discovered the joys of pulling himself upright and now unless his feet were planted on the ground, he complained. Joyce sighed exaggeratedly at Joe and placed him carefully down. The baby clamped on to Seppe's trousers and started his trek to the vertical.

'Billy.' For a minute Seppe thought Joyce had forgotten his name. 'He'll be with us again soon, Seppe.'

Would anyone have wanted him, Seppe, back this dearly? Alessa, maybe. He looked down at Joe's curls. And here was someone else who hadn't met Billy, but loved and needed *him*. Seppe swallowed, reached down for Joe and pulled the baby up close. Joe giggled, patted Seppe's cheek with fat fingers. They were cold from the ground so Seppe tucked them under his chin and Joe giggled again.

Frank filled another tankard, handed it to Seppe.

'Things can go back to normal with our Billy back.' He looked over at Amos. 'I reckon we might stand a chance of persuading him to stay above ground with me now, old butt, what do you think? No need for him to go back down those drift mines.'

'You know our Billy, Frank. He'll do as he darned well pleases; always has, always will.'

'Aye, but it's worth a shot, isn't it? Your Billy knows his way round these trees better than most.'

Seppe took a long draught, the cider scorching his stomach. Frank needed more fellers for all these rebuild quotas that were pouring in. There was nothing to read into this.

'I'll need to keep a closer eye on my chickens an' all, once Billy's home and bringing back every waif and stray he can find.' Joyce's voice contained the same warmth as Amos'. 'Be just like him to bring in a fox cub because it looked lonely.'

Amos laughed. Laughed! 'Aye, and our Bess'll have to get used to sharing the rug again with whatever creature he's wrapped up and put there to get warm.'

'I can't remember a time when he didn't do it. Do you recall that . . .'

Their conversation was smooth as a stone from the brook. They span round and round the core of their memories, binding the knot that would hold fast now Billy was coming back. Seppe joggled Joe and watched them. They would be whole again, in ways they hadn't even realised they were fractured.

Joe wriggled to get down and Seppe bent to swoop him to the ground, his cider tipping with the motion. Joe crawled over to the apple tree and levered himself upright yet again, laughing at his own brilliance. It wouldn't be long before the baby was walking. Time was moving and Connie was missing it, missing her own child. If Seppe was working a long shift and didn't manage to see Joe for a day, he raced down the next day, could see a change in the child almost perceptibly. Connie had missed layer upon layer upon layer of change, the infant she'd left behind growing into this laughing, expressive non-stop child. He didn't know how she could bear to be without him. He missed her still, but in a more abstract way, missing a Connie that perhaps didn't exist as much as the one that did. Whereas nothing was less abstract than Joe, his sticky fingers in your hair, his milky breath hot on your cheek as you swooped him into the air to hear him giggle.

Seppe looked back at Amos. He'd left his crook to one side, had put down his cider tankard to describe something with his hands. Everything had been freed in Amos. His movements, his stories. Amos was never going to be Gianni – and just as well, since one Gianni was more than enough some days – but he was lighter now.

He couldn't talk to Amos, nor to Frank nor Joyce, about staying. It would be wrong to ask to stay, he saw that now. They had been kind to him, so kind – he felt for the whittling knife, safe in his pocket – but one of their own was coming home, and in watching this he understood how he could never belong.

He drained the cider, stepped round the bench and put the tankard onto the window sill beside Amos's.

'It was delicious. Thank you. And Amos . . .' He put out a hand. Amos looked confused, but shook it anyway. 'It is very good news that Billy will be home soon. I am very pleased for you all.'

'Not off, are you, lad? You've only just got here.'

He nodded, sadness loading into him with the movement. 'I must – ' He waved vaguely in the direction of the forest behind them, but Amos, already full up with his own joy, wasn't really paying attention.

'Aye, well see you in the morning, then.'

Seppe couldn't risk saying goodbye to Frank or Joyce in case it betrayed how little space they had for him now, too. He bent to kiss Joe, the long grasses around the tree tickling his neck as he did so. 'See you tomorrow, *carissimo*.' Joe gurgled and turned back to his inspection of the tree trunk.

Back at the camp, jubilation still reigned. A guard and an Italian staggered past Seppe as he passed through the truck stop back to the parade ground, hand clamped either side of some big object. It was only as he reached it that it hit him what they'd been carrying. That was one of Gianni's moonshine vats.

The parade ground was one big party. Someone had pulled Seppe's benches from the mess and guards were sitting knee to knee with campmates, matching them drink for drink by the looks of things. A line of men in wigs and costumes pilfered from the theatre congaed past. Everywhere there was singing, dancing, weeping.

Where was Gianni? But no – today wasn't going to be the day to get any sense out of him. Sorrow tugged again, laced now with a bitter anger. Why was Seppe always so out of step with everyone around him? Today should be a time for elation, he saw that, but the home that didn't want him no longer existed, and the home he thought he had here had turned out to be borrowed. Amos and Frank didn't need him, not now Billy was coming back. He'd been ridiculous to think that he could stay. It would only take another day or so and Amos would see that Seppe's hut was intrusive, that the last thing a British soldier would want at the end of his garden would be one of the enemy.

Seppe couldn't – wouldn't – voice this to Amos, nor to Frank. To say something would be to force them to confirm the rejection and they had been too good to him for him to put them in that position. He needed to be gone and not their concern by the time Billy returned.

And what about Joe? He stood stock still in front of the bulletin board, the names blurring before he'd even found his own. Joe's room was Billy's room first. Now that Billy was coming back, life was returning to normal – and normal didn't include Joe any more than it included him. Bloodlines must come first.

Blood came first. Seppe dug down hard on the knife in his pocket as he thought it through to the end. He needed to take Joe to Connie. She couldn't do this to Joe. She didn't know what she was missing, what Joe was missing. He, Seppe, had tried – would keep trying – to be the parent that Joe needed. But Seppe couldn't stay here. The gap in the forest that had opened up and let him in was only there because of circumstance, like a strut propping up the trunk of a sapling until it was strong enough to bear its own weight. Now the war was over, the forest was shedding its temporary occupants, regenerating from the old-growth. Gianni was full of fine words about staying and marrying Mary, but he had no way of knowing if this would even be possible. And Gianni was Gianni – the Foresters would long to retain him here; he brought joy to every situation. He, Seppe, had served a purpose but now that purpose was eradicated, unnecessary, and he would need to move along.

His hand shook on the blade as he thought of packing up, leaving the hut almost finished. He couldn't bring himself to picture leaving Joe. The Forest was closing back in on itself, displacing the invasive species. It was time to go.

Fifty

London

THE MINISTRY FOR RECONSTRUCTION was worlds away from the forestry HQ, further than the distance between the Forest of Dean and London could ever suggest. But the queue of men looked so familiar that Seppe saw with ease and regret how Connie would have thrived on the move from one to the other. Seppe shifted Joe onto his other hip and tried to find a spot on the wall to lean against without knocking off any of the posters or official-looking lists of instructions. Joe snuffled and snuggled into Seppe's shoulder, grounding him. When Seppe was agitated, like today, the baby seemed to divine it and pull in tighter.

It was a mark of how used they'd all got to handing over the baby for the early mornings that Amos hadn't seemed to think anything of it when Seppe showed up just before dawn. He had merely said a quick 'thank you' and strode off to check on the late lambs. Amos's mind was more than half on Billy now. It had been an easy enough task for Seppe to slide in, parcel together a few things that Joe might need. He hadn't told Amos of his plans, kidding himself it was because he didn't want to bother the older man. Actually it was because he couldn't bear to see Amos's reaction. Amos would need Joe's room back for Billy; rationally, Seppe knew this. But to see Amos relieved at the prospect of a burden removed; that would be too much. Better not to mention it to any of them, to just slip away.

The queue shuffled forward, Seppe with it, toeing before him the parcel in its brown paper and tarpaulin. Many of the men carried their own tools in heavy cotton bags contained between their feet; they'd have a surprise if they could see into his own wrapped bundle, containing not hammers and nails but half a dozen napkins and a battered knitted teddy Joe couldn't sleep without these days. On closer scrutiny, this workforce was nothing like the timber-work detail. Nobody seemed to be speaking English, or speaking much at all really. Heads were down and there was none of the chatter and jostling Seppe knew from the camp or from Frank's timber workers. A close-shaven man with searching eyes had eyed Joe closely when they'd entered, but had looked away when he saw Seppe watching.

Seppe looked now at the man in front of him, older than Seppe, more Frank's age. His jacket and trousers hung loosely, had seen better days, but there were no black patches sewn on. These weren't prisoners of war, though it was clear they weren't local either. Seppe tipped his head to hear the odd angle of a word spoken here or there, but it was sharp, muttered; he could get no purchase on it. Not a language he'd encountered before.

Joe squirmed in his sleep, knees drawn up to his chest, head resting in the crook of Seppe's shoulder, where it had found comfort ever since Joe was a tiny infant. The weight and warmth of Joe's body was an anchor, pulling Seppe into life, keeping him rooted when all else threatened to set him adrift. What was going to happen to him once he and Joe were separated? *Don't think about it,* he repeated to himself, as he'd needed to often this last week. *People need their families, not artificial facsimiles that can't last. You're doing what's right for the boy, that's the important thing.* He rubbed his spare hand over his eyes to get rid of the thoughts and the tiredness. Neither shifted.

'Next!'

Their turn now. He ducked into the flimsy chair. The woman opposite him kept up with her paperwork better than Frank; this was a desk that looked like it might even sometimes see polish. She had her head down, ticking off a series of boxes on a list. The all-familiar quota sheets. Frank would appreciate this. The war in England was still being fought by quotas according to an exasperated Frank, even though peace had been declared. As Seppe scraped his chair towards the desk, she extended one hand, her eyes still on the check boxes in front of her.

'Work order?'

He glanced quickly around. Sure enough, every other man clutched a sheet of paper. He straightened up, and Joe squirmed again, squeaked softly in his sleep.

The woman across the table sat up sharply at the noise. 'Is that a baby?'

Surely this wasn't a question that needed an answer. He waited. But the woman waited too.

'Yes.'

Another pause.

'We are not here to work.'

'Well no, I'd hope not, not with a baby.'

Seppe bridled, was about to tell her how good Joe was out felling, but now wasn't the time. The woman looked down at her checklist with what appeared to be longing for the order it brought, then looked up again somewhat impatiently. 'Well?'

Seppe frowned, and she leaned forward, exasperated rather than angry. 'If you don't want work, what do you want? This is a construction allocation office, not a church hall.'

He started. 'I am looking for – for a woman.' He pointed at Joe. 'His mother.'

The woman softened, smiled at Joe. 'Daddy's brought you to say hello to Mummy, has he?' She didn't wait for an answer. 'Well, tell me your wife's name and I'll have a look for where you can find her today.' She looked up expectantly.

Your wife. 'Connie. Constance Granger.' His skin prickled to say her name out loud to this stranger.

'Granger, Granger . . . ah yes, here goes.' The woman scribbled something on a piece of paper and handed it over. 'Granger. Over in Finsbury Park today – can you find that? Bus is probably easiest from here – number 19 all the way up from Piccadilly Circus.' She smiled at Joe. 'Won't be long before he gets to see Mummy again.'

Somehow Seppe managed to nod his thanks. He hoisted Joe back up, curled the parcel under the other arm and made it out onto the street. The noise and smells attacked him. His skin prickled still and his heart raced as if he'd run to London. He felt in his pocket, not for the knife this time but for the few shillings he had spare. Should he buy a cup of coffee, find a kindly café owner to warm up Joe's bottle? He looked around, saw a brown awning across the street.

Stop delaying. He stepped back onto the pavement, narrowly avoiding a bicycle, stubbing his toe on the kerb. *Come on, Seppe. You've come all this way, it has to be done.* The last couple of weeks, since his revelation, had been a maelstrom of covert planning. Gianni had some vague notion that it might be possible, under the terms of

386

one treaty or another, to stay in Britain. That was enough for Gianni. In Gianni's position, it might have been enough for Seppe, too. But it was too ephemeral to hold the weight of Joe as well. And watching Amos's quiet, mounting joy at the prospect of Billy's return consolidated one thing for him above all else: parents needed their children, even if they pretended not to. Joe needed to be with Connie.

He turned around and set back off towards the bus stop.

The bus seemed to take as long to cross London as the train had taken to cross half the country. He sat downstairs so that he wouldn't miss their stop, had tried to ask the conductor to let him know when to alight but the conductor had just clipped his ticket without meeting his eye and Seppe's courage had failed him. The window above him had a screw loose in the hinge; it clacked an incessant tale of indifference as they trundled up grey streets, and he itched to fix it. Is this what Livorno would look like now, the dust of a hundred bombs steeped into its people? But Livorno had sunshine, not this streaky light that left you not knowing if it was raining or the world was ending.

In his lap, Joe stirred, and Seppe stroked his head, downy hair flattening under his palm, until the baby fell back to sleep. He didn't know how long this bus journey would be and there was nowhere to warm a bottle; best that Joe stay asleep for now. Seppe stared at the windowpane, his view funnelled inward. In a matter of minutes he'd see Connie again. What would she think of him, showing up without warning? He'd thought about asking Joyce for her home address – they were still in touch, he was certain of it – but unless Connie had changed completely from the girl he knew, she would be softer outside, more herself. And if he needed this to work for Joe, he needed Connie to be at her most receptive.

Looming in front of him he saw a red circle stuck through with a blue rectangle and the white words declaiming FINSBURY PARK. Seppe shot to his feet, patting frantically for the bell. Joe woke up, outraged by the sudden movement, and started to yell.

They stepped off the bus into grey mist that seemed almost vertical, and a tidal wave of people who all knew exactly what they were doing. Seppe halted, watching the throng in front of them, Joe's wailing adding to the hubbub.

'Shh, shh, little one.' The people jostling past didn't seem to notice or care. He was struck again by the comparison with Livorno, a city where it was impossible to cross the road without someone knowing about it and telling others. This was a relief.

Joe flailed, his distress building, and caught Seppe in the cheek. He captured the little balled fist, swung it gently, considering. He couldn't return Joe to Connie like this, scrunched up and bawling. He stood in the street, parcel hooked around one arm, jiggling Joe, but it was fruitless. Joe's face was red, tears bouncing off rounded cheeks, and he beat his fists without looking, implacable.

'You know what, baby? I think now we will buy that coffee.' Thank heavens for Gianni and his insistence that Seppe be paid in English money, not camp tokens, for the pipes he carved for the guards.

There was another brown-awninged shop down the street from them. Was this standard for all English cafés? He'd never been to one in the Forest. Perhaps it was yet another unbelonging thing he hadn't learned.

The café owner glanced up from the newspaper but didn't get off his stool. Seppe rummaged in his coat pocket and found the bottle, miraculously still upright. 'Can you please help me and warm this up? For –' He gestured at the baby, as if that wasn't obvious. Seppe straightened up again. So far London had involved a lot of demonstrating he was respectable. The café owner shrugged. 'Fair enough. And what'll it be for you? Tea?'

He nodded. It was easier.

Joe settled down after the bottle. Seppe risked the ire of the proprietor and took the baby to the lavatory to change him. He knelt down on barely clean tiles, Joe balanced on the toilet seat. What should he do with the dirty napkin? He could hardly greet Connie with her son and a napkin full of faeces. In the end, he stuffed it deep into the parcel. He would remove it when he handed everything else over to Connie, take it home and wash it. No – he would dispose of it – they wouldn't have Joe at home any more, wouldn't need it. Joyce's voice played in his head: *waste not, want not, Seppe lad*. But what would it matter? They wouldn't have the baby, and he was going to need to find a new life. His shoulders sagged again. He couldn't think of that, wouldn't let himself go near it, until he knew Joe was all right. Until he'd seen Connie again, and coped.

On the way out of the bathroom he caught sight of himself and Joe in the mirror. The baby was perfect again now, rosy-cheeked, giggling up at Seppe with Connie's eyes. Who would be able to resist him? Seppe glanced down at his own best trousers, last worn at Christmas, the day he'd – well . . . The trousers were pressed and clean, but still bobbled and frayed. Shame fretted him like a saw.

He stepped back out into the noise and grime and turned down the first street he came to. Devastation covered every spare inch. The sky, the ground – everything was grey, thick with dust and dirt. Seppe pulled his coat jacket over Joe's mouth and held it firm despite Joe's protestations.

He walked slowly down the middle of the street. The bombs had had no mercy. Entire houses had been ripped apart, unrooted. Wallpaper hung from jagged edges, greens and yellows shrieking against the uniform grey of destruction. Is this what Livorno looked like now? Is this what had happened to his family's home? In Africa, war hadn't looked like this. War had been sandstorms and burning heat, and endless, sightless swathes of desert. War hadn't been a street of rubble, homes abandoned. All those people with nowhere to go, nowhere to sleep; all those letters which would come back undelivered, meals which could never again be cooked on the stove. How could he have wished this for his own city? What would there be to go back to, even if he had wanted to?

Seppe turned left again, on to the next street, paused on the corner to hike up the parcel more securely.

As he did, he heard her.

His head shot up and he peered down the street. There she was, at the top of a pile of rubble, an enormous joist balanced on one shoulder, shouting instructions to whoever was at the other end of it. *That should be me there with her.* She shouted again, confident, in charge, and Seppe's hands started to sweat. How badly he wanted her back, wanted those easy times back. But they were gone.

'OK, Joe, let's go and see Mamma.' He took a few steps towards Connie. He was almost lightheaded with the shock of seeing her, even though this had of course – of course – been the point of the trip. He bent his head towards Joe's, his cheek against the softness of Joe's hair. If Joe went back to Connie now, he wouldn't remember these last few months, would only remember having a mother. This would be better for him, and better for Connie too. Seppe only needed to persuade her. But Seppe would miss Joe more than he could bear, would miss his giggles, his shrieks of laughter when Seppe held his hand with an extended forefinger and helped him to walk from one tree to another.

Ahead of him, Connie laughed as if at the thought of it, an enormous belly laugh that even from here looked like it might send the whole pile tumbling. She was relaxed, that much was clear from her stance. She looked happy. She was in her element.

Seppe stood stock-still and looked around. Jagged pipes stuck out from heaps of rock; shards of glass were embedded into filthy puddles of rainwater collected in the dimples of bricks. What had he been thinking? This wasn't a place Connie could bring Joe to work. This wasn't like felling work, where the baby was safe on the forest floor; here there would be every danger of him climbing onto one of those piles and setting off a landslide. Connie would need to stop working and look after Joe – and then how would she manage? In crept the secret thought. *She will need me again.* But Seppe's shoulders straightened before he'd finished the thought. He wouldn't do that again, wouldn't accept Connie's best try because she saw him as a way of making things stable for Joe. She needed to want him. If she didn't want him, then just needing him could no longer be enough.

Connie perched on the end of the joist to drink from a flask, her head tilted back, confident. Seppe moved back to the shadowed corner where she wouldn't see him. He felt sick; his hands had started to shake. He jammed them in his jacket pockets. If he took Joe to Connie, he would wreck everything for her. She was happy, anyone could see that. She had left, and he needed to accept it. And she'd left Joe behind. It didn't matter if family was best: if your family didn't want you, you needed to find another one.

Seppe turned back towards the bus stop, determined now. Joe needed to stay in the forest – of course he did. That was his home. And what Seppe had learned from today was that it was his home, too.

He had to find a way to stay.

Seppe risked one last glance at the woman on the rubble, allowed the secret admission momentary life. He'd needed to see Connie again, needed to see her to know if there was still a chance. It had been selfish, and to pretend even to himself that this trip had only been about Joe was wrong.

He knew now. Better to remember Connie happy than to compromise her life again, or impel her to compromise Joe's. He sighed, and turned back down the street.

Fifty-One

IT WAS GETTING DARK now, you could only see as far as the first apple trees. Joe hadn't been brought home for his tea. Amos would have put two bob on them being back for feeding time. He'd left the food there, a chop for Seppe since it didn't sound like meat was making its way into that camp yet, and a plate of mash for Joe with some bits of Amos's chop beside it. And carrots, for that babba loved carrots. But here it was, almost time for the owl in the far oak to greet the night, and no sign of them yet. Amos paced beside the window, willing them to show up. Where could they have gone?

Footsteps came round the side of the house and his shoulders dropped. Here they were. Thank heavens for that.

'No sign, Amos?'

'Joyce. No. Thought you were them, actually.'

Joyce came in, went over to the range. 'I'll put the kettle on. Didn't say where he was going?'

Joyce wasn't going to start chattering on, was she? Amos shook his head and went back over to the window. If he'd wanted a cup of tea, he'd have made one. Couldn't be having a drink at this time of night, not at his age.

More footsteps. Busier than Coleford on market day, this was getting. He didn't move this time – bound to be Frank.

But it wasn't. It was Seppe, looking for all the world like he'd seen a ghost – and Joe. Joe was back. Amos took two strides forward, beat Joyce to the babba for once. Joe's eyes opened, just a fraction, and he smiled up at Amos. Amos smiled back – not something you could help, not with this one – and aimed his words at Seppe.

'Where the heck have you been?' All the worry had balled up, was bulleting out.

The lad didn't answer, wouldn't look up. Joe wasn't going back to sleep neither, by the looks of him. Those blue eyes were wide open, staring up with all the answers, if he could only spit 'em out.

'Here we are, then.' Joyce bustled two mugs of tea on the table. 'You eaten, Seppe?'

'No.'

Oh, so the cat hadn't got his tongue then, not when it came to food. He'd be better off telling them where he'd been, gallivanting off with the baby.

'I'll just heat this up.' Amos could hear Joyce flitting around at the range but he couldn't take his eyes off Joe.

'You going to tell us where you've been?' He hadn't been able to settle to anything, not once he arrived home and discovered no Joe. All that pacing was coming out in his words now. He could never make words do what he needed them to do.

Joyce reappeared at the table, setting down the plate and pulling out the chair for Seppe. She sat down beside him. *Make yourself at home in my house, why don't you?* Amos moved over to the chair beside his fire, settled himself in with Joe still cradled on his lap. Bess, half-asleep herself at the hearth, shuffled over to nose at the baby on his knees and Joe giggled, pushed stubby hands through the dog's fur. Amos stared into the fire.

Behind him, a fork was scraping on the plate – Seppe must have been proper hungry.

'I went to find Connie.'

It was so quiet Amos thought he'd made it up. He sat upright in the wing chair, his head titled towards the kitchen table.

'Aye, lad, I wondered if it was something like that.' Joyce's voice was lamb-soothing quiet, leaving the gaps for Seppe to fill. You had to admire the way she had of getting people to tell her things. Why couldn't Amos do it like that?

'But I came back.'

'We can see that.' Another pause. Joe gurgled at the dog and it took all Amos had not to shush him.

'I thought – I thought – I thought, with Billy back and the camp emptying I had better find Joe his mother, his proper family.'

It was as if someone had slogged Amos right in the gut. How were they not Joe's proper family, him and Seppe and Joyce? Give the babba back to Connie, who could barely look after herself, never mind a baby?

'What do you mean, his *proper* family?' Joyce was as shocked as Amos, then. That was something.

'This – this is all nice but I know now it cannot last. You have all been kind, so kind, but now the camp is closing and the forest will go back to being just you, being empty of us incomers.' Amos had given up any pretence now, was earwigging good and proper. 'And I –' Seppe raised his chest '– I cannot wait until you tell me it is time to go. You have been too good to me; I will not be impolite and outstay this welcome. But before I go, I must find Connie for Joe, so that Billy's room is Billy's room again and things can go back to how they were.'

Oh, that was *it*. His blood roaring, Amos spun round. 'You telling me I haven't got it in me to take care of this one and our Billy?'

Seppe's head came up. Was the lad going to contradict him?

'Of course you can manage. But Billy is your flesh, he was born here. He needs this space now.'

Amos snorted. 'Space? Take a look around you, lad. Thass something we've got plenty of here in the forest, is space. Our Joe's a Forest kid through and through; take him anywhere else and that's when he becomes the outsider, you ask me.' How could Seppe not see this? Amos felt it through his blood, rushing like the brook in springtime. He didn't have the fancy words but he couldn't go losing the babba. Nor the lad. He looked at Joyce, helpless. Now he knew how them ewes of his felt when he came across them caught up in a bit of bramble, waiting on him to sort their way out of the mess.

Joyce had her hand on Seppe's arm now, gentle-like. 'And what's this about you leaving? I thought you were staying on with Frank as and when this blessed war ends – heaven knows he's still got the quotas pouring in.'

'That was before Billy was coming back. An English soldier won't want the enemy living at the bottom of the garden.'

Amos had all but forgotten that Seppe had never met Billy; in his head they were almost brothers. He came over to the table, stood off to the side beside Joyce. 'Our Billy ain't going to see you like the enemy. He's not like that, you'll see. Knowing Billy he'll probably start agitating to build a hut like yours beside it; I'd watch out, if I were you.'

Joyce patted Seppe's arm. 'Amos is right. Our Billy coming

back don't change anything. The thought hadn't even entered my head – nor Frank's nor Amos's, I'd wager. We need you here, son – Frank for the trees and Amos to have a hand with Joe. You might be an incomer, but you're dug in now, part of the soil.' She paused, but this time it was just to catch breath. 'Look. I don't know what went on up there with Connie, and to be honest, I don't want to know. That's between you and her. But you're back now, and so's our Joe. Back where you belong. You stay here, and we stick together and sort it out. Lord knows the Forest's suffered enough losses in the name of this war; you and that babby are two of the rare bits of good to come from it, and your home's here. We don't want to hear any more of this nonsense, do you hear me? Ain't that right, Amos?'

Seppe's shoulders were square, but his neck was tense, like Bess when she was getting ready to sprint. He stretched his hands out in front of him as if protecting himself from an unspoken force. Skin spanned tautly over sinew and bone, hardened and sun-scorched. Amos had heard there were people who found the answers in palm-reading, but for him, the real measure of a man was on the other side of the hand. And this man, this man before them, had thought they didn't want him around any more.

Amos had to swallow twice before finally he found the words. 'Joyce is right, lad. This is your home now. Yours and the babby's. It'll take some bumping along, but we'll get there.' He put his hand on Seppe's shoulder, rested it there until he felt the trembling halt. There was stuff Seppe wasn't telling them about that London, about that Connie, he was sure of it. But Amos didn't need to hear it, not now. The boy would tell in his own time, or he wouldn't if he didn't have a mind to. That didn't matter. What mattered was that he was back. They were home.

Fifty-Two

July

CONNIE LEANED DOWN HARD on the joist until it tilted. 'Come on, get the other end of the bugger!' Sweat was dripping into her eyes and her fingers were fat sausages of heat. The crew had sworn at her when she'd told them to meet at daybreak, but she'd been right to insist. They'd got the frames sorted across the terrace before they were all burned to a bleeding crisp.

Her sleeves had come loose again and were sticking to her arms. She shoved them back up, her skin all prickly. The lads were working shirtless, had been for a month now. It didn't harm the working day, let's put it like that. She had half a mind to join them and strip off too – that'd put the cat among the bloody pigeons.

Misha had got behind the joist, swinging it up like it was his girl and they were jiving. He was all right, Misha. Spoke a bit of English, too, so he could help her get through to the others.

Connie pulled the nails from her belt and hammered them in. That wasn't going anywhere now.

'All right, lads, that's us for the day.' They stared at her, five broad blank faces, and she sighed, flapped at Misha. 'Tell 'em.'

When were they going to start picking up English? It wasn't that hard – look at Seppe and Gianni and that lot. Spoke it better than the Foresters half the time. Connie smiled to herself. Seppe had barely known what to call a tree in English when they'd first starting working out in the forest, had called the wedge the 'widge' for a week before he'd nailed it. But it had only taken a couple of weeks for him to know all the English names of the most complicated bits of kit, the stuff that sometimes baffled her still now, like the billhook. He'd got pretty good at other words too – her smile deepened into a grin, remembering the things he'd whisper to her if they got a moment alone in the trees, especially in the later days. Oh, he was pretty confident about expressing himself by the end.

The grin faded, doused by guilt. If she'd given him half a chance, explained how she felt, he'd have had all the words he needed for it, she was sure. This lot could surely manage more than they did.

She chucked the hammer into the barrow and one of the blokes carted it off to the lock-up. The tool belt was hers, meant more than any bit of jewellery.

Connie raised her hand high in salute to the crew. 'See you in the morning, same time.' She could count on this lot. They didn't seem to have anything else to do with their lives, so they'd be there all right when she rounded the corner tomorrow. She stopped now and looked back from that same corner, grinned to herself. Elfield Row was coming together, getting shape to it. You could see new roofs, new walls now where before it was rats and rubble. Filthy bleeding work it'd been when she'd first arrived. Every bugger was nose to the grindstone on the front or in the munitions factory. The sorry few who'd volunteered were crabby and overrun, and half the time they had to knock stuff all the way down before they could build it back up. Her first day on the job she'd stepped on a rotten joist, plunged to her knees into stinking scum and gashed her arm on a nail that was jutting out. She'd almost packed it in then and there, gone back to the forest after all and pretended she'd been away for Women's Things or something else Frank wouldn't question. She'd barely dared write for a bit then, in case she'd given in and gone back.

She gave a half-salute to Elfield Row, soppy cow that she was, and started home. She was good at the work, she'd give herself that. Once they'd got onto shaping and sawing, she'd recognised the rhythm, felt the weight of the wood catch on the teeth, and smiled for the first time in weeks. One afternoon she'd refitted three windows and the foreman had stopped her at the end of the shift.

'Good little worker you, ain't you?' She'd thought of Frank, how he'd taken no shit from her, shown her how to love the work, and she'd dashed her shirt sleeve against her eyes when the foreman hadn't been looking. And here she was now with her own crew, her own patch of houses to rebuild, proper nice little digs and a bit of spare cash in her pocket.

To begin with, she'd blown the cash every week, beside herself at all the choice. She went to the pictures and saw the latest show, not whatever had trickled down to that bleeding backwater of a cinema in Coleford. She went dancing with Vi, thrilling at the novelty of a proper dance hall again.

It'd been a stroke of luck, bumping into Vi that time early on when she'd been outside that dress shop trying to talk herself into spending Mary's coupons on a couple of serviceable frocks. Vi had not only found her a bloke who did a roaring trade in black market coupons, but she had offered Connie digs too, proved to be a right diamond.

There was another dance tonight. That was the thing with London, there seemed to be dances every night if you wanted them. They just weren't all that much cop, not once the first thrill of being out had worn off. Her feet killed her by the end of the working day and all the blokes were not right in the head and hadn't been able to fight. She'd heard of a couple of clubs that were mostly for GIs stationed over here; maybe she'd persuade Vi to give them a go one of these days. London was tougher than she'd thought but that Hollywood still looked worth a go, so sunny and shiny. Catching back up with the GIs would keep her on track, remind her why she'd come up here.

Connie had reached the stairs to the Tube. It was going to be like a sauna down there, a stinking one, too. Not so bad now there hadn't been so many raids, but the smell must be bled into the tiles, didn't ever seem to change. Better to think about the dances. She put her hand lightly to the stair rail and sashayed, kicking out her feet at the ankles.

'Mind where you're going, willya?' Had she kicked that bloke? No, there was no way she'd reached him from here – he just wanted her to be miserable too. That was the trouble, she was coming to realise, all this grey and bombing. It got into you, made you feel like your insides were rain and the cloud was pressing down on you. When you tried to keep yourself going, do something a bit daft maybe, there was always someone in the city ready to shut you down, not wanting to see the way out. Coventry hadn't been like that; she'd belonged, knew everyone on Hillview Road and everyone on her factory line, too. She'd often felt herself hemmed in by the way everyone in the forest seemed to know each other – or be related – but it was only when she moved here that she copped on to how nice that could be sometimes, too.

She didn't have to wait long for the train, but there weren't many carriages again. She swayed with the rhythm of the train, feet planted wide apart as if she was going to get down an oak, not breathe in some bloke's armpit whilst he tried to cop a feel. Her overalls stuck to her in a way she didn't even know they could and her hair was full of sawdust, except here it didn't smell fresh, the way a tree did when you sawed into it. Must be baking in the forest too, weather like this – but at least they had the stream. Did Joe have a bonnet, to screen him from the sun? She couldn't remember. Next time she sent Joyce some money for Joe she'd check, just in case. Seppe would know, too – but she hadn't heard a peep from Seppe. Couldn't say she could blame him, but she hadn't counted on how strange that felt. Seppe had snuck under her skin, the way a blister heals and leaves the area stronger. She hadn't known he was making her stronger until she ripped away from him all at once. She'd always been able to be so honest with him and now she was back in a place where nobody knew the whole story and she noticed, really noticed, that that protective layer he'd provided was all gone now. It hadn't even been this raw when – well, when the bomb hit.

Those first few nights here, in the manky B&B before she'd moved in with Vi, she'd jolted awake and banged her head on the mouldy wall, choking on the panic of her dream. Seppe and Joe were in danger – trees were falling like mortar shells, just tilting down willy-nilly without her there to organise it all – and however hard Seppe ran, he and Joe were going to be squashed by one. She knew it, just knew it, screeched upright in bed, Joe's desperation in her throat. She hadn't been able to do a thing without bumping into a memory of her son. Every spoonful of porridge she expected to be interrupted by him grabbing the spoon, or the bowl, or demanding a mouthful himself. The first two weeks of being up here she stopped every time she left the house, patted herself down to figure out what it is she'd left behind before realising it was the babba she was missing, had barely gone anywhere without him for months. She could eat porridge and leave the house now without him appearing in her head, but he was never far away. And where Joe was, so was Seppe.

Still, she'd made her bed and now she had to lie in it, even if it turned out being in London wasn't all that after all. Since the war had ended all that hope seemed to have gone. They were just as mired in gloom and grimness as before, and now there was nothing to blame it on.

The train slowed into her station and she got off, preparing to swap this indoor, swampy heat for the dry blast of sun outdoors. She couldn't be doing with the dance tonight, she just couldn't. Vi would mither on, but she'd find someone else to go with – one of those girls from that office of hers, where they'd spent all day in crisp shirts not having to deal with the sweat dripping down their backs or the nails getting so hot they'd burn your skin the minute you tried to get one in place. But try as she might, Connie couldn't imagine ever being the person working in the office, either. This was her world, outdoors. And London, after all, was only her stepping stone to America. If she missed the odd dance, the world didn't stop turning.

September 1945

Fifty-Three

THE HOUSE WAS QUIET when she got in from the building site. Vi was still at the office. That was the good thing about this grimy city sunshine: days started at dawn, and early starts meant early finishes. Connie had the house to herself for an hour at least.

The door was stuck again with the heat so she gave it a good shove, glass rattling in the pane as she did so. It was stuffy for September. Even though she loved being on a terrace again for the most part, it wasn't half hot. Not like Amos's cottage; those walls were a mile thick and all the trees had scared away the sun anyway. Here she could barely breathe sometimes, in the mugginess, even though it was supposed to be the tail end of September.

When she'd first moved in, Connie had opened all the windows to get some air in and Vi had arrived home and screeched:

'Are you trying to get us robbed in our beds? The looters'll bite your arm off for easy pickings like that.'

407

They hadn't known each other long at that point. Connie tutted at Vi's paranoia, but the windows stayed shut.

Connie had felt faint all day today and her head was pounding. Maybe it was this heat. A bath would sort her out, and she'd still have time to get the job done. She went straight to the bathroom, set the taps going and stripped off, dropping everything on the floor. Next door's wireless was blaring through the wall again; outside the window, the trains were rattling past and the neighbour's kids were playing a hollering game of British Bulldog in the street. Some of them were right little tots; another few months and Joe might be big enough for that sort of thing now. *But you missed his first birthday. You've got no right to imagine him playing games.* She swallowed.

'Yoo hoo! Connie! Are you back?'

She started, shocked, and bashed her knee against the side of the tub. For a second that sounded just like Joyce. Her face split with a beam and she scrabbled to hoist herself out of the bath.

'Con? Where're you hiding?'

Oh, *Vi.* Connie sagged. Stupid of her, really, to imagine it could possibly have been Joyce, who rarely went further than Cinderford. This was a bit early for Vi to be home, though.

'In the bath.' She hopped in quickly and lay back. The water was more than a bit nippy and she shivered as the door banged open and Vi burst in.

'A bath in the middle of the week? Look at you, Lady Muck!' Vi perched on the lavatory seat and poked at the water with shiny red toenails. 'Lady Mucky, more like – look at that scum.' She removed her foot sharpish. Good.

'Some of us do actual honest work for a living, not pushing bits of paper around and flirting with delivery boys.'

'More fool you, then!' Vi grinned and picked up Connie's tool belt. Vi thought the belt was hilarious, couldn't for the life of her understand why Connie had saved up so long for it.

'What's in the belt of delights today?'

'Hammers – you can see that. We're fixing joists this week; row of houses not far from here, as it happens. If you line up all the nails then knock 'em in quick enough, it sounds like a woodpecker – rat-a-tat-a-tat.' Connie had got all teary the first time she'd recognised the noise, but there was no way she was telling Vi that.

'A woodpecker? More like ack-ack fire, lovie. We didn't all spend our war hidden away in the back of beyond, you know.' Vi dropped the tool belt and it rustled the bag hidden beneath Connie's overalls. Connie tensed, but Vi was already nosing around. She pulled out the bag.

'Ooh, so you did go to Woolies after all! That's more like it. Get any good slap?'

Connie half rose from the bath, but Vi held the letter away from her, tilting it towards the light to see through the envelope.

'Stationery? Pens and paper? What are you up to? Got a sweetheart I don't know about, have you, Connie Granger?'

'There's plenty you don't know about.' Connie pushed under the water, where she couldn't hear Vi's comeback. The mental checklist in her head added on another item. People in the Forest had the sense not to ask constant questions.

She splashed out of the bath, accidentally-on-purpose getting water onto Vi's fancy skirt, and marched past her in a towel.

Wait, she needed that stationery. 'I'll have that back, ta.' Her hand shook and the paper rustled. Vi opened her mouth and Connie legged it to her room and shut the door as firmly as she could without actually slamming it in Vi's face. She bent down under her bed and her towel fell off. She'd dry quick enough in this heat.

The sock was where she'd stuffed it, between the mattress and the springs, a rustling pile of envelopes and a crafty bottle of mother's ruin alongside it. The sock was as lumpy and bumpy as a Christmas stocking, and her heart swelled a little bit. *I did that.* She reached inside it and pulled out a couple of crumpled notes and the latest envelope. Babies weren't cheap, though Joyce never asked for any cash and certainly never made mention of Amos passing any comment. But in that last picture she'd sent of them all out picnicking, Connie had seen that Joe had on a little cap and blazer, not the sort of thing Joyce could have knitted. Must've cost a bob or two, even with coupons.

Well, maybe she'd find out for herself soon enough. Connie swallowed hard. No number of nails going into rafters month after month had tapped out the message of what she should do. After those first few weeks of what she'd thought was freedom, the doubts about London life had built up and up like sediment. But she'd stuck it out; the beginning of anything always felt a bit odd and that wasn't a reason to give up. She was a city girl, she just had to get used to it again.

Then one morning, a month ago, she'd arrived at the rebuild site just after dawn and found herself listening out for Seppe's humming. Into the disappointment that filled the silence, the answer had arrived, as shining and decisive as any blade she'd ever handled. The only way she'd know what the future looked like would be to go back and find out for herself.

Connie pulled an envelope from the packet and took a quick swig of gin. Her palms were sweating. Must be the heat.

Fifty-Four

AMOS HAD BANGED ON the hut door this morning before the blackbird had even started chirping. He often deposited Joe with Seppe first thing whilst he went and checked on the sheep, and even though it was the end of September and the nights were starting to very gradually draw in, Joe was still waking with the light. Seppe didn't mind; it gave him more precious hours with Joe before handing him over to Joyce for the morning. Most nights he scrambled back from felling in time to help bathe Joe, tell him a story and feel his warmth before tucking him in upstairs at Amos's. It worked out well for all of them.

'Bright one today. Cobnuts are ready, hazelnuts too. When I'm back from the sheep we'll get going.' Joe pushed past Seppe into the hut, chattering nonsense in his sing-song voice, and Amos nodded after him. 'Had his porridge, he has. Don't let him fool you.' Amos was lighter now, younger since they'd had the letter from the War Office. Billy had followed it up with one of his own, full of excitement at being back before Christmas. Billy, who had called this forest home before Seppe had even known it existed. And now he'd be back. Seppe would meet him. A brother in arms.

Joyce, mind reader that she was, had taken Seppe aside when the letter arrived. 'Don't you be fretting with Billy coming back. You'll never hear our Amos say it, but you're family too now, you and Joe. And Amos is fierce loyal to his family, you know that.' Joyce had long since given up trying to talk to Seppe about the letters she got from Connie. At first she'd left them around for him to see, even underlined the bits where Connie asked after him. But as far as Joyce and Amos could tell, Seppe resolutely never even glanced at them.

When Amos returned from his morning round, they'd gathered baskets and left the oaks behind, gone down towards Pillowell to a place Amos knew. It was clear and crisp today, the leaves rustling their scarlets and ochres in anticipation of impending release. Joe had fallen over, laughed and thrown up a handful of leaves, only wanting a carry right towards the end.

Seppe bit into a hazelnut and was back in Italy, sitting at the table whilst his mother made *torta di nocciole*. They were sweet, the memory and the nut, time ripening them both. Mamma would have been happy, in the end, to see this life he had made. And she was safe from the Major now, and would not have feared the end because in her mind it would have meant reuniting with Alessa. Seppe sighed, smiled.

He reached for another nut, arm extended to full sinew, stretching out the aches of woodcutting. Beneath Seppe's feet the rung of the ladder wobbled; below, Amos adjusted his stance and the ladder was firm again. Connie would have loved this; he smiled to remember how much she'd enjoyed the apple picking last year. But even without her, these small acts of harvesting brought their own pleasures, made their own memories. He looked down at Joe, who grubbed for a nutshell and hurled it at Amos, giggling. Joe's wrists were already poking out from his pullover again. Amos joked it was all this sunshine, growing him faster than a sapling. Seppe would talk to Joyce about unravelling a couple of his sweaters to knit something bigger for the child this winter.

Earlier in the summer they'd gone out for a picnic to celebrate Frank's birthday. Joyce had borrowed a camera from someone she did some sewing for, was insistent that they get a record of the day even though Frank himself said he'd rather not mark the passing of the years, thank you very much. She'd arranged them all together and taken their picture and something in the way she'd been fussing, making sure Joe was in full view, made Seppe sit up straight in realisation at who she was sending the picture on to. Would Connie have recognised this giggling little boy, the baby in him receding almost weekly?

Would she recognise either of them? For Seppe, too, had grown. Those hundreds of napkins changed and washed, the nights of pacing amongst the oaks rocking Joe out of a nightmare he couldn't yet express: it had pulled him up, made him stronger.

That first winter, he'd lived in the shadow of his desperate need for Connie's return. He'd glimpsed her a thousand times, lurking behind the trunk of an oak as he raised the axe to it, skipping down the slope towards the cottage in a breeze. After his trip to London, it had got worse, not better, for a while, his mind taunting him with images of her laughing on that joist, content. *Without him.* But when the leaves unfurled fully in the summer sunshine, he'd unfurled with them.

Now he cast his own shadows. Connie's absence was

413

there every time he looked at Joe, but it wasn't a hole any more. Now it was a knot in the wood that marked what had gone before. They had got through that winter, him and Amos and Joe, and *this* is who they were now.

Seppe pinched a hazelnut where it joined the branch, the soft vole-like fur of its casing a promise against his skin. No need to rush getting down the ladder; the basket would only tip and they'd have to start all over again. Amos took it off him as he stepped down onto the ground.

'Time to get this one home for some tea.'

'Yes, it must be.' Seppe lobbed the empty shell casing at Joe who ran squealing behind the trunk.

Baskets full, they made their way back home. Seppe looked up at the leaves, pellucid against the inky sky. That had been a good afternoon. Who knew what happened next to the nuts? Amos or Joyce would doubtless show him. Or he could rack his brains for the *torta* recipe, maybe check with Gianni, married now to his English Mary and helping to run the Bell. The others had all gone back to Italy, the camp dissipating and with it the final vestiges of threat, of the homeland. Gianni visited often, cooed at Joe in Italian. 'Aren't you teaching Joe? He can have his own private language, this little Italian Forester.' Gianni was devoted to Mary, settled here now for the rest of his days, but he was desperately homesick, clung to any vestige of home that he could. But Seppe had smiled and shaken his head. His life was here now, he had no need of the language that bound him to the past.

Joe picked up a fallen twig, cupped his hand into the cleft, and pointed it at Seppe.

Where had he learned this? Seppe grinned at Amos and fell to the ground, wounded, possibly fatally.

'No, no stop! You have me captive!' He writhed, the ground pulsing with the dregs of summer. 'Oof!' Joe landed on top of him, pudgy hands claiming his victory. There was only one thing for it. Seppe leaped up, swinging Joe like an axe. The child shrieked with laughter and Seppe's heart filled.

Seppe paused when they reached the hut, picked up a fallen branch and shot Joe once for luck. 'I'll come to the house in two minutes.'

It was cool inside the hut, despite the wood overlain with brush to keep out draughts. He'd need to start thinking about how to heat it, maybe do some overtime now he could be paid for it and buy one of those tortoise stoves like Frank's. It had been frigid in here over the winter, ice latticing the windows in the mornings, colder even than the sardine bunks in the Nissen huts despite the four blankets Joyce had insisted he take. It was always cosier, though. His bed, built into the side of the wall, boasted not one but two of Joyce's blankets, their mismatched knitted squares ensuring Joe could learn every colour just by pointing at one and repeating the word; on the narrow table Seppe had built against the opposite wall, a small box contained more wood, offcuts waiting for his next carving project.

No time for carving now, though. Seppe splashed water on his face from the jug, scrubbed at his hands and left. He paused at the gate into Amos's garden as he often did. *Family.* From here, in the half-light, the view into Amos's kitchen was illuminated like a painting by the gas light within. Joe was running backwards and forwards by the range, playing soldiers with Bess now. Where was Amos? Seppe walked closer and Amos came into the frame, over in the corner by the scullery. He was stilled, staring at something in his hand. Seppe stopped walking to watch.

When he got going again, the garden was longer than usual, the oaks whispering from the edges. Amos met him at the doorway, still holding the object in question. It was a letter.

'Has something happened to Billy?'

'It's not our Billy. Look. You want to have a read of this one, lad.' Amos thrust the letter at Seppe. Was that fear or curiosity in his voice?

The envelope was fat and its whisper matched that of the oaks above. Seppe turned it over, saw the scrappy handwriting.

Still in the same fearsome rush.

His stomach lurched.

SEPPE STEPPED OUTSIDE. THE trees bent to greet him, draw him forward, the promise of autumn steady and sure. Seppe strode into the gloaming. A breeze gusted the leaves, flung a rainbow of bronze and scarlet from the beeches above. Beneath his boots, twigs cracked like bones.

416

Fifty-Five

IT WAS ONLY WHEN she changed trains at Gloucester and got on the two-carriage chugger that her stomach had unclenched. They'd curved round the river where it was as broad as the sea, gulls swooping down on the mud flats as the train had leaned into the turn. Connie pressed back from the window until they'd left the bends behind and nosed their way up the hill.

The trees had been thickening around the railway sidings for a good few minutes now, wrapping the train into the Forest. Connie looked at her hand where it gripped the open window. It was cast again in the amber of autumn-diluted leaf-light that she'd stopped noticing until she'd moved up to the city and realised how grey everything was there. She put the other hand up to join it. There! Now she was wearing orangey-brown gloves.

They had slowed right down now, the wheels juddering on the rails. Connie ground her teeth. Was she going to be sick with nerves? That'd be a pretty way to arrive.

Think about something else, Granger. She swallowed hard

once, twice, and stuck her head right out of the window, forcing the thought into the breeze. Her hair flapped into her face and she closed her eyes. You didn't need to see the trees to know this was the forest. She breathed sharply in – there was that furniture polish smell again. God, but she'd missed that. Vi had come in one night, caught Connie sniffing at the tub, and thought she'd gone doolally.

The train jolted to a halt and she almost came a cropper against the side of the window. An old gent behind her reached out and gripped her by the elbow. 'You all right there, wench?'

There was that Forest of Dean burr, as round and tippy as the tree-covered hills. She beamed and the poor bloke stepped back, doffed his cap and beckoned for her to get off the train before him. His face was a picture. *Get a grip.* Scaring the locals was the last thing she wanted to do.

But she couldn't help twisting back and smiling again as she shouldered her bag and stepped onto the station platform. That voice. He sounded like Amos, like Frank. Would Seppe have a hint of that now?

Would Joe?

She plonked down her bag whilst she got her bearings. It was a battered kitbag belonging to some old flame of Vi's, less of a pain to lug around than her suitcase, especially since it was only half full. She hadn't told Vi what she was up to, not exactly, just asked for a borrow of the bag to 'pay a visit to old friends'. Vi's mind had gone instantly to the gutter like it always did, and this time Connie had been happy to leave it there.

She'd have known this was Cinderford, even without the sign outside the station. It still gave you a shock, seeing all the place names uncovered now that Jerry was no longer a threat. And it wasn't like it made any difference out here – no stranger would have the first clue how to get through the trees, however many signs went up. She laughed out loud and got a strange look from a woman walking past, dragging a shopping trolley with one hand and a squawking kid in another. Must be the nerves.

Connie strode down the main street and paused at the butcher's. What should she bring them? She'd saved her coupons specially. God knows they'd been feeding Joe these past months; in that photo that Joyce had sent he was real bonny now. She hugged her arms to her with the excitement of soon getting to pick him up again, see for herself. *What if he won't let me pick him up any more?* She hugged herself tighter, squeezing away the thought before it took hold.

But the queue snaked out round the counter and nearly to the door. Someone would see her and get word to Amos – and Seppe – faster than she could say, 'pound of sausages, please'. She shrugged the kitbag higher and moved on out of the town.

She'd forgotten that the trees made great big arches over the roads. Connie skipped, the kitbag bashing her between the shoulder blades. Good job Vi couldn't see her now; she'd think she'd fully lost her marbles.

There was a rustle from the side of the road and Connie turned, just caught sight of a white flash of tail bounding away. She'd never been able to keep straight all the different types of deer. Maybe Seppe could teach her – it was the sort of thing he'd have clocked right away.

She was jumping ahead of herself.

Above the treetops a hawk orbited a target only it could see, biding its time. Crows clacked around it, black wings beating. She stopped to watch, her heartbeat matching the crow's wingbeats, not quite sure who she was rooting for.

The hawk moved in for the kill, its wings back as it plummeted between the treetops, the crows banished.

Connie sharpened her pace.

The road stretched in front of her, long and straight and lined with oaks.

Acknowledgements

Never one to do anything without excessive overthinking and discussion, I've been ridiculously lucky to have incredible support from so many people.

Huge thanks to my editor, Eleanor Dryden, for your glorious mix of unflaggable enthusiasm and razor-sharp talent. This book wouldn't exist in this form without your ninja skills. Enormous thanks too to my agent Juliet Pickering for such talented editorial acumen and bottomless patience expertise and friendship. Thanks to all at Blake Friedmann and at Bonnier Zaffre, particularly Alex Allden, Sarah Bauer, Emily Burns, Tara Loder and the miraculous sales and marketing team.

Dave Franklin has lived with this project for years and to call him 'supportive' doesn't come close. For getting me out of my own way more times than I can count, for brilliant, brutal feedback on several iterations of the manuscript and for never, ever failing to believe that I'd finish it: thank you.

Carys Bray is the friend every writer – every person – needs. I'm so glad that our words on the page led us to meet. Thank you for endless conversations about ways to describe trees, for reading the manuscript in its various stages of development and for your insightful advice on so very much.

Jenn Ashworth's mentorship and friendship have both been just like Jenn: fierce, kind and extraordinarily intelligent. Thank you doesn't cover it. My gratitude, too, to the Arvon/Jerwood Foundation for the support which led to this opportunity.

Rachael Beale, Susie Hales, Simon Hepworth, Scott Pack and Grahame Williams all read various iterations of this manuscript and offered their views: thank you.

To my friends: thank you to those of you who know this path all too well and have been such understanding company along the way: Sam Baker, Alison Barrow, Stephanie Butland, Anna Carey, Jon Courtenay Grimwood, Lissa Evans, Shelley Harris, Alison Hennessey, Jason Hewitt, Francesca Main, Sarra Manning, Julie Mayhew, Cliff Shephard and Craig Taylor. And for your unquestioning cheerleading of my peculiar need to stay in and scowl at adjectives: thank you Ann Allen, Carrie Baker, Elisabeth Baker, Ilona Blue, Lisa and Nick Cheek, Sue Crosbie, Sue Franklin, Kate Harper, Steve Hay, Melanie Martin, Karen O'Neill, Jason and Bee Noble, Mel and Marc Pullen, Andy Richards, Jane and Adam Scott, and Jo and Martin Sutton.

Thanks to Janice MacNamee for space and time to write the book. Thanks also to the staff at Gladstone's Library and to Deborah Dooley and the late Bob Cooper at Retreats for You for literal shelter for parts of the writing of this. My colleagues and students at Oxford Brookes have provided excellent distraction and been overwhelmingly enthusiastic on my behalf, as have the brilliant team at Blackwell's in Oxford and the Short Stories Aloud gang.

Thank you to my parents, Neil and Lynette Harper, for support throughout and for instilling in me a love of books and the forest that sustain me wherever I am.

And thanks (again) to Dave, and to Jonah and Lucas, for encouraging me despite my endless half-sentences and for making it hard to sit down and write because I'd rather be hanging out with you. You are all my favourites.

Author's note

Though I've used real locations and place names in this fictional account of the Forest of Dean, some liberties have been taken with geography; a transgression I'm hoping any Foresters will forgive. Similarly, some licence has been taken with depictions of the bombing in Coventry.

The following resources have been of huge interest and use to me during the research that underpinned this novel.

The archive room at the Imperial War Museum in London was the source of several first-hand accounts of lumberjills and Italian POWs.

John Belcher and the Dean Heritage Museum in Soudley kindly opened their archives and talked to me both about POW camps in the Forest and about the lumberjills. John was of further help in furnishing me with an account of an Italian POW, Bruno Porciani, who was resident in the camp.

Gratitude is due to Manfred Hahn for generously sending me the translation of his uncle Willi Bungart's self-published book, *War Captivity*, also depicting life in both Camp 61 and other British POW camps. Further information about POWs in the UK came from Sophie Jackson's book *Churchill's Unexpected Guests*.

Nicola Tyler's account of the World War Two landgirls, *They Fought in the Fields*, contains an illuminating chapter on the Women's Timber Corps, as does *All Muck, Now*

Medals by Joan Mant. W.E. Sherwell-Cooper's *Land Girl: A Manual For Volunteers in the Women's Land Army*, was similarly useful. Russell Meiggs' *Home Timber Production 1939-1945* contained several references to the Forest of Dean and was illuminating as an overall picture of the necessity of the lumberjills to this vital war effort.

Several sources provided material for both the location and the time period. *The Forest of Dean in Wartime*, by Humphrey Phelps, contains many first-hand accounts of life in the Forest during the war years. Joyce Latham's *Whistling in the Dark* is a great first-hand account, too. The archives of the *Dean Forest Mercury* – now the *Forester* newspaper in Cinderford – were also invaluable in this regard, my thanks to Tina, Andy, and the staff there for their help and hospitality. Though tackling the time immediately after the war, Dennis Potter's *The Changing Forest* has shaped my thinking for decades and undoubtedly brought me to this material. Similarly, I can't remember when I first read *How We Lived Then*, Norman Longmate's exhaustive account of daily life in Britain in the Second World War, but it was as engrossing now as it was all those years ago.

And thanks must go to my father, Neil Harper, for humouring me as he has done on so many occasions, and marking on an Ordnance Survey map the locations of the camps and GI activities he remembers from his wartime childhood.